WATERMARK

PHANTOM ISLAND
4

KRISSI DALLAS

Cover design by Kristen Verser
Interior design by Caypeeline Casas
Edited by Katrina Elsea

Published in the United States of America

ISBN: 978-0-99973-113-0
1. Juvenile Fiction / Fantasy & Magic
2. Juvenile Fiction / Action & Adventure / General
13.08.01

For Katrina Elsea
Thank you for being the first person to
walk through that portal with me.

RECONNAISSANCE

THE SOAP OPERA CONTINUES

Whitnee was gone. Again. That meant we were on an all-out man-hunt for her. Again. Caleb couldn't decide if he was afraid or angry. Again.

And I was sick to my stomach...*again.*

It had been absolute chaos in Jezebel's house for the last few hours. I woke up in the quiet, early morning light with sharp stomach cramps and a killer headache only to find Whitnee's spot in the bed empty. I didn't worry at first because, well, I was so sick I had to bolt to the bathing room before I made a nasty spill on Jezebel's precious flooring. I also figured there was probably a logical explanation for where Whitnee was...Boy, was I wrong.

When I finally emerged, telling myself that I was only sick from indulging in so much food the night before, I tiptoed around the dark house. Most everyone was still sleeping. Thomas had been on guard duty with Gabriel—he would be exhausted by now. I figured I would find Whitnee and then see what he was up to next. But there had been no Whitnee.

And that was when events started moving too fast for me to completely remember. First, our old friend Tamir stole in through the front door, taking me by surprise and causing Seth to stir on the couch.

"Morgan, it is good to see you again!" Tamir bowed to me, and I bowed back with a smile.

"When did you get here?" I asked the tall man.

"Just now, actually. Levi called for me last night, and I came as soon as I could. How are the others?"

"Pretty good. Caleb is asleep, and Whitnee is around here somewhere."

"Amelia and Kevin did not make it back this time?" He grinned.

I shook my head. "We couldn't risk bringing them back—not after everything that happened last time. But I'm sure they would love to see you again, if they could."

"Could you two keep it quiet? I just want a few more minutes of sleep," Seth, a Geodorian Herbal Technician, grumbled from the couch.

"Hey, Morgan, where's Whitnee?" Caleb's groggy voice came from the door to the bedroom. He hit a switch, bathing the room with soft light.

"I don't know—" I paused as Thomas threw open the front door, looking flustered.

"Did Gabriel and Whitnee come through here? He is supposed to be on duty with me, and now I cannot find him."

"So much for quiet," Seth growled and sat up, defeated.

Caleb and I exchanged meaningful glances. "We just woke up," I said.

"Was Whitnee *with* Gabriel?" Caleb wanted to know.

Thomas explained, "Well, yes. She woke up a few hours ago and they wanted some private time together, so I left them alone." At this news, I tensed up on Caleb's behalf. His face had fallen.

"I wonder if she has her memory back," I mumbled.

"She does," Thomas nodded. Caleb's expression became irritated then. "They went out back and talked to the prisoners, and the next thing I knew Whitnee ran off and Gabriel went after her. Apparently something upset her."

"He let her talk to the prisoners?!" Caleb was aghast. "What was he thinking?"

"Is it not obvious how easily Whitnee can persuade Gabriel? He cannot deny her anything," Thomas replied suggestively, and I really wished for Caleb's sake that Thomas would shut his mouth. "But that was a long time ago. I finally went looking for them in the cave and they are not there. I am sure they are somewhere close because Gabriel left his satchel outside."

After that, we woke up the entire house and nobody could find either of them. Still, panic didn't set in until Jeremiah, an unusually quiet Pyra, came sprinting through the house with bad news. He had reported for duty out back, but all four of the prisoners were gone. That was when we all knew something had gone terribly wrong.

Jezebel, that drama queen of a Pyra, freaked out and made Jeremiah escort her outside to have a look for herself. Eden immediately started organizing search parties—both for Whitnee and Gabriel *and* for the kidnappers we had just caught the night before. She also instructed everyone to evacuate Jezebel's house and remove all evidence of our presence there. It was just a matter of time before the escaped prisoners led the Palladium to our location. We had to get out of there.

I was in the bedroom collecting our things when I had to make another dash to the bathing room. This time there was a lot of blood involved. More than I had ever seen before.

I knew then that I had not healed myself after all. My body was still dying.

I sat there on the floor, reeling with emotion. I was devastated, scared…then mad at Whitnee for always disappearing and being busy when I needed her. And when Whitnee was in a bad situation, she took Caleb away from me too. He would always worry about her first. Then I felt guilty for being so selfish. After all, I was the one who hadn't told them the truth.

So I just gave myself over to the loneliness.

Without treatment, I knew I would not have much time left. And with treatment, my life would be prolonged temporarily, but at what cost? What hellish nightmare would I have to endure in order to live? Suddenly, seventeen years felt so short.

And how had I really spent those years?

Being afraid. Sitting in the background of other people's ambitions. Riding the coattails of my family, boyfriends, Caleb, Whitnee... anyone who would let me hitch a ride for part of their own exciting journey.

Sure, I had dreams of college, getting married, having kids... but those seemed so generic. My dreams had never taken on a life of their own. If you asked me if I wanted to go to college, I would wholeheartedly say yes. But ask me where or what I wanted to do there, and I had no answer.

Because I had never thought that far.

Maybe I had always known I would die young. Maybe it was a blessing I never had ambitions for the future because, well, the future was just a fading wisp in front of me now.

I felt cold...like I was halfway in the grave already.

I stood perfectly still and stared in the mirror for so long that my own reflection felt like a stranger. A knock at the door forced me out of my darkness. It was Thomas.

"Eden just questioned me until I thought she would run out of breath. Geos are so suspicious of everything." Thomas went to the sink to wash his hands. "I swear I do not know how those men escaped! I certainly was not the one who—" He grew quiet when he met my eyes in the mirror. He dried his hands on a towel and turned around to confront me.

"Morgan, are you sick again?"

It wasn't worth lying anymore. I nodded, directing my gaze to the floor.

"Very well. I am taking you straight to the Healing Center. Whatever is wrong, they can fix it. You remember meeting Lilley last time? She is a very gifted Healer. She studies rare illnesses—maybe she has heard of yours. I will tell Eden."

"No. We need to find Whit—"

"There is very little you can do to help Whitnee right now. But you can help yourself."

"Thomas, I've been living with this for a while. Another day or two won't hurt me. I can't go to Hydrodora until I know Whitnee is okay."

"If she is with Gabriel, she will be fine—"

"Exactly. *If* she's with Gabriel...We don't know that for sure."

"Then I suggest you tell Caleb what is wrong with you. He will probably agree with me."

Just tell Caleb...*Sure.* Thomas had no idea what kind of news I would be giving my friends. I knew the moment I spoke the word, they would understand exactly how serious my situation was. I couldn't tell them...not yet, anyway.

"You promised not to tell anyone. I need you to respect the fact that I'm not ready to share this with my friends." I sighed and walked out of the bathroom with Thomas following close behind. "I never should have told you. You don't even know what we go through back home with this stuff...I mean, what was I thinking?" I started stuffing clothes into my bag. "I can barely handle the reality of being sick... how can I expect anyone else to know what to do about it?"

"What do you *want* me to do? Clearly I do not understand, so tell me what to do."

"I want you to..." I stopped. What exactly did I want from Thomas? Why did I tell him the truth instead of telling my best friends?

Because in his life, I was here-today-and-gone-tomorrow anyway. And because our relationship was nothing compared to my attachment to family and friends. Maybe it was unfair to him...or maybe he was exactly who I needed during this time. I met his clear blue eyes and asked for the one thing he could give me right then.

"I just want you to hold me."

He swept me effortlessly into his arms, cradling me as if I were a small child. As he lowered himself to the floor, my hands crept around his neck and I dug my face into the dip between his neck and shoulder. I allowed myself to feel everything about the moment—the smoothness of his arms, the steady rhythm of his breathing, the tension of his muscles, everything that made him *alive*.

"I am afraid for you," he whispered. His hand found mine and once our palms flattened against each other, I felt him give me the very essence of life—the power of Water.

It was refreshing. It felt *right*.

But it didn't fix me.

Swallow it down, Morgan. Just swallow it down.

Caleb was thinking aloud, and I was feeling the gag reflex again. Stomach cramping had intensified. I knew there was nothing left to throw up. Except maybe a lung. Come to think of it, my lungs had been rather useless this summer too. Maybe if I coughed one up, I'd have more room in there to breathe. But my ribs ached, and I wasn't sure I could handle any more heaving.

"Either those prisoners knew a special way to escape armbands," Caleb mused, "or somebody let them go in the middle of all the chaos...but who would do that?"

I just shook my head, worried that if I opened my mouth, it wasn't words that would come out.

"And where do you really think Whitnee went?" he continued. "If this was one of her careless I-just-wanna-be-with-Gabriel moments, I might throw up."

Me too.

"I know you said to give her space, but I can't believe she got her memory back and then went straight to *him*. She didn't even have the courtesy to let us know!"

"Maybe whatever she remembered was something Gabriel needed to know immediately," I suggested weakly. This caused Caleb to sit back and frown.

Jezebel was listening in on our conversation; she had been strangely quiet the last few hours. Seth was packing up his kit of herbs and bottles. Eden was on and off her zephyra in contact with the search parties. Sometimes she would leave the room to speak privately. Thomas had opted to stay with Eden to help "protect" Caleb and me, and I was extremely grateful he had finagled that. He was currently resting in the bedroom, trying to compensate for his sleepless night. We were the only six left at the house, hesitant to leave in case Gabriel and Whitnee showed up.

After eyeing Seth shuffling bottles around, I finally asked, "Hey, Seth, do you have anything in there that might help a stomach ache?"

He opened a little leather box and pulled out a triangle that looked like it was made of crushed leaves. "Chew on this and drink Water."

"Are you sick?" Jezebel spoke up, watching me dubiously as I nibbled on the green stuff. It had a strong peppermint flavor.

"Morgan has a nervous stomach," Caleb explained dismissively. "When things stress her out, she gets sick."

Interesting how Caleb had been interpreting my behavior...I just nodded, thankful for his explanation, even if it wasn't the whole truth. I drank Water and averted my eyes from the others as I directed the life force to my stomach. I might not be healing the real problem, but it seemed to help alleviate the symptoms temporarily. While I was concentrating, I happened to be the only one who saw the zephyra on the table light up.

"Jezebel." I pointed to the flashing silver cube. She immediately answered it, and the voice that came through on the other end made the entire room freeze in fear.

"Hello, Jezebel. I hope I did not wake you this morning," Abrianna said. As cool as can be, Jezebel held her hand out to her side where Abrianna couldn't see it and gave the rest of us a "stay still" signal. I wasn't sure the range of vision a zephyra offered, but none of us happened to be sitting near Jezebel.

"Not at all. I was already up early. My Firelight sculpture was *damaged* so I am starting designs for a new one." I exchanged glances with Caleb, who had visibly tensed up. "Is there something you needed, Abrianna?"

"I am trying to find Gabriel. Did he spend the night with you?" Abrianna asked casually. Caleb's eyebrows shot up and he mouthed "*what?*" to me. I shrugged, probably thinking the same thing he was. Did Gabriel regularly make a habit of spending the night with Jezebel?

Jezebel was a very smooth liar and didn't miss a step, even with us making faces in front of her.

"No, not last night," Jezebel replied, and actually yawned as if the subject bored her. "He contacted me yesterday to cancel our plans. I really needed him to help me clean out a few things in my storage house. Maybe when you find him, you could remind him to come over here soon?"

"Of course, dear," Abrianna answered coolly. The thing about Abrianna was that we could never tell what she was really thinking. Was she buying Jezebel's story? "And I apologize for running off so quickly last night when you came to visit. I had some important matters that needed immediate attention."

"I understand."

At that moment, Eden bustled into the room, her zephyra in hand and her mouth opened to speak. Caleb jumped up and pulled her far away from Jezebel while Seth and I made motions to be quiet. She appeared confused until she heard the Guardian's voice in the zephyra.

"I must admit I was surprised when you came to visit with Eden and Hannah. I did not realize they were friends of yours." Now Abrianna was definitely fishing for information.

But Jezebel was ready for her. "They are *not* my friends. I am just making nice with them because Gabriel wishes it so. Eden especially irritates me," Jezebel said disdainfully, not glancing up at Eden's own irritated expression. "But she is the best Scent Artist on the Island and you know I love pretty things. Which reminds me, how did you feel about the dress Hannah designed for you?"

I was amazed at how Jezebel was handling Abrianna. I also suspected that most of what she said was the truth.

"It was beautiful. We will have to remember Hannah when it comes time to design your wedding dress. You will need to look exquisite for my son! I suppose we all need to sit down together soon and decide when to make the public announcement. Gabriel has been difficult to pin down lately."

Holy. *Beep.*

Judging by the faces in the room, Caleb and I were not the only ones surprised by this news. Eden's head snapped back like she'd been slapped, and Seth frowned. Jezebel ignored us, but she did shift uncomfortably in her chair.

"Yes, well, if Gabriel does not find time for me soon, there might not be a wedding." She flipped her hand dramatically, and I recognized the acting now. "I am not easily ignored."

Abrianna laughed lightly. "He is a strong-willed man, like his father, but I am confident the two of you will be very happy together."

"I suppose we shall see..." Jezebel sighed and rolled her eyes.

I was really sick now. What would Whitnee do when she found out about this? And why didn't Gabriel tell us he was engaged? And, oh, for the *love*...did Jezebel know about Whitnee and Gabriel?

This was worse than a soap opera.

"If you would like, I can send a few Palladium guards to help you today."

"Thank you, mistress, but I will just wait. I am not in the mood today. But you are always so kind to think of me." She smiled into the zephyra adoringly.

"Well, if you change your mind, they are yours...and Jezebel, dear, if you hear from Gabriel before I do, will you please notify me immediately? It is very important."

"Of course."

And then the conversation was over, and Jezebel slammed the zephyra shut. The four of us stared awkwardly at her, not sure what to say or who should say it first.

"*Wellll*," Caleb breathed. "That was weird."

"Jezebel, it might not be safe for you here. She obviously knows the truth and was testing you. Now she knows you cannot be trusted," Eden fretted.

Jezebel stared off into space for a moment. "I am not so sure. She was hiding something, yes. But think about it. Why would she bother asking if I had seen Gabriel if she knew he was still on the Mainland?"

"I was thinking the same thing," Caleb said.

"Abrianna is a manipulator. She knows we helped Gabriel back through the portal and that Whitnee escaped her guards. That was her ploy to see how Jezebel would respond," Eden replied.

"I am telling you that I know Abrianna very well, and there was something wrong," Jezebel insisted. "She was trying too hard to act natural with me. When she is manipulating someone, she is completely in control. *That* was Abrianna fighting for control."

Eden looked doubtful, and I wasn't sure what to think because, *hello*, I was still hung up on the whole Jezebel-in-an-exquisite-wedding-dress-for-Gabriel image.

"If we leave here, where will we go?" Caleb asked, and Seth and Eden glanced surreptitiously at each other.

"We have a meeting place," Eden said. "But we need Gabriel and Whitnee. Everything about this whole operation revolves around the two of them."

"What is your real motive here, Eden? I thought this whole party you have been putting on was about protecting the Travelers and finding the missing father. What does Gabriel have to do with it beyond that?" Jezebel sounded haughty.

This caused all of us to look at Eden in confusion. Jezebel did have a good point. What exactly was Eden planning? Was there more going on than we knew?

Eden remained silent as if contemplating what to say.

Jezebel stood. "You now know that anything involving Gabriel involves me too. If you have a secret, I will find out about it. He tells me everything."

I suddenly spoke up. "How long have you and Gabriel...?"

"There has never *not* been a relationship between Gabriel and me," Jezebel responded as if adding a *duh* to the end of her sentence. Across the room, Caleb heaved a sigh and rested his hands low on his hips. When he looked at me, I could sense his mistrust of Gabriel growing again...and a multitude of other emotions.

Jezebel looked back and forth between the two of us. "If you think I am concerned about your little golden-haired friend, I am not. I know Gabriel thinks he feels something for her, but he is unlike most Pyras. In the end, his sense of duty is far greater than his emotions. "

"And marrying you is his duty, not his choice?" Eden clarified, at which Jezebel bristled visibly.

"That is none of your concern. Unless you want to explain to me what you are really trying to accomplish here." The two of them stared each other down for a moment.

Finally, Eden spoke coolly. "I do not believe that a secret betrothal to our future Guardian means that you should be privy to everything involving him."

"Then maybe I have earned it because I have let you use my house, and I have lied to my future mother-by-marriage for the sake of your foolish plans!" Jezebel's temper was rising. I flashed back to the exploding wagon and decided I personally did not want to see her out of control again.

But before Eden could respond, her own zephyra started flashing. She left the room quickly and the most awkward silence settled between Jezebel, Caleb, Seth, and me. I tried to catch Caleb's eye again, but he was trying to listen for Eden's voice in the other room.

Almost as abruptly as she had left, Eden stormed back in. "We found them. Time to leave."

"What? Are you serious?" Caleb cried. "Well, I want to talk to Whitnee. Call them back!"

"Sorry, Caleb, not on the zephyras. You never know who monitors communications," she told him. "You will see her soon. Somebody go wake Thomas. We need to leave."

"I am going with you," Jezebel declared. When Eden gave her a doubtful look, she said, "I have transportation you can use."

As if she was calling a truce, Eden said, "Thank you, Jezebel. I do appreciate your help."

Jezebel tossed her hair. "I am not doing this for you."

LIST OF LASTS

Jezebel's "transportation" was a hot air balloon.

Well, that's what I would relate it to on the Mainland. She called it a Fireport. Hers was made of gigantic palm leaves with a wooden base where the passengers sat or stood, and she actually controlled it with Fire. In the center of the platform, there was a red glass cube that glowed like the Firelight sculpture Whitnee had destroyed. When Jezebel pressed her hands to it, waves of heat blasted upward and filled the leafy balloon. Jezebel had given the balloon part her own unique design. There were swirling, looping flames painted along the massive leaves. I was not much of an artistic person, but I was really starting to appreciate the way Jezebel introduced beauty and design into her own little part of the world. And Hannah wasn't kidding...Jezebel was beautiful enough to be a work of art herself.

Every time she released more heat, the inside of the big leaf filled with little floating lights, reminding me of the lightning bugs back at camp...only these lights were completely visible and brilliant in the sunlight. I felt ridiculously sad every time they eventually burned out, until more lights would fill the empty spaces and propel us higher.

When I could tear my eyes away from the workings of the Fireport, I was amazed at the view of Pyradora in the daytime. The city was set on a mountain, linked in a crazy pattern of twisting and winding trails. Jezebel's house was secluded near the top with the best view, but everywhere below, there was activity and movement and brilliant colors—both in the buildings and in the vegetation that grew along the mountainside. I could not find one logical pattern to the layout of the village—even the buildings were unique and artistically set apart from one another. I supposed this trait fit the emotionally-driven personality of the Pyras. They must have built their city however they had *felt* like building it at the time.

"It is too bad none of you are Aeros. We might get there faster," Jezebel commented as she pulled on a lever connected to a long tube. A gust of Wind emitted from the tube high above us and gave us a little shot in the right direction. "The Wind propeller does not work that well yet. Wind is so difficult to harness in an instrument...more difficult than Fire. We still have much to improve with this model."

"Is this a new thing on the Island?" Caleb questioned, carefully staying away from the side of the platform. He wouldn't admit it, but I was pretty sure he had a little fear of heights.

"Yes, it is a project Gabriel and I imagined when we were younger...childhood fantasies of leaving the Island, you know," she smiled slightly to herself and fixed her gaze out on the sky. "Gabriel did a lot of the construction whenever he found free time over the years. But once we actually got this one to work, Eli took our designs and had a few more constructed for entertainment in Pyradora. It is purely recreational. Though sometimes I confess that I take it up by myself and pretend I am floating away forever." Then she rolled her eyes as if to make light of what she had just admitted. "It would never happen—I would crash in the ocean once I left the Island."

Eden had a faraway look in her eyes. "I remember one time at a festival in Geodora—when Gabriel and I were about ten years old— he shared with me the idea of the Fireport. He said he dreamed of going to the Mainland someday and leaving the Island." She paused and thought for a moment. "I could not understand why. I have never desired to leave the Island. I love it here and I resented him for say-ing that. He was our future leader and he wanted to leave..." She shook her head slightly. "I understand better now."

Nobody knew what to say after that. I pondered the relationships of the people on the Island and how interwoven their lives were. We came here as a tiny blip of interruption on the grand timeline of their lives. And for what? Gabriel and Jezebel had real history together, even though I didn't understand it. I had no idea how to break the news to Whitnee that Gabriel had lied to her—again. And, yet, I hadn't really heard Jezebel say that she loved Gabriel. It sounded like she was *resigned* to marrying him.

And then what about Eden? While she seemed to have her own irritations and memories with Gabriel, there was still a level of genuine care and concern for him. But did that just extend as far as the fact that he was the Island's coming leader? Or did it go further? She and Gabriel reminded me too much of Caleb and Whitnee just a couple of years ago.

I watched Thomas, who was now pointing out landmarks and trading stories with Seth. What did Thomas actually feel for me? Was it just a fascination for me because I was a Traveler? And if that's what it was, could it be that Gabriel couldn't help being fascinated by Whitnee? Yes, she was pretty and, yes, she was a lot of fun to be around. But she was also super powerful—with abilities that scared all of us sometimes. How did you know the difference between real love and a simple fascination just because somebody introduced something new and different into your life?

I turned my gaze on Caleb, sitting beside me. When he felt my eyes, he turned toward me and tried to smile, but it wasn't real. I reached my arms around his neck and gave him a hug, suddenly overwhelmed with how much I cared about him. Plus, he just looked like he needed it. I whispered in his ear, "Are you okay?"

He returned my hug and said, "I'm pretty irritated. But other than that..."

"You know you're gonna have to let go of that before you see Whit."

"Depends on what she has to say." His voice sounded cold, but I knew he was just hurt. "I mean, how did they get on the other side of the freaking mountain? It sure looks like she just ran off with him again and got herself in a bad situation she couldn't control."

"Be fair. Eden said that Gabriel was hurt. So we know something unexpected happened," I said quietly, not wanting the others to hear our conversation. "Look, I can't tell you how to feel, but I still say she needs space to make her choices."

"Looks to me like she's already made her choice, Morgan. She went to *him* first. She remembered *him* first. And I can't be the one to tell her about Jezebel and Gabriel...it just makes me look jealous."

No way did *I* want that job, either. "No, you're right. Gabriel needs to tell her," I agreed.

Eden spoke up. "Morgan and Caleb should probably move to the floor as we are rounding the mountain. The Palladium has instruments in the Dome that they use to scan the skies, and we do not want them to see you here."

"By that measure, you should probably disappear then, too, Eden. It does not make sense for you and I to be taking a ride together," Jezebel said.

I took one last glance at the breathtaking view stretched out all around us. I added *hot air balloon ride* to the mental list I had found myself making of Morgan's Lasts—a list of the amazing moments left in my life. It was right up there with *finding a magical Island* and *kissing a Hydrodorian boy named Thomas*. I still had to find a way to accomplish what had snuck its way to the top of the list—*do something brave, for a change.*

Being afraid was just a waste of my time now. I had nothing to fear anymore—because there was nothing to lose that wasn't already about to be gone.

According to Jezebel and Eden, we landed somewhere north of the Watch Tower ruins between Aerodora and Geodora. The foliage in front of us looked pretty thick, and I hoped we would not be hiking far. I was definitely not up for that.

But Eden stopped sharply in front of us and pressed both her hands to the ground. With illuminated green eyes, she scanned her surroundings as if she were listening for something. Apparently satisfied, she stood again and faced the deep foliage with her left hand extended. Suddenly the thick, overlapping plant life collapsed inward on itself like a crowd of umbrellas snapping shut and disappearing at the same time. A smooth path was now visible through the trees.

It didn't matter how many startling things I had witnessed on this Island; I was still always amazed.

"Where are we?" Caleb asked as we followed Eden curiously down the new path shrouded by tall plants and shrubbery. Seth stayed behind to hide the Fireport.

"This used to be an old Geodorian sacred ground," Eden explained vaguely. "But now we use it as a sort of…headquarters. That means the protections put into place are somewhat more involved than before."

A wide line of trees whose enormous trunks were twisted unnaturally around each other stood resolute at the end of the path like silent soldiers. They created a thick wall of bark and branches that stretched high enough to block out the mid-day sun. Eden tapped one several times.

The two trees directly in front of us shuddered and groaned as their trunks separated and uncurled, opening up a gap wide enough for us to enter. I smiled at Caleb whose eyebrows were lifted in an expression of awe.

We stepped through, but Eden thrust her arms out to halt our progress.

"Wait," she commanded. I felt the Wind before I saw it. Directly ahead, about a foot away, was a silvery, wispy substance rushing past us at incredible speed. The whooshing sound coming from it was high-pitched. This looked like a bigger version of the Wind Blocker

Whitnee had learned last time we were on the Island. It worked kind of like a force field that repelled an intruder or an oncoming attack.

The trees groaned as they started wrapping around each other again, leaving us stuck in a corridor between tree and Wind. But as soon as the outside light was sealed off, the section of the Wind Blocker in front of us changed directions and made an ever-widening circular gap until it had opened up a hole that we could walk through. Eden went first and Caleb and Thomas waited for Jezebel and me to go next. As each person crossed through, a great gust of air encompassed us in swirly silver sparkles. Then a sound like an abnormally large bell chimed loudly, as if announcing our arrival.

"Aeros and their inventions…so dramatic," I thought I heard Eden mutter as she smoothed her hair down.

I pushed my bangs out of my eyes and took in the scene before me. I had the strange feeling that I had just stepped inside Willy Wonka's chocolate factory—minus the chocolate waterfall and Oompa Loompas. The blooms on the plants and trees were so wonderfully colorful that they seemed edible.

And there were Dorians scattered about who stopped to stare at our arrival. Tents were set up everywhere, and while it was bright like daylight, it felt different than it had outside. I looked up and found that the huge trees in and around this place also twisted their branches together above us, obstructing the view of the sky—and giving me the feeling that I was in a protected arena.

Tamir approached us quickly.

"Where is Whitnee?" Caleb wanted to know immediately.

"The fourth tent on the right." Tamir pointed. "She will be glad to see you. For some reason, she had a difficult time trusting us."

"And Gabriel?" Eden and Jezebel asked at the same time.

"Second tent. Michael is attending to his injuries."

Caleb marched off without a word. I scampered after him. When we approached the second tent, I slowed and caught Gabriel's eyes through the flaps. He was lying on his stomach, and Michael was working on his back. I wondered what had happened to him and jerked with the urge to go find out. But then I saw Gabriel's eyes shift to Caleb.

The two of them glared at each other as Caleb passed by with purpose. That was when we spotted Whitnee, standing outside of the tent ahead of us and looking over a set of poster-sized yellowish papers with Levi. She was no longer wearing the pink dress but still had pink stripes in her blonde hair. It struck me then how much she appeared to be the exotic, foreign one. Not the dark-haired, tan Dorians. She almost had a gleam around her...like she reflected light differently than the rest of us.

Weird.

As if she sensed something, Whitnee glanced up and looked around until she zoned in on Caleb and me. Shoving the papers at Levi, she jogged toward us and threw her arms around Caleb forcefully enough to knock him backwards. I barely had time to notice Caleb's hesitance to hug her back before her embrace transferred to me, and I was engulfed in the scent of fresh wind and lavender.

"Oh my gosh, you'll never believe everything that has happened!" she exclaimed as she pulled away. "I have so much to catch you up on! Gabriel and I found all kinds of crazy stuff—"

"Are you okay?" Caleb interrupted her.

"Well, yeah," she said, her eyes bright with an excited energy. "A little tired, but—"

"That happens when you run off in the middle of the night," he stated flatly, and she visibly deflated a little.

"I'm sorry about that. I woke up and my memory was there and—"

"You immediately ran to find Gabriel," he finished for her. She took a deep breath and gave me a knowing glance before meeting Caleb's eyes. I had a feeling things were about to get ugly.

"It wasn't like that, Caleb. I had questions for him...things involving my kidnapping."

"You could have at least told one of us...Where did you two go?"

"Look, I want to tell you," she said quietly, glancing suspiciously around her, "But I don't want to discuss it out here in the open...not until we know what's going on around here."

"What's going on is that everybody here is trying to *help* you, Whitnee."

"*Actually*, we don't know that—"

"*Actually*, let's focus on what we *do* know. Starting with your memory..." Caleb's voice was sharp. "When you were kidnapped, did you leave the cabin on your own or did someone take you from there?"

She looked confused. "I felt the portal, and I went down to the river. They found me there..."

"You went down to the river. Without us," Caleb confirmed. She nodded slowly. "And when you woke up this morning, did you really ask Thomas for alone time with Gabriel?"

"Well, yeah, but—"

"And when you two pulled your disappearing act, did you choose to leave...or did someone force you to?"

Whitnee seemed increasingly irritated with his interruptions. "What are you trying to say, Caleb? We were exploring, but we never intended to be gone for so long—"

"But that's the thing, Whitnee." Caleb's voice was low, despite the intensity of his emotion. "You always jump into things without thinking first. You left the cabin, you went exploring...it all seems so innocent to you. Meanwhile," —he gestured between himself and me— "we're left behind *worrying* about you."

"Well, I couldn't exactly control the kidnapping—" she protested.

"But you could have controlled what happened this morning!" His voice was growing louder, and I looked around nervously to make sure no one was listening in. "Whitnee, you were kidnapped and then you *died*. I held you in my arms and you were just...dead! And when you woke up, you looked at me like I was a *stranger*. Do you know what that felt like? Can you even stop to imagine what Morgan and I have been through because of you?"

Her gray eyes became glossy as she looked back and forth between the two of us.

"Y'all, I am *really* sorry..."

"I don't want you to be sorry!" Caleb exploded. "I want you to change! I want you to keep your promise that things would be different this time!"

That was when her face fell, and she shook her head, not meeting his eyes.

"Caleb," I warned softly, wanting him to calm down. After all, we didn't know everything she had been through, either. And truthfully, something in Whitnee's expression had me on alert.

Unfortunately, Caleb noticed it too. "What is it? What is that face, Whit?" he demanded. "Why do you look so...?" Then he stopped and pulled back like he'd been hit in the face. "Did something *happen* between you and Gabriel?"

Oh, no.

It was all over her face. Whitnee couldn't lie to us no matter how hard she tried. She shut her eyes for a moment and pressed her lips together as if gaining the courage to say something. Then she reached out and grabbed Caleb's hand. "Don't do this...not until I can explain everything," she whispered. He cast her hand away from his. With a disgusted look he turned on his heel and stalked away. "Caleb!" She started to follow him, but I pulled her back.

"Let him go," I suggested, and she actually listened to me. We watched him disappear behind a tent. "He's been a complete wreck since camp. Just give him time to think."

"Morgie." She looked at me, her expression pained. "I'm sorry."

I sighed. "Listen, there's something I have to tell you. I don't know what happened with you and Gabriel, but he's not being honest with you. We found out something..." I trailed off, worried about hurting her, but deciding she needed to know...especially if she was already going down that path again with Gabriel.

"You mean that Gabriel's engaged to Jezebel?" she finished, taking me by surprise. "Actually, Gabriel has been more honest with me than you know."

I studied her for a minute. "I *really* want to know what's been going on with you," I finally told her.

Her face changed a little at my words. "And I *really* want to know what's going on with *you*," she said pointedly. "And I think you know what I mean."

She remembered our conversation back at the cabin. She remembered something was wrong with me. I don't know why, but that comforted me. Maybe she hadn't forgotten me in the midst of everything else.

"Well, we should talk later," I answered lightly, already dreading the moment I would tell her the truth.

"Whitnee!" Levi called out. "It is almost time."

Whitnee's face turned grim. "Okay." She started forward, looping her arm around mine and pulling me with her. I noticed all the other Dorians were moving and gathering where a semi-circle of wooden benches was set up facing a grassy slope. It was as if the ground and plants had formed a natural stage and backdrop. "We're having an important meeting, apparently. They were just waiting for y'all to get here," Whitnee whispered, and I saw her eyes darting around. She might have been looking for Caleb or maybe Gabriel. I didn't know. But she was tense.

"A meeting about what? Do you know?" I asked.

"No." She shook her head. "But we're about to find out. Listen, you need to know something immediately…someone here is a traitor. I want you and Caleb to be very careful."

"A traitor? What does that mean?"

"It means that someone we know helped kidnap me…I didn't see him, but I know it's a *him*. That's why I went to find Gabriel when I first woke up and remembered. There was someone at Camp Fusion who knew me, and that same person could be here…*with us*."

"Oh my gosh," I breathed, my mind turning over this news. "Maybe he was the one who freed the prisoners back in Pyradora?"

Whitnee froze dead in her tracks and yanked me back to her side. "What?" she hissed.

"They didn't tell you? The prisoners, the ones who kidnapped you, escaped—"

"You mean Saul is out there somewhere...free?" She looked distraught.

"Who is Saul?"

"Um, the Island's version of Satan," she replied dramatically. "Morgan, that's bad news. I'm telling you—"

"I think they are ready for us, Whitnee," a deep voice resounded behind us. It was Gabriel. If Whitnee was casting a special light around her, Gabriel looked more like he had just been through hell and back. You could just tell when someone was ill. I wondered if I looked like that too.

"Gabriel." Whitnee released me and grabbed him by the forearms. "Are you better?"

"Michael works miracles." He smiled slightly at her.

She bit her lip. "Morgan just told me Saul escaped."

"Yes, I heard," he said grimly. But then with a tender hand, he brushed her hair out of her face and assured her, "He will not find you again. I promise I will not let him hurt you."

She didn't look too positive. "Maybe we should tell Eden everything...I don't know. Morgan thinks the traitor might have helped the prisoners escape."

"It is very possible." He lowered his voice and leaned in confidentially toward Whitnee. "Whatever happens in this meeting, though, we are not saying anything about where we have been or what we found. Not until we know who to trust here."

My curiosity about those exact things was spiking. I was about to ask more when I spotted Caleb coming back around the tent toward the meeting place we were now standing in. My eyes met his between Whitnee and Gabriel's linked arms and, well, it just looked really bad. He shook his head and moved to the back of the crowd as if he hadn't seen the two of them leaning intimately toward each other like that. I was torn over my loyalty to both friends as I watched his retreating figure. Sometimes Whitnee just didn't think through everything...and sometimes Caleb just thought too much.

A tired sigh escaped me just as Eden called, "Whitnee, Gabriel, we want you up here." She gestured to the top of the slope. "If you refuse to tell us where you have been, then maybe what we have to say will change your mind."

Gabriel gave Eden a frown. Whitnee hesitated and looked to me. "Find Caleb for me?"

"He's here," I stated flatly and nodded toward the back. Caleb stood there staring straight ahead, his arms crossed over his chest.

Whitnee sighed heavily. I squeezed her hand, and she motioned for me to sit in the front row of benches where Thomas and Hannah had a space for me. I watched her move gracefully up the slope, as if she was floating. But I wasn't the only one staring...it seemed like everyone in the arena was watching her even though nothing had officially started yet.

Once the two of them were standing on that slope together, Whitnee and Gabriel's physical differences both contrasted and complemented each other. He was massively muscular, and Whitnee's petite frame only made his presence seem more commanding. She made him look important. His darker features made her lighter skin and hair seem almost otherworldly. Like an angel...like a pure and innocent being you would instinctively trust. Combine that with the subtle glow that I swear was still about her, and the two of them together in front of everyone like that presented a powerfully striking impression.

I had this strong sense that I was looking at two people whose lives were about to change...if they hadn't already.

WILL THE REAL REBELS
PLEASE STAND UP?

Fear was something I'd never given much attention to in my life. Granted, I'd always had a ridiculous fear of fish, but that was more like the panicky, disgusted kind of fear that you knew was slightly irrational and probably unfounded. Real fear—like the kind I knew Morgan struggled with on a daily basis, the kind that affected your choices and your emotions—had just never held me back enough to worry.

Before yesterday, I had never been threatened and overpowered by another person; my personal safety and security had never been rocked that dramatically. Even when Abrianna and Eli had tied me up last time, I had still felt like my safety was in their favor.

But I knew fear now. And his name was Saul.

I was honestly afraid of what that man could (and would) do to me if given the chance. I considered myself lucky so far that there had always been someone to protect me from his awful plans, whatever they might be.

So Morgan's news of Saul's mysterious escape sat like a rusty weight in the pit of my stomach. And I was so sure that someone we knew had helped him escape—giving him potential access to me—that it made me suspicious of everyone. This was not a game we were playing. There was real evil out there.

And I seemed to be the target.

"What are you thinking? You look terrified all of a sudden," Gabriel whispered, resting his hand at the small of my back.

I cleared my face of emotion and swallowed hard. "I guess I'm just wondering what's about to happen here. I want some explanations."

"You and me both," he agreed.

Just as Eden joined us on the slope, the entry bell chimed three times, announcing the arrival of three more people. In the short time I had been there, I was already growing accustomed to the sound of the bell. However, I saw Morgan jump and peer around, which drew my own attention to the back...where Caleb stood. Not looking at me. Acting as if I didn't even exist.

If I could just go back to Camp Fusion a day ago, before I was kidnapped...

Caleb was right. I should have stayed at the cabin. Things would have turned out so differently had I waited for them. If I had stuck with the plan and not rushed off...*Ugh*. I needed a Do-Over button.

A ball formed in my throat as I imagined what Caleb and Morgan must have felt when they figured out I had been taken, what it must have been like to think I was dead. *Gah*. Maybe some people wondered how their friends would react once they were gone, but death was just too real of an issue for my friends and me.

I had an instinctive urge to bolt from that grassy stage and throw myself into their arms again just to tell them how much I loved them both. For the briefest moment, I actually wished I could transport us away from all this madness...to where we could just sit on the porch of the cabin at Camp Fusion. And Caleb would hold my hand again, and not look at me like I had just betrayed him. And Morgan wouldn't be sick and keeping secrets. The three of us would watch the sun set on the familiar Texas landscape, and life would just be a good kind of normal.

"Are you sure you are okay?" Gabriel interrupted my thoughts again.

"Yeah," I choked, accidentally peeking back at Caleb again. When it was obvious he just wasn't going to look at me, I sighed again. It was too late by the time I realized Gabriel had followed my line of vision. He pretended like he didn't notice, but I knew he did.

Finally, Eden addressed the small crowd, and I was impressed not just by her posture and clarity of voice as she called everyone to attention, but by how everyone reacted to her. It was obvious now who was in charge.

"Loyal Dorians," she said loudly and clearly. "Thank you for gathering here on such short notice. Each of you has taken an oath to uphold the ancient values of this Island and to protect the sacred laws of the life forces that govern our existence. And that oath is why we are here today."

Okay, I was already lost. I glanced up at Gabriel, who had his eyes intensely trained on Eden.

She continued boldly, "The time for action and change is upon us. Everything we have been working and planning for is about to be put to the test. I know many of you have questions" —her eyes slid sideways toward Gabriel and me— "and together we hope to answer them. But, first, I believe it is the proper time to inform Gabriel, our next Guardian, of who we are and what we are trying to accomplish."

Gabriel took a small step forward, and I watched as all the Dorians briefly nodded their formal bows and then broke out into tense whispers. Despite their dutiful show of respect, they were obviously more hostile to Gabriel's presence than I had understood.

"Dorians!" Levi commanded from the side, and there was immediate silence again.

"What is this about, Eden?" Gabriel murmured.

Eden turned to face Gabriel straight on, and in front of the crowd, she announced to him, "We are here to help you, but some believe we are taking a great risk by bringing you into our plans. Until recently, our presence has been kept secret from your parents and all of those affiliated with the Palladium. However, I believe

it is time you know the truth…And the truth is that we are—"
She paused.

"The rebels? Like Tamir said?" Gabriel's voice was tinged with
brewing anger.

"No," Eden replied. "We are not at all the same group responsible for such terrible acts on the Island. We are those who remain
loyal to the Island—to those prophecies and teachings that were
not created by men, but by a greater Purpose. We are more like…
Pilgrim Protectors."

A hush fell over the arena at the word *Pilgrim*. All eyes were
back on me.

"What does that mean?" Gabriel growled.

"As you know, the Pilgrim represents the perfect incarnation
of the Island—a savior to bring peace. And we believe that we are
living in the time of the Pilgrim. A time of change."

The perfect incarnation of the Island?

I started sweating.

Gabriel shook his head. "We do not know that Whitnee is
the Pilg—"

"Let me start from the beginning, Gabriel," Eden insisted calmly.

He hissed at her, quietly enough that only I could hear from
where we were standing: "I cannot let you jeopardize Whitnee's
safety in front of all these people, Eden. I do not understand what
game you are playing, but the things you speak of so openly can
cause a lot of trouble."

She did not back down or give any sign of fear on her face.
"Please trust me."

That was when I stepped forward and rested a gentle hand
on Gabriel's upper arm. "Listen to what she has to say. There's no
going back now, Gabriel." He looked back and forth between the
two of us and then finally took a step back beside me to show his
acceptance. But his body language was closed off after that.

I looked out into the crowd again. So many different people
there…a few in heavy cloaks, some dressed like they just stepped
off the beach, others dirty and drab like Seth…even their ages

seemed varied. And then there was Caleb at the back, watching everything with cold collectedness. I stared hard at him.

Look at me, Caleb, I begged inside. *I need you.*

Nothing. That stubborn jerk. I found Morgan's pale, weak frame in the front row. She gave me an encouraging look from tired eyes, even though she seemed as confused as I was.

Eden began. "We know that Whitnee's father was a native-born Dorian. We know that years ago some believed him to be the prophesied Pilgrim, and that he did not just disappear as once thought, but chose a life on the Mainland. We now know that the Guardian developed a portal between the Mainland and the Island and has kept it secret all these years. A few months ago, before Whitnee found the Island, we intercepted messages over zephyras that mentioned the Pilgrim—a name we have not been allowed to use here on the Island for the last thirty years. You can imagine how that raised some interest for us."

Gabriel raised his eyebrows at her, but did not interrupt.

"We formed a small group of spies at that point," she explained. "We needed to know more about what the Palladium was planning. The next thing we knew, Whitnee and her friends arrived on the Island, and you remember what happened then."

"Why didn't you tell us all of this when we were here before?" I jumped in.

"We did not know then what we know now. We certainly did not know of your father until after you were gone, and we put all of our information together. We also did not expect the way events unfolded. Do you remember the day you were running in the rain to the Palladium, Whitnee?"

I did remember. It was the day we left Eden, Thomas, and Levi behind at the dock to head to the Palladium. It was also the day I transported back to the Mainland unexpectedly.

Eden looked at me. "I tried warning you that day. I tried to send you a message through the Earth that you were heading into danger. Do you remember?"

I thought for a moment. "That was you? But the rebels...I thought the Earth life force was telling me to run from the rebels in the woods."

"No. It was *our* people hiding in the woods, waiting to see what would happen. Ready to fight for you if you needed us. I was trying to tell you the Palladium was dangerous."

"That was why you did not attack when the Guardian sent me outside," Gabriel realized. "And when I came back later, you were gone."

"So there are *two* sets of rebels..." I mused.

The good ones and the bad ones. Surely we were with the good ones, right?

"The rebels Gabriel has been hunting for the last few years are possibly led by Saul. They have destroyed parts of the Island. They are responsible for the people in every tribe who have gone missing recently. We also believe they are the ones holding Whitnee's father captive. And, Gabriel, can you guess who we think is protecting them?"

I sucked in my breath, and Gabriel just slowly shook his head, as if resigning himself to the truth.

"The Guardian," I whispered.

"It is the only thing that makes sense," Eden stated. "We do not understand all of their purposes, nor do we know how extensive their influence is...but, yes. We believe the other 'rebels' are working for your mother."

Everything Eden said was making sense...except for the fact that I knew the Guardian did not know of my kidnapping. If these rebels really worked for her, then why would they hide what they were doing from her? Unless they had gotten so powerful on their own that they were now operating without her.

I pictured Saul uninhibited, uncontrolled...and my blood ran cold.

I opened my mouth to say something, but Gabriel jumped in.

"So that is what this is about? Are we here to plan a way to subdue the rebels?"

Eden glanced out in the crowd, as if looking for someone, before continuing. With a quick breath, she turned her big green eyes on Gabriel. "No, what we are here to do is bigger than that." Then her words fell like a slow-motion bomb on my comfort zone. "We need to subdue your parents. And we need your help. Both of you."

Mumbling spread through the crowd, and I distinctly felt Gabriel's body temperature rise.

"What exactly are you asking of us?" he clarified.

Eden didn't flinch. "Nobody can deny that your parents' control of our government has become corrupt. Your mother has all the power she could want—both with a husband in the Council and a son who will be taking her place in the next year. The recent events involving Whitnee and her friends only shed more light on the problem. We know that the Guardian has become obsessed with an unnatural manipulation of life force power...We have a spy inside the Palladium."

"Who?" Gabriel demanded.

"Michael," she admitted, glancing at the quiet Hydro who had healed Gabriel earlier. He stood near Caleb at the back, and I watched as he nodded slightly at Gabriel. Gabriel had explained to me that Michael had been his personal attendant most of his life. Michael was the only other person in the world he seemed to trust—in fact, Michael had been the one to suggest Gabriel's back-up plan for returning from the Mainland just in case his parents shut down the portal on him. Apparently, Gabriel had trusted the right person. Eden said, "Through Michael, we know that Abrianna and Eli frequently employ violence as a means to get what they want. We know that you have seen this first-hand—"

"Enough!" Gabriel practically shouted. His face flushed, and he looked angrier than I had ever seen him. I had no idea then what Eden meant or how Gabriel took it. But clearly he was not open to discussing his parents' cruelty. "Just tell me what you want."

"We want your loyalty, Gabriel." Eden had softened her voice. "And, in turn, we offer you our loyalty. We offer you a chance to be a real leader…one who rids our government of corruption. One who balances out the power that has been usurped by your mother. We have reason to believe Abrianna will try to extend her Guardianship, thus eliminating you completely, Gabriel. We want you to help us gain control of your parents and then help us renew the system of government we have set up—with you as the leader of the people, as our rightful next Guardian."

The silence was so thick after that…I think most of us had forgotten to breathe. I could see Gabriel warring with the consequences of doing as Eden asked. When he finally did speak, I recognized the vulnerability there.

"Why me?" he asked her, and then he addressed the crowd, his words laced with the insecurity I knew was deep inside of him. "Why would you want me to be your leader? I am their son! Do you really believe for a moment that the same corrupted blood that runs through my parents does not run through me? I am sorry, but I am the wrong person for such a task. Maybe I do not want such power."

Someone yelled from the crowd, "I told you he would not join us!" Others began shouting and arguing with each other across the meeting area.

"This is foolish!" another shouted. Eden tried to regain control as the Dorians' arguments increased in volume.

I ignored them and yanked Gabriel down to my level. "*What are you doing?*" I looked hard into his eyes, remembering all the talk Abrianna had given me last time about setting up a *new kind of government*…that had sounded suspiciously like a dictatorship. "Honestly, Gabriel, Eden is right! Do you really believe Abrianna is going to just step back and hand over the Guardianship to you? If you don't do something, I'm afraid she's going to make her own changes—and they won't involve *you*. It's time for you to make a choice here."

Fiercely, he spat, "I am not who these people think I am—"

"You're right—you're much better! Do you remember my dare? To change your world? This is your chance, Gabriel. You can do this."

"This is crazy!" he protested.

"Sometimes the crazy thing is the right thing!" I turned my attention back on the crowd. "Listen up!" I yelled. I shot my hand up in the air and conjured a forceful gust of cold Wind that rippled viciously through the crowd.

That got their attention. And they didn't look too happy about it.

"Uh, sorry…" I took a deep breath and spoke from my heart. "If you want to make a change, then you have to be united. Please quit arguing and just listen." My heart was pounding. "Eden is right. Gabriel is the man to help you. He is smart and resourceful. He knows each of your tribes and respects the different cultures of each one. And he is *not* like the Guardian." I flashed a look at his incredulous face as he watched me speak. "Trust me, I *know*. He values life here on the Island; he cares about people and about doing the right thing." My thoughts flitted to my dad and what Ben had shared with me this summer about Dad's hesitancy to rule the Island so many years ago. The similarities between Dad and Gabriel struck me profoundly. So I added, "If anything, Gabriel's hesitance to join you is proof that he doesn't take the power you offer him lightly. That quality alone makes him a good leader. He has seen that too much power corrupts a person."

Eden picked up on my efforts and addressed Gabriel: "You already are a Pilgrim Protector, Gabriel. Look at all you have done to ensure Whitnee's safety. Not only that, but your parents left you stranded on the Mainland. Clearly, they see you as a threat to their power. You have nowhere else to go, Gabriel. You need us…and we need you. The *Island* needs you."

The crowd was quiet, tension hanging heavy in the air. I traded glances with Eden as Gabriel appeared to be thinking.

"If I were to join you," he finally said, "how could you ever accomplish such a thing? The Guardian has power and control everywhere. She has her own group of spies too—most of whom you would never know. You have maybe seventy-five, eighty people here? You cannot control her with that many."

That was when Eden's face broke into a smile. "These people you see before you? These are just the fighters, Gabriel. Our numbers significantly increased after Whitnee left. We have a network of people in every tribe all over the Island working for this cause. How do you think we have been able to track and pull together so much information in so short a time? Trust me, we have the followers…we just need the leader."

Gabriel gave her a look that bordered doubt and respect. "You look as if you are doing a fine job leading on your own, Eden," he pointed out. And, well, he was right. My admiration for Eden was growing dramatically the more I listened to her. She could be so girly and yet so authoritative. The girl made and sold perfumes but then kicked butt at a competitive game of coconut launch. I had seen her laugh and play with her little siblings like a normal person and yet now she was commanding the respect of an entire network of spies.

Yep, Eden was pretty amazing. And maybe Gabriel was starting to notice.

"But I am not you, Gabriel," she replied with sincerity.

"I still say that is not enough. What about the Tetrarch Council? What about those already in power? Do they know anything of your plans?"

Eden glanced again at the crowd. She looked uncertain for the first time since we started the meeting. "That is unimportant. I just need to know if you will consider—"

"Answer my question." He looked suspiciously at her.

"I…I do not—"

"It is all right, Eden," a booming, jovial voice called from the crowd. "The time has come. We cannot hide our involvement any longer." Three of the cloaked figures in the back lowered the hoods covering their faces. A few people gasped. The wide, bearded figure who spoke was Joseph, Eden's father—the Councilman for the Geodorian Tribe. "Gabriel, you have support from most of the Tetrarch Council already."

His companion, the tall, wispy figure with the long, silver hair was…

"Ezekiel!" I exclaimed.

My grandfather was *here*. And trailing behind him was my grandmother, Sarah.

I ran down the slope to meet them as they made their way in our direction. I threw myself into Ezekiel's arms and couldn't control the happy tears that filled my eyes at seeing the majestic man who I now knew was my own flesh and blood.

"Hello, Granddaughter." He greeted me with a surprisingly powerful grip for such an old man.

"I have so much to tell you!" I whispered into his chest.

"Likewise, my dear."

"And Sarah!" I transferred my embrace to the graceful, willowy woman with the wise pewter eyes. "I got your letter…I tried to come back, but everything went wrong…"

She smelled like sweet powder, and she patted my head softly with her small hand. "I hope you know I could not tell you the truth earlier because of the threats to Ezekiel and to our tribe. Abrianna has her guards posted everywhere in Aerodora to ensure our silence. But I had to try."

"I figured it was something like that." I looked up into both of their aged faces, finally seeing a small resemblance to my own features. Our coloring might be different, but Ezekiel's eyes were my dad's eyes. "I've missed you!" I confessed. With reassuring arms around me, they led me back up to the grassy slope.

Ezekiel faced Gabriel straight on, and the crowd quieted again. "Gabriel, my granddaughter speaks wisely. I have always suspected your potential for greatness, but after you came to me in confidence about Whitnee and her father, I *knew* you were the one we needed to turn this government around…and to help recover the family that was lost to me so long ago."

Joseph clapped a meaty hand on Gabriel's shoulder. "We know that asking you to turn your back on your parents is a big decision, Gabriel. It is one we do not take lightly, nor do we expect it to be easy for you. But you have the support of Geodora and Aerodora." He looked out into the crowd as if asking them to confirm his words. Aeros and Geos raised their fists and grunted in agreement. Gabriel already had a good relationship with Joseph, and I could detect the effect Joseph's words had on him—almost like the support of a father.

"What about the Hydros and Pyras?" I asked.

Ezekiel answered, "Simeon gives his unofficial support and has allowed us to rally different Hydros to the cause. Our new friend, Thomas, has been instrumental in bringing Hydros into our plans slowly and secretly. But Simeon prefers that Hydrodora remain outwardly neutral for as long as possible, and he is right to protect that appearance. Even if it is just that—an appearance."

"We have recruited some in Pyradora, but that has been difficult given their allegiance to your father, Gabriel," Joseph told him. "We are hoping you will help us with that. You must know more about your father's affiliations than we do."

Gabriel still appeared hesitant. "Do you have a plan for how to accomplish all of this?"

Everybody looked to Eden for an explanation. "Well, as we said, we are first Pilgrim Protectors. So the first priority is to retrieve Whitnee's father. He is too much of a powerful bargaining tool for them."

Ezekiel gave her an approving nod and squeezed my shoulder. Even Sarah's eyes lit up. My heart gave a little hopeful jerk as Gabriel and I exchanged glances. "I believe we might have some information that will help with that," Gabriel told Eden quietly. "But Whitnee and I would prefer to share that in private. Is there any other reason why we must continue this big meeting?"

"Actually, yes. We have told you what we want from you, Gabriel. But Whitnee is just as important in our plans."

"Me?" I repeated stupidly. "Eden, maybe you should hear more about my father before you—"

"We know enough about your father," she assured me. "And, Whitnee, we will find him and put an end to the Guardian's control over his life. Once we do that, though, the implications of what the two of you mean to this Island and to our people are pretty serious."

"O-*kay*," I said slowly. "So what exactly do you want from us?"

I looked at the solemn faces of those around me—Joseph, Ezekiel, Sarah, Eden, and Gabriel. Then I found Caleb's face at the back. This time he met my gaze, and his face was so intensely focused on mine that I think he knew what was coming next... even before I did.

Then Eden said it.

"Because of the Pilgrim prophecy and what it means to our survival, we want you and your father to consider staying on the Island...permanently."

My body jolted at her words. Stay here *permanently*? That was not in my plans. No, I was supposed to find Dad and reunite him with Mom and live happily ever after on the Mainland. I mean, I had my senior year ahead of me and college and...staying on a magical Island as their...Pilgrim or whatever...was not my future.

My life was meant for the Mainland...wasn't it?

Suddenly, I didn't know what to do with myself. I thought about bolting out of there and hiding from all the people staring at me, waiting for my response. Gabriel must have sensed my upheaval because he said softly, "Surely she does not need to decide that right now. Could we take a break here and plan out our next step?"

Ezekiel jumped in, "Eden, you have done a fine job, but Gabriel is correct. Let us take a break." He waved his hands at the crowd. "Dorians, we will meet again in a few hours. You are dismissed for now." My grandfather carefully started down the slope with Sarah's arm tucked in his.

Joseph followed with Eden, suggesting, "Perhaps we should go to my tent."

I stared after them, my feet having a difficult time uprooting themselves from where I stood. Gabriel extended his hand to me. With an expression that seemed as hesitant and overwhelmed as my own, he asked quietly, "Shall we go now? The others should be informed about what we know. And I believe I owe Tamir an apology."

I blinked at his extended hand and hesitated. My eyes drifted to the back of the meeting area.

Caleb was gone.

But Jezebel was watching us, and my stomach fluttered with apprehension.

"Whitnee." Gabriel said my name with such insecurity that I rested my gaze back on him. "Are you with me? I cannot do this without you."

With a small nod of my head, I took Gabriel's hand and we descended the grassy slope.

Together.

THE BEST LAID PLANS

"Tunnels under the Watch Tower ruins?" Joseph repeated incredulously. "Of course! Nobody goes to the Southern Beach or the ruins. They would have had years of privacy to build whatever they wanted there."

"Makes me wonder now if the rumors about it being haunted all these years were formulated for a reason," Levi grunted as he and Gabriel pored over Gabriel's holographic map of the area. "Thomas, show us again about where they disappeared with Whitnee last night."

Thomas pointed to the southernmost tip of the ruins. "Somewhere around here, I think."

"Do you remember any defining landmarks there?" Gabriel questioned.

Thomas frowned and stared off into space for a moment. "I remember a tree that grew out of the tower foundation. And the rock was really uneven. But that defines most of the ruins, does it not?"

"Maybe," Gabriel mumbled.

Morgan turned to me and whispered, "Remember spending the night at the ruins the first night we came here? How weird is it to think that your dad could have been that close?"

My thoughts had already led me there, but I just shrugged. I remembered the foggy, formless dreams that had awakened me that first night. Hadn't the slamming of a door woken me up? But I had soon become distracted by Gabriel and our little training session out on the beach. I had been so intrigued by him that night…and so full of questions.

I was still full of questions. Just different ones.

My eyes flashed to Caleb across the tent. He was concentrating on the map and still largely avoiding me. I was pretty sure I had overheard Morgan whisper to him earlier: "I said give her space, not act like a jerk." Of course she was trying to help. The longer Caleb went without talking to me, though, the more it was starting to upset me.

"I am interested in this theory of Nathan being on a boat. Saul did allude to the idea that he was no longer on the Island, correct?" Ezekiel pointed out.

Gabriel nodded. "Yes. But Saul has always spoken in riddles. The fool thrives on sowing confusion and doubt."

"But it would make sense. Perhaps the tunnels lead to a docking station or a place where they could easily access a boat that stayed somewhere off the coast," Ezekiel suggested. "I will send out some thunderflies to scour the perimeter of the Island. It will likely take them the rest of the day and into the night."

"They cannot veer too far from the land, though," Tamir pointed out.

"Yes, but neither can a boat…unless it wants to be lost forever," Ezekiel agreed.

"I think our best chance at recovering Whitnee's father is to act immediately. I say we wait no longer than tonight," Eden suggested.

"I agree." Gabriel lowered his hand and the map dissolved. "They have to know by now that I am here and not on the Mainland. Saul and the others must have reported back to the Palladium with the identities and locations of all our people. But as far as Saul knows, Whitnee has no memory of anything about the ruins. We cannot waste another night waiting around."

"Wait a second," I interrupted. Everyone in the tent—those that made up our closest circle of trust—turned to me. "We don't know that Saul and the others report to the Palladium. I have serious doubts that Abrianna even knows I was brought to the Island."

Caleb scoffed, "I find it hard to believe that Abrianna is not *somehow* involved in all of this."

Not the support I wanted, but at least he didn't ignore me...

"Whitnee," Eden addressed me. "Let us assume she had nothing to do with your kidnapping. We still have the problem of the rebels, and you said yourself that Saul knows where your father is being kept. We can deal with Abrianna later. Right now, we need their most important weapon...your father."

I looked to Gabriel for support. "I just don't want us fighting the wrong enemy here."

"They are all connected somehow," Gabriel shrugged. "Eden is still right."

I frowned. Was I the only who cared about this little glitch in their theories? If Abrianna controlled the rebels, then how did they kidnap me without her knowing? Unless I just misunderstood...just remembered the conversation in the ruins wrong. I suppose that was possible.

"So tonight we put all our focus on the Watch Tower ruins," Gabriel continued, pulling up his map again. "I suggest we take separate teams and approach the ruins from the north, west, and east." He gestured with his other hand. "We need to concentrate on looking for secret entrances or passageways—"

"Like the 'screen' thing you described in Jezebel's cave?" Caleb asked. Everybody's heads snapped back like they hadn't even thought of that. If Jezebel had been allowed in the tent (which Gabriel and Eden both had forbidden), I probably would have found myself sneaking a peek at her reaction. I was more than curious to find out if she knew what was on her property.

"Yes, Caleb, a screen would be an obvious clue, but they are hard to find. You will have to touch most everything in the area to see if it is real," Gabriel conceded.

Eden added, "I think it would be prudent to bring a few boats down from Hydrodora to surround the area by sea. Just in case the boat theory has some validity. Thomas, could you organize that on such short notice?"

"Tonight? Are you both forgetting the Festival of Springs commences tonight?" Thomas asked.

"Oh, yes. I did forget..." Gabriel's eyebrows furrowed.

"What is the Festival of Springs?" I piped up.

Thomas explained, "It is an annual Hydrodorian celebration in which we give thanks for the provision of Water."

"Giving thanks? More like throwing parties every day and night for three days," Eden smirked.

Thomas grinned boyishly and winked at Morgan. "That is the best part."

I turned to Morgan beside me. "Sounds like Fiesta week back in San Antonio. Papi would be proud." She gave a short laugh. My friends had seen Papi during Fiesta week. The man was even more, um, boisterous than usual. Not that his alcohol intake had anything to do with it...

Gabriel expounded, "Every tribe has a festival at some point in the year for the purpose of celebrating and giving thanks for their particular life force. The Hydros happen to put on the largest festival and usually have the highest attendance from all tribes. It will be chaotic in that village for the next three days."

"Even better," Eden remarked as if it wasn't a big deal. "Most of the Island's activities will be centered around Hydrodora. Even the Guardian herself makes an appearance at each festival. It provides a perfect distraction, which means our enemies will not expect us. Of course, the crowd will expect to see you there by her side, Gabriel, will they not?"

"Given the fact that my parents left me on the Mainland, I am certain they will already have an excuse for my absence," Gabriel replied darkly.

Eden nodded and added, "I still think it would be wise to have at least one boat down south."

Thomas bit his lip doubtfully. "I will contact a few people, but I cannot promise anything."

"Do your best, Thomas. Eden, those are good thoughts. Now, if we have boats in the ocean, thunderflies in the sky, and teams on ground, what else are we missing?" Gabriel may have been addressing all of us in the tent, but I did not miss the way his eyes went first to Eden for her opinion. I wondered if he realized he was actually working *with* her now instead of *against* her.

Ezekiel chimed in. "I would like to send someone to investigate the cabin where Whitnee claims her father has been living."

Gabriel nodded, but said, "That is probably wise, but I feel very strongly that nobody outside of this group in here should know about the cabin or the cavern we found. We have good reason to believe that someone Whitnee knows is secretly working for the Palladium. Does everybody understand?"

We all nodded.

Ezekiel said, "Tamir, I would like you to escort my wife back to Aerodora and then travel immediately to the place you found the cabin. I trust your tracking skills to fully explore its purpose. I want to know what exactly they are hiding there in the mountain too. If there is another portal, we need to know about it."

"Of course, sir. Whatever you ask." Tamir bowed respectfully.

"Watch out for the drakons," I muttered.

"By the way, how did you know where to look for Whitnee and Gabriel?" Caleb suddenly questioned Tamir with a skeptical face.

Tamir shifted his eyes carefully toward Gabriel. "Jezebel suggested it. She told Jeremiah to search the other side of the mountain, and I went with him. That was where we found the cabin."

Gabriel inhaled deeply and his eyes found mine across the tent. Did that mean Jezebel knew about the passageway and where it led? Caleb vocalized what I was thinking. "Are you sure we can trust Jezebel?"

"Yes." Gabriel did not hesitate with his answer. "But I will speak with her about this."

Eden warned, "She knows now what we are doing, Gabriel. See to it that her loyalty stays with you, regardless of what she knows or does not know about her property. Understand?"

Gabriel nodded.

Tamir redirected the conversation. "Are you sure you do not want my help at the ruins tonight?"

"No, I believe they have more than enough help. Leave in the next hour. Tell no one where you are going," Ezekiel decided.

Tamir bowed again in a sign of obedience. Observing the tall guard, I felt guilty all over again for doubting his loyalty and motivations back at the cabin. *But you knew there was a traitor somewhere, and he did seem threatening at first*, I told myself in defense. In retrospect, Tamir had been falsely concerned that Gabriel would take me to the Palladium. His behavior made complete sense now that I knew the whole picture.

But thoughts of the traitor had me scanning the room again… surely it was not someone in here.

Surely. *Not.*

Hannah and Eden were safe because they were female. I knew the traitor was a man. Gabriel was a man, but, well, we'd already been down Mistrust Lane, and I planned to avoid that route at all costs. Morgan and Caleb…obviously not one of them. Joseph, Ezekiel, and Sarah were a *duh*, too, based on the fact that they were heading up a secret rebellion already. That left Thomas, Levi, and Tamir.

If it had been Tamir, he would not have passed up the golden opportunity to take us to the rebels when he found us in the cabin. I really didn't think Thomas was capable of turning on us…he seemed too playful and innocent and, okay, he was clearly a little distracted with Morgan most of the time. Although…he was the one on duty when the guards escaped. And I had just found out that he was not recruited into this cause until the day we left the Island. But most of the Dorians out there had only joined the ranks since we left six weeks ago. It hardly seemed like enough evidence against Thomas. Plus, I just didn't get that feeling from him. He had been the most suspicious of me since I came here. If he'd been Abrianna's spy, he would have been a little less obvious, right? Ever since he witnessed the healing I performed on Caleb, he had been adamant that I was the Pilgrim and had been convincingly loyal ever since.

So only Levi remained under suspicion. But, again, he was one of my grandfather's most trusted Aeroguards, a man in his inner circle. Out of all of them, Levi had trained me the most on using the Wind life force, empowering me to fight against enemies. I trusted him the *most*.

No. Whoever our traitor was, he wasn't in this tent with us.

So, who is it?

"…Whitnee and Morgan will stay here tonight. Caleb, would you like to stay with the girls or go to the ruins with a team?" Gabriel's voice brought me back to the rescue plans.

"Oh, I'm going," Caleb replied automatically.

"Wait, what?!" I interrupted, shaking my head emphatically. "I'm not staying here while you guys go find my dad!"

"Sorry, Whit, but it's not safe for you to be there," Caleb said and looked to Gabriel for back-up.

"Agreed. You are staying," Gabriel confirmed.

"I am *not!*" I cried. How dare they team up against me! *Boys.* I turned to Morgan. Her big blue eyes said she was not really keen on arguing the point with me.

"I am sorry, but you are the one they are trying to find," Gabriel reasoned. "If we rescue your father, but lose you, then we have gained nothing."

I glared back and forth at the two boys I cared about the most. They both had their arms folded in front of them and were staring me down with the same stubborn looks.

I changed tactics. "Fine. Go without me. I'll just meet you there later."

Caleb didn't blink; years of friendship had only strengthened his capacity to withstand my threats. But Gabriel sighed. "You will have a hard time finding a way out of here—"

"*Will* I?" I narrowed my eyes at him. "You remember what happened in that cave…you think you can keep me in here?"

I could use all four freaking life forces for crying out loud! *Try and stop me.*

"Whit, quit acting like we're just trying to control you. It's about keeping you safe," Caleb said, and his face held genuine fear this time. "I'm sorry, but after all that's happened in the last twenty-four hours, I do not want you in danger again."

"How do you think *I* feel about *you* walking into a dangerous situation, Caleb? Do you want to put me through the same thing? This is dumb." I turned a desperate face to Ezekiel who was watching me curiously. Surely he understood. "Ezekiel, you know how important this is to me. It's my father! This is the whole reason I came back here! Please tell them—"

But it wasn't Ezekiel who suddenly jumped to my defense.

"Let Whitnee go with you." It was Morgan. She rose to her feet, and my mouth fell open, stunned.

Caleb shook his head in exasperation, as if Morgan had just betrayed him. "It's a bad idea."

She looked him straight in the eye and in a very un-Morgan-like way, she stated passionately, "It's a bad idea to *not* have her with you, Caleb. She's the most powerful person on this Island. *She's* the one who has gotten us this far in finding Nathan. And don't forget that he's found ways to contact her on more than one occasion. You'd be stupid not to take her with you." She thrust her chin out. *Go, Morgie, go,* I thought. "Besides, if you don't, she'll go anyway…and I swear I'll do whatever I can to help her." Her voice shook a little, and her face flushed. I stood up and linked my arm tightly with hers. Together we faced the rest of the tent.

Gabriel gave in first. "Very well. It looks like we are all going."

Nobody looked happy. Especially Caleb.

I gave a satisfied nod while Morgan's arm trembled in mine.

GREEN-EYED BOY AND
GRAY-EYED GODDESS

"If you turn your arm like this and step into the forward motion, it will create more distance," Levi explained, curving my arm and demonstrating the position for me.

I followed his instructions and stepped forward, projecting the Wind life force as sharply as I could. I watched as the purple lightning arrow soared from my hand across the field. It barely missed the dummy target, and exploded instead into the protective Wind Blocker behind it.

"Dang," I muttered.

"That was good. Your distance was much better…now just combine that with a better aim at your target and you will have it," he encouraged.

"The aim is all in the wrist, Whitnee," Hannah offered. "Keep your wrist in alignment with your target, and the arrow will always go where you want it. Power and distance are important, but consistency in your aim is what makes you successful."

I gave a quick nod and took the position again. It was one thing to stand still and aim at something. It was quite different to be moving in their strange martial arts positions and still get my aim right. And then what would I do when my target was moving too? This offensive fighting stuff was much more difficult than I expected.

I shot again…and missed again. I grunted in irritation.

"Keep practicing," Hannah smiled. "When you get comfortable with it, the three of us will do some combat practices."

I chanced a casual glance at Eden and Caleb several yards to my left. Caleb was intensely focused and apparently having a lot of success with the Earth life force. Nine times out of ten, he hit his target effortlessly. And earlier he had made roots shoot up out of the ground and lunge for Eden, who had just as easily sidestepped and subdued them. Pathetically, I wished he were as distracted by me as I was by him. This was the first time I remembered Caleb intentionally avoiding me. And it was infuriating.

Morgan was working with Thomas and Michael where a spring had been created for training practices. I watched her control and manipulate the Water into powerful weapons of attack. At one point, she had even risen up high into the air on the strength of a wave that then dropped her gracefully on the ground before curling back into the spring. She was a complete natural.

And yet, there I was shooting lightning arrows that couldn't even hit their stupid target. Granted, Caleb and Morgan only had one life force to understand and master. I had *four*, and they all came from different places within me, utilizing a multitude of different feelings.

The arena we were in had its own training field and facilities, an upgrade Eden had made once this place had become their official headquarters. And even though nobody truly expected a fight to break out tonight, we were still nervously practicing attack techniques anyway. Levi and Hannah were coaching me while Gabriel was off somewhere attending to the details of our mission.

My eyes wandered away and found Ezekiel and Joseph sitting on the side, watching our progress and whispering together. Ezekiel smiled encouragingly at me when our eyes met. I smiled back and focused again on the different weapons I was learning within each life force. Lightning arrows, Firedarts, Earthstones,

Water spears…to name a few. All of them were what Levi referred to as "focused shots of energy." They required a bit more skill than just conjuring one gust of Wind that covered a wider area. These were smaller, but more intensely powerful. I was getting better switching back and forth between the life forces. It was just my technique, body movements, and aim that needed work.

Hannah and Levi stepped back to observe while I pushed myself harder. I shot over and over again, most of the arrows detonating on the Wind Blocker. One hit a target I wasn't actually aiming at.

Using offensive life forces was almost like a dance…an angry, punctuated dance.

"I wish I had some rap music," I commented in between shots. The steady rhythm of a good hip-hop song might actually help me.

"What is rap music?" Levi asked.

I grinned. "The kind my mom doesn't like." I paused to slow my breathing. "Actually, Morgan is the closet rap fan. In fact, do me a favor…" I threw a look back at Morgan flirting with Thomas in the Water. "Sometime when she least expects it, tell Morgan these words exactly…'I like big butts and I cannot lie.' It'll make her smile."

It would actually prompt her to kill me. But it would be *so* funny.

"Okay," Levi agreed with a puzzled smile in Hannah's direction.

I turned back and concentrated on that annoying target way out there. I pretended there was music, some kind of rhythm my movements could follow. I executed a Firedart, but it was obvious immediately that my aim was off. As if I had some strange reflex reaction, my hand shot out again, and the Firedart unnaturally veered to the right from its straight course. In an explosion of flames, it hit the center of the target.

That gained the attention of everyone on the field. Even Caleb.

"You did it!" Hannah cried.

Levi seemed intrigued. "Yes, but you manipulated one life force with another…very smart."

"I used what you taught me about moving objects with Wind. It just happened to change the direction of the Firedart," I explained.

"Do you think you could try that with a moving target?" he asked.

"I guess." I never seemed to know what exactly I could do until I tried it.

"Eden!" Levi called. "Run out there and see if Whitnee can hit you."

"What? No, I can't hit Eden…what if I hurt her?" I cried.

"Eden is the best at deflecting hits. She will be fine," Levi assured me.

Eden left Caleb and began running across the field. Okay, so it was definitely more nerve-wracking trying to hit a real person—especially someone I liked. I observed her speed and movements for a moment and finally swung my arm back. I shot a Water spear, using the Wind to redirect it. She saw it coming and changed directions deftly. But I was quick too. Almost comically, the spear began chasing her at my command. When she ducked and it shot over her head, I turned it back again. She conjured a shield just in time. The spear hit the shield and burst like a deadly water balloon.

"Brilliant!" Levi commended. Morgan clapped and whistled. Caleb made an unimpressed grunt and turned away. I suddenly wanted to launch a Water spear at him and see if *he* could react that fast. What a *turd*.

"Maybe we should work with moving targets now…" Hannah mumbled.

"I need a break for a minute," I decided and uncorked my bottle of Water. I took a swig and marched over to Caleb. "Can we take a walk?"

He wouldn't meet my eyes. "Not now. We're training."

"Caleb, we should talk."

"It can wait…we have a lot to do right now." He turned his attention back on Eden across the field and called out, "Can we try more of the Earthshaking?"

Grr.

I jerked his arm so that he would look at me. "Fine. You don't want to talk. Then fight with me."

"What?"

"Let's go. You want to train, right? Train with me."

"I don't think that's a good idea."

"Because you're scared of me?" I raised my eyebrows in a challenge.

"Whatever." He rolled his eyes.

I backed up a few steps. "Come on." I shot a gentle ripple of air his direction. He pressed his lips together in annoyance. But he moved out into the field with me.

I was so annoyed that I attacked first with a lightning arrow, and he barely blocked it with a quick shield. "*Geez*, Whit. At least warn me," he growled.

I shot an Earthstone, calling, "Your enemy won't warn you. Why should I?" He deflected it again. I was about to hit him with another one, but he shot first this time. I couldn't make a shield fast enough, so I dove on the ground to avoid the oncoming attack.

"Crap! Are you okay?" he yelled. Instead of answering, I released a gust of hot Wind at him. He fell back several steps, and I used the distraction to pull myself up and move closer to him.

"I know you're mad at me for a lot of reasons, but you didn't even let me explain what happened!" I huffed.

"You didn't have to explain. Your actions say enough."

"So you admit this isn't about me running off all the time? This is really about *him*. Caleb, you don't even *know*..." I was hardly thinking about the life forces now. I sent a mini-whirlwind at him with a sharp flick of my hands. He blocked it and launched another Earthstone, which I effectively blocked with my own shield.

"Whitnee, I don't need to know what happened because I know *you*. I was stupid for thinking things could change."

I dropped my hands in surprise. "Things *have* changed. Things *are* different this time, Caleb. If you would just stop being mad at me and let me explain—"

"I'm not mad at you."

I snorted at that. His hands dropped to his side too, and the green glow of his eyes slowly changed back to normal. "No, really, I'm not. I'm mad at myself."

"Why? I'm the one who screwed everything up."

"Yeah, well…I'm the one who allowed myself to have hope." He looked down at the ground and rested his hands on his hips. "I set myself up for this…I *knew*, Whitnee. I knew that you cared about him, and I didn't respect that at all this summer. I knew when we came back—well, you know what I mean. I know where your heart is. And it's not with me." He said it so emotionlessly, so matter-of-fact. My eyes wandered around the field, noting distantly that Jezebel had joined the sidelines of people. Everyone was trying to look occupied, but I'm pretty sure we had an audience. Caleb turned his back on me and started to walk away.

As if this was over!

He called dismissively over his shoulder, "We've got work to do—"

I darted into his path, and in a haughty voice, I said, "How can *you* know where my heart is when *I* don't even know that?!" He looked surprised, but I was fuming. "You think you know everything, Caleb Austin! But you don't!" I shoved him lightly in my frustration. "You don't know what it's like to wake up and have no memory of your life or the faces in the room except these really strong feelings for the green-eyed boy who is holding you and calling you 'baby' like he belongs to you and you belong to him!" I started pacing in front of him. He stood frozen like a statue. Maybe he thought I had forgotten the "baby" comment he had made during all that. "You don't know what it's like to want to murder a man for what he did to you and then while you're hating yourself for being such a monster, the first person you think of is that same green-eyed boy because he makes you feel good about yourself when you hardly feel good enough for him!" I turned to face him again and poked a sharp finger at his chest. "And you don't know what it's like when another guy, who you really care

61

about, kisses you and…and all you can think about is the green-eyed boy and how special he is to you and how you don't want to lose him!" I think I heard Caleb's sharp intake of air, but I couldn't stop. "There is so much you *don't* know. And I don't know how to tell you because I hardly understand it myself! But I cannot function without that green-eyed boy. I *need* him."

After my rant, we just stared at each other for a minute while I caught my breath. I know my face was probably red—and not just from my frustration. I was starting to feel embarrassed for admitting all of that. But, well, it was the truth. I was sick of lies and secrets. I didn't want them between my friends and me anymore.

"Say something!" I finally spat.

When he looked at me again, there was a slight twinkle in his eyes. "So, uh, who is this green-eyed boy? I think I might have to kick his—"

"Caleb." I shoved him again, but this time playfully. "I was being serious."

He reached out and rested both of his hands around my neck and tilted my face up to look directly at him. The gentle pressure of his hands was soothing, and I think I kind of leaned my cheek toward one of his palms. The spicy scent of wood and earth lingered on his skin. With a sigh, he said softly, "There's that expression on your face again…the one I can't read yet. It's been around a lot this summer."

"Maybe it's the one reserved for you."

He smiled like he hadn't thought of that. "I'm just trying to give you space to figure things out, okay, Whit? But I'm still *here*."

"Okay." I nodded, refusing to look away from those green eyes that I loved so much. "Then stop ignoring me. I don't want that much space from you."

"Fine." He ran one thumb gently along my jaw before letting me go. "And just for the record, I can totally go the rest of my life without *ever* hearing about another guy kissing you. Deal?" His tone and words were light, but I saw the hurt in his face.

"I'm sorry."

"Hey." He held up a hand. "Just friends, right? Wasn't that the last thing we agreed on at camp?" That smile was back.

I groaned loudly. "Yes, I believe it was…"

"So technically, I am a free agent," he continued, mischief coloring his tone. "And it's a good thing too. These Island girls just can't get enough of me this time around. Everywhere I go, it's like 'Caleb, make out with me'—"

I didn't let him finish. The gust of Wind knocked him over before he even knew what was coming.

As he lay flat on his back, trying to catch his breath, he choked, "Good gosh, Athena. Give a guy a break."

"Athena?" I repeated, as he pulled himself up on his knees.

"The gray-eyed goddess. You remember seventh grade Mythology, right?"

"Of course I know who Athena is," I scoffed. "I just wanted to hear you say that you think I'm a goddess."

He cocked one eyebrow, the one with the scar.

"No, really," I teased. "I think that is how you should greet me from now on…'Hello, my goddess. What can I do for you today?' Go ahead. Practice it."

"You are *so* full of yourself. I think you need to be taken down a notch."

And then his eyes lit up in that glowing neon green color, and he slammed his hands down. The ground beneath me actually roared and rippled like an ocean wave and shook so violently that I fell forward and landed hard at his feet. With a stunned expression, I raised my face to find him laughing at me.

"What *was* that?!"

"Aww, Whit…did you just *fall* for me? Did the *Earth* move beneath your feet in my presence?" He laughed harder at his own jokes.

"I gotta learn how to do that," I muttered.

"Admit it, goddess. I know how to *shake* things up, get it? Huh?"

"Shut up."

He was still laughing as he helped me to my feet. Then, as naturally as always, he pulled me into his arms for a hug. I let my arms slide around his waist and up his back. Our laughter started dying down, and I got that tickly feeling in my stomach again. Despite our circumstances, despite the danger that lie ahead, it felt like everything was going to be okay. Funny how Caleb could make me feel that way…

I pulled my face back to look up at him, but he wasn't letting go yet. He gazed down at me with such longing that I grew a little nervous. One of his hands moved to brush my hair back…

And then we were completely engulfed with a freezing splash of Water. It was so cold that we could only blink in shock at first while the Water trickled down our bodies.

We turned around to see Morgan riding proudly atop a wave that was at least twelve feet high. She waved mischievously and giggled before sending another splash our direction. I was ready, though.

With one hand out, I met the cascading Water with a blast of frigid air. It froze in midair and then crashed to the ground in icy chunks.

Morgan gaped at us. "Oh, it is so *on*." She grinned as she descended like a water nymph from her little spring.

After that, the whole field erupted into hand-to-hand combat practice…competition in its truest form. We were shooting and deflecting back and forth, all the elements and their colors crashing and dancing around us. Somewhere between shots, I realized Gabriel had joined Ezekiel and Joseph. I had no idea for how long he had been watching…but he did not appear entertained, and he did not jump in to play, either.

NOT-SO-SILENT GARDENS

Sleep. It was all I wanted. I had pushed myself to the limit. I had eaten. I had guzzled about three bottles of pure Water. Now I just needed to lie down. We were leaving in three hours for the Watch Tower ruins, and I was so exhausted I couldn't even dredge up any kind of feelings about it, good or bad.

"Come, my child." Ezekiel offered me his arm. "I will walk you to a tent where you can rest. I can sense you need it."

With a yawn I linked my arm in his, and we strolled toward the tents, leaving the others mingling and talking. "Since you are my grandfather, what should I call you?" I asked Ezekiel. "What do Dorians call their grandparents?"

His wrinkled face broke out in a wide smile. "Whatever you wish! Most children simply call them Grandfather or Grandmother... sometimes even by their given name. Parents are even called by their given names at times. It just depends on the person."

"I call my other grandfather Papi. But what do you think about Poppa Zeke?" I asked shyly. I liked nicknames because they were personal. And I thought it was cute when Sarah referred to Ezekiel as Zeke.

"Poppa Zeke..." he repeated. "I love it!" He used his other hand to squeeze mine, which was resting in the crook of his elbow.

"Whitnee Skye Terradora…you are well-named. Your father must have known something to choose such a name for his daughter."

"My mom said it was just something he came up with, a name he liked. And according to Ben, Dad didn't remember anything about the Island until he started having dreams the year or so before he disappeared."

His face darkened at my words and he looked out in the distance as if he were seeing something not really there. "My brother, Benjamin…how is he?"

"He's okay, I guess. I don't know what I would've done if he hadn't been there to explain everything. He is a complicated man, though, isn't he?" I watched Poppa Zeke curiously.

"Yes. Unfortunately, I wronged him a long time ago. And I never had the opportunity to make things right," he told me sadly.

"He never said anything about that."

"It was a long time ago, my dear, and nothing for you to concern yourself with now. Just two old men who did not see eye-to-eye about things. For whatever it is worth, though, I do believe he was always trying to do the right thing, and his own compassion blinded him."

"Does this have anything to do with Abrianna and my dad?" I questioned. "What exactly happened the night Ben disappeared?"

He gave a sigh that was heavy with the weight of years and experience. "We, the Tetrarch Council at the time, chose Nathan over Abrianna to be our ruler. There was something special about Nathan—and I do not say that just because he is my son. He was unnaturally unique—even Sarah could testify to unexplainable dreams and sensations she experienced when she was pregnant with him. And everybody who met Nathan knew he was special.

"But Benjamin was torn over the Council's decision. He loved both children—and rightfully so. He had helped raise both of them. He knew Nathan did not want to be the leader, and he knew that Abrianna did. I never could see it, but Benjamin believed in Abrianna's goodness. We had a terrible argument over the issue, and I said some things I regret. I suppose I had always perceived Abrianna as a self-serving, spoiled child even though Benjamin swore that there was more to her than that. And perhaps there was…until Nathan left the Island aboard that boat. I truly believe once he was gone for good, she chose a destructive path for her life."

I was dying with curiosity then. "What happened the last time you saw Dad?"

He closed his eyes for a moment, as if remembering. "I put him on a boat with that odd little boy he had come back to find and they sailed away from here. I feared then I would never see him again."

"Why? Why did they leave by boat? Why not transport back?"

"Goodness, it all happened so fast…When he was about twenty years old, Nathan disappeared for a short period of time. I knew Abrianna was guilty. She had only been the Guardian for about four years then. I confronted her, and she tried to convince me that Nathan had chosen to leave for the Mainland. When he came back a few months later to retrieve the boy who had transported here, he was different. Being on the Mainland had ignited something inside him. He had fallen in love with your mother." He smiled at me then. "He barely said anything about the Mainland that did not have something to do with her. But then some awful things happened…things only he could explain. All he would tell me was that he had destroyed the portal—that it was a curse on the Island. And he felt strongly that his presence here made things worse. I never knew what exactly he meant, and nothing I said would convince him otherwise. But he assured me the portal would no longer work, and we would not be able to find him again. That was why your presence here this summer was so shocking."

If he destroyed the portal, then Abrianna must have rebuilt it…

"That had to be so terrible to watch him leave," I sympathized, remembering the day I watched my dad drive away for his fateful trip to Hawaii.

"It was worse knowing that if he survived the journey, he would not remember anything about the Island. And between you and me, I think it was what he wanted. I implored him to tell Benjamin that I forgave him and that it was not worth risking the love of a brother…But I am pretty confident that Benjamin never got the message."

I resolved then that when I saw Ben again, I would pass it on.

"Poppa Zeke." I lowered my voice. "Do you believe Dad is the Pilgrim, or do you think it's me?"

My words hung in the air between us. He frowned and shook his silver head. "I do not know. I was always so confident that Nathan was our promised Pilgrim…until I met you."

"Ben said it would come down to our choices in the end."

"Benjamin is probably correct." But his face was troubled as he mumbled, "I fear the day that we know for sure…"

"Why?"

His expression changed immediately, almost as if he hadn't meant to say that out loud. "Never mind. Just the fears of a silly old man. I simply wish for a long, happy future for both you and your father. Promise me you will be extremely cautious at the ruins. I cannot stand to lose you again, either." His grip tightened on my hand.

"Of course. I promise." I leaned my head into his shoulder briefly. We stopped at a tent and Ezekiel held the flap open.

"I believe Gabriel has requested you use this reserved tent for sleep." He sighed as if slightly amused. "It is very obvious how much he cares about you. Sometimes I think you are the real reason he is agreeing to our plans."

"Oh." I didn't know what to say. I moved into the tent and lowered myself to a cot. Zeke was about to walk away until I called out to him. "Poppa? Would you be disappointed in me if I wanted to go back to the Mainland when this is all over?"

He paused and thought for a moment. "It has been your home for the last seventeen years, so I would not be surprised. But I would ask if you would be disappointed if you could never return to the Island."

Hmmm…that was a tough question.

"But my mother—"

"—could very easily be brought to the Island too," he pointed out.

"I guess."

"Whitnee, I will not lie to you. You and your father were not born by accident. I believe we—the Island and all of its people—need both of you. But for what purpose and for how long…That I do not claim to know."

I nodded slowly.

"It is time for you to rest."

"*Almost* time…" Gabriel's voice sounded from behind him.

Poppa Zeke excused himself, and I waved weakly at him. Gabriel came into the tent and closed the flap behind him. "How do you feel?" he asked.

"Exhausted." When I studied his face, though, he was the one who appeared exhausted. "Are you okay?"

"Of course." He knelt by the cot, and I gave him a skeptical look.

"Are you sure all of the drakon venom is gone? Let me see your back."

"It is healed, I promise." I don't know why I thought he was lying to me, but I didn't push it. I had no strength to argue with him, especially when he said, "Lie down."

Once I curled up on my side, he pulled the blanket over me. His eyes were troubled, and I tried to keep my eyes open while waiting for him to say what was on his mind. "I know you are scared about everything Eden brought up in that meeting," Gabriel said quietly.

I turned my face up to his. "I know you are too."

"Yes, but for the first time, it feels as if I might have a purpose now," he admitted. "I've spent my whole life dreading the responsibility ahead of me. But with this kind of freedom and support… it could be different."

"It is different. And you will be great. I just know it."

"What about you? How do you feel about Eden's proposal for you to stay here?"

"Uh…I don't know. I'm wondering if I really have a choice in all of this or not." I tried to keep the shakiness out of my voice.

"A very wise and beautiful young woman told me that there is always a choice." A slow grin spread across his face. "I cannot make you stay on the Island, and I do not believe anyone here would force you to stay, either. I know that you are set on finding your father and leaving again as soon as possible…" His fingers traced a hot line along my cheek. His eyes were that warm, dark chocolate color again, and I think I shivered. "However, you should know that I am going to break off my betrothal to Jezebel as soon as possible. It does not make sense anymore."

"Gabriel, please don't." I pulled away from his touch.

"I am doing it because it is the right thing to do, as you so wisely suggested. And I would be a liar if I did not admit that I *want* you to consider staying on the Island permanently."

"I-I…" I stuttered.

How in the world was I supposed to respond to that?

"I know you do not understand what you feel toward me right now. But you do feel something. We cannot ignore that, Whitnee. Imagine how much we could accomplish. Together."

The way he said *together* connoted a lot more than just a friendly *partnership*.

I buried my face in the pillow with a groan. Gabriel and I had a unique connection…a positively electric attraction too. But was a life here with Gabriel something I wanted? For some annoying reason, all I could think about was Abrianna's words of warning to me on the beach last time. *Imagine if he had the Pilgrim by his side as he ruled…*There was just so much power there. Did Gabriel and I make the right combination? Or would we run the risk of ending up just like Abrianna and Eli? Two powerful and corrupted people?

And then there was Caleb. Could I leave him behind…forever? Sensing my frustration, Gabriel patted my shoulder and said, "You have time to decide later. Things might seem different around here once you are reunited with your father." At that, I lifted my face to look at him. His mouth tried to turn up in a reassuring smile, but he faltered. His expression turned dark as he rubbed his chin. "Whitnee, is there anything I can do or say that would change your mind about going with us tonight?"

"No," I answered honestly. "Why are you so worried? You saw me practicing out there. I know what I'm doing."

"It is not that. I just have a bad feeling." He rested his powerful arms on the edge of the cot and stared at me. I blinked slowly at him.

"It'll be okay. You have a good plan. My biggest fear is that we'll get there and find nothing and be back at square one." I snuggled into the blanket and found my eyes closing on their own.

But then I felt Gabriel's lips lightly brush my cheek. My eyes fluttered open with the stupid rush it gave my heart. "Thank you for believing in me," he whispered and stood up. Before he exited the tent, he reminded me, "I will be preparing potential escape routes and contingency plans with the others. I will wake you later."

I was still too fuzzy-brained to respond before he disappeared.

Why, why, why was I so weak around him? I willed my heart to stop thumping, and I was about to doze off when Morgan came tiptoeing in. I lazily opened one eye and watched her crawl into the other cot with a goofy smile on her face.

"Why are you smiling like that?"

"Oh." She giggled. "Thomas is just an amazing kisser."

"Morgie!" I exclaimed, raising my head an inch off the pillow to focus on her. "Y'all kissed?"

She nodded excitedly. "Go to sleep. I'll give you details later."

I rolled my eyes and dropped my head back down. "You should really rethink getting involved with one of these Island boys. Trust me. Not a good idea."

"Life's too short to worry about it," she replied, and I smirked.

"Whatever. We'll talk later." I rolled over on my other side. "Sweet dreams."

"You know it…"

I wished then that I could be as laid-back as she was about relationships. With me, everything felt like the beginning or end of the world. With Morgan, it was just so simple.

I wished for the millionth time that I was more like my best friend.

I dreamt again of that blurry concrete-looking room from the last dream I had of my dad. The lighting was dim, and this time I discovered bars like a prison cell. I had the same unsteady feeling, like the ground beneath me was rocking ever so slowly. A pesky ringing was sounding in my ears when I *felt* him…not in a physical sense, but like the sixth sense that sends a shiver down your spine. You can't see it; you just know something's there.

"Dad?" I looked around, trying to find him. "Where are you?"

I started to realize I was the one inside the cell with nobody else visible. But I knew he could hear me. It was like he was *inside my head*.

"If you can hear me, we're coming for you! To the Watch Tower ruins…Is that where you are?"

There was no response except for that ringing in my ears that was growing louder and becoming more like static. "Dad!" I called through the noise, but the room began to fade. I woke up in the little tent.

Morgan was sitting up in her cot, watching me with a horrified look. "What is it?"

"I just had a weird dream again." I used my shaking fingers to comb through my hair as I sat up. It was darker in the tent now, so we must have been asleep for a while. I did feel more rested even if my heartbeat was a little wild at the moment.

"Your eyes are glowing…but they're not normal," she informed me with that same expression on her face.

"What do you mean?"

"They're two colors. Gold and silver. Did your dad contact you again? Were you using life forces in your dream?"

"No." I dropped my face into my hands as I leaned over the cot. "I was in that same room from before, the one I saw in my dream that night in Hydrodora. Remember that?"

"Uh, yeah…the night you almost blew up the whole boat? I definitely remember. You woke up with glowing eyes then too."

"The boat…" I pondered aloud. "I thought the rocking sensation had just been me standing on the waterbed, but this time… it was rocking again." I snapped my head back up to look at her. "Morgan, I think my dad really is on a boat!"

"Really? Are you sure?"

"Well, no…but I'm pretty sure wherever my mind just went was where he is. I could feel him there, but he didn't say anything. Maybe he couldn't? But the ground was creaky and unsteady. Like a ship!" I grew excited at this clue. "I need to go tell Gabriel!"

I jumped up and ran out of the tent. There were not as many people around as before, and it was definitely night; there were soft little floating lights like lightning bugs high up in the air. Each tent was flanked with torches of beautiful, crackling Firelight. For a moment, I panicked and thought everyone had left without us. But then I spotted Hannah a few tents away.

"Do you know where Gabriel is?" I called out to her.

"I believe he went to the Silent Gardens," she answered. When I looked confused, she pointed. "Opposite side of the training grounds."

Morgan peeked out of the tent. "Wait for me."

Together we dashed in the direction of the Silent Gardens. There was such a thick gathering of trees and blooms that the moment you stepped into the Gardens, the other sounds of the arena became muted. Tiny flickering lights floated through the air, and there were little trails that wound inside. I followed one with Morgan behind me. "Man, this place is gorgeous."

The path came to an abrupt end and opened up into what could only be described as a sanctuary of flowers and plants. It was like entering a cathedral where it was silent and echoing at the same time. In the center of a shimmering beam of light was Gabriel, kneeling alone on the ground. I almost called out to him, but there was something so reverent and private about his demeanor that I grabbed Morgan and pulled her behind a colorful bush with a sharp floral smell.

"Is he praying or something?" she whispered. I just shrugged, thinking maybe we should just wait for him outside the Gardens. Whatever he was doing, it didn't seem appropriate to interrupt him, no matter how important my news was. I was about to tiptoe back down the path when we heard Jezebel's haughty voice ring out from the other direction.

"There you are, Gabriel! Are you going to continue ignoring me?"

We hunched back down behind the bush and peered out through the gaps to see what was happening. I knew eavesdropping was wrong, and I probably should have left, but I was sinfully curious about Gabriel and Jezebel. Apparently, Morgan was too.

Gabriel slowly rose to his feet, and took a deep breath.

"I am sorry, Jez. I have certainly been preoccupied this afternoon. But I do wish to speak with you." His voice was so calm and controlled.

With her hands on her hips, she said, "I hope you do not expect me to go along on your little adventure tonight. It is the most absurd idea I have ever heard."

"No, I want you to go home. It could be dangerous, and you should be far away from here," he agreed. Morgan and I glanced at each other. Geez, he certainly was protective of her. Curse the tiny pang of jealousy that coursed through me!

"I am not going home. Your mother contacted me again and invited me to accompany her to the Festival of Springs tonight. She asked again if I had heard from you."

He frowned at this news. "Surely you are not planning to meet her."

"What else am I to do? I do not wish to go home *alone*." She arched one perfectly shaped eyebrow at him suggestively, and I couldn't help rolling my eyes.

"Speaking of your home..." Gabriel expertly sidestepped her implications. "Jezebel, tell me the truth—did you know about the secret passageway inside your cavern?"

She smirked. "Of course I knew there was something there."

"And you never told me?" He was genuinely surprised. And so were we. Morgan's eyes looked about ready to pop out of their sockets.

Jezebel just shrugged. "Because it is my father's business."

"Do you not care what your father is doing? Or, more particularly, what he is protecting?"

"I care nothing for his affairs. You know that." She shook her head at him as if he was ridiculous for thinking it was a big deal. "I know how to play the game, Gabriel. My job is not to ask questions or try to change the system. I just do what I am told, and then I get what I want. In the case of my cavern, I was given access to whatever supplies I needed as long as I just ignored the little screen in there."

He grabbed the back of his neck with one hand and grew more irritated. "Do you know what they are hiding down there? Do you know where it leads? Because Tamir said it was *you* who told him to look for us on the other side of the mountain..."

"I swear I do not know what is in there, but I had a feeling it led out somewhere on the other side. There have been instances where people have shown up on my property from nowhere... people who work for my father." She peered at him curiously. "Why? What did you find?"

"I found the reason why you have been betrothed to me all these years," he muttered.

"What is it?"

"I do not know yet. But it is important...and I know my parents are involved." He turned his full gaze on her. "I believe it is best if you do not see or speak with my mother until we have more information. I do not trust her. She might try to use you against me, Jez."

"Gabriel, I truly believe that she does not know all that has happened since yesterday. Surely she would not ask me to join her tonight if she did. However..." She slinked toward him with a pouty face. "Maybe if you came with me to the Festival, it would make everything better. We could leave here and pretend none of this happened. You could work these issues out with your parents directly instead of sneaking around, and surely Whitnee can find her father without you. You are not really serious about all these plans of Eden's, are you?"

"They are not just Eden's plans." He bristled at her words. "And, yes, I am very serious about it. There is no such thing as just 'pretending' now. Things need to *change*."

"What are you saying?" She gave him a piercing stare.

"I am saying that..." He paused. "Everything is changing now...even us. If these new plans are successful, then there is no need for you to marry me. You are free."

She didn't move. "And if your plans are *not* successful? What then?"

"Jezebel, did you not hear me? I am giving you the freedom you have always wanted. Even if all of our plans fail, then it still will not matter. I will either be imprisoned or killed, and you cannot marry a dead man."

"Gabriel!" she hissed. "Abrianna would not allow that to happen to you."

"Do not be naïve! You know I was left on the Mainland... You know how manipulative, how cold my parents are. We both know that I was never born out of a loving relationship between two people. I was bred for power and control. We *both* were." She recoiled at his words, and he softened his tone again. "It is not right for us...for you and me...to be together. We have always known that."

I sucked in a breath and Morgan looked over at me with raised eyebrows. Gabriel was actually doing it. He was breaking off the engagement! I tried to sort out how I really felt about this.

"This is about *her*, is it not, Gabriel?" Jezebel snapped. "You do not really believe in all these ancient laws and prophecies! You are just doing this for Whitnee."

"That is not true—"

"Oh, stop lying to yourself!" Her voice was raised and punctuated with emotion. "Look at her. Do you think she really loves you, Gabriel? Have you seen her around her little Mainlander boyfriend? *He* is the one she loves! Not you! She is just using you to find her father!"

Using him? I held back an indignant gasp. She didn't know me well enough to say such things!

"Jezebel—" Gabriel's voice was brewing with anger.

But she continued in a heated voice, "And what do you think is going to happen if she does find her father? Do you really believe she will stay here on the Island...just to be with you? I am not the naïve one here, Gabriel!"

"I am warning you—"

"No, *I* am warning *you*! Whatever you think you feel for her is not real. And these games you are playing with all of your little friends and your asinine rebellion...You and I both know your parents cannot be defeated. It is a mission destined for failure! How can you even consider it?"

"Because it is the right thing to do!" he exploded. "I am tired of my life being dictated to me! I am tired of feeling like I am always on the wrong side. For once, Jezebel, I want to take control of my own future. Why can you not understand that? You know what it is like..."

I was shocked to see that Jezebel had started to cry—real tears. "I do know what it is like, Gabriel!" she cried passionately. "Which is why you cannot change the plans on me—you are all I have in this world." She cupped his face with her long, slender hands and made him look at her. "Do you know that you are the only person who takes care of me? The only one who stops by just to make sure I am even still alive? My parents do not care what happens to me or what I do with my time. If I were to disappear, I am certain they would not even notice. Do you know how many times I have thought of ending my own life because I am so lonely? My future...the one I have with *you*...is the *only* thing that stops me, because I keep hoping you will make this whole forsaken life better." Her voice cracked through her tears, and she stood in front of him like a beautiful broken doll. For some odd reason, an image of Amelia wading into the river with tears running down her face popped into my head as I listened. "I know that we might not have chosen each other if it had not already been chosen for us. But I still need you, Gabriel. You cannot leave me...you cannot—"

And then she completely lost it. I watched Gabriel reach out and pull her into his arms. She leaned into him and sobbed, and I was compelled to look away. I felt like I was watching a movie of the two saddest people in the world. My own eyes prickled as I tried to avoid Morgan's concerned looks.

"Shhh," he comforted her. "It will be okay. I am not leaving you. Just because we are calling off a marriage does not mean I will stop taking care of you, Jez."

"But it does," she moaned. "If you marry someone else, things will never be the same between us."

"You know you do not want to marry me. We do not love each other...like that."

She jerked away from him suddenly. "You do not know anything about how I really feel, Gabriel. I love you the only way I know how."

He sighed heavily. "I know."

She wiped her eyes and tried to compose herself. "Are you really serious about this? I need to know now. Are you telling me you do not want me in your future as your wife?"

I'm pretty sure Morgan and I stopped breathing. Gabriel watched Jezebel carefully as he responded: "Yes. I am sure."

I didn't think I could take anymore of this. I laid my hand on Morgan's arm to signal that we should leave. But Jezebel's words interrupted me.

"Very well." Her voice grew hard. "Then nothing is stopping me from joining your mother tonight and letting let her know your plans. I could tell her everything...about the ruins, about Whitnee and her father, about this little rebellion. I can even list the names of every person involved—including all your new friends this summer."

Gabriel just stared at her, as if deciding whether she was making a sick joke or telling the truth. He called her bluff. "You would not do that."

"Would I not?"

"Jezebel, stop playing games with me. I am not trying to hurt you. I thought you felt the same as I did."

"Gabriel, this is simple," she said. "Just assure me that I will still be your wife, and then you can go off and try to save the Island or whatever noble thing you believe you are accomplishing. I promise I will be a good wife...I will be whoever you want me to be. I will look the other way and give you your *freedoms*." She sounded completely emotionless, except for the tiny catch in her voice as she added, "Just do not leave me alone the rest of my life."

"This is completely mad, Jez! I do not understand you!" he bellowed with frustration.

"The truth is, Gabriel, when all of this falls apart and Whitnee goes back to her home and all of your *loyal* followers realize they were wrong...I am all you will have in this world too."

He rubbed his hand over his face. "Please do not do this," he begged quietly.

"Then do not force me to," Jezebel told him. I thought back to Eden's words of warning regarding Jezebel…*See to it that her loyalty stays with you.* Would Gabriel do whatever was necessary to retain Jezebel's trust?

I had heard enough. I crawled away from the bush and then ran out of the Silent Gardens as fast as my feet would carry me, hoping Gabriel and Jezebel didn't see me. Once I was back out in the arena, I gulped in deep breaths and tried to control my raging emotions. I felt intensely sorry for Gabriel. The guy just wanted to do the right thing, and he was met with opposition everywhere he turned. And somewhere deep inside, I felt pity and compassion for Jezebel, and it irritated me. She reminded me too much of Amelia. I tried to squelch those feelings and concentrate on how much of what she said was true. I had never thought about what Gabriel's future held if—when—I left the Island. If he really was doing all of this for me…and I knew I wasn't staying…

"Oh my gosh," I breathed and leaned over on my knees.

"Wow," Morgan exclaimed as she joined me outside the Gardens. "What do you think?"

"I, um…" I stuttered, still concentrating on my breathing. "Morgan, am I…I mean, do you think I'm screwing up everybody's lives around here? Am I being selfish? I just want my dad back. I…I didn't ask for all of this…"

Morgan didn't respond immediately and then Jezebel came barreling out of the Gardens. She caught one glimpse of our deer-in-the-headlights expressions, and I think she suspected we had heard something. I tried to look away and pretend like nothing had happened.

She marched up to me and pointed her finger in my face. "He is risking everything…*for you.* If you are really the good person Gabriel thinks you are, then *let him go.* Or this is all going to end very badly."

With that, she stormed away, snapping her fingers and shooting sparks into the air.

The sick thing was…I knew she was right.

SICKENING SURPRISES

When Morgan and Caleb and I were campers five years ago, we pretended that Camp Fusion was actually a training ground for future government spies. I suppose that it sounded better to us than admitting we were at a "therapy camp" for kids who couldn't seem to cope. We took our game so far that one night we actually snuck out and met at the river for our first "mission." Morgan had been ready to chicken out from the moment the idea was born. But in my mind, the game was so real that I had convinced myself I would be failing my mission if I didn't go through with it.

So we dressed in the colors of the night, even smearing black mascara across our cheeks, and embarked on our first adventure together. With a terrified Morgan in tow and my little trinket clutched tightly in my hand, I had darted down to the river only to find a nervous Caleb waiting for us.

I could still see young Caleb in my mind. He first looked relieved that we had actually shown up, then amused by our black faces, and finally repulsed when we told him it was mascara. "Everybody have their 'evidence'?" he had asked, taking charge. We had held up our symbolic trinkets and set out to get the job done, making up the rules as we went.

The whole experience had always resonated in my memory because the spirit of adventure and change had felt so alive in the summer night air. In retrospect, our self-assigned "mission" had actually been a very cathartic experience for each of us…Nobody knew then that the best therapy we received that summer was each other.

And here I was again…with a nervous Morgan in tow, all of us dressed in black, minus the mascara smears. Our new "spy" team trekked quietly through the jungle with Gabriel and Thomas in the lead and Hannah and Levi bringing up the rear. We were approaching the ruins from the eastern side, which forced us to curve around toward my usual landing spot on the beach.

Adventure and change were again on the horizon. My whole body vibrated with electrified energy. All of my senses felt alert and finely-tuned to my surroundings. I had a feeling that my use of all of the life forces this afternoon had both strengthened me and given me a new awareness of my abilities. Life force dripped and rippled outward from every living thing around me, including my friends. Even the night air itself had a pure quality to it that was only enriched by the approaching saltiness of the Southern Beach breeze wafting our way.

I suddenly remembered those moments I had used life forces on the Mainland. The frightening dream of Elon, Eden's petite little sister, came back in vivid detail.

"Hey, Eden," I called to the girl trudging in front of me. "I had a dream about Elon back on the Mainland. How is she?"

Eden almost came to an abrupt stop at my words. Even Gabriel slowed and glanced stiffly back at us.

"What did you dream about her?" Eden questioned, a stunned expression on her face.

I was taken off guard by her reaction. "It was weird. I was walking through the fields of Geodora and there was this flower…a golden flower. And it transformed into her, and she was warning me that 'they' were coming for me. And then dark shadows of people started coming after us, and I threw out my shield to protect her and...I woke up."

Something kept me from revealing the fact that I had woken up to a green shield illuminated in my room. That was a question I had for my dad, and I guess I didn't want to hear their confusing theories about the phenomenon. Caleb and Morgan both gave me knowing looks, but they kept their mouths shut.

"That is bizarre, indeed," Eden agreed and picked up her pace again. Her voice came out robotically. "Elon has been sick."

"With what?" I asked in surprise.

"We do not know exactly. Her only symptoms are extreme fatigue and no access to her life force."

I heard Levi suck in a breath. When I looked back, his eyebrows were furrowed and Hannah's face had grown more solemn.

"What does that mean? Is that a common sickness on the Island?" I wondered. Gabriel kept tossing cautious, almost empathetic glances back at Eden.

Eden remained emotionless as she explained. "It is not uncommon for children who are extremely ill to experience a disconnection with their life force, but it usually comes back as they grow healthy again. But you have seen Elon—she is more delicate than the rest of us. If someone in my family is going to get sick, it is usually her. But this time there is nothing to heal. She was playing out in the field three weeks ago—working to create her treasured 'Whitnee' flower like your hair, actually—and she faded right on the spot. She was asleep for almost two days and the HydroHealer could find nothing wrong with her. When Elon finally woke up, she could not connect with the Earth..." Eden's voice caught.

Three weeks ago made for a curious coincidence with my dream—and with my own strange connection to the life forces from so far away.

Hadn't I heard somewhere that a Dorian could not survive on the Island for long without life force? No wonder everyone seemed so grieved about this news. Gabriel was apparently already aware of the situation because his tone was reassuring. "I am sure it is temporary. Like you said, this has happened to her before, and she was fine once it passed. This time it is just lingering."

Eden nodded and swallowed before addressing me. "Gabriel says that there have been a few other instances of this happening with children in other tribes. Seth has been treating her regularly with herbs he crafted to give her some energy. So perhaps it is just something that will go away soon."

"Probably," I agreed, even though I had no clue. My heart constricted for little Elon. How upsetting to think of children being physiologically attacked by something that could take away their life forces and ultimately their *lives*. What could cause such a phenomenon? For some unexplainable reason, I had a sudden fear that these sicknesses were my fault...but that made no logical sense, of course.

My gaze rested on Gabriel's back as he led our way through the thicket. I didn't know what his response to Jezebel had been, but she had disappeared. I was insanely curious to know if she had gone home or joined the Guardian in Hydrodora, but I felt it was inappropriate to ask. If Gabriel didn't feel the need to volunteer the information, then maybe I didn't need to know. All I knew was that his demeanor toward me had changed slightly even in her absence...as if he was putting emotional distance between us. It might have been because of the things she said about me, or it could have just been the stress of everything else.

But I supposed a little distance between us was okay. I needed to focus on our current mission. My dad was out there somewhere; I was so sure of it even though I could not prove it. When I had finally been able to tell Gabriel of my recent dream, he had broken the news to me that the thunderflies had not discovered any boats off the southern coast. And yet, I knew what I had felt in my dream. There had been water involved...an unmistakable rocking. And my dad was *there*. How could I describe to my friends the feeling of knowing something without really knowing it?

Thomas and Gabriel came to a sudden stop in front of us. "It was right past that wall where I last saw Whitnee with Saul and the other guy." Thomas pointed to the ruins in the distance. I stepped forward to see what he was pointing at, trying to avoid those dark memories of my kidnapping. If only I could have seen where they took me…and who the third person had been.

I knew the ocean was somewhere off to my left because I could hear the unmistakable lull of waves crashing rhythmically against the shore. There was no stirring but the soft wind in the trees and overgrowth that had sprouted up around the ruins. From the distance, it didn't even look as if the place had been touched by a human in years—save for the night we spent there.

"I think a few of us should ensure there is no danger before we all go," Eden suggested, and Gabriel turned his attention on me.

"You and Morgan stay here. Wait for our signal; then you can join us." I didn't argue. He glanced at Caleb as if giving him a choice. "Caleb?"

"I'll stay with the girls."

The three of us hunkered down and watched our Dorian friends cautiously approach what was left of the once-beautiful Watch Tower. The history of the Island was as complicated as the real world we came from—full of its own good and bad moments. The Watch Tower had originally been constructed as a lookout point for the arrival of the Pilgrim. Its current decay was very symbolic of the Dorians' neglect of the ancient prophecy and its promises.

In the faint moonlight, I watched Thomas lead the others around the old rock pilings. They started to separate and filter cautiously out around the area.

"Morgan," I whispered, staring keenly into the night. "You trust Thomas, right?"

I just needed to hear someone else confirm my own thoughts.

"Of course she does," Caleb muttered to my right.

"Why would you ask me that, Whit?" I felt Morgan's eyes on me from the left. "Do you *not* trust him?"

"I *want* to trust him," I sighed. "But somebody is not being honest. And he's the one who saw me out here first and somehow lost me with the kidnappers."

"Whitnee, that's ridiculous. Thomas is not lying."

"He was on guard duty when the prisoners escaped," I pointed out. I could sense her annoyance festering, which was something I was afraid would happen. "Look, I don't want to believe it's him, either, but how stupid would we be if we ignored the obvious—"

"How is that obvious? Look, every time we've been on this Island, he's been with me. Don't you think I would have noticed—"

Caleb interrupted. "Wait, didn't you say, though, that you thought someone else was in the jungle when we found y'all making out in the spring?"

"Well, now I know that it was one of the Pilgrim Protectors. They had people everywhere and Thomas had to keep their presence a secret from us on Eden's orders—"

"Time out." I made a 'T' sign with my hands and turned my attention on the defensive Morgan. "You and Thomas *made out*? In a *spring*? Annnnd…where was I?"

"Kidnapped and drugged," Caleb answered flatly.

"Caleb!" Morgan snapped. "Quit making it sound like I didn't care about Whitnee. You were distracted at Camp Fusion too when she was taken…"

I cast jealous eyes on Caleb. "Wait. Nothing happened with Claire, did it?"

He made a disgusted face. "Of course not." I gave him a stern look in return, ignoring the fact that something had happened with Gabriel and me, and I technically had no right to be upset with Caleb. *Whit the Hypocrite.* That should be my new name. "But I'm not the one you should worry about…Claire was totally hitting on your Island boyfriend."

"What!" I hissed. "Claire hit on Gabriel? You better be kidding me—"

"Oh, good. I'm glad you knew who I was talking about when I said Island boyfr—"

"Tell me what Claire did."

Morgan gave a short laugh. "She offered to show him around and then, get this, she gave him her phone number! Gabriel didn't even know what it was."

Gah! That girl had some serious nerve! I glanced back at Caleb, whose expression probably mirrored my own distaste for the situation.

"Does it bother you that she had a thing for Gabriel?" I questioned.

"No. Does it bother *you?*" he returned pointedly.

"No." But it did bother me. A little. "I can't believe I'm just now hearing about all of this. What else did I miss?"

"Did I tell you about the part where Caleb tried to beat up Gabriel the first time we saw him at camp?" Morgan grinned wickedly again.

"Morgan, please," he sighed.

I tried picturing a fight between Gabriel and Caleb…

"It wasn't funny at the time, but now I—" She stopped speaking and her face turned white. She made a horribly pained expression, squeezed her eyes shut, and then doubled over.

"Morgan?" I reached out, confused by her sudden reaction.

She fell on the ground for a moment, and I watched in horror as she placed her hands on her stomach. A blue glow spread from underneath them, and when she opened her eyes, they were illuminated in the darkness.

"What just happened?" Caleb interrogated as we both leaned over her on the ground.

"Just a stomach cramp," she said, slowly straightening up. Her breathing was irregular.

"She's lying." Caleb looked at me and tapped his head. "Geo instinct."

"Time to tell the truth, Morgie. What's wrong with you?"

She hugged her knees to her chest, which really accentuated how small and bony she had become.

"Nothing…just a nervous stomach." She looked trapped. I raised my eyebrows questioningly at Caleb.

He shook his head. "Still lying."

Morgan's face turned angry. "That is really getting on my nerves."

"Then stop lying," I challenged her. "You were just healing yourself, Morgan. What's the deal?"

"Okay, fine!" she blurted and shrugged her thin shoulders. "I've got a stomach problem that won't go away. But I promise when I get home, I'll see a doctor about it and get it fixed up."

I looked again to Caleb, and he made a face like he wasn't convinced. However, he didn't accuse her again. Maybe she was telling enough of the truth for it to sound right...

"I thought you just saw a bunch of doctors—" I started, but an unmistakable snap of brush sounded from behind us, and I jerked my head around.

We grew still and silent, ears straining to hear, eyes darting around nervously.

Tamir's tall figure emerged out of the darkness. I let out my breath. "Tamir! You scared us to death! What are you doing here?"

He gave a small grin at our obvious relief. "I decided to delay my plans. I might be of better use here tonight. The cabin can wait." Briefly, I wondered what Poppa Zeke thought of this change in plans. "Where are the others?" Tamir wondered, his eyes scanning our surroundings intuitively.

"Uh, out there making sure it's safe." I gestured toward the ruins. "Maybe we should—wait, where did they all go?"

I couldn't see anyone in the darkness.

"There's Gabriel." Caleb pointed, and I could scarcely distinguish his bulky figure as he crouched awkwardly over the ground examining something. "Why don't I take Tamir and see what's going on? Whitnee, I'll wave at you if you're clear to follow." He raised his eyebrows at me meaningfully and nodded in Morgan's direction, obviously communicating his ulterior motive in giving me some alone time with her. It was time to openly confront whatever was happening to Morgan.

Once Caleb and Tamir had slowly moved away and everything appeared to be safe and uneventful, I became aware of Morgan's ragged breathing beside me. She still sat on the ground, staring off into space.

"Morgie."

Her eyes refused to meet mine. In that moment, I wanted to yell at her to snap out of it and start being honest with me. But before I got my chance, she spoke.

"Can I ask you something?" Her voice was distant. I nodded, even though her eyes were fixed on some unknowable point in the darkness. "When they asked you at the meeting to consider staying on the Island…you looked surprised. As if you had never thought of that possibility before."

I waited impatiently for her to get to her question.

Finally she looked up at me with her luminous blue eyes set into a gaunt face that appeared ghostly in the darkness. "Well? Would you ever live here…permanently? I mean, what if we found your dad tonight and we could bring your mom here? What if we all stayed here together?"

"You're not serious, right?" I scoffed. But she was serious. A chill ran down my spine. "First of all, that's ludicrous. Why would *you* want to stay here?"

She cast her gaze to the ground and didn't respond.

"Geez, Morgan. Is this about Thomas? I know you guys kissed and the new romance is fun and all, but—"

"No, it's not about Thomas. I don't know, Whit…" She paused for a moment. "Sometimes I just *feel* better here. Sometimes I think I feel like Amelia and just want to disappear."

I stared at her in frustration. "What is *with* you?!" I exploded. She was not acting like my best friend. Like my *Morgan*. "You've been so different this summer, and I don't get it!"

"Well, you've been different too! People change, you know," she snapped back.

"If I've changed, fine. But at least I'm still honest with you. You, however, have turned into a liar! If we don't have trust between us, then what do we have, Morgan?"

"Forgive me if there has never been an ideal time to sit down and talk about *me*. Your summer has been one big drama…to the point where maybe other people don't feel like there is time to actually have an honest conversation with you!"

"What—But—" *Oh my gosh.* That was completely unfair! "Don't give me that crap, Morgan! I have given you plenty of opportunities to tell me what is wrong with you, but you chose to lock me out of your life this summer. I *know* you. And when something's wrong, you keep it all inside until you're about ready to combust. I've tried to wait patiently until you decide to tell me the truth, but this has gone too far. Are you depressed or something?"

She laughed petulantly as if I had just made a huge understatement.

"So that's it?" I clarified. "You're dealing with depression? Over what? I don't understand…"

"How could you *ever* understand? I'm not like you, Whitnee." She pulled herself up from the ground and threw her arms out. "I'm not driven to do great things. I've always been in the back seat of *your* adventures. My life…it's nothing. It's inconsequential. It always has been."

"That is not *true!*"

"Oh, come on. We found an Island whose entire existence seems to revolve around you." She looked away to dust herself off. With a biting undertone, she added, "I just happened to pick a best friend who will always be more important than me. When I'm gone, it will make no difference to anyone."

When she was *gone*? What in the world was she talking about? I was speechless. Her words about me were upsetting enough, but beneath them lay something even more disturbing. Morgan had a very sad, very messed-up idea of herself. I had never seen it before then.

"What is wrong with you two?" Caleb called, waving his arms in the air. "I've been trying to get your attention! Let's go."

Without a word, Morgan stalked away and left me there in the darkness.

"Morgan!" I called out. She didn't turn around, but marched right past Caleb toward the shadows of the ruins.

Caleb crossed his arms over his chest and stared after her with concern. "Is she okay?"

I took a deep breath and tried to swallow down how upset I was. "No," I told him honestly. "No, she is definitely not okay."

"What is it?"

"Ask *her*," I muttered and brushed past him too. Caleb sighed with the frustration any guy shows when he doesn't understand girls and their problems.

When I approached the ruins, our team had reconvened. Gabriel and Eden were pointing out the worn tracks of recent activity in the crumbling rock and intruding plant growth. Thomas and Morgan were whispering off to the side. I allowed my stare to be obvious, trying to read what she was saying. It almost looked like Thomas was trying to reason with her, because she was shaking her head and clearly trying to brush him off.

"…spread out and look for any possible entry points. Anything suspicious or unnatural…" Gabriel was saying. I refocused my attention on the task at hand, trying to shake off the fact that Morgan blamed me for her problems. All I knew was that she was sick, depressed, and mad at me. Those just seemed like symptoms of a greater problem.

"If there really is an underground facility here, then wouldn't there be at least a few people guarding the area? Like lookouts? It's too deserted out here," Caleb remarked.

"I agree," Eden nodded. "Hannah, go with Caleb to the upper levels of the ruins and see what you can find. We have another team that should be arriving from the west soon. Tamir and Levi, I would like a word with you." The group started spreading out.

Eden was frowning as she moved hesitantly away with the two men. Caleb joined Hannah with a last warning to me to be careful. I watched him fade away into the maze of stone and plant life before I noticed Gabriel motion to me with a jerk of his head.

Before joining him, I glanced again at Morgan and Thomas still talking softly, encompassed by the shadows of a huge tree that had grown into one towering side of the ruins. Morgan was growing more upset. I could tell by her hand gestures. And it made me wonder how much Thomas had to do with her current emotional state. With an aggravated sigh, I met Gabriel.

"Please stay close to me out here. I cannot explain it, but something feels wrong," he confided quietly. He definitely had a pensive look about him.

"But all the signs point to us being right about this."

"Exactly."

I wanted to reach out and smooth the worry lines from his face. I knew his burdens were great, but I felt like he was overreacting. Before I could respond, Eden called out to Gabriel. Two things registered in my mind at the same time: First, Eden's voice seemed pinched with uncharacteristic emotion. Second, the way Gabriel turned his body to face her was very unnatural…almost like his back and neck were stiff and he was trying to hide it.

Without warning, I reached for his tunic and lifted the back of it. He jerked away when he realized what I was doing, but he wasn't fast enough. I saw the puffy flesh and the spidery dark lines that had spread further.

"You said that Michael healed your back!" I exclaimed, accusation coloring my tone.

"He did," Gabriel growled as Eden joined us.

"But it looks worse—"

"The flesh is no longer open. It is fine for now."

"Eden! Have you seen Gabriel's back?"

She looked back and forth between the two of us. "Gabriel, just tell her the truth," she said, which caused me to glare at him expectantly. It was the first time I felt a sliver of jealousy at the fact that Eden knew something important about Gabriel that I did not.

He wouldn't meet my eyes. "Drakon venom is not as easy to heal…the effects can be long-lasting."

"Effects? What effects?"

"It varies depending on the amount of venom and how long it is in the body. It could be as simple as a slight stiffness in the arms and legs for a few days." He shrugged as if it was not a big deal.

"Or it can cause permanent damage, inability to move the rest of your life, deterioration of your body's primary functions…eventually death," Eden interrupted bluntly, a hollowness in her voice.

I was horrified.

"How could you not tell me that?!" I slammed my hand down on his arm, gripping him too tightly. "You shouldn't be here, Gabriel! You should be getting help in Hydrodora…professional healing. A transfusion or…or surgery or *something*! We have to get that venom *out*!" My voice was growing in pitch as I realized the horror of his situation. The venom had been in his system for hours…Hours! What was too long? What was too much?

"Whitnee." He pried my death grip from his arm and turned the full force of his eyes on me. "The venom is gone. I feel fine right now."

"You're lying!" I cried. "You can hardly move your back. It's getting worse. I can tell…Gabriel, please…You don't have to do all this for me. I mean, you don't have to push so hard with these plans. We can't risk something happening to *you*! Not if there's something that can be done—"

"Shhh. There is nothing more we can do at this point." He gently cupped my face with his warm hands. "Nobody else knows about the venom. I would like to keep it that way. But I need you to trust me."

He had to pull out the trust card again…*dang him*. I involuntarily let out a little moan and squeezed my eyes closed for a moment. First Morgan, now Gabriel…I pulled his hands away from my face, but didn't let go of them. How did we do that little magic tranquility thing again? I desperately needed a dose of it.

"Speaking of trust," Eden glanced cautiously around as she spoke. "I need you to stay calm about this, but I think I know who our traitor might—"Then she silenced herself and perked her head up as if listening for something.

Alerted by her behavior, I shifted to look around and realized the three of us were completely alone. Morgan and Thomas were no longer in sight, and the ruins were alarmingly quiet.

My heart slammed against my chest. "Morgan?" I called out. Where did she go? I jolted into action, running toward the tree I had last seen her under. Gabriel shouted at me to stop, but whatever Eden suddenly felt, I had felt too. "Morgan!" I called again and nearly tripped on a body lying unconscious on the dark ground.

My stomach lurched. It was Thomas.

Eden and Gabriel were close on my heels. While Eden knelt to check on him, Gabriel threw one powerful arm out and swept me close behind him while projecting his other hand defensively. The flames danced off his outstretched fingers like a blowtorch ready to fire up. He backed us up against the wall and stared out into the darkness while Eden dragged Thomas to a safe place.

"Where's Morgan?!" I screeched. Where were all the others, for that matter? Something was terribly wrong. Horribly, fatefully wrong. It was so obvious now.

Eden knelt into a defensive position, scanning our surroundings. "Thomas was hit on the head, but he is breathing," she whispered to us, her nuclear green eyes unblinking. She had one hand pressed to the ground in concentration. All was quiet except for the pounding of my pulse in my ears and a soft whistle of ocean breeze through the crumbling structures around us.

"I found Morgan!" Tamir's voice broke out from across the expanse of ruins. He came around the corner of the dilapidated stone that backed up to the other side of the tree. And he was carrying Morgan.

"Oh, thank God!" I cried, escaping the shelter of Gabriel's protective body to meet Tamir halfway.

"Whitnee, no!" Eden yelled sharply. I was too focused on Morgan to register the commanding tone in Eden's voice...too distracted to recognize her warning for what it was. Instead, I helped Morgan out of Tamir's arms. She groaned and put her hand to her head. I saw a small trickle of blood running down her cheek.

"She was over there!" Tamir was breathless as he pointed back the direction from which he had just come. "Somebody must have attacked her when we were not looking."

I will never know what might have been said next or who would have said it. Because at that moment, an eruption of Firedarts exploded out of the sky like meteors—heading right for me.

Tamir deftly knocked Morgan and me to the ground before sweeping his arms out with a gust of Wind current that shifted the Firedarts off their target. Their damaging explosions still detonated on the ground around us, blocking my view of Gabriel and Eden.

I crawled to Morgan on the ground beside me and conjured an Earth shield to protect us from the flying debris.

"Whitnee!" Gabriel yelled.

"I'm fine, I'm fine!" I called back through the smoke.

There was an ominous moment of silence as the smoke settled before another launch of life forces came at us from invisible attackers in every direction.

"We are surrounded! Watch the trees!" Eden screamed as she and Gabriel began fighting back, aiming their attacks blindly.

The rebels must have known we were coming. They had been hiding, watching and waiting for the right moment. My mind returned to our traitor…Had Eden figured out who it was?

Morgan groaned beside me.

"What's going on?" She sounded groggy.

"We need to move, Morgan! Can you run?" I dropped my shield and pulled both of us to our feet. She was a little slow, but she was trying. I watched as Eden manipulated a tree into violent tremors that shook a few attackers from its branches. Gabriel was casting Fire-powered shots into the darkness while Tamir continued to deflect hits that seemed aimed at Morgan and me.

"Whitnee! Where are you?" It was Caleb's voice this time, echoing in the distant parts of the ruins. I froze. *Oh my gosh. Don't come this way, Caleb!* I thought, resisting the urge to call out to him. I didn't want him anywhere near danger. I saw his face peek over the crumbling balcony to view what was happening. Then I spotted one of the attackers who came out from behind a tree to aim up at the balcony—right for Caleb! Reflexively, I shot a lightning arrow at the stranger and was shocked when it exploded on his side and he fell to the ground.

Holy crap. I had just hit somebody...*did I just kill him?!*

There was no time to freak out.

The wall to my right exploded and thousands of tiny rock shards raked across the right side of my body. Slivers of cuts instantly opened up and hot blood seeped out of my arm, neck, and cheek. I saw the spreading dark spots on my skin before I felt the pain.

"Whitnee, we need to get you out of here!" Tamir bolted my direction and practically swept me away from where I was standing in a daze with my wet fingers pressed to my cheek. I had the sense to drag Morgan with us—and with good timing too. Not a moment later, a huge boulder crashed on the exact spot where I had just been standing. I stared in horror at what was happening. The ground was on Fire—life force shots combusting everywhere, branches falling and waving dramatically, debris flying dangerously in all directions. People were fighting back and forth. Gabriel... Eden. And there were Caleb and Hannah shooting from higher up across the ruins. I wondered where Levi was...and if Thomas was still lying there unconscious. It was complete bedlam.

Before I could clear my head enough to act, Tamir shoved us into a gap between the towering tree and the rock wall.

"Do not move!" he commanded and turned his back on us again. I had to shut my eyes momentarily to block out the dirt that flew around us with Tamir's powerful Wind. Morgan was holding on tightly to me. I couldn't stay behind this tree. I needed to know what was happening. I needed to be out there fighting...

"I have to go," I finally told her. "Stay here."

Her grip tightened. "Don't leave. Don't go out there."

"Morgie—"

"Whitnee, no! It's you they want!" I tried pulling away from her.

"Let go!" I yanked my arm out of her grasp. That was when she jerked on me with a surprising amount of strength and caused both of us to tumble backwards...into the rock wall.

The good news was that we did not crack open our heads on the wall. The bad news was that we fell through another screen. But this time, there was such a steep incline on the other side that we both rolled at uncomfortable angles, kicking and crushing each other all the way until we hit the bottom.

Catching my breath, I untangled myself from Morgan, pulling my ankle out from its painful position under her. I peered around in awe at the dark tunnel we were now in.

Morgan stirred slowly and tried sitting up.

"Where are we?" she mumbled, her voice echoing in the stillness.

"Um," I breathed. "I think we just found the entrance to the tank." Another explosion from outside shook the floor beneath us, and I threw my arm out to keep steady. "We have to tell the others!" The shouts and the chaos of the battle outside were oddly muted in this tunnel. But I heard enough to know it was bad. And people were probably getting hurt. "Come on, Morgan..." I started to ascend the slope we had just tumbled down, but the low grating sound of a heavy door scraping closed stopped me. With a final thunderous slam that struck me with familiarity, the sounds outside completely faded.

"Who's there?" I called out. Heavy footsteps descended closer. I threw a trembling, bloody Firelit hand out in front of me...just in time to see Tamir step into the light. "Tamir, what's happening out there?!" I cried. "We need to go help them."

He just shook his head. "No. They are on their own now."

"What do you mean?" I still wasn't getting it...still wasn't putting the clues together.

"Oh, no," Morgan breathed, her voice pinched with fear. I felt her hand slide into mine and pull me back. "Tamir, it was you. You were the one who attacked Thomas up there...weren't you?"

He didn't answer her, and I gave both of them a bewildered look. "Wait, what?"

Morgan continued, her voice growing in volume and panic. "You told the rebels we were coming tonight...You've been working with the Guardian all along! This is all your fault!"

In a flash of reflexes, Tamir yanked Morgan by the neck and held her against him, his other glowing hand mere inches from her terrified face. "Whitnee, do not make this any more difficult than it already is. If you cooperate with me, I will not hurt Morgan."

What the—?

Tamir was the traitor? After all that?

My hands were already extended, the Fire dripping a scorching lava-like substance around my feet. Red hot anger burned inside me. I could kill him. I really could...but not when he had Morgan by the throat.

"Morgan is not part of the plan—she should not be here. But I will spare her if you just do as I tell you," he repeated.

"Don't believe him, Whitnee!" Morgan cried, tears pooling in her eyes. "He just sent our friends to their deathbeds up there! Take him out! Don't let him use me—"

He tightened his grip on her throat, and her eyes bulged as she gasped for air.

"Stop it!" I screamed. In the span of a second, I considered my options: Try to aim carefully and blow him to pieces...possibly injuring Morgan just as badly. Or cooperate and preserve everyone's lives for the time being...

"Lower your hands, Whitnee, and I'll let her breathe! She does not have to suffer like this." His silver eyes were unflinching. Morgan was trying to shake her head, trying to tell me not to back down. But she was braver than me. I couldn't watch her suffer.

I dropped my hands and the Firelight extinguished, plunging us into darkness again. But Tamir's glowing eyes were still there, illuminated with determination.

Morgan wheezed again and inhaled as he loosened his grip. "Turn around and start walking, Whitnee."

"No—!" Morgan choked in protest.

"Morgan, just shut up!" I commanded before he could rough her up again. If she didn't calm down, he would keep hurting her. I turned away and started walking carefully in the dark without knowing what was in front of me.

"Won't the others find the screen, Tamir? They'll be down here soon…maybe you should rethink what you're trying to do here," I suggested. I could hear him shuffling behind me with Morgan still imprisoned against him.

"There is no screen there anymore. They will only find a wall," he answered. So that was the door I heard slam shut. "The only way to save your friends now is to give yourself up to the Guardian. Now, keep walking!"

NEGOTIATIONS

"So it's starting to make sense now, I guess," I thought out loud, my voice echoing around the tunnel walls as I trudged ahead of Tamir and Morgan. "You've been Abrianna's spy this whole time. Someone last time had to have been keeping her informed—she was always a step ahead of us. She knew about my life force abilities because you *told* her. And *you* helped stage Amelia and Kevin's kidnapping, conveniently showing up to rescue them from the hands of rebels…just so Abrianna could manipulate the situation and bring the kids to the Palladium! *Ugh.* To think we all thought you were our hero…" I spat, disgust dripping off every word. "And speaking of kidnapping…Want to go ahead and just admit that was you on the Mainland? The one they wouldn't let me see?"

"Correct on all counts," Tamir replied.

"I don't get it. You have protected me so many times, Tamir. Even from Saul on the Mainland…Why?"

"My job was to ensure your safe delivery here. The Guardian preferred you were alive and well—for obvious reasons."

"Right." I gave a mirthless laugh. "Obvious reasons being she wants to take all of my life force abilities. And who knows if that will permanently damage me or not…"

He remained silent.

"Why didn't you just bring me in today at the cabin? You had Gabriel and me both right there. Nobody would have known." I should have trusted Gabriel's instincts then.

"It is about the big picture, Whitnee. Bringing down a rebellion takes patience and planning. After tonight, there will be significant losses to their cause. They will not be able to recover in time."

"So you freed Saul and his kidnapping buddies this morning before you came to find us…and you're the reason Abrianna's been able to keep Ezekiel on such a tight leash with her threats," I muttered, considering the extent of Tamir's involvement. "I bet you've been feeding her every secret from within Ezekiel's own personal circle of trust! How could you betray him like this?"

"Ezekiel is the one betraying our Island! Not me!" Tamir growled from behind me. I nearly stumbled at his words. "He has been forming a rebellion against our ruler…sneaking around and spying on her. Do not speak to me about betrayal. My loyalty to the government of this Island supersedes my loyalty to a man like Ezekiel."

I had to stop then and turn around to face him in the dark. "Are you telling me you trust Abrianna over Ezekiel? That you put your faith in the ideal of a government that no longer works?"

"I am a true Loyalist. Abrianna is our Guardian—a sacred position given only to the one the Island ordains in the stars. Perhaps you do not understand what that means," he said, tightening his grip on Morgan, who moaned in pain.

"I understand that she is a corrupt Guardian! I understand that she has manipulated a lot of good people for her own selfish motives. Don't tell me that you are loyal to her just on the basis of principle! You can't just blindly follow a leader because they say the things you want to hear! I don't care whether she was ordained by the Island or elected by the people—she made her own choices!" I argued.

"She has only sought to bring peace to our Island. And she believes that your abilities will help bring a better life to the tribes."

I snorted in derision. "Peace?! Is that what you call what's happening outside right now? Violence? Death? Lies? Fear and mistrust? She is tearing this Island apart. Tamir, you have to listen to me. She does not want my abilities for some greater good of the Island—and if she really believes that, then she's kidding herself. What you believe about her is not the truth—"

"Enough!" he barked fiercely and Morgan cried out in pain again. I backed down, unable to see clearly enough what he was doing to her. "I am doing what I have been instructed to do. After that, I wash my hands of the mess. I trust the Guardian to do the right thing."

"You can wash all you want, but your hands will still be guilty, Tamir," I pointed out harshly. "And if something awful happens to one of my friends, don't be surprised if I go all Jack Bauer on your twisted patriotic *'loyalist'* excuse for a man."

I think he might have grinned at my empty threat. "I suppose that might frighten me if I even knew what a jack bauer was."

"He's a person. Who gets rid of guys like you," I muttered. No need to clarify that Jack Bauer was a *fictional* person who brought down entire terrorist networks within a twenty-four hour period.

I heard Morgan wheeze, "Oh, Whitnee." Okay, the Jack Bauer reference was melodramatic and wasted on Tamir. But he had crossed the line now. On the Mainland, we do *not* negotiate with terrorists.

With a startling boom, a door behind me was thrown open and blinding light spilled out into the tunnel. I blinked wildly, trying to see. I was seized and dragged into the next room before I could even react.

The door slammed shut again behind us, and someone griped, "You were only supposed to bring the one girl! Who is this?" I recognized the voice. I focused my vision on the man who was now gripping Morgan tightly by the jaw, inspecting her face.

"It could not be helped," Tamir responded.

"Then get rid of her. We cannot have any distractions."

"Don't touch her!" I cried and tried yanking myself out of the arms imprisoning me. The man pulled away from Morgan to peer at me. His eyes were a cold shade of blue. I did not know his face, but his voice was so familiar…

"I would keep her around," Tamir suggested lightly. "Whitnee will cooperate for Morgan's safety."

"You already brought the collateral we need to make Whitnee cooperate."

Tamir shrugged. "One more will not hurt."

"You!" I gasped at the Hydro. "You were the one who drugged me! What collateral are you talking about? Just let Morgan go, and I'll do whatever you want, okay?"

"Oh, we cannot let her go," the Hydro laughed. "She knows too much now. You can say your goodbyes in just a moment. Take them to the tank."

Say goodbye?! Were they going to kill her? My fear suddenly increased exponentially. I glanced at Tamir for signs of mercy, but his expression was indifferent. Adrenaline kicked in as I turned my eyes on Morgan's. I was shocked when I saw no fear there. She looked absolutely calm…and resolute.

"Tamir!" I spoke in a rush. "You think you kidnapped me for the Guardian, but she doesn't know! After you left me with Saul, this guy right here—the one who drugged me—told Saul that the Guardian could not know I was here. I really believe she has no clue! She sent Gabriel to the Mainland right after you, thinking *he* was going to bring me back! You have to listen to me! Whoever is giving your orders is lying to you—"

Smack! Someone backhanded me, and the jarring blow blurred my vision for a moment and stunned me into silence.

OUCH.

"Oy! Nobody touches her without permission! Understand?" the Hydro barked at someone to my left.

"What is she talking about?" Tamir wanted to know, a hint of suspicion in his tone.

"I have no idea. She was delirious and incoherent when they brought her to me. Do not worry, Tamir. You have done your job well, and the Guardian will reward your loyalty."

"I would like to speak to the Guardian myself, then," Tamir responded.

"Obviously, she is not here right now..."

At that point, I thought I heard Morgan whisper to me.

"Did you say something?" the Hydro leered at her.

Her eyes never left my face. "Jack...Bauer..." she said hoarsely. It was a call to action. And it was all I needed.

Perhaps combining all life forces again was what this situation called for...I only hoped Morgan was prepared. I mustered my waning strength and pulled from every known sense within my body. Then with a shout, I thrust my hands out where they were gripped behind me and...

Nothing happened.

I could not conjure a life force. At all. The confusion must have registered all over my face. Even Morgan looked dumbfounded.

"Release her." The Hydro motioned with his hand, a sarcastic smile on his face. I felt my captors let go of me. "Go ahead. Try using a life force here."

I just stared at him, knowing it would not work. That was when I actually observed my surroundings. The walls, floor, and ceiling were coated with a silver material that looked something like metal...but with a dull sheen. It was the mountain rock—the frozen kind that Gabriel said could block access to a life force. I could not connect with my powers in here.

Which meant it had to be blocking theirs too.

In a desperate move that I'm pretty sure I should have thought through first, I launched myself at Tamir and tried tackling him to the floor, hitting him with as much force as I could. "Tamir, you have to listen! Don't let them do this!" I screamed like a wild banshee.

Yeah, that didn't work at all.

Surprisingly, Tamir did not fight back—only blocked my ill-aimed and pathetic punches. But the others were upon me instantly. "Get her to the tank! Now!" the Hydro ordered with annoyance.

And I was dragged away screaming down a long, silver corridor that was strangely damp and creaky.

We passed doors and rooms and corridors on what seemed to be an abnormally long journey underground. But when we finally came to a dead end with one of those wheels you have to spin to open a vault, my curiosity was winning over my fear.

We stepped into a vast pentagonal chamber that was cold and clinical in nature. Through the bluish hue of the room, I noted immediately only one other door out of there—also sealed with an air-lock wheel. The small window above the lock was pitch black on the other side.

There were geometrical patterns that ran along the floor and led to a prison-like cage across the room, the metal bars extending from floor to ceiling. I felt like I had been sucker-punched the moment my eyes rested on the bars…the concrete-like surroundings…

I had been here before. In my dreams with my dad.

Only I had been seeing it from inside that cage. However, it was obvious we were not on a boat right now. I had been wrong about that. But I had been right about the tank and my dad. No wonder Will Kinder had called the ruins the *tank*. He had been here; he had known all along that this was here.

My mind turned over all the possibilities, and I was careful to guard my expressions as they shoved Morgan and me into the barred area and locked us in. Then they retreated from the chamber, leaving two unknown guards by the door. I breathed a sigh of relief, knowing that at least for the moment, Morgan and I were together.

"Are you okay?" I immediately went to her and examined her neck and head.

"I guess. I don't think I look as bad as you," she mumbled, gesturing at my open cuts.

I frowned. "Is my face messed up?" Not that it was a good time to be vain and worry about scarring, but, well…focusing on injuries right then seemed like a sane, normal thing to do. Now that I was taking inventory of my afflictions, it did feel like my right eye had swollen. Though most of my cuts had bled extensively, they seemed rather shallow.

"Geez, Whit…Use your shirt to wipe off all that blood so we can see the real damage. Are you in a lot of pain?"

"I think I'm kind of numb right now." I did as she instructed and began dabbing at my exposed skin. "I *promise* I won't let them do anything to you, okay? Don't be scared."

"I'm not," she replied and attempted a feeble smile. The weird thing was…I believed her. She had some kind of calm about her that did not make sense to me. "Listen, Whitnee…you need to know this. If you get the opportunity to pull off your superpower moves and take these people out, just do it—even if I'm in the middle of it. Don't let me be the reason you give up."

"Whatever. I'm not doing anything that could hurt you too—"

"Whit, I'm serious. You should know that if you can't save me, it's okay. I'm not afraid to die if it means you can save yourself and the others."

"Morgan!" I snapped. "I don't want to hear any talk of anyone dying, okay?! I know you're pissed at me for a lot of reasons, and you don't think you're important or whatever, but you're the most important thing to *me* right now! You are not dying here. *Nobody* is dying. Got it?"

I stared her down, unable to read the exact emotion on her face. She looked as if she was battling with opening her mouth again and arguing with me. Instead she looked away and retreated to the wall, slid down to the ground, and hugged her knees to herself.

With a sigh, I also moved to the wall and slumped to the cold ground, resting my head and closing my eyes for just a few seconds. I couldn't entertain fatalistic ideas of what was happening above ground right now. I had to believe in my friends' abilities to protect themselves. And we had other teams that were supposed to be showing up. Right? Unless Tamir had also tipped them off about that part...which he probably had. I shuddered inwardly, praying constantly for protection over Caleb, Gabriel, Eden, Hannah, Thomas, Levi...The list of people who mattered to me was quite extensive.

Morgan and I sat in separate silence for a few minutes, listening to the low creaks in the foundation. It was almost like we were swaying slightly in a treetop or something...

"Do you feel that?" I finally spoke.

"Yes." She was staring off into space, concentrating on something.

"It's like we're..."

"Rocking?" she supplied at the same time I said, "Moving."

"How is that possible underground?" I mused.

"Don't freak out, Whitnee." Morgan's voiced was hushed.

"What?"

"Judging by my sense of direction...which, granted, isn't that great most of the time...but taking into consideration all the signs, I don't think we're underground anymore." She spoke slowly. "I think we're...underwater."

I let her words sink in as I considered the possibility.

"You mean you think we're somewhere out in the middle of the ocean...off the Island?"

"Makes sense to me," she replied. "Put us in a 'tank' where we can't access a life force. And then surround us with ocean water and a mythical water beast that guards this place...it's like the Island's version of a high security prison."

The water beast...Yep, I think I had intentionally forgotten that part of the story.

A wave of nausea hit me like a truck.

I groaned, leaning over and dropping my head between my knees. I was not good with underwater. Not good at all. And the lightheaded sensation I was now experiencing was only adding to my panic.

"I told you not to freak out."

A perfectly-timed shudder of the foundation below us echoed through the chamber, confirming my fear. I stared hard at that other door in the room—the one with the window. Was there nothing but vast, deep, dark ocean water on the other side of that window? There was a tight pressure in my chest now, and I was seeing black spots all over the room.

"Morgie…I can't…" I gulped in air, trying to keep myself conscious. But I was fading…I think I felt her hands on my head.

"Hey, hey, it's okay. You've lost a lot of blood, so you're probably just a little woozy."

"But…w-we're underwater…there's a beast…and our friends are…Caleb is…" I stuttered weakly. Saying Caleb's name did me in.

"Just keep breathing, Whitnee…Somebody, help!" Her voice was drowned out by a loud ringing in my ears. Then there was tunnel vision…

And I was gone.

"Finish cleaning these wounds! She is waking up."

My head pounded with a whoosh of awareness as I tried to open my heavy eyelids. I could feel myself being poked and scraped, and the right side of my body burned with whatever they were doing.

I jerked reflexively and opened my eyes to see the icy blue eyes of the man in charge down here. "Where's Morgan?" I rasped.

"Over here. It's okay—they're helping you," she called from the corner of the prison cell.

"I'm sorry, Morgie," I told her weakly. Tamir was holding her back, watching me with cool calculation. I gave him a contemptuous look.

"Drink," the Hydro commanded. When I just stared back at him defiantly, he added, "It is only pure Water. Will help you with the fading…we need you awake right now."

He pulled me into a sitting position, and I discovered several blood-soaked rags on the floor around me. A couple of women pulled away from wiping at my face and neck. I sniffed the bottle of Water before swallowing in small doses. "When we leave here, we can heal your wounds. For now, we cleaned them up as best we could. Now, look at me."

I shifted my gaze to him, noting that even though his hair was unruly and he was roughly-shaven, he might have been a good-looking guy once upon a time. Too bad hanging with the wrong crowd makes you ugly.

"Good," he affirmed as he studied me clinically. "Your eyes look a little better. Now your friend tells me you have some kind of issues about being underwater. You will not have to stay here much longer if you just cooperate. Understand?"

My stomach quivered again at his words. "So we actually are underwater? I mean, is there any chance that…you know, water breaking in…drowning—?" I paused, visions of sinking to the bottom of the ocean inside this prison forcing their way into my thoughts.

With a nod at the other exit to the chamber, he remarked, "Just avoid that door and you have nothing to worry about. At least nothing that the ocean can do to you." My gaze shifted again to the darkness of the window, and I could already see bloodthirsty sea creatures swimming on the other side, waiting to feed on me as the ocean water crushed me to death…

The Hydro snapped his fingers in front of my face. "Focus! You have some important decisions to make. We have already wasted valuable time. Are you ready?"

"What is your name?" I asked. If I was going to have to deal much longer with this guy, I needed a name.

He watched me skeptically for a second, as if trying to decide how important that information was. "You can call me Jude," he finally replied.

"Is that short for Judas Iscariot? Or would that be *Tamir's* real name?" I grumbled. I wasn't sure how much biblical knowledge these Islanders had, but at least Morgan would know I meant the worst betrayer in history. She pressed her lips together, and Tamir remained motionless.

"Just Jude." He narrowed his eyes at me. "Now, according to Tamir, you seem to know quite a bit about why you are here. So I will not waste time. You have something that we want, and I daresay we have something that you want."

"What I want is for you to call off your people from attacking my friends outside!" I responded heatedly.

"That might require a bit more negotiation. Besides, I do not know how much longer they will survive out there anyway. You might want to ask for something a bit more...long-lasting." He had a glint in his eye as he stood. At a motion from him, the two women cleared up the rags, and they all left the prison cell. I stood unsteadily. "Tamir, go tell him that she is ready," Jude called back from outside the bars.

The tall man who I had thought was my friend, the one who still bore the symbol of a loyal Aeroguard on his clothing, made his way out of our cell. I grabbed his arm as he passed by, throwing myself at his mercy. "Tamir, please do not let them hurt all those people outside. You can stop this," I pleaded softly. He did not meet my eyes, but there had to be something in him that felt bad about this. He didn't seem to enjoy the violence...not the same way that creep, Saul, seemed to feed on it.

"Tamir!" Jude yelled. "Go!"

I released his arm, and he walked out without a backward glance. The cage door slammed shut, locking Morgan and me back in. I pressed myself to the bars, my fingers poking through as I watched them turn the wheel on the outer door for Tamir and Jude to leave. They were gone just a few moments when another man came strolling arrogantly in from the passageway.

He let out a cackling laugh when he spotted me. With his arms thrown open wide, he called, "There is my pretty girl! I told you we would meet again!"

I shrank back from the bars, my stomach turning horrible flips at the sight and sound of Saul's scarred face. "Oh, please tell me he's not their negotiator…"

Morgan whispered beside me. "Is that…?"

"Saul," I answered, bile rising up in my throat. "Morgan, do *not* mess with this guy." I warned her under my breath. He marched purposefully to our prison cell, and with a few clicks, yanked the door open wide. His face was alight with a sick joy. Instinctively, I placed myself in front of Morgan and tried not to show my terror. He seemed to thrive on the fear of others.

"We are going to have fun now." He smiled sinisterly as he moved into our cell.

"Really? The last few times haven't been so fun for you, Saul… maybe you should keep your distance this time. Wouldn't want another ugly scar on your face." I held my ground bravely, but my insides felt like jelly that might come spilling out at any time. If he took one step closer, I might lose it.

"That is fine with me. I like it when you fight back." He licked his lips, and I heard Morgan whimper in disgust behind me.

"I want to talk to Jude. He can kiss my cooperation goodbye if you touch either of us, Saul."

It was the wrong thing to say. He was looking for a challenge from me. In one swift move, he reached out and yanked me away from Morgan, slamming my body against him. Morgan started screaming and pummeling him with her fists. With one meaty hand, he punched her in the gut and sent her flying back against the wall. I watched helplessly as the breath was knocked out of her, and she crumpled to the floor in shock.

"Morgan!" I shrieked hysterically.

"I told you there would be nobody to stop me this time." His face was in my hair, his putrid breath hot against my neck. His hands were gripping me tightly enough to make bruises. I cried out in pain and humiliation, my fists ripping at his hair. If I could just bring my knee up to his...

The voice of my salvation was certainly not the one I expected at that moment.

"SAUL!" a deep male voice shouted with authority, detestation thick in his tone. "Who let him in here?" Saul froze momentarily as Eli, Gabriel's father and the Councilman for the Pyradorian Tribe, entered the chamber with a forceful presence about him. I took immediate advantage of Saul's hesitation and thrust my knee upward as hard as I could in his groin area.

As he doubled over, I sidestepped his reaching arms and ran to Morgan. Her face had gone white and tears leaked from her tired eyes as she lay there curled up in a fetal position against the wall.

"Oh, Morgie," I moaned. She looked up at me with clear pain in her expression, unable to speak as she wheezed for each breath. I spun around and shouted at Eli. "Morgan needs help! Please!"

Saul looked about ready to lunge at us again, but Eli took control of the situation. Saul was immediately subdued by the guards and dragged away from us. "Make him cool off!" Eli instructed the guards as they escorted Saul from the chamber.

"She keeps getting lucky! Just wait!" Saul was raving on his way out. "I get her when you are done..." Eli ignored the angry Pyra and stepped through the cage door, ducking slightly. Though I could see a resemblance between Gabriel and his father, I had forgotten just how dark Eli's eyes were...how sharp his features were in comparison to his son's. I didn't trust Eli the first time I met him and I still didn't. He was big, bald, and intimidating.

Tamir hovered near the entrance to the chamber, watching with solemnity. I wondered what he was thinking…if he was questioning what he had done. I took a chance at proving he was on the wrong side.

"So, you're the one behind all of this?" I spat at Eli, my chest heaving with emotion and physical exertion. "Does Abrianna know what you've done? Does she know how you've betrayed the government of the Island? And what about Gabriel? Does she know that he's probably out there fighting for his *life* because of you?"

Eli stared hard at me for a silent moment, then crossed his huge arms over his chest—a habit that reminded me too much of Gabriel.

"Abrianna is not innocent," Eli responded darkly. "Does she know I was the one who sent them to take you before Gabriel got there? Not yet, but she will figure it out. And as for Gabriel, he chose sides and will face his own consequences. If he had been smart, he would have stayed on the Mainland where I left him." He grinned mockingly at me. "Stop looking so worried, Whitnee. My son can take care of himself." If I hadn't been afraid to leave Morgan's side, I might have flown at him in rage then. What kind of father lures his own son into a trap that might kill him? These people were sick.

"I want out of here, Eli," I told him, hating that my demand came out sounding more like a plea.

"Then we both agree on something, Whitnee," Eli proclaimed. "I want you and your father off this Island—forever."

My heart stopped. "Where is he?"

"Closer than you think. The problem is that my wife is a little too attached to Nathan. I cannot afford to lose everything I have built up over the years—including the government of this Island—to her pathetic weakness." I think I frowned as I thought about what kind of attachment he was referring to. "Not only that, but you have been an unnecessary distraction for my son. I want *you* gone, and I want *Nathan* gone as soon as possible. You see how we want the same thing, even if we want it for different reasons."

I wasn't wild about having something in common with Eli, but…"What's the catch? I'm pretty sure there's always a catch with you people."

"Once the situation above ground is over, we leave here immediately for the White Mountain—the place we were originally taking you before your little friends interfered. I know you and Gabriel discovered our secret in the mountain." He paused for effect. I decided not to let on that I was confused about what I had found. Was it another portal or something else? "There you will transfer your life force abilities to me permanently. Then I will send you and Nathan—and your worthless friend here"—his gaze flicked to Morgan's struggling figure on the ground— "back to your home."

So it wasn't a portal…it was some kind of device used to transfer life force from one person to another. I thought back to the tables on the floor and the straps…and I shuddered. "What about Caleb? He has to come with us—"

"Caleb is probably dead by now. You would be wise to accept that."

It suddenly felt like I had been the one Saul punched. I couldn't breathe at Eli's words. Just hearing him say it brought the panic to a whole new level. Even Morgan's breathing changed, like she was fighting back sobs now. Desperately, I cast a glance toward the chamber door, but Tamir was no longer there.

"I don't believe you," I whispered. "I want to see my dad first."

"You are not in much of a position to bargain, Whitnee," Eli smirked triumphantly. "In the tank, you have no access to the immense power that you take for granted every moment you are on this Island. You are hardly in much physical condition to fight back. Your friends are either dying or being captured as we speak…You really have no right to negotiate anything other than your return home with your father."

I thought about my situation, about my friends, about every moment that had led up to this one. And then I remembered something important.

"Oh, really?" I narrowed my eyes at him. "Because if what Abrianna once told me is true, you can't just take my life forces from me without my consent. I have to actually give them to you. Right, Eli? So I guess how all of this goes depends on how badly you want my abilities."

That was when his face darkened, and I knew I had just found my bargaining chip. He made a motion with his hand, and his guards exited quickly. Then he stepped closer, his powerful frame casting a large shadow over me. I tried to meet his glare without flinching, but it was difficult. Something about the vast emptiness in his shadowed eyes made me feel cold all over...like maybe deep down there was nothing good inside Eli. Nothing good at all.

He gripped my arm—the one that was tender and cut up. His huge hand wrapped completely around it and squeezed tightly. That deep voice came out distorted with violent emotion. "You do not make demands here, Whitnee. Last time, Abrianna was the one protecting you. This time she does not even know you are here. You believe that stubbornness will get you what you want, but I can make you hurt so badly that you will be begging to give me those abilities of yours. I brought you here this time, and I can see to it that you never see your mother or your friends again." His grip tightened, and fresh drops of my blood started seeping out around his fingers. I bit down on my lip to keep from crying out. "When your father comes through that door, you do whatever convincing it takes to get to that mountain and off this Island. If you or Nathan give me any trouble, I will make it hurt, Whitnee. Not just for you...but for her too." He nodded at Morgan. "Do you understand?"

I wanted to spit in his face. And I wanted to break down and cry like a baby. Saul scared me because he was uninhibited and unpredictable. But Eli scared me more—because he was *smart*.

I don't know what my reaction would have been to his threat, because everything came to a sudden, chilling stop when a voice rang out crystal clear, piercing the damp air like the trumpet of an archangel.

Just five words that dropped like an airstrike missile to my heart.

"LET GO OF MY DAUGHTER!"

THE WHITE LIGHT

I'm pretty sure time stood still, because it would have been impossible for the million and one thoughts, feelings, and sensations to course through my body in the millisecond it took to process his voice. All I know was that a heavier weight of authority seemed to register throughout the room at his words. His was a command so pure, you didn't want to be the one on the wrong side of it. Eli's face changed right before me. Was that a flicker of fear? Annoyance? I couldn't read it before he had composed himself.

The pressure on my arm released, and Eli stepped out of my line of vision and turned around.

"We were just having a friendly chat, Nathan," Eli responded coldly, wiping his bloody hand roughly on the back of my tunic as if I were a disposable rag. "You and your daughter are more alike than I ever knew."

With shaking hands, I brushed the stray hair out of my eyes, and searched for the reality I had only dreamed of.

It was no holographic image this time. He was *right there...* walking forward boldly, his familiar face struggling with expressions of righteous anger and disbelief. The guards grabbed him by the arms and stayed his progress. "What have you done, Eli?!" The two men glared at each other, but I could not take my eyes away from him. The heavy silence that fell on the chamber felt thick and suffocating. Eli calmly exited the cage, leaving the door open behind him.

"I am giving you five minutes alone with her and then Jude is bringing in the drug," Eli informed him as he passed by. "Remember, we can hear everything. Choose your words wisely, Nathan." Then without a glance back, he commanded, "Put him in and lock it up."

The guards escorted the blond-haired man with piercing gray eyes into the cage, locked the door behind him, and then left the chamber with a resonating slam of the door and click of the wheel. The foundation creaked ominously again, and then it was just Morgan and me...and him. Alone.

With slow, unsteady feet, I moved forward as if in a fog, staring with astonishment at the father I had not seen in six years.

He also took a few steps closer, but then paused. "Baby Doll, are you all right?" His voice was no longer angry. It was tender and cautious.

And that was my breaking point.

"Daddy!" The sob ripped out of me, uncontrollable tears spilling down my cheeks and blurring my vision. I stumbled forward and fell into the arms that had rocked me as a child. He was *real*. His embrace was strong, a long-lost fatherly cocoon of safety. Though I was taller now, my face still found a hiding place in his chest.

Even after all this time, I had not outgrown my daddy's arms.

"Oh, my Whitnee...my baby girl!" Dad pulled back enough to cradle my wet face and stare into my swollen eyes—so like his own. I reached up and covered his hands with mine and there was no question then that something magical happened. It felt like an electrical pulse shot through my body the moment our hands fused together. His eyes flashed a white light at me. Just once. Then they were normal again. My face registered confusion, and I saw him mirror my expression. He had felt it too—and perhaps my eyes had done the same thing.

"Did you feel—?" I choked through my tears, but his eyes widened, and he shook his head in warning. Oh, yeah...they were listening. But something had happened...something neither of us had expected. I followed his lead and tried to mask the sensation of power that was slowly spreading through me the longer I held onto him. Tears pooled in his eyes then as he carefully pressed his fingers to my damaged cheek. "You're hurt...I'm so sorry..."

"Daddy, I'm so confused..." I tried to slow my sobs as questions began forming in my mind. "I...I thought you were a prisoner here. We were coming to rescue you...but everything went wrong—"

My voice faltered because suddenly it really did dawn on me that this was not quite what I had pictured. Dad looked perfectly healthy, his appearance clean and...strong. He was not bound in any way, nor was there one mark or bruise visible on him. In fact, he looked nothing like the image I had seen of him on the other side of the river or in the forest...when he had been unshaven and unkempt. He was handsome as ever, even if there were a few gray hairs mixed in with the blond.

"I know you don't understand. I'll explain what I can as soon as—" But then his gaze wandered past me, and his expression grew so compassionate, even sorrowful, that I had to turn to see what he was looking at.

Morgan.

She had found a way to stand up, deliberately keeping herself at a distance from us. But as she leaned wearily on the bars, holding her stomach and watching our reunion, silent tears rolled endlessly down her pale cheeks.

"Morgan," I breathed, releasing my dad to move to her side. The powerful connection that had surged through me earlier deflated the moment I lost contact with him. I threw one arm around Morgan and guided her forward. My voice wavered. "Dad, this is my best friend in the whole world. Morgan, this is..." I lost my voice because at that moment, a huge smile broke out through her weeping, and she just sort of leaned in like a small child— right into my dad's surprised arms.

"It's nice to finally meet you," she whimpered weakly, her eyes closing in exhaustion. At that point, she seemed to lose her ability to hold herself up. Dad was quick to catch her wilting frame and lower her gently to a sitting position on the floor. He cast a glance at me once, deep concern registering on his face. I was a little taken aback by her behavior. It was like all her defenses just completely fell down...like she had been waiting for the right moment to fall apart.

I watched in fascination as Dad knelt down in front of Morgan and rested his hand lightly on the top of her head for a few seconds. She stared back at him unabashedly through glazed eyes. "Hi, Morgan," Dad said softly as if he was talking to a five-year-old. "I can tell that you're very sick. But we're going to get you help as soon as we can, okay? Can you just sit here and rest for a little bit?"

She nodded with absolute trust and did not argue with him. Nor did she deny being sick. I felt a slight shiver—both at her behavior and at his ability to read her so quickly and accurately. That was when I stepped back and saw Morgan through different eyes...as she might have appeared to Dad for the first time.

A girl who looked deathly ill.

"Whitnee, come here. We don't have long." He held out his hand to me from where he knelt on the ground. The moment our palms connected, that white light flashed in his eyes again. This time, Morgan raised her eyebrows and gave a tiny gasp as she looked back and forth between Dad and me.

"Look..." she mumbled somewhat deliriously. "He glows too. Kind of like you...in that weird all-over way..."

I glanced at my dad in confusion. Other than his eyes flashing, I didn't see whatever glow she was talking about. Something was really wrong with her.

"Dad, Eli said he can get us off the Island tonight—" I started desperately.

"I know what he says." His voice was low and his face troubled.

"But, listen, my friends are out there—fighting off Eli's rebels. We thought we were coming to rescue you, but Tamir—Ezekiel's Aeroguard—was telling Eli everything we were planning all along. They set a trap for us…and Tamir thought he was doing all of this for Abrianna and at one point maybe he was, I don't know…but Abrianna doesn't even know I'm here…" Dad nodded as if none of this was news to him. Clearly, he knew a lot more about our situation than I understood. "And, Dad, you don't know him, but my other best friend, Caleb, is out there. He came here with us and I'm *not* leaving without him. He—"

"He loves Whitnee…more than just friends," Morgan interrupted in a weak, sing-song voice. She gazed at us with a drunken half smile. "Whitnee loves him too, but she's not ready for a commitment…but she'd be lost without him, even if she doesn't know it yet…" And her eyes fluttered again like they wanted to close.

Dad cocked one eyebrow at this, and I'll admit my sigh was a little annoyed. I mean, really, did Morgan have to go all weird and loopy and expose the Caleb drama with my dad *now*? The man hadn't seen me in six years…I didn't exactly have boyfriends when I was eleven! With one hand I squeezed her shoulder gently in warning—because God help us if she said a word about Gabriel—and I jerked on my dad's hand to take the attention off Morgan before she could open her big mouth again.

"The point is that we can't leave this Island without him. We can't leave all of our friends out there like that—you have to negotiate with Eli to make it all stop." I turned wide, fearful eyes on him, and a familiar ringing in my ears suddenly returned.

I understand, Whitnee. There are a lot of things that must stop on this Island. I could hear his voice, but his mouth wasn't moving as he stared back at me with intense focus.

"Ummm…" I was confused.

Talk to me through Wind communication—with your mind. As long as our hands are touching, our life forces are connected. I can't explain it, but it's there. Don't you feel it? Don't let go of me in here, no matter what.

I nodded but didn't know how to tell him that I had no earthly idea how to communicate with him that way. I didn't have that special gift like he and Abrianna did.

"Whitnee, I know this must be very hard for you," Dad said aloud for the benefit of whomever was listening in. "But I don't see many other options at this point. The most important thing is to get you and your friends back home; I agree with that."

"But Dad, I can use all four life forces...I can even combine them together. And Eli wants those abilities for himself. Says there's a way to permanently gift another person with them. But I don't even *know how* to do everything with them or what I'm capable of...some things *I've never tried*. You know?" I raised my eyebrows at him meaningfully.

You know how to communicate with me in your mind—you've done it twice before on this Island; you just didn't know that's what you were doing. The communications between us have not been dreams. I even heard you in here today when you told me you were coming, but I couldn't warn you. My powers are not strong enough alone to overcome this tank. You're clearly more powerful than I am. Tell me exactly where your friends are and how many are out there.

I shut my eyes in frustration. "I just want to help my friends in the *Watch Tower ruins*..." I emphasized the answers to his questions. "There were *so many* surprises that I can't believe all of this happened...like people coming in at least *three directions* with *back-up*...but we *never saw them*. And it's really annoying to know that I *can't communicate* with them!" My final words were full of frustration. *Ugh.* How was I supposed to cast a thought in *his* mind? Maybe it was just easier when I was asleep.

Hurry—we're running out of time, Baby Doll! Our minds are like frequencies on a radio—and every person's frequency sounds and feels a little differently. You have to find mine through your other senses. Once you're connected, project your thoughts into my head. It's really important you learn how to do this...like, now.

"Don't worry about your friends right now...I'm sure if we cooperate with Eli, he will call off his fighters. Abrianna developed a way to permanently gift another person with a secondary life force. But it's dangerous and the results have not been successful. She and Eli believe that, because you are half-Mainlander, it won't hurt you to give up your abilities permanently."

But there is no way I will let them try! Taking another person's life force like that is a serious offense to the Island. Not only that, but Eli has lied to Abrianna and is trying to steal your abilities before she can. Go along with what I'm saying out loud for now. I think I have a plan to get us out of here before they come back...

"Well, I suppose that's good news," I muttered at both his audible and inaudible words, meanwhile wondering what his plan was. I tried concentrating on my thoughts and finding Dad's "frequency." It actually wasn't that hard once I shut up and listened for a moment. Perhaps being bonded through the life forces helped. I closed my eyes again and focused on the sound of his voice in my head. And then he was just there—in an abstract sort of way. I could feel him and see him—or the essence of his mind, I guess. His frequency connected to mine in soft, white light with the calmness of a gentle breeze.

Can you hear me? I projected my thought into the light.

His face broke into a smile. *You're still a fast learner. Good girl. Now, listen...I want you to place your other hand on Morgan while we talk. Give her some healing energy—she will need a HydroHealer for the other problems, but she's going to need to be very awake if my plan is going to work.*

Why do you think we have life force power together like this? I asked.

Because we're gifted differently by the Island. And we share the same blood. Every time you're on the Island, I can sense you. Could you sense me?

I thought about that for a moment. *Yeah, I guess. Not directly. But you never felt more alive to me than when I was here. On the Island.*

I felt him freeze at my words. Then, with something like regret in his expression, he reached out with his free hand and cupped my good cheek.

I'm so sorry you never knew what happened to me...I don't even know what to say.

Just say you're coming home with me, I answered.

I watched him carefully for a reaction, but his expression was hidden.

Let's worry about getting out of here first. Just follow my lead.

His hesitation to confirm going home with me made me feel uneasy, but I knew I would get answers from him later. "Is Morgan a Hydro?" he asked casually. I nodded as I obediently laid my free hand on Morgan's head first and then along her stomach. I had learned earlier today that healing internally where there was no open flesh didn't require Pure Water...but it didn't seem to work as strongly or as precisely. She stared up at me in confusion as my eyes lit up blue, and Dad immediately said aloud, "Try not to move, Morgan. Just rest until they come back in here." His eyes conveyed a deeper message to remain quiet at what she was seeing and feeling. Fortunately, I think she picked up on it even through her haze of delirium.

When I tried to alleviate her stomach pain from Saul's attack, it was more like I had to search around for it instead of having Water to guide me directly to her injury. And then I felt something unexpected...a blockage of some sort. It was like the Water life force came up against a wall and wouldn't let me go any deeper. She jerked in pain for a brief moment and then relaxed as I set about working in the areas it would let me strengthen. I finally came to a stop when her eyes and expression became more lucid and she sat up straighter. When I pulled away and felt the familiar trickling like a water pipe shutting off, my own stomach felt a little nauseous.

"Thanks," she mouthed, and I gave her a quick, half-hearted smile.

"So, what do we do now, Dad?" I asked aloud.

"I think we only have one choice right now, Baby Doll..." Dad said, giving me a look I suddenly recognized as the I'm-about-to-tell-you-some-bad-news look. I had seen it before—when he had to tell me my pet hamster died and when I got my first B on a report card (stupid math class) and when he realized I broke my toe running barefoot from a wasp at the pool…

He glanced back at the other door in the chamber—the one with the window. The one that led to the deep, dark ocean.

And then came the bad news through my head like a news ticker broadcasting the latest national tragedy.

I think we're gonna have to swim out of here.

"Um, are you *crazy*?!" I blurted out loud without thinking.

"What? What are we gonna do?" Morgan asked, her eyes wide and alert now.

"Apparently, something has fried your brain in the last six years," I told him, ignoring Morgan's confused looks. "I still have major issues with…you know." I waved my free hand side to side like a fish swimming.

"Whitnee, your cooperation is important here," Dad reminded me with a double meaning.

There is no time to argue. His voice broke into my reeling mind. *We have to escape before they come back in here. If they separate us, then we've lost our chance! By combining our life force powers, we can break through this cage, use Wind power to turn that wheel on the door, and flood the chamber—*

I half-yelped at what I was hearing.

No WAY! If screaming into someone's mind was possible, I might have just done that.

Whitnee, do you really think Eli is going to let Morgan live through the night? He will get rid of her as soon as he can no longer use her to threaten you—maybe even when he comes back in here! Dad's tone was authoritative and forceful now. I glanced at Morgan in fear. Her eyebrows were puckered as she scrutinized our faces, probably realizing there was some other communication going on that she wasn't privy to. *Do you really think he'll call off his people out there—even for the sake of his own son? You don't know Eli like I do. Trust me. We have to act now. We flood the chamber and they'll be forced to keep the door sealed off. Once it fills up completely, we can swim out—*

"I can't do that," I mumbled, shaking my head in denial.

"Can't do what?" Morgan questioned.

We're not that far from the surface or from the Island itself…swim straight up and then toward the land. As you get closer, your life force will come back to you fully. You can both use your Water life force to propel you faster.

What about the water beast?! I shrieked inwardly, knowing that was probably just a myth, but still…even if there wasn't a beast, there were still fish swimming around…sharks…piranhas…

I haven't heard him around here in days, and he shouldn't hurt you if you don't threaten him first. Besides, he can't get too close to the shore, so you just head for shallow water—

"Are. You. Serious! Not a chance—!" I jumped up to pace, forgetting I wasn't supposed to release his hand. Every part of me was trembling at his scenario. That was his brilliant idea?! Drown us or let us be eaten by a beast?! There was no happy ending for me here…Even if I survived, I'd have serious psychological problems the rest of my life.

"What's wrong with her?" Morgan rose to her feet too.

"Whitnee, you can do this," Dad said and grabbed me by the shoulders, forcing me to stop pacing. "*We* can do this. Together." Our hands connected again. I felt the surge of power, but it did nothing to make me feel better.

"You know, Dad…maybe you forgot some things about me over the years…weird phobias and all," I protested.

"I haven't forgotten a thing about you, Whitnee. I promise."

"Whatever he says to do, Whit…just do it," Morgan spoke up confidently.

"Easy for you to say!" I moaned.

Is Morgan a good swimmer? Dad asked.

Oh, yeah…she's a great swimmer. Far better than me! I threw back.

"Okay…are you ready?" Dad's eyes searched my face.

"No. But I'll never be." I was going to throw up at the anticipation.

"Morgan, hold on to the bars, okay? Be ready for anything," Dad whispered. She did exactly what he said and grasped the bars.

What do I do again? I asked him, trying to swallow down the fear.

But we were too late.

The chamber door started opening with a screech.

"Whitnee, they're coming!" Dad warned, but I was distracted and paranoid.

Nothing prepared me for the next surprise to come through that chamber door.

Her bloodshot, hazel eyes were wide with fear as Tamir shoved her into my view. And then it clicked...*She* was their collateral, their *insurance* that I would cooperate...and they were right.

"Stop!" I think I meant for only Dad to hear me, but my voice echoed across the chamber.

"Oh, dear God," Morgan moaned beside me.

I was not really seeing this. This was *not* happening...

They had Amelia.

AS IF I NEEDED ANOTHER
REASON TO HATE FISH

How did they get *Amelia* here?! I watched her drive away from Camp Fusion the other night—in that same outfit she was wearing now. *Please just let that be a holographic image meant to deter me…*

Eli strolled in behind Tamir, and Saul followed quickly with a manic grin on his face.

"Now, how did I know you might need just a little more convincing, Whitnee? I warned you that it would hurt if you did not cooperate…" And he nodded pointedly at Amelia as she struggled against Tamir.

"Shut up, Eli!" she screamed at him with that recognizable preteen attitude. And that confirmed the reality we were in, because I knew from experience that their Pyra images couldn't talk. That was the real Amelia. "Whitnee, please tell me you didn't fall for it too?! It was Tamir—you should never have trusted him! He's the spy! And he hurt Ben—"

I let go of my dad and flew at the bars in rage. "What is she doing here? Tamir, don't touch her! Is Ben here too? What is *wrong* with you?"

"No, he just brought me—" Amelia spat, and Tamir shushed her.

Dad rushed to my side. "Eli, this is too far. We've already said we'll cooperate with you. Let the girl go."

"Nathan, you are a terrible liar," Eli responded.

Tamir's eyes were still a solemn gray as he held the feisty twelve-year-old girl back. I had to give it to Amelia. She was showing no fear...just a lot of indignation.

"I'm sorry, Whit," she called out in frustration. "I shouldn't have gone back to camp. It's just that I had a feeling you were planning to go to the Island and I convinced my parents I left my cell phone there and had to go back. It all happened so fast! I went to Ben's cabin when I couldn't find you, and then *Tamir*" —she stomped down hard on his foot— "showed up and I thought he was there to help until he knocked out *Ben*" —she elbowed him in the stomach, eliciting a small grunt from him— "and took me instead! What a liar, Tamir! If Ben dies back at camp, I hope you rot in—"

"Oh my gosh, Eli. I swear you won't get a thing from me if you hurt her or anyone else," I yelled fiercely.

"But, Whitnee," Eli's tone was condescending and heartless. "Sometimes pain is the only way to help make up a person's mind. You obviously do not care about your own pain. So how about hers? Would it matter to you if we snapped her neck right now? If you watched the very essence of life disappear from her just... like...that?" He snapped his fingers. "Maybe then you will realize we are not playing a game here."

"No!" I cried as Eli approached Amelia and ran one finger along her delicate, stretched neck.

"Eli, enough! She's a child—" Dad began, but I was done with this.

"I'll go with you! Right now, Eli. You and me. You can have all of it. I don't care anymore. Just don't hurt anyone else." I was grasping at straws. "Lock Amelia up in here with Dad and Morgan. Take me to the mountain. And right before we make the transfer, I want you to let them go."

"Whitnee, what are you doing?" Dad interjected. He turned to face me, his eyes flicking intuitively all over my face, and I slowly reached out for his hand. Right before we connected, we closed our eyes so nobody would see the white flash.

"Dad, just trust me. It's the only way," I replied dramatically. *I do NOT negotiate with terrorists*, I told him. Then aloud to Eli, I continued, "You have to promise, Eli! I will give you my abilities the moment you can confirm that you've released them from here. I'm ready now. Do we have a deal?"

Eli was definitely suspicious of my proposition. Knowing that Pyras were sensitive to emotional climates, I tried to give off a vibe of fear and desperation...not entirely too hard to do, given the circumstances.

Surprisingly, Tamir spoke up. "She will do anything for their safety, Eli. I have seen it firsthand. I do not believe she is lying." I hid my confusion at his sudden willingness to vouch for me here. Eli searched my face through the bars.

"Please," I begged again, looking him straight in the eye.

After a longer hesitation, Eli declared, "Very well. Put the girl in the cage. Take Whitnee to Room Two. Tell Jude it is time."

"Whitnee, this is a bad idea!" my dad reprimanded me loudly as Saul approached to open the cage for Tamir and Amelia. "Eli, I won't let you separate me from my daughter!"

"She made the choice," Eli shrugged.

Dad, as soon as they open that door, you take out Saul and I'll grab Amelia. Then we bust that door open and swim the heck out of here. Let Eli and the others drown...

His thoughts came back at me without hesitation. *Already there. I could read you like a book, Baby Doll*, he assured me. *But it's going to take both of us to turn that wheel...*

I waited, barely breathing, as Saul made the clicks on the door and sneered, "Well, well, well...I will be escorting you to the mountain once again. Only this time, you will remember *everything* that happens to you." He was practically salivating. I felt Dad's fingers tighten protectively around my hand. I avoided making eye contact with Saul, and instead focused on Amelia through the bars.

"It will be okay, Amelia…just do everything my dad tells you to do, okay? I promise I'll get you out of here." I tried to reassure her, making note of the fact that Eli was still near the chamber door, watching from a distance.

"Oh, this sucks," Amelia responded with annoyance. "And Ugly Dude—yeah, you with the scar face!" She directed this at Saul. "Brush your teeth! Geez. I'm so sick of the nasty breath on some of these people…"

Oh my word. Only Amelia would continue hurling insults in such a situation.

Saul barely gave her a second glance, for which I was grateful. The door made its final click, and every muscle in my body was tight like a wind-up toy ready to pounce.

And then Tamir spoke my name softly. It threw me for a moment as I risked a glance at him. But all he said was, "Jack Bauer." And then he gave me a barely perceptible nod of assurance. Amelia cocked her eyebrows and looked confused as she tried to wiggle around to see his face.

Saul was hardly giving Tamir any attention, his eyes focused only on me as he swung the door open wide. But then things played out like a perfectly rehearsed scene in a movie. Tamir shoved Amelia at me. Without hesitation, I sent him flying several feet in the air with a gust of Wind. He was somewhat surprised, but didn't fight back as he allowed himself to be propelled so far. Dad did the same with Saul, who was actually astonished. He was thrust away from the open cage entrance and pinned against the wall with Dad's life force strength.

Morgan quickly gathered Amelia to herself—and out of our way.

Eli just stood there, stunned. "How is that possible—?" He thrust his own hands out, but of course, nothing happened. He turned to run several steps away, shouting for more help. Dad sent a force that knocked his feet out from under him.

"Now, Whitnee!" Dad shouted.

With mirrored motions, we stretched our hands out toward the other door and silvery Wind blasted across the chamber, encompassing the wheel in a swirl of strength and spinning it wildly. Water started spraying out of the sides as the pressure increased. Saul caught his breath, and Tamir rolled and jumped to his feet.

"What—?" Eli realized a moment too late what was about to happen. "He is flooding the room! Nathan, you fool—!"

The three men sprinted to the door that led to the rest of their headquarters. "Grab Whitnee!" Eli shoved Saul away from their exit. "We need her—"

"But—" Saul protested with a fearful glance back, but then the ocean door flew off its hinges, and the water cascaded violently into the chamber. Saul lunged for the other exit door and slammed it behind Tamir, Eli, and himself—just in time. We were locked into my worst nightmare now.

"Go, Amelia!" I heard Morgan cry, just as the full strength of the first wave hit us. I immediately lost my footing. Dad tried to hold me up, but the water was too strong. We were both thrown against the outside bars of the cage, losing contact with each other and the life force. Morgan had shoved Amelia out of the cage, but she herself was tossed further inside the prison, against the wall.

"Morgan, get out of there!" I yelled over the crashing sounds.

"I'm trying!" She struggled to walk forward as the water surged up to her waist and slammed up the sides of the walls.

"Dad, can't we control the Water?"

"Possibly…but ocean water will be difficult. Can you grab my hand?" I reached out for him but we couldn't get a good grip with wet hands from this distance. "It will be easier to manipulate the ocean water the closer we get to land. Remember, don't swallow any of it!"

"Uhhh…Whitnee?" Amelia was clinging to the bars several feet away from me as if her life depended on it. Fear tinged her voice for the first time. "Was this part of a plan or something? I'm not a great swimmer in deep water…not without a life vest!"

"Dad, you're gonna have to help Amelia!" I looked to him for support since he was closer to her; he was already moving in her direction.

Amelia reached out for him and exclaimed, "Nice to know you aren't really dead, Mr. Terradora. I'm Amelia…Whitnee's favorite camper and an extremely talented Pyra."

I didn't miss the amused smile that broke out on Dad's face. He wrapped an arm around her, explaining to all of us, "We have to wait for the chamber to fill up before we can swim out easily. Everybody just stay calm until then and keep your head above water. We'll take one big breath together and then swim through that door and straight up. It's not far as long as you keep kicking and pushing forward. Amelia, stay close to me! Whitnee, you and Morgan help each other."

I pressed my face to the bars and looked in at Morgan, who was still having a hard time moving. She appeared ridiculously tiny fighting against the pounding water. "I'm coming!" I told her and started pulling myself along the bars to the entrance of the door. It was alarming how fast the chamber was filling up and how strong the water was as it poured in.

"Oh, yuck! Something just touched my leg!" Amelia squealed, and I froze for a moment as the water swirled up to my chest. *Don't look down, Whitnee. Just keep moving.* The water wasn't terribly cold, but the chill of our situation was creeping up my throat like ice blocking off my lungs. *You just have to survive,* I told myself.

The foundation suddenly let out a deep groan and then without warning, one side of the room jerked and tilted sharply downward, sloshing all the water to one side. I screamed and all of my weight, plus the pressure of the shifting water, was shoved painfully against the bars. Amelia and Dad were tossed further away from me but found a way to hold onto the cage, trying to maneuver to a safe distance atop the water's surface.

But Morgan…

She was still in the cage, and I watched helplessly through those blasted bars as she vanished underneath the churning water.

The sudden shift in weight and pressure in the chamber caused the cage door to slam ominously, its force vibrating deep inside my chest.

She was closed in. I couldn't get to her now.

"Morgan! Morgan!" I choked, spitting out the salty ocean water. *Please come up for air.* I begged silently. I heard Amelia's screams of terror as we shifted further down again.

"The pressure of the water is collapsing the room…" Dad muttered as he surveyed our situation.

And then Morgan's arms broke the surface and her face came up, gasping for air. I reached my hands through the bars. "Morgie, over here! Grab on!" She swam to me and our fingers touched as she gripped the bars again. That was when she noticed the door had closed on her, and she turned wide eyes on me.

"It's okay, it's okay," I assured her loudly. "I'm gonna go open it. Just hold on." It felt like I was fighting molasses to get there, and the water was definitely getting deeper in there.

Morgan followed me on the other side.

I took a deep breath and went underwater, trying to feel for the lock…hoping it hadn't really clicked into place. Hoping I could just pull the door open for her.

I struggled with it and yanked and pulled for as long as I could hold my breath. It didn't budge even a millimeter. When I came up for air, Morgan's face was leaning into the bars and watching me expectantly.

I called out, "Dad! How do I open the door? It's locked, and Morgan's stuck in there!"

"There's a combination of some sort…I don't know it!" Dad called back to me, the weight of his words visible in Morgan's expression. "Hold on, I'm coming!" He was swimming our way and Amelia was pulling herself across the bars in our direction.

"Whitnee…" Morgan started crying.

"Don't get upset, Morgan. We'll just blast it open if we can't unlock it," I told her, trying to reassure myself at the same time. Trying to ignore the fact that we were majorly running out of time.

Dad came to my side and then submerged himself underwater. I ducked down again, and we both tried pulling on the door together with no luck. Back on the surface, we gulped in breaths.

"Give me your hand. We're gonna have to break her out of here!" I grabbed onto him and the pulse of life force power was there but it was fainter this time. Dad nodded in agreement, but I read a shadow of doubt in his expression.

"Move away, Morgan!" I commanded and counted to three. We launched an attack at the metal bars, but it was weak. It was *so* weak, it did nothing. "What's happening? Why are we losing strength?! Dad, are you really trying?" I cried.

"It's the ocean water, Whitnee." We were starting to tread water now to stay afloat. "We're not as strong in it."

"Well, let's try again! We have to get her out of there!"

He hesitated. "Let me think for a minute." His eyes roved around the chamber again as if looking for something. "Maybe I can figure out the lock..." And he dropped below the surface again.

I turned back to Morgan who was staring at me sadly now. Because of the leaning room, the water was flooding her side first. "Don't be scared...We're gonna get you out, Morgie!" I reached my hand through the bars and she held onto me with trembling hands.

"Whitnee, I'm so sorry for everything I said outside in the ruins!" she sobbed. "I didn't mean it—I am so blessed to call you my best friend. You've always taken care of me, and you've taught me so much about what's important in life. And I'm proud of you for following your instincts and finding your dad!"

"Don't say all of this...please. We can talk about everything once we're out of here." My own salty tears were mixing with the ocean water. I knew what she was trying to do and I refused to accept any closure on our friendship or on her life.

"You don't have much time left...you have to leave soon—" She was trying to get a grip on herself. I watched her swallow with difficulty, her bright blue eyes reflecting the swirling water surrounding us.

"And you're coming with me! Morgie, I'm not leaving you!"

"Whitnee, in a few minutes, you're going to swim away and leave me in here. And it's going to be okay because I've been sick for a long time, and I'm already dying. I'm halfway there, Whit. I can feel it. I'm sorry I didn't tell you before now, but I'd rather go like this than die in a cold, lonely hospital bed in a matter of months. At least for now, I'm still *me*."

"No…no, no. You're lying…" I stuttered, but I knew she wasn't.

"Whit, you have to *let me go*."

Dad came back up and shook his head in frustration. Morgan gave him one look, and when she cast her eyes back on me, her face was resolute.

"Don't you give up on me, Morgan Maye Armstrong!" I screamed at her, recognizing that look in her eyes. The more panicky and emotional I became, the calmer she was growing. "If you don't care about your own life, fine! But what about me?! You can't leave me like this—I *need* you, Morgan!"

"Morgan…" Amelia was crying hysterically now from a few feet away. "Please don't give up! Please!"

"I love both of you so much!" Morgan coughed and sputtered as the waves came up to her mouth. "It's okay…I promise it's okay. Tell Caleb—" But her words were cut off as she struggled to keep her face above the rising water.

Something inside me snapped when I realized she really was resigned to a dark, watery grave inside that cage. "Dad, hold onto me and give me as much life force as you can, okay?!" I shouted, throwing my arm out toward him. "We're going under."

Dad didn't question me. With a deep breath, we dove beneath the surface.

If we can't break the bars, maybe we can bend them! I tried communicating to him through our thoughts, but the connection was fuzzy. I wasn't sure he heard me until I guided his free hand to one side of the bar and I placed my free hand on the other side. He knew then exactly what I was doing.

With every bit of strength left, I accessed power from each life force, combining them all into one focused beam of energy. In the cave, I had felt superhuman enough to break through rock. Well, now I just needed to bend some metal enough for her to swim out.

I think an electrical current rippled through the water, because I felt it in the metal gripped tightly in my hands when I combined all four life forces. Ignoring the shock, I heaved against the bar, tugging with everything in me. I was concentrating so hard that I almost missed the jerk of Dad's hand taking me back to the surface.

Morgan was still gasping for air up above.

"Morgan, there's a gap down there—it should be wide enough for you to swim through!" Dad instructed her while I caught my breath.

She shook her head. "No. Just go!"

"Dangit, Morgan!" I yelled and banged my fist against the bars between us. Now I was just mad. If she let herself drown in here, I would never forgive her. "You don't get to quit just because you want to! That's not what friends do! Get your butt down there and swim out. NOW! All that weight you've lost should help you fit through the small space!"

"I can't, Whitnee…I can't…" she protested weakly.

I was going to scream at her again, but Dad's calm voice came out first. He thrust a hand through the bars and grasped her fingers. "It's not time for you yet, Morgan," he told her gently. I had no clue what he meant or why he said it, but it made her pause.

All that could be heard after that was the rushing water, our panicked breathing, and Amelia's child-like sobs. Morgan's eyes met mine one last time, and she let out a cry before disappearing beneath the rising water once and for all.

I held my breath. What had she just done? I could feel my pulse thumping in my temples as Dad and I waited, treading water away from the now completely submerged cage.

"Where is she?!" Amelia cried out, peering into the dark water. I couldn't see anything. I couldn't even process my thoughts. I know it was only about a minute or so that passed, but it felt like years before Morgan suddenly broke the surface behind us with a big splash.

"Well," she said between gasps. "If it's not my time, then maybe there's still some use for me somewhere…" Amelia gave a shout of joy, but I was confronted with too many emotions at once. She was going to let herself *die*. How could she *do* that to me?

"Five years of friendship and that's how you were gonna end it?! Glad you listened to my dad who you've known a grand total of five seconds!" I retorted, even though relief flooded through me at the sight of her. "I might drown you myself for putting me through that!" My tears had become angry tears, mixing violently with the saltwater dripping down my face.

"I'm sorry…I heard everything you said, Whit," she assured me and squeezed my arm under the water. "And you freaking bent that metal bar like a beast…Any smaller and I wouldn't have fit through."

I rolled my eyes and choked back my sobs. I squeezed her arm in response to show she was forgiven. We would deal with her other issues once we survived the depths of the godforsaken ocean.

"Okay, girls, time to move!" Dad swam to retrieve Amelia, and the four of us paddled across the chamber, fighting the current spilling in from the vault door. "I'll go first with Amelia and you two follow closely behind. Remember, swim out and *up*! You can do this!"

I don't know what he saw in my expression, but it caused him to smile sympathetically and say, "Everything in life's an adventure, right, Baby Doll?" I could think of fifty other moments in my life that Dad had made that exact comment to Mom and me. It was his way of keeping things positive, keeping the enthusiasm up no matter the circumstances.

"Wow, you two are so much alike…" Morgan remarked.

"I don't want to do this," Amelia whined as she clung to Dad's shoulder, and for once I was in complete agreement with her. However, now that we were just hanging onto the wall, waiting,

I was becoming claustrophobic. The water was becoming darker and more menacing. I felt trapped in a situation with danger on both sides. Even though there was a greater chance of surviving outside of the collapsing chamber, I still didn't want to face what was on the other side.

As if we needed more prodding, the room shifted down again, and the sound of metal trying to break off screeched deafeningly through the remaining air. Amelia cried out, "Never mind! I want out of here. *Now!*"

"Time to go!" Dad agreed. "See you up there..." I received one last encouraging look from him. Then he counted to three, and he and Amelia went under. I panicked the moment he disappeared.

"Morgan! What if I can't hold my breath long enough or I swallow too much ocean water? What if I forget how to swim or...or can't find the surface?" My voice rose an octave. "It happened last time when Gabriel found me...I don't know if I can do this. What if there are sharks!?"

Another groan vibrated *through* the water this time, causing the surface to ripple in a very unnatural pattern. It was not accompanied this time by the sound of metal creaking. And the room didn't shift again.

"What was that?" I gasped, my head whipping around in all directions, trying to pinpoint the origin. I could feel my imagination starting its usual tricks at the sight of all the deep, dark water, and I tried to stop it, I really did, but, well, how did I know there weren't sea creatures *already in here with us?* Morgan was totally freaking too, by the look on her face, but she shook her head in denial.

"We gotta go," she reminded me tensely.

"But that didn't sound like—"

"Take your own advice, Whit." She shook one of my shoulders and made me look her in the eye. "Don't think; just get your butt down there and swim! One...two...*three!*"

If she was going, so was I...

I gulped in as much air as I could and then we took the plunge into the muted twilight of foreign ocean water. Morgan went first, and I felt with my hands along the wall and pushed after her out the door. Kicking against the current, I listened for the swishing of her legs to guide my path. The pressure on my head was uncomfortable, and I was only then aware of the sting from the saltwater on my wounds.

My wounds! *Shoot.*

Weren't sharks attracted to *blood?* I had open wounds! Why didn't anyone think of this before we flooded the stupid chamber? My dad and his brilliant ideas! Suddenly I wished I had just taken my chances with Eli...

My thoughts raced in a million directions and had me kicking harder and faster to the seemingly unreachable surface. I hated being in the wild, uncontrollable ocean. I thought of Morgan and all the scuba diving lessons she took on her family vacations... How could she feel so uninhibited in a world where I felt completely suffocated?!

And speaking of suffocation...how much further until I could breathe again? I couldn't sense Morgan's presence anymore, and I now had to ignore the other unknown sounds of the deep.

Just keep swimming. Just keep swimming...

What was that?!

Something groaned again under the water—like a tuba blast that rattled my eardrums. It was exactly like the last time I had fallen into this ocean. A powerful presence with the strength to create that kind of deep, resonating call was out there *in the same water as me.* I didn't know how close or far, but I was sure. Morgan had to have heard it too.

Wildly, I sort of hoped that I was still passed out back in the tank. Maybe this was all just a dreadful nightmare! Which would also mean I hadn't really found my dad yet. I could just hear him in my head again...*Oh, I haven't heard the water beast around here in days...he won't hurt you unless you threaten him first...Yeah, right, DAD!*

But then, guess what? I hit the surface of the water! Sweet relief—I had made it to the top!

Too bad I didn't know then that the real nightmare was just beginning.

Relieved to see Morgan treading water not too far from me, I made a quick scan for Dad and Amelia. They rode atop a wave farther away, beckoning for our attention. I waved one arm to signal we had made it too, and was forced to take a second to just float on my back and try to soothe the pressure in my lungs. My eyes were still swollen and stinging, which is why it took longer than it should have to register the odd orange light reflected on the surface of the waves around me. I blinked enough to focus my eyes on the starlit night sky above me.

When I jerked my head up and the water drained from my ears, I finally heard what was really going on. Shouting. Splashing. Waves crashing. I searched for the shore, and my heart dropped into my stomach. It wasn't just that the beach was far enough away that we might not have the strength to make it there. No, the horrific part was that the gorgeous, lush vegetation of the Southern Beach around the Watch Tower ruins was ablaze with Fire. Trees had fallen, and the ones that still stood were being eaten alive by the destruction. Huge billows of smoke blocked the view of the sky over the land. And in the midst of it all, the crumbling rock of the ruins was a hovering apparition in the distorting heat waves.

No trace of human life was distinguishable in the bright flames.

"Look!" I pointed, but Morgan had already started a desperate swim toward the burning Island. I followed after her, chanting in my head, *Please let them be okay…please…*My muscles were burning, and exhaustion threatened to slow me down even as Morgan plunged ahead of me.

Then I heard Amelia's call over the roaring ocean, and I stopped to look back.

A boat. There was a boat in the ocean. It was pretty old-looking and moving slowly, but I could see people aboard. The question was, were they good or bad people? As I stayed afloat with weary muscles, a light suddenly appeared from the boat and began moving along the surface like a searchlight.

I froze. What if these were rebels looking for us? My eyes found the dark spots in the distance that were Dad and Amelia. It looked like they had stopped swimming and were trying to float inconspicuously in one place.

I quickly decided that if the light came to me, I could just duck underwater, but then I realized Morgan was still swimming further away. They would see her...and then what would happen to us? I risked calling her name. She turned back to find me, and the Fire on the land cast her in silhouette. I don't know what her expression was, but she screamed my name in warning and pointed behind me.

O-kay...kind of an overreaction on her part. There was no way the people in the boat wouldn't hear that—

But the boat wasn't what caused her reaction. No—I turned around just in time to see a huge, horned *thing* emerge like a submarine moving at a deliberate pace through the water behind me. The ocean waves rippled away from it, almost as if it was splitting the water in half as it approached...closer...and closer...

Its cry thundered around us before a big blast of air and water shot up out of the top of it. The sight and sound of the beast were so immense that I felt like I had really only seen an eighth of its complete mass above water...which threw me into a complete panic. I thrashed about wildly with no real idea of which direction to move or how to avoid meeting my doom.

Just when I closed my eyes and braced for the impact, I felt a magical swirl of water around me, and my body floated completely up and away.

When I opened my eyes, I was soaring on a wave that had risen up unnaturally out of the ocean...and right out of the line of contact with the giant in the water. The fish-beast chugged past me like a steam engine on a one-way track. Then it submerged as quickly as it had appeared.

I stared down in shock at Morgan, whose hands were upraised and whose blue eyes blazed like a Water princess in the night. She wasn't even treading Water, just sort of floating half in and out of it herself. I was pretty sure she had just saved my life…or at least prolonged it a few more minutes.

The bright light from the boat blinded me for a second. "Whitnee, is that you?! *Why* are you—what the heck?!"

Oh my gosh, it was *Caleb*…on the boat! "Caleb! Get us out of here!" I screeched.

"Hold on, we're coming!" He shouted instructions. The boat turned and started heading toward us.

"No, get Dad and Amelia first!" I had the presence of mind to shout.

"Um…*who*?!"

"Over here, Caleb!" Amelia waved both her arms in the air.

I thought I heard Eden's voice over the waves as the boat veered in their direction. My body broke into tremors as any visible signs of the Water Beast above the surface had completely disappeared.

"Whitnee, we have to move before that thing turns itself around. That was one *big* fish…or monster…or I don't even know what that was. It was so fast." Morgan sounded incredulous as her illuminated eyes searched the depths. "I'm bringing you down, okay? Use your life force to swim to the boat."

"Do I have to?" I said with a shaky voice. Not kidding. I preferred Morgan's Water tower at the moment. But I knew she couldn't sustain it for long—I couldn't imagine how much life force strength she was exerting *in ocean water* to keep me afloat. Dad was right about it being stronger the closer we came to shore, but still…

Carefully, she lowered me back into the ocean, and the comforting swell of her life force dissipated around me. I watched them pull Amelia up onto the safety of the boat. But just as Dad was about to board, the roar of the beast sounded again, and I saw Dad hesitate and look for me. I didn't wait around any longer.

I swam as fast as I could, having a difficult time manipulating the Water life force to help me. I was tired and more than a little preoccupied with trying to watch out for the creature. Morgan sped effortlessly past me. But then the horned thing shot up out of the ocean right in front of us, its underbelly bright white and shiny in the night, obstructing our path to the boat. Morgan and I came to a halt and stared up in horror as it rose higher and higher into the air, its vastness taking my breath away. Then it came crashing back down like a tidal wave, slapping its horrid tail against the side of the boat and pitching it dangerously sideways. I didn't even have time to take a breath before I was sucked back under in the violent wake of its splash.

I was flipped around and tossed about so badly underwater that I didn't know which way was up. My chest burned as I swallowed the salty water by accident. I collided with something huge—perhaps the beast itself—and the impact jarred me enough to send me floating in another direction. I was vaguely aware that I might be sinking, because I definitely wasn't moving anymore…and I certainly wasn't breathing…

…until the Water wrapped around me again, and the backs of my eyelids flashed with blue swirls. And then I was above the surface and breathing again. All I remember was Morgan's face somewhere in all the madness, her flashing blue eyes concentrating as she moved at an unnatural pace alongside me. Was she swimming? The Water moved around her like it was part of her body…like it had given her wings. And then I flew out of the Water and landed right in Caleb's soaked and steady arms aboard the boat.

I coughed and wheezed for air, trying to make sense of how I ended up there. Caleb steadied me with one arm while the other brushed my wet hair from my face. He was speaking, but I was too rattled to understand him. Then Morgan rose up on a wave, much like she had in training that day, and dropped gracefully onto the deck. Her eyes were aglow as she caught her breath. Thomas had no sooner gathered her in his arms and planted a relieved kiss on her forehead than the whole boat jolted again as if we had hit something—or, more likely, that we had been hit. Caleb toppled backward, and I landed on top of him with a grunt, his arms still around me.

The water beast growled in frustration again beneath the surface. "He will capsize the boat if we do not leave!" someone shouted.

"Nathan is still out there…" Eden righted herself and stumbled to the side.

"What?! Dad didn't get on the boat?" I panicked. Amelia was holding on to a post, her eyes wide in the moonlight. Levi was standing by protectively. I dragged myself out of Caleb's embrace and tottered to the railing.

"He jumped back in to go after you," Eden explained as we scanned the rough water, the boat still rocking violently. "And then the beast…"

My heart was thudding wildly in my chest. Caleb came up behind me with the light, searching over the water. I called out for my dad. We listened, but there was no answer.

Instead, the beam of light fell on the massive creature, which had surfaced again and was barreling full speed ahead toward the side of the boat. "Brace yourselves!" Eden yelled. I had a feeling we were all about to end up in the water again very soon.

Caleb was yanking me away from the railing when I thought I saw a white light moving like a missile under the water…on a collision course with the beast. "What is that…?" I cried, but Caleb didn't hear me, and I was forced to back away. Everybody was holding on tightly to the boat, faces and bodies tense, as we awaited the blow of the beast's attack.

But it never came. Instead, we heard another wail and felt the stirring of fresh waves. But there was no impact that sent us hurtling. Confused, we looked around at each other. Had it just missed us? How was that possible?

I took a shaky step forward, but Eden called, "Wait!" Caleb kept a firm grip on my hand and all was silent onboard except for the wind and the slap of waves that kept us rocking.

It wasn't until a pair of dripping hands grasped the railing and Dad's face appeared that we moved into action. Caleb pulled him onto the deck with a firm grip, and then I threw my arms around him as he caught his breath.

"I am getting way too old for this stuff," Dad remarked as he hugged me. He looked as if he had gotten some sort of rush from the whole experience.

"This was not funny in any way!" I scolded shrilly. "We were almost eaten by that thing!"

"He was just playing with us…" Dad waved me off, and I honestly couldn't tell if he was joking or not. "We should, however, get out of his territory now while he's taking a break."

"Head north!" Eden shouted and soon we felt the boat surge forward again.

"What was the white light in the water?" I questioned suspiciously.

Dad shrugged. "I didn't see that." I noticed his response wasn't necessarily a lie, but it expertly avoided answering my question. We glanced up at all the curious eyes watching the two of us, and then I finally noticed there was something alarmingly wrong with this picture.

"Where's Gabriel?" I searched the distraught faces surrounding me. "And Hannah?"

Nobody spoke at first until I rose and faced Eden, the sensation of dread shooting daggers into my heart. "What happened?" Her face struggled to mask her emotions. I had no patience for their foreboding silence.

"Eden…*where is Gabriel?*"

RECOVERY

THE ISLAND E.R.

Silently, the group parted as Eden led me to the helm of the boat. I stopped and stared, paralyzed by the fear of what I was seeing. One...two...three bodies.

She exchanged a whispered conversation with the Hydros keeping watch. With sorrowful glances my direction, all but the one steering the boat left us alone.

The third body was Gabriel. My friend, my first real kiss, my guardian angel...just lying flat on his back in the semi-darkness, the fading flames from the shore casting a slight glow over him.

"Is he—?" I couldn't ask it, couldn't bear to even think it.

"He fought for a long time...but the drakon injury made him slower, weaker." Her voice was very soft and reverent as she spoke, and I felt my knees buckling. "I saw it happen...the attack came from behind, and he was not fast enough. It hit him full force, knocked him to the ground...I thought he was dead—"

"You mean, he's alive?" Hope flared in my heart.

"For now."

I stumbled forward and knelt at his side, almost afraid to touch him. He looked so peaceful without any emotion or expression on his beautiful face. Tears sprang to my eyes. This was so wrong. This was exactly what I had feared...if I hadn't pushed so hard about exploring that cave or gotten us trapped in the tunnels or even activated the portal thing and upset the drakons…There were just so many things I could have done differently to prevent this moment.

Eden added, "We are fortunate Thomas arranged for this boat of reinforcements to come. Our other teams never made it to the ruins. Not even the thunderflies showed up for extraction. We would all have ended up like this had the boat not arrived with help."

"This is all my fault," I whispered. The guilt was so powerful that I actually felt fifty pounds heavier and ten times more exhausted. Very gently I splayed my fingers over his forehead and traced a line to his thick, damp hair. As I allowed those shortened curls to run through my fingers, I willed him to open his eyes and look at me. *Wake up and tell me you'll be okay, Gabriel.* Too bad I couldn't cast my thoughts into his conscience the way I could with Dad. He didn't stir at all. My eyes finally shifted to the other bodies lying there. One person I did not know, but he was a bloody mess. The other was Hannah. I winced at the blistering burn marks that ran up one side of her body; her clothing had melted into the ghastly wound.

Eden explained quietly, "They gave her a sleeping draught until they can heal the burns. She was in a terrible amount of pain."

"Eden," I started, wiping away the fresh tears in my eyes. "How and when did you figure out Tamir was the one—"

"When he met us at the ruins." Her voice grew hard. "He lied when I asked why he was there. I do not understand why I never caught it before. Apparently, he has been telling enough of the truth so that I could never sense the lies."

"He helped us escape down in the tank. I think he realized he was fighting for the wrong side…" My voice trailed off in exhaustion.

"I need to know everything that happened. Everything that you learned about what they are doing and why…and how you ended up in the ocean." Eden was all business again. I think it was how she dealt with her fear.

I nodded in agreement. Tenderly, I took Gabriel's hand in both of mine, alarmed by how cool his skin felt. "Gabriel is going to be okay, right?" I needed her reassurance. Eden wouldn't lie to me. She hesitated, and for a moment, I think we were both feeling the same sorrow—except I seemed to be the only one with the freedom to express it. With detachment, I wondered if there were other more personal reasons influencing Eden's loyalty to Gabriel all this time.

Caleb's voice interrupted us. "Eden, they're waiting for your instructions on where to go, what to do." When we turned, there was Caleb with my dad coming up behind him—a sight I never thought I'd see. Slowly, I released Gabriel's hand and blinked my eyes several times to clear my vision from the threatening tears.

Eden stuttered in Dad's presence, or maybe she was more emotional over Gabriel's state than she wanted to admit. "I…I do not know…"

Dad glided carefully among the injured bodies, pausing thoughtfully over each one. An intense look of concentration was on his face, and something about his mannerisms caused Caleb, Eden, and me to remain still and silent while he made his inspection. When he came to Gabriel, he knelt down and peered into his face.

"This is Gabriel…Abrianna and Eli's son," I told him, trying to hide my emotion.

Dad glanced at me curiously before answering, "I know who he is." I'm not sure why that surprised me. Lightly, he rested a hand on Gabriel's head like he had with Morgan. His expression was unreadable. With a sigh, he rose again. Caleb and Eden were standing side by side, waiting.

"You are Joseph's daughter, Eden?" Dad asked.

Eden seemed surprised. "Yes."

"And you must be Caleb…" Dad said.

I held my breath. *Please don't say anything embarrassing. Please be cool...*I pleaded inwardly, remembering what Morgan had blabbed back in the tank.

Caleb extended a hand out, an expression of awe on his face. How weird this must be for him to meet my father for the first time. "Yes, sir. I've heard a lot about you." *Don't say you've heard a lot about him too...please.*

I was only thinking to myself, but when Dad's eyes shifted slightly to me in amusement, I think I had accidentally cast my thoughts into his head. They shook hands firmly.

"Thank you for what you have done...for risking your lives to find me." Dad's voice was gracious. "If I might make a suggestion... I believe it is imperative that we go immediately to Hydrodora."

Eden's face was surprised again. "But, sir, the Guardian is there...for the Festival of Springs. With so many people, it will be impossible to keep our presence a secret."

"With so many people, it will be easier to blend in with the crowd...and your friends here need the kind of help that only the Healing Center can provide. We should be able to make it there before dawn," Dad pointed out rationally.

Eden looked as if she was thinking this over, but before she responded, we were all startled by Amelia's cries for help.

What now? I couldn't help thinking as I reluctantly left Gabriel to see what was happening.

It was Morgan. She was slumped over the railing like dead weight. Thomas pulled her away and slid to the deck with her cradled in his arms. Amelia dropped to her knees beside him, crying helplessly as she brushed Morgan's wet hair from her face.

"Whitnee, she's throwing up blood," she told me shakily.

Thomas picked up Morgan's limp hand, and a faint blue light emitted from his palm. "She is not taking it..." he muttered. "Morgan, wake up. Take the life force!"

Morgan's eyes were open, but she seemed catatonic. Caleb and I knelt down beside them, while Thomas grew more panicked.

"She made me promise not to tell you, but I cannot let her suffer like this."

Caleb glared at him. "What are you talking about?"

"Morgan is sick," Thomas confessed.

"With what?"

"She did not give it a name. But she said it was incurable on the Mainland. She said she was in pain all the time. She did not want you to worry about her, but I tried...I tried to make her go to Hydrodora for help...I tried to get her to tell you. She would not listen."

Caleb looked to me in confusion. "What do you think it is?" I just shook my head and tried to stay calm.

"Morgie, can you hear me?" I reached out and wiped away the small spatter of blood near her mouth. I cupped her cheek with my hand and tried to get her to look at me. Slowly her eyes found mine in the dim light. "Hey, Water Princess." I smiled comfortingly. "You still with me?"

"It hurts..." she whispered.

"I know...we're going to get you help," I promised. "But I need to know what you have, Morgie, so I can help you. Please tell me what's wrong with you." Her eyes threatened to close, and I shook her slightly. "Hey, hey..."

"Let's talk when we're out of the tank, okay?" she replied weakly.

"We are out of the tank, Morgie, remember? We swam out? And you saved my life...from that beast in the water. I panicked, and you were the brave one." My voice caught with emotion as I stared down at her.

"Oh, yeah." One corner of her mouth tried to turn up in a smile, but it was obvious she didn't have the strength. "I'll have to add that to my list..."

"What list?" I repeated, but she was fading. I shook her harder. "Hey, Morgie...don't leave me! Keep talking, okay? Caleb, help me, please! Don't let her pass out...we need to know—"

Dad's hand rested firmly on my shoulder. "Let her sleep. She's exhausted."

"She's dying! And you know it, Dad!" I cried, my words startling Caleb beside me. I jerked away from Dad's hand and jumped to my feet. "Somebody bring me a bottle of Water! I can heal her. I can fix this. And then I'll heal Gabriel and…and Hannah… Nobody has to die around here. I mean, what good are all these abilities of mine if I can't use them to help? Caleb, get up!" I barked, running my hands through my wet hair manically.

"Whitnee, let's just calm down—" Caleb said gently.

"Don't tell me to calm down! This is serious! She probably has internal bleeding from what Saul did to her…I felt a blockage or something earlier when I was…" I gestured wildly, my emotions spinning out of control. "If someone doesn't stop it soon, it could get worse. I just need a freaking bottle of Water! Why isn't anyone helping me? We're not giving up here!"

"Whitnee." Dad's voice was forceful.

"Dad." I spun on him angrily. "If something happens to Morgan or to *any* of them, I will never forgive myself."

"It's not your fault." His voice was still calm, but firm. And something about that annoyed me. "There is nothing you can do for any of them right now. What they have is not a quick fix. That's why we're going straight to Hydrodora. Trust me."

"Oh, *trust* you!" I repeated bitterly. "Last time I trusted you, we were chased by a monster and almost drowned in the ocean! Really, Dad? *Really?!* Maybe you didn't know it's *your* fault that I have issues with the ocean in the first place…maybe you didn't realize what it does to a person to worry for six years that her dad drowned!" I snapped.

That was when Caleb picked himself up and grabbed me by the elbow. "Okay, Whit, that's enough. Come on." He started to direct me away from the gathering of people.

"No, I just meant…" I glanced at Dad in frustration, knowing I never should have said that. His face only held compassion as he stared back at me. "I didn't mean that, okay, Dad? I'm just freaking out here and—"

"I know, Baby Doll. I understand," Dad replied, and he glanced at Caleb and then back at me. "Why don't you go rest for a little bit? I think I need some time to chat with Eden about the current state of things."

"Well, I should be here for the plans, shouldn't I? And Morgan needs—"

"No, Whit," Caleb jumped in firmly. "Let your dad and Eden handle this now. And Thomas has Morgan. She's just sleeping." Thomas nodded weakly, barely taking his eyes off Morgan whose head now rested in his lap.

"I'll stay with her too," Amelia said softly. "I don't feel tired."

I turned watery eyes on my Dad. "Why won't you let me fix this?"

"Because you can't." The truth of his words only frustrated me further. "And you need rest too."

How could you possibly know what I need right now? I flung the angry thought into his mind. *You have no idea what I can do...You haven't been around!*

Dad's intuitive voice came into my head. *I want you to go with Caleb because he seems to know how to calm you down better than I do. I promise, you and I will talk soon...after the shock of the last few hours has worn off.* There was nothing in his expression to make me think he was lying or that he wouldn't make good on his promise.

Fine. But I have a lot of questions for you...

I know. He nodded once and then turned away to address Eden. I stared at his back, thinking how many times in the last six years I had involuntarily searched for that figure in a crowd... always wondering if he would appear again someday. Caleb gently pulled me away before I could protest again.

Even after we were out of sight and hearing distance from the others, we remained silent. I don't think either of us knew where to start. I collapsed onto the deck, leaning against the side of the boat, and he joined me without a word. I was thankful he sat so close, allowing our sides to press against each other. Now that I was calming down, I found that being soaking wet in the night wind was kind of chilly.

We still hadn't said a word when I reached one arm over and wrapped it around his stomach. There was no hesitation as he lifted his arms to encircle me, allowing me to snuggle in against his chest. Not only was it warmer that way, but it was also comforting for both of us.

"So." His chest heaved with a big sigh. "You found your dad. Amelia is…*here*. Tamir was the traitor all along. The water beast is real. The tank is real. And Morgan is *dying* of some mysterious illness. Anything else?"

"Eli ordered my kidnapping. He controls the rebels. The Guardian doesn't know I'm here. I can talk to my Dad through our minds. Gabriel was exposed to drakon venom that could leave him paralyzed the rest of his life…or kill him. I think that's it." My turn to take a deep breath. Thoughts of Gabriel's still body on the other side of the boat brought sharp pains to my chest.

We were silent again, both processing the situation in our own ways.

"I'm so glad you're alive," I told him with a squeeze. "Scariest moments of my life…worrying I'd never see you again."

"Ditto. I thought I was seeing a ghost when you suddenly appeared on top of the water." He sounded so tired.

"Morgan shouldn't have used up all of her strength on me like that. I'm sure that's why she collapsed…" I felt so guilty. Poor Morgan was now practically in a coma from trying to protect me from my worst fears.

"Your dad was right—whatever is going on with her is *not* your fault, Whit. And seriously, is she really that sick? Or are you just overreacting?"

"I *wish* I was overreacting. Caleb, she was going to drown herself in the tank." I shuddered openly and wished I could permanently erase that memory of Morgan saying goodbye to me. "She believes she's dying. She was going to just give up and leave me…"

Caleb's arms tightened around me, and I felt his chin rest on the top of my head. "Are we sure *she's* not just being dramatic?"

"Morgan doesn't get dramatic."

"*All* girls can get dramatic."

"Probably true," I admitted. "But look at her. Something is seriously wrong. Even my dad noticed it immediately. I hope the Healers can fix it." Dad seemed to notice everything...like he could see to the heart of a person beyond just their physical appearance. I always remembered him being a good judge of character, but here it seemed like more than that.

"Caleb?"

"Hmm?"

"Did you see Gabriel...get hit?"

"No, I didn't. But I'm sorry that he did. Really, I am." When I was silent at his words, he added, "Don't worry...I'm sure he'll be okay. Gabriel is super tough, you know."

I blinked hard a few times and tried to push away the fearful thoughts. "So, what do you think of my dad?"

"Um...yeah. Your *dad* is *alive*. You were so right about everything, Whit. I'm sorry I ever doubted you." He gave me a quick, apologetic squeeze. "I'm completely intimidated by that man. I mean, he's your *dad*, you know? I want him to like me and all that."

I smiled at his sincerity. "Everybody likes you, Caleb."

"Not always true...And dads are super protective of their daughters. Maybe I shouldn't even be touching you right now."

"I don't think you have to worry." Caleb didn't know that Dad already understood a lot about him...his quiet observation earlier about Caleb's ability to calm me down was proof. "I'm so scared, Caleb. I don't know how I'll ever be able to close my eyes again and not see so many horrible images...how I'll ever sleep again without being afraid somebody will come take me or hurt someone I love."

"Well, you're safe on this boat right now. And I won't let go of you, if that helps. I promise. You can take a nap right here," he suggested, his voice warm with affection.

"I'll make you a deal." I actually yawned just thinking about sleeping. "I'll take a nap if you take one with me."

"Kind of hard to protect you if I'm asleep too," he teased.

"I thought you said the boat was safe," I pointed out.

"Touché." He yawned then too. "Maybe I can justify a little rest...before we get to Hydrodora."

And I think that was the last thing we said aloud, because it wasn't long before the boat rocked us to sleep in each other's arms.

Caleb woke up first. I'm not sure he ever achieved the depth of sleep I fell into, but he was the one who stirred me out of my dreamless state. It took all of five seconds for me to remember everything...and realize the nightmare was my reality this time, not a horrifying dream that would just fade.

A group of Hydrodorians boarded our boat a little south of the Hydrodora harbor on the Blue River. They brought cloaks and costumes to match the festivities that had continued in the village all night.

Eden had insisted that we separate into smaller, less conspicuous groups that would each be responsible for transporting one of the four injured or sick people to the Healing Center. She also believed it wiser for Dad and me to split up just for the short trek, insisting it was easier to protect us that way. Dad was hesitant about this at first—as was I—but he finally agreed when Amelia proclaimed she wanted to be in his group. I think he realized that too many Travelers in one group might draw attention.

"Hydrodora is the safest village," Eden had reminded him.

"No village is safe," Dad had responded with a dark look. But he went along with the splitting up plan as long as Caleb and Thomas were in my group.

Because of Gabriel's status on the Island, they didn't want to risk anyone recognizing him. He was lowered into an empty wooden crate marked *HydroHealing Center Supplies*. He barely fit inside, and as they closed the lid, it felt like watching him disappear into a coffin. I wanted to throw up at the thought. Several men had to carry the crate on poles to get it to the Healing Center. They left the boat first once we docked in the village, and I watched as Eden marched stoically along with them. We would meet them at the Healing Center.

Morgan was placed carefully on a stretcher, her frail body covered by a blanket, and a decorative pearlescent masquerade mask strapped onto her face to hide her identity. If questioned in the village, we were supposed to act like she had just gotten sick at the festival—a common scenario during these events, apparently.

A heavy black cloak was given to me, the strands of my blonde and pink hair tucked carefully into the hood so no one would see. My mask was pink and gold with glittery swirls all over the face. Amelia, Caleb, and Dad were similarly dressed. It was a little disconcerting once everyone had donned their masks, their expressions hidden behind the vivid painted colors. Thomas did not dress up, but stayed as he was, loyally carrying one end of Morgan's stretcher while Caleb took the other. Hannah was covered by a blanket on another stretcher, and she tried to stir into awareness when they moved her. My heart broke as she moaned in pain until Dad rested his hand on her head and she went back to sleep. He stayed by her side, and Amelia accompanied him and two other Hydros from the boat.

"We have to take different routes to the Healing Center," Dad reminded us. "Thomas, you know where you are going?"

Thomas looked haggard as he nodded. "Lilley is meeting me at the back of the Healing Center. She and her mentor Healer are prepared to work on Morgan."

I remembered Lilley from the first time we visited Hydrodora. She was the little sister of Thomas's best friend. All I knew about her was that Thomas believed she was somewhat of a prodigy when it came to healing. I certainly hoped so.

"We will take Hannah through the front where the others are waiting for us. The other group will escort Malachi a few minutes later so we don't all arrive at the same time," Dad continued. I assumed Malachi was the bloody guy I did not know. "Everyone, be on your *guard.*" I saw his eyes slide to me meaningfully through his mask.

You contact me immediately if there is any sign of a problem, understand? Dad's worried voice entered into my thoughts. Aloud he said, "Caleb, protect my daughter." I couldn't see either of their expressions. Maybe I was the only one who found it weird to hear my *dad* say that to *Caleb*...And why did he trust Caleb so much? Not that Caleb wasn't trustworthy, but how would Dad *know* that?

"Yes, sir," Caleb grunted. And then we split up.

As Thomas, Caleb, and I approached the heart of Hydrodora, it was obvious that the first night of partying at the Festival of Springs was slowing down. People were picking up trash, and new tents were being set up. Dawn was breaking over the sparkling expanse of the Blue River. I could see several ships lined up on the opposite shore. Each was decorated to look like an exotic, colorful sea creature. They were gargantuan which made me shudder, remembering what had happened in the ocean just a short while ago.

"Thomas, what exactly goes on during the Festival of Springs?" I questioned as we maneuvered as quickly as possible through sleepy, stumbling party-goers and workers getting ready for the next events.

He was distracted as he explained, "Last night was the traditional opening with the Fountain of Lights. The Pyras and Hydros team up and create a display of Water and light in the Blue River that tells the story of how Marah was created...how the First Ones who came here were thirsty and the Island provided twelve springs. How the Island itself whispered the secrets of purifying and healing with Water."

"Dang," I muttered. "I would have liked to see that."

"It is incredible. The whole river comes to life with the story. After that, there are food, games, and a lot of dancing in the fountains. Today will be the children's festival where Hydrodorian children show off their trained Water pets and receive awards."

"Water pets?"

"Fish, turtles, sea horses, crabs…There are many categories of competition. The children work all year to train for it. The older ones can compete in dolphin races and shark-taming competitions, which I did a few years ago. Believe me, it is no easy feat to beat a dolphin in a race."

"It's like a Water rodeo!" Caleb exclaimed as if that was the coolest idea he'd ever heard. I pictured the stock show and rodeo at home. But instead of traditional bull riding, I imagined bull sharks bursting forth from underwater stalls, flailing riders on their backs…

I shuddered again. I would probably stay far away from the children's festival.

Thomas finished, "And tonight is the Lost Ceremony where we honor those who have gone before us. Tomorrow is the parade that kicks off the Waterpark activities, and then everyone is allowed to swim in the river. The festival ends after three days."

I suppose the boats across the river did look more like floats for a parade. I was keenly reminded of the riverboat parades in San Antonio during Fiesta week. How could the Island be so similar to my world and yet so different at the same time? A sharp pang of homesickness hit me.

"What are the masks for?" Caleb questioned, his eyes wandering around. Some people wore them, some didn't.

"Part of the festivities includes dressing up like different Water creatures. You will see most of that tomorrow night during the parade." I peered more carefully at Caleb's mask and discovered it did have clown-fish orange and white stripes on it. *Yuck.* "Part of celebrating Water is celebrating the animal life that depends on it for survival. The masks are just souvenirs from each festival."

"What is Morgan's mask supposed to be?" It featured pearlized blue streaks, and I didn't see how it was a creature.

"Hers is fashioned after a seashell," he replied matter-of-factly. "Yours is designed after an octopus. The swirls are like the tentacles."

I don't think Caleb had to see my expression behind the mask to know I was not exactly pleased with that. I heard him chuckle.

"Oy, Thomas! Where have you been all night?!" A slurred voice called out from a group of young adults lazing around under a tree. Caleb and I tensed up, and Thomas slowed his pace to look over. The group waved and smiled at Thomas like they all knew him. I recognized a few of them, especially the speaker.

"Mark." Thomas grew uncomfortable as he addressed his best friend. "I have been out on delivery, remember? Just returned."

Mark paused in confusion, then waved it off like swatting at a fly. "Who is that with you?" He was a little tipsy as he stood to his feet to peer closer at us.

"I do not know them exactly," Thomas glanced uneasily at us. "I just offered to help move their sick friend to the Healing Center. Probably too much wine to drink…like you, my friend." Thomas forced a knowing grin at Mark.

Mark laughed loudly. "Probably so! Do not tell Lilley, or she will lecture me later. Oh, I do believe she is working at the Healing Center this morning. If you see her, tell her that her big brother will not allow her to work during the whole festival this year." He leaned over and whispered conspiratorially, "Sometimes I think she is really a Geo, born with the wrong birthmark…the girl has strange ideas about fun!" He winked at us.

"You probably have enough fun for both of you," Thomas replied dryly.

"True statement, my friend! Promise you will rescue my sister and come party with us later?"

"Yes, you must!" The group echoed with giggles. Mark's mannerisms were so exaggerated by his generous wine intake that I had to stifle a mocking laugh when he stumbled over nothing.

"Yes, yes. I will find you later," Thomas called back over his shoulder impatiently and rushed us away.

Once we were out of earshot, Caleb remarked, "I just had a flashback to why I avoided prom after-parties."

Caleb had always made it clear he would never touch alcohol—not now, not ever. Not when his father had been killed by a drunk driver. I had made my own unspoken commitment to avoid it too, out of loyalty to Caleb and the heartache I knew such a temptation had caused him and his family. Even at school, the underage party drinkers seemed to respect his stance on it and never pushed the issue. Besides, most of our close friends stayed clear of making stupid choices like that anyway. "Guess some things are the same no matter where you go in the world," I mumbled. *At least Mark can't drive on the Island*, I thought but didn't say aloud.

"Speaking of prom," Caleb continued as if the thought had just occurred to him. "You should be my date this year. You know, since it's our last one…"

My mouth dropped open, but of course I couldn't see his expression to know if he was serious or not. Was now really an appropriate time to ask me that? While we carried our dying best friend to a hospital on an Island, dressed like a scene out of an underwater medieval masquerade? And, um, prom was practically a year away…Who knew what would happen in a year?

"Or not…" he said after my awkward silence.

"Caleb. Are you kidding me?"

"Well, we just technically 'slept' together for the first time… Prom seems like a good next step for our relationship—"

I whacked him on the arm. "You are so inappropriate! I swear, if you say anything like that around my dad, I will kill you," I warned. "Let's suppose I thought for a second you were *seriously* asking me to prom…Do you think this is how a girl wants to be asked?"

"What is prom?" Thomas jumped in.

"An event I will apparently be dateless for next year," Caleb responded pointedly.

"Whatever. I'm sure Laura would go with you—"

"Okay. Forget I brought it up." Now Caleb's tone was sharp. Maybe he really had been serious about asking me...and that irritated me too. Why would he spring something like that on me? We settled into frustrated silence. Just as we rounded the back of the Healing Center, Dad's voice echoed in my head...*How much longer until you get here?*

Coming in now, I replied. *Delayed a little by Thomas's friend.*

Good. I will come find you in a little bit. Do not leave this building under any circumstances. His tone was commanding, so I didn't argue.

The HydroHealing Center was the biggest building I had seen on the Island—bigger even than the Palladium. It was one story tall with mirror-like windows along the sides. Lilley was pacing near the back exit. She was about my size with long, straight black hair pulled back into a simple ponytail. Dressed in a soft blue tunic and cropped pants, she seemed too young to be a Healer. As soon as she spotted us, she immediately pressed her fingers to a blue gel-like pad on the wall, and the back door swung open. Thomas hurriedly led us in.

"We have the east wing blocked off with rooms for the Protectors. There are already Hydroguards posted at the end of each hall," she whispered loudly. So she knew what was going on...but her brother, Mark, had seemed clueless about Thomas's involvement with the Pilgrim Protectors. Of course, he had also been drunk. "Turn left and take her to Room 14. Priscilla is all set up for her in there."

Once inside, I took off my mask and hood so I could see better. I tried to observe my surroundings as we rushed down the halls. I was expecting a cold, clinical hospital setting, but the Healing Center was much more comforting than that. It felt more like a posh day spa on the coast somewhere. The walls were a cool blue and the accessories were made of the white glittery mountain stone. We passed an aquarium of exotic fish built into the wall, and I sort of jumped as I almost backed into it. Okay, so not everything was *that* comforting.

"Lilley, did Gabriel make it here okay?"

"Yes," she nodded as she pointed Thomas to Room 14. "Michael just arrived to work on Gabriel in Room 3 at the other end. Your father is with them. He asked me to show each of you to your rooms so you could clean up and eat first."

"Our rooms?" Caleb echoed.

"He said you had injuries that needed work too." She glanced curiously at the cuts I had forgotten about on my face. "I will send Sapphira to your room, Whitnee. She is specially trained in cosmetic healing so you do not scar…and she is a Protector. You can trust her."

We entered Room 14 and I was surprised at what we found. Instead of the big hospital bed I was expecting, the focal point of the room was what looked like an above-ground hot tub made of stone. A couple of stairs on two sides gave easy access into the water. The room carried an aroma of fresh rain. Priscilla was stirring the Water in the tub with her hands. Without exchanging introductions, she formally instructed Thomas and Caleb to lower Morgan onto the floor by the tub first.

I made a quick inspection of the rest of the room while they settled her. Beside the tub was a cart of bottles and metal instruments that did not seem familiar to me at all. There was a window with a breathtaking view of the Blue River. On one end of the room was a cushy bed with white linens and blue blankets stitched with the Hydrodorian tribal symbol of the angelfish set into four waves.

Lilley removed Morgan's mask carefully and pulled the blanket away from her while Priscilla spoke. "I was told she has been vomiting blood and having stomach cramps. What else?" She was feeling for Morgan's pulse as she talked. Lilley began dabbing Morgan's forehead and face with a cloth soaked in a green substance.

"Um, diarrhea…severe weight loss," I added. "No appetite. Fatigue. And sometimes I think she's not breathing right."

"She is in a lot of pain. And she told me what she has is not curable on the Mainland," Thomas threw in.

I did not miss the look of concern that passed between Lilley and Priscilla ever so briefly. My own concern jumped to an alarming level as I wondered why Morgan would tell Thomas that. "Help us lower her into the pool, and then you will need to leave," Priscilla told us.

"I really don't want to leave her...can't I stay in here?" I asked fearfully as Thomas and Caleb lowered the stretcher into the Water. The corners hooked into four levers inside the tub that seemed to allow the Healer to raise or lower the person as needed. Why wasn't Morgan waking up with all the movement?

"Nobody is allowed in the room while we work on a patient. I am sorry," Priscilla replied briskly, not even looking up at me. Something told me she really wasn't that sorry about it, either.

I was about to protest again when Lilley ushered us out the door with a sympathetic look. "I will come get you as soon as we have some answers," she assured us. "Whitnee, you are in Room 17. Caleb is in Room 18. Unfortunately, you are to go to your rooms and stay there until otherwise notified. Even though there are guards, it is safer if no one wanders in the halls. You will have bathing rooms and food and beds waiting for you." She pointed down the hallway. Then she reached out and inspected Thomas's neck a little closer, curiously, like a doctor would. "You have quite a bruise back here," she mumbled. "Go rest in Room 11, and I will come fix this for you as soon as I can."

He reached out and gave her an exhausted, brotherly hug. "Thank you, Lilley. I knew I could depend on you for help. If anyone can fix Morgan's problem, it is you."

When he pulled away, she was beaming at his words. "I will try."

"Mark says you are not to work during the whole festival. He wants us to meet up with him later," Thomas informed her as he started trudging dutifully to his room.

"Mark is not my priority right now," Lilley said, nervously smoothing down her tunic, her exotic blue eyes dancing everywhere but directly at Thomas.

"Yes, but we have to keep up appearances too. Your parents might be Protectors, but Mark is still unaware." Thomas yawned. "And it might do you some good to get out later, Lilley. You know you can only heal so much before you need a break. Maybe Morgan will feel well enough to go too." I didn't want to cast doubt over Thomas's optimism, but I had a bad feeling about Morgan's sickness. It would certainly make me happy if she was completely healed by tonight.

"Perhaps," Lilley seemed flustered. Right before he disappeared into his room, she called out. "When you saw Mark...was he intoxicated?"

Thomas paused. He glanced at Caleb and me before responding with a shrug, "You know how your brother is at a party."

When her expression turned to annoyance, Thomas said with a smile, "Do not worry about him. Go do what you do best, Silly Lilley."

"You know I hate that name," she replied, but she smiled anyway. Then she excused herself with a slight blush on her cheeks.

I barely caught a glance of my best friend lying lifelessly in a pool of Water before the door shut again.

TIME HEALS EVERYTHING...RIGHT?

The peaceful combination of a clean bath, delicious pastries, and some time alone to process the recent turn of events really helped my ability to relax. I won't lie—I shed a few exhausted tears the first time I saw my reflection in the mirror. The right side of my face and neck had been torn up—it looked worse than it felt. I don't know why I hadn't healed it myself. I suppose it had been the last thing on my mind once I had life force ability again. But seeing the disfigurement of my face reminded me of the terror in the tank, and my tears came out in little bursts even as I sat in the bathing tub and stared at the ceiling. The emotions coursing through me were overwhelming and continued to shift every few seconds. After indulging myself in the vulnerability that only a private moment could afford, I pulled my weary, bruised body out of the tub and changed into the fresh hospital clothes laid out on the bed. The first wave of intense drowsiness didn't hit, though, until I was sitting on the small bed, drying my hair with Wind. Despite the persistent questions about Gabriel's status that I kept putting out there for Dad, he had remained silent. It felt like I was one of those annoying children whose parent just kept ignoring questions from the back seat of the car.

If you don't answer me, I'm coming down there! I finally threatened. I knew he could hear me...right?

Whitnee, stay in your room. Gabriel is still sleeping and so is everyone else—including Amelia. Why are you so concerned about him when you should be using the time to rest?

Whoops. Maybe I was pushing too hard. I don't know why I feared my dad knowing anything about the short history between Gabriel and me...I just had a feeling he wouldn't approve.

He's my friend! And the Pilgrim Protectors need him for their plans, I replied somewhat truthfully.

Dad didn't answer back, so I pulled the blanket over me and lay on my side where I could watch the Water rodeo taking place on the river outside my window. I figured that would distract me while I waited on Dad to come down here for a long-overdue talk. I did not, however, count on the heavy sleep that overtook me in a matter of minutes.

When I finally did wake up, my stomach was growling, and the light in the room told me it was early afternoon. I blinked a few times and yawned before realizing Dad was sitting in a chair by my bed, his face resting in his hand while he dozed. I sat up, and my movement woke him.

"Hey, Sleepyhead. How do you feel?" he questioned, stretching his arms above his head and yawning.

"Physically better..." I answered, noting the cuts on my arm were healed. I pressed my fingers to my face, and the skin was smooth and cool in temperature. Even my achy body felt revived. I guessed Sapphira had come in and done her work as I slept. "I didn't mean to sleep so long." I yawned again. Dad stood up and leaned over me, planting a kiss on my forehead.

"When you sleep, you look younger...like the way I remember you," he said softly before lounging back into the chair again. "Don't feel bad about the long nap; the pastries had a light sleeping draught in them. Everybody needed some uninterrupted rest, and the Healers prefer the patients to be relaxed before treatment."

"You know, I'm really tired of being drugged by people on this Island."

Dad gave me a sympathetic grin. "Speaking of people, Eden left for Geodora. She is trying to rally what is left of the Protectors—yes, she told me everything. Pretty impressive organization, actually. I gave her all the information she needed about the tank and the rebels and Eli. Ezekiel and Sarah will be attending the Lost Ceremony tonight, and Simeon will bring them here to see us. Eden could only communicate a few cryptic details with them by zephyra. I have not spoken directly with them in years…" He heaved a big sigh as if seeing his parents again was going to be difficult. I kind of knew how that felt. "Gabriel has still not woken up. Michael has done everything he can for his internal injuries, but the drakon venom has complicated the situation. They won't know how extensive the damage is until he wakes up from the coma…that is, *if* he wakes up from the coma."

"Oh my gosh," I whispered.

"Michael explained that there are two different outcomes—there's a chance he could die within a matter of days." My heart stopped at his words, and I almost felt like Dad was stating it bluntly like that just so he could observe my initial reaction. I tried to remain expressionless, but my breath still caught. "Or he could just wake up and be completely fine…maybe sore for a few weeks but with no devastating effects. Obviously, outcome two is what we are all hoping for, but we just have to wait."

Outcome two…it would happen. I had to believe that for now, or I would not be able to contain one more emotion.

"And Morgan?"

"They are still working on her. I asked them to do a complete body analysis. That means they will check everything and fix whatever they can find. It is very thorough, but it takes almost a whole day. Lilley will come get us in a while, I'm sure."

"Okay." I nodded, taking a deep breath and exhaling slowly. "They'll be okay, right?"

"I hope so. Hannah and Malachi are already doing much better. They will probably get to leave in the morning." Well, that was good news, at least. Dad raised an eyebrow at me. "You doing okay, Baby Doll?"

"Sure...yeah. I'll just feel better when everyone else is better, you know?" I said honestly. "What about you?"

He leaned forward in his chair. "I have to know something, Whit." *Oh, great.* What was he going to ask me? Where did we start with the questions and answers after all these years?

"What?"

His eyes lit up expectantly. "Did you get the part?"

I was confused. "What part? What are you talking about?"

"The part of Mary Poppins!" He smiled like he couldn't believe I didn't understand his question. "Remember, you had auditioned for the part of Mary Poppins in the summer drama camp production? The last time we talked on the phone, you had just finished the callback and you really thought you nailed the solo! But then, well, everything happened, and I never knew. It has bugged me all these years not knowing..."

I just stared at him in shock. *That* was the first question he had for me? After everything that had happened? "Um, yeah. I got the part," I replied slowly, thinking back to that horrible summer after fifth grade.

"Of course you did! That's great, Whit!" He sounded so excited, as if this had just happened yesterday. As if he was still on the phone with eleven-year-old me. "How did you do? Was the production amazing? I wish I could have seen it—"

"There was nothing to see," I cut him off flatly. "I gave up the role and didn't go to drama camp after you..." I was going to say 'died,' but that word didn't really ring true anymore.

"Why would you do that? Why wouldn't your mother make you—"

"Dad, come on." I frowned. "The search for your body went on for six weeks. The investigation lasted longer than that...it made national news. You were and still are a missing person! My life changed dramatically after you were gone."

He deflated visibly at my words. "What did the investigation conclude?"

"Nothing," I muttered. "The hotel clerk said he saw you with a woman before you disappeared. Now I realize her description fit Abrianna. But for six years, Mom and I never knew who she was. There were rumors that maybe you were...having an affair. That your disappearing act was a setup."

"No..." His eyes glazed over as he stared into space. "Poor Serena...surely she wouldn't believe that. Surely she would know—"

"I have never heard Mom doubt your loyalty to her," I assured him. But I couldn't tell him out loud that *I* had doubted him. That I had never been sure...never had peace about his motivations and actions. When he finally looked at me again, I wondered if he saw the doubt in my expression. If he was so good at reading people, could he see through to my hurting heart? Did he know what his choices had cost me?

I couldn't look at him then. "After a while, they finally released all of your belongings from your hotel room." I cleared my throat, because I did not want to cry. "There was a brand new necklace with all of your stuff...Mom gave it to me because she assumed it was a gift for me."

"I remember that. Of course it was for you." His voice was low. "That was our tradition every time I went on a trip, Whit. I always brought home a new necklace for you from a new place."

I nodded quickly and picked at the invisible fuzz on the blanket. "I wanted to believe that...but I kept wondering if you had bought it for *her*...for the mysterious woman. There were just so many lies in my head." My voice broke, and I cleared my throat again. "I only kept the necklace for about a year...until I was at Camp Fusion."

He was very still as he listened to me. "One night, Caleb and Morgan and I decided we needed to do something real—something concrete—to help us let go of our bad memories. We were just kids, and I...I guess the necklace was always associated with bad memories of you." I paused, remembering again that night we had snuck down to the river with our little trinkets. "We pretended like we were spies destroying 'evidence' against us. Caleb had a little stuffed dog that was given to him when he was recovering in the hospital after the car wreck. Morgan had a statue of an angel that Carrie's parents had given to her at her funeral. Morgan refused to get rid of the whole statue, so she broke off one of the angel's wings...To this day, she still has that little angel with the broken wing on her dresser." I felt my eyes filling up as I opened up my heart to the past. We had been such broken, innocent kids. "And I had that necklace...The stupid thing made me angry and guilty every time I looked it. So we counted to three, and we threw our 'evidence' into the Frio River and watched it float away and drown...forever. It was *that* night...not the memorial service, not the move to San Antonio...but *that* moment that I finally said goodbye to you. I haven't even worn a necklace since then."

I had to stop there. With a whisper, Dad asked, "Do you remember the charm that was on that necklace, Whitnee?"

I nodded and squeezed my eyes shut, trying not to cry as the pieces of the past fell into their proper place. "It was a dragonfly," I choked.

"The same shape as a thunderfly." He spoke so gently, I almost couldn't stand it. "It was the symbol of my lost heritage. And I bought it for you in Hawaii, determined that I would come home and tell you everything I had discovered...everything about myself and everything about your own legacy, Whitnee Skye Terradora. I didn't realize that I would never make it back home."

Six years he'd been gone...so much lost time. It was unfair. He took my hand in his, and I felt the flash of energy between us. Those deep gray eyes that had haunted my dreams for so long searched my face. "Whitnee, I'm so very sorry you went through all of that...that you never knew the truth and that you had to question my integrity all these years. I love you *and* your mother— nothing has or ever will change that. I promise you, Baby Doll. I *promise...*" I couldn't hold back the tears any longer, and we both leaned forward at the same time. He held me tight as I wrapped my arms around his neck and let loose a flood of emotion.

"You don't know how badly I've wanted to hear that, Dad," I confessed.

"It's the truth. I need you to believe me." His voice was tinged with sadness too. When he pulled away, he wiped my tears with his thumbs. "I love you."

"I love you too," I said. To my *dad*. To the man I thought I'd never get a chance to see again.

His smile was the most precious sight to me right then. "I can't believe it's been six years. You're a teenager...almost an adult. Look at you, pink hair and all. Is that, like, the style nowadays?"

I laughed through my tears. "Just bringing back the eighties, Dad...for a performance at Camp Fusion."

"I like it. Suits you." He smiled as one tear fell from his eye. Then he pulled away and sat down again. With fervor, he begged, "Tell me everything, Whit...I want to hear about Camp Fusion, middle school, high school...everything you can think of to tell me!"

I sniffed and gave a small laugh, wondering where to start. "So sixth grade was a bad year..." I began and briefly described how Mom and I had coped with his absence. I gave him a few details about the memorial service we had held for him, but to be honest, I just didn't remember much from that year of my life. However, my stories grew more animated when I told him about Camp Fusion the next summer and all the adventures Morgan, Caleb, and I had. From that point forward, there wasn't a story worth telling that didn't involve at least one of them. He listened avidly, laughed out loud several times, sympathized in all the right places, and asked clarifying questions whenever he could. I don't think either of us were aware of time passing because it just felt so good to be together again. It wasn't long before six years felt like six minutes. We recalled our own good memories as a family. He quizzed me on the lyrics to his favorite Van Halen song and made me assure him I still had all of his old CDs...which I did, of course. He wanted to know who the current president of the United States was and what major historical events he had missed.

As we munched on the snacks left in the room, he finally asked, "So...how is your mother? Does she ever...miss me?"

"Every single day," I said without hesitation, remembering Mom's words just a few weeks ago. He smiled sadly, and the look on his face made it harder to confess the next part. "She started dating someone this summer...while I was away at Camp Fusion."

Dad tried to sound nonchalant. "That makes sense. Your mom deserves to be happy. She's a beautiful, caring person with a lot of talent...I'm surprised she didn't find someone before now." He cleared his throat.

"Whatever!" I blurted. "She doesn't really like him! She's only dating him because...well, I don't know why exactly. It's stupid and we got in a fight over it when she told me—"

"Whitnee," Dad scolded. "You better not disrespect your mother."

"But, Dad!" I defended myself. "She's just trying to get over you! I mean, *hello*. She picked a man who is the complete opposite of you. Boring, unattractive, nerdy, bad dresser..." I could have kept going with the list, but I controlled myself. "Once you come home, Robert will be old news. Trust me. Even Caleb didn't think it was that serious...I think she's just afraid of me leaving for college next year."

Dad grew quiet, his face thoughtful. "And she knows nothing of the Island? You didn't tell her anything that happened?"

"Well, no..." I said. "She would never have believed me."

"You might be surprised. Your mom is really smart. And strong. And she can see through the lies to the truth." He spoke passionately when he talked about her. And I loved that about my parents. Six years of separation and they still stuck up for each other. They still believed in the goodness of the other one. I wanted a marriage like that someday—minus the separation.

"Maybe, but I think it would be more exciting to tell her the truth with you there," I admitted. "You have to come home, Dad... we need you."

"It sounds like you and your mom have done really well for yourselves without me." He didn't say it in a pouty way, but more like he was genuinely proud of us. I just stared at him expectantly... waiting for him to just tell me we were leaving here together. That was when he sighed. "We'll see, Whitnee...not everything is as easy as you think it is."

"Explain that."

"Not right now. I'm enjoying our time together too much to get into all the other problems at the moment," he told me honestly.

"But you said you'd answer my questions—" I pointed my finger at him accusingly, and he held up one hand to silence me.

"Patience, young grasshopper." His tone was light. "I still have heard nothing about boyfriends yet, and I'm wondering why..."

I rolled my eyes and shrugged my shoulders. "Because I don't have a boyfriend."

He put his hand over his heart and acted like he was taking a deep breath. "While I'm *so* relieved to hear that, I'm also wondering what Morgan meant about this Caleb kid."

"Oh, *geez*." I could feel my face flushing. "She was just delirious..."

"Whitnee Skye, are you lying to me?" He raised his eyebrows.

"Dad, come on...are we really going to talk about boys right now?" I pretended to be really thirsty so I could hide my expression as I drank from my Water bottle.

"What? Just because I'm your dad? You used to tell me everything."

"Yeah, about stupid jokes and homework and music and all the other unimportant things kids want to talk about...I'm seventeen years old now. There are some things you probably wouldn't want to know." At the shocked expression on his face, I backtracked, "No...that's not what I meant. I mean, I'm a good girl, Dad. I promise..." I thought of Gabriel and the raw attraction between us and how I didn't always *feel* like being a good girl around him. And thinking of Gabriel and our, um, *inclinations* reminded me that he was one of the things my dad would probably not want to know about...I guzzled more Water to hide my blushing face.

"You are still eleven in my mind, and it completely floors me to think of you dating," he admitted. "But as your father, I need to know the real story—especially since Caleb is here on the Island with you. If he's important enough to know one of your biggest secrets, then I should know more about him..." I really didn't want to discuss Caleb with Dad, either. But at least he was a little easier to explain than Gabriel. "If it helps, just consider it girl talk between you and me. Pretend I'm Morgan..." He crossed his legs, and in a high-pitched girly voice, he said, "Let's dish, homegirl!"

That did it. The Water I was drinking spewed from my mouth as I dissolved into a choking fit of laughter. Oh my gosh, my dad was still a dork! I jumped up from the wet bed as Dad let out one of his big guffawing laughs at my reaction.

Then he tried again, still in his girly voice. "Now, is that really how a lady behaves? No wonder you got no boyfriend, homegirl!"

"Stop that! And nobody says 'homegirl' anymore, Dad!" I finally rasped. "Ugh, I think the Water went up my nose..." And that released another set of giggles, which were interrupted when the subject of our conversation rapped on the door and poked his head in without permission.

"Whit? What are you—?" Caleb stopped when he saw it was just Dad and me bent over laughing. "Oh, sorry..."

"Hey," I greeted him, lunging for a towel to clean up my mess. "You can come in." I spun around and flashed a warning look at Dad. He sat up straight with his legs still crossed, folded his hands over his knee, and wiggled his eyebrows conspiratorially.

*Please don't embarrass me...*I begged, wiping my face with the towel and dabbing at the bed. Dad just smiled back innocently.

"You two look like you're having fun in here," Caleb remarked, remaining hesitantly near the door.

"Yeah…just catching up on the last six years. Oh, and I had an accident with the Water bottle," I explained, glancing at Dad to make sure he was behaving. "Did you get some good sleep?"

"Actually, I did." Caleb nodded, rubbing his face as if he was still waking up.

Because he was dreaming of you… Dad teased.

I ignored his internal commentary and sat down on the bed, my back to Dad. "They drugged us in the pastries. These snacks are safe if you want something."

"Have we heard anything about Morgan yet?" Caleb wanted to know as he walked to the cart by the bed and shuffled through the remaining food choices.

"Not yet. Hopefully soon," I answered.

"So, Caleb," Dad said, uncrossing his legs and acting normal. "Whitnee tells me you're an athlete. What sports do you play?"

"Football, basketball, track…but basketball is really my favorite. I love the constant action," Caleb replied, chewing on some crackers.

"He's really good too…on the Varsity team since freshman year," I bragged. "Go lucky number thirteen! My favorite jersey." I was a faithful presence at Caleb's home games (and even most away games when Morgan was up for a road trip).

"Whit, you don't play any sports, right?" Dad questioned, already suspecting the answer. When had I *ever* shown a talent for athletics? Caleb made a scoffing sound.

I turned on him defensively. "What? You have something to say about that, Mr. Austin?"

Caleb grinned at me, swallowing down his food first. "I'm just remembering that one time you convinced me to teach you how to play basketball…Oh my gosh. Never again." He laughed and turned toward my dad. "You know, there are few things that your daughter can't do. But when it comes to basketball, wow…"

"First of all," I jumped in, "I do not like people all in my face like that, and I'm really not that competitive. If you're going to invade my personal space for a stupid ball, I'd rather just give it to you."

Caleb shook his head. "The game doesn't work if you just hand the ball over—"

"*Second* of all," I said, ignoring him, "I might have a small problem with aiming—"

"And depth perception, and controlling the ball, and taking advice on how to shoot right—"

"Which is why I don't play!" I gave up and shot him a dirty look. "Geez, you make it sound like there was never any hope. I could have learned if I'd really wanted to…"

"Of course you could have…but then there would be nothing I could do better than you. And that's not good for a guy's ego," he teased, elbowing me affectionately. "Don't look at me like that. I've always admired you for trying things even when you don't know what you're doing. It's cute."

"I don't think 'cute' was the word you were thinking after that first lesson," I retorted, even though his words meant a lot to me.

"Oh, yeah…you were *real cute* when you nailed me with the basketball and stormed off the court calling me a 'turd'…"

"You were making fun of me!"

He rolled his eyes at Dad conspiratorially. "I can only imagine what she was like as a child, Mr. Terradora."

I glanced back at Dad, who was resting his chin in his hand as he listened to our banter. He had an unreadable expression on his face. But at Caleb's words, he smiled and said, "Oh, there was never a dull moment with Whitnee. I still remember the potty-training days—"

"Do *not* go there, Dad."

He gave me a harmless look as he said, *I see exactly what Morgan meant now. This boy has a thing for you, which means I'm going to have to place him in armbands and question him until he cries for his mommy…*

I launched the pillow at him without thinking.

We're just friends, I replied sharply. Dad easily deflected my attack. Caleb made a funny face at the two of us.

*Sure. I remember when I was just your mom's friend too...*He winked at me.

Out loud, I stated, "I think we should change the subject to... oh, I don't know...how about what *you've* been doing the last six years, Dad?"

I watched Dad's expression morph from amusement to reluctance.

*I know you don't want to talk about it, but I have to know the truth about everything...*I reminded him firmly. Caleb and I both waited for his response, but he was temporarily saved from answering me again because Lilley knocked on my door.

Morgan was awake.

"Morgan did suffer a serious injury to the stomach at some point last night, which was causing severe pain and excessive internal bleeding," Priscilla explained in a monotone voice, peering at her notes. "It appeared to have been partially healed before she got here which slowed the bleeding and just might have saved her life."

"That was Whitnee's work," Morgan mumbled. Her eyes skipped my direction, and I remembered what Saul had done to her and how many times she had been roughed up in the last twenty-four hours. I squeezed her hand.

She looked a little better now that she was all cleaned up and clear-minded again. Her mannerisms and voice seemed incredibly exhausted to me, and she still looked too pale and weak. But compared to how things had been on the boat...this was an improvement.

"In addition to the stomach injury, there was a broken rib, some contusions in the neck and throat area, as well as several distressed muscles. All of this was relatively simple to heal," Priscilla continued.

"That's good news," Thomas breathed. He was standing protectively on the other side of Morgan's bed, his arms crossed over his chest as he listened.

"Is that why she was throwing up blood?" Amelia asked quietly. She had been summoned from her long nap, and she sat on the floor listening and watching with sleepy eyes.

"Perhaps," Priscilla answered, her eyebrows knit together in concentration as she looked over her notes.

I decided to speak up. "When I was healing her, I felt something strange. Like a blockage or something. It seemed to cause her a lot of pain, and I couldn't touch it with the life force. Was that the stomach injury or what?"

My dad took a step closer to Morgan's bed, and Priscilla dropped her notes on the cart with a tired sigh. I felt Morgan's hand tense up in mine.

"Did you do the complete body analysis on her?" Dad wanted to know, and I heard the uneasiness in his voice. What was he expecting them to find?

"Yes," Priscilla answered and finally gave us her full attention. "And what Whitnee felt is what we feared…She has the Poison."

My dad briefly shut his eyes and exhaled slowly at this news.

"No!" Thomas exclaimed, his face registering shock and denial. Even Lilley seemed sorrowful at Priscilla's diagnosis.

"What?" I looked around the room at the different reactions. Caleb and Amelia were the only ones who seemed as confused as I was. "You mean like food poisoning? She *has* been sick to her stomach…"

Dad shook his head slowly. "Where is it?" he questioned quietly.

Priscilla rested her hand above Morgan's stomach. "We found the largest accumulation here. But it is also here" —she rotated her hand around Morgan's entire upper abdomen— "and here, where she breathes" —her hand glided up to Morgan's chest— "and in patches in several other places." Her face was set in a grim mask, and Thomas just stared down at Morgan in horror.

"I'm confused..." Caleb murmured.

Dad looked Morgan straight in the eyes, and his voice was gentle. "That's pretty advanced, Morgan. How long have you known about this?"

Her face crumpled, and she started crying. She hid her face in one frail hand and the other one just went slack in my firm grip. I didn't know what to say because I didn't understand. Caleb and I traded bewildered glances before he spoke again. "Is this like that drakon venom or what?"

"Do you want me to tell them?" My dad was still only addressing Morgan.

"Tell us what, Morgie?" I wanted to know. She wouldn't look at us, but she barely nodded through her sobs.

I turned fearful eyes back on Dad, and there was that look again...the one that told me bad news was coming.

"Morgan has cancer."

MY TRICYCLE

There are defining moments in life when everything suddenly comes into sharp focus. It's like a blurry view through a camera lens. All it takes is one word from a doctor or one phone call with bad news or one tragic moment...and then the lens finally focuses in on the subject, offering a crisp, poignant snapshot of what's really important. Maybe that's what people call "gaining perspective." And I desperately wished that we wouldn't wait for those moments to see what's really in front of us.

"Morgan," I breathed sadly and dropped my face onto the bed, pressing the back of her limp hand to my forehead. I squeezed my eyes shut, trying to compose myself. The compelling desire to be strong for her kept the tears at bay.

"I'm so sorry I didn't tell you," she sobbed.

"How long have you known?" I heard Caleb repeat my dad's question, his voice filled with heartbreaking tenderness.

"We just found out for sure this week," she admitted. The mysterious appointments, the phone call to her parents...Everything made sense now. "But I've *known* something's been wrong with me for a while. I just ignored it until it got so bad my mom noticed and forced me to see doctors. I'm supposed to go back for more tests next week to confirm how extensive it is. The first scan showed masses in several places…the colonoscopy results were bad…" She broke down again and her hand tightened desperately around mine. "Whitnee, please don't be mad at me."

I brought my head up and looked into my best friend's eyes. "Oh, Morgie, I am not mad at you. What an awful secret to hold all by yourself."

"Why didn't you tell us?" Caleb wanted to know.

She looked around the room hesitantly. "I guess there was never a good time. And deep down I hoped that once we got to the Island…once I could see a Healer…" The three of us glanced hopefully at my dad and Priscilla.

"There are some things that not even pure Water can break down," Priscilla responded robotically. I shifted my gaze back to Dad for confirmation.

"It's true." He nodded solemnly. "Poison is their word for cancer, and it's not very common here. But just like on the Mainland, there is no way to heal it." I caught sight of Amelia crying quietly on the floor.

Thomas appealed to Lilley. "Is this not one of the diseases you have been researching? Is there nothing at all that can be done?"

Lilley shifted uncomfortably behind Dad. She hesitated, her blue eyes darting nervously toward Priscilla. "Nothing that I have found…" she answered quietly.

"Whitnee." Thomas turned bloodshot blue eyes on me. "I have seen what you can do. You are the Pilgrim! There must be some way you can help her. You are so gifted—"

Priscilla interrupted adamantly. "The Poison comes from a dark place that we do not understand. There is *nothing* on the Island to cure it."

I regained my voice and tried to keep my tone hopeful. "Well, okay then…We need to get you back home for those appointments. On the Mainland, they can do surgery or treat it with—"

"No!" Morgan cried passionately. "I am not going back there. I don't want to be cut up and treated with chemicals that will make the time I have left completely miserable…I just want to die and be finished with it."

Caleb and I looked at each other, astounded.

"You can stay here on the Island, Morgan," Thomas assured her. "I'll take care of you for as long as you need it. They can do regular Water therapy to help with the pain—"

"Thomas!" I exclaimed, indignant at his agreement with her. "Morgan is not staying here to *die*! She has a family and friends and…we have to *graduate*. It's our senior year…we have all kinds of activities and traditions…"

"If I go home, I will miss most of our senior year because of treatments. I'll be lucky if I make it to graduation—"

"You don't know that!" I argued. "It sounds like the doctors are just at the beginning of exploring the problem—"

"They'll only dig deeper and find more. Priscilla even said it was all over my stomach and in my lungs…the lymph nodes…" Morgan ripped her hand out of mine as she said, "I can't put my parents through all of that—medical bills and treatments and sickness that will only lead to the same end—a grave for their daughter! I saw what Carrie's parents went through—it almost destroyed their family!"

"Oh, so you'll put them through your random, unexplainable disappearance?" There was an edge to my voice now. "You'll let them spend night after night wondering what happened to you? Spending money and time and tears trying to find you? Is that really a better fate for them, Morgan? Because I've been on that end of it—and it's a horrible way to live! You *know* what it did to me. What you *don't* know is just how bad your cancer is…you might get to all those tests next week and find out it's not as bad as you think!"

"I'm telling you the truth, Whitnee!" Morgan argued. "Even if the doctors haven't confirmed it, *I* know my own body. I. Am. Dying. Why can't you just *accept* that?!"

"Why do you so *easily* accept it?!" I snapped back.

Caleb rose to his feet then, resting one hand on my shoulder as if signaling me to be silent. "It's time for everyone to leave the room. I'm sorry, but Whitnee and I need some time alone with Morgan." After a pause, Dad gave a short nod of agreement. Priscilla picked up her notes and turned to leave. Thomas stood by stubbornly. Caleb firmly reminded him, "Don't you and Lilley have somewhere to be?"

"I am not leaving—" Thomas began, but Morgan interrupted him.

"It's okay, Thomas. Just go. I'll still be here." He stared down at her with concern before finally relenting. We watched as he leaned over and kissed her on the cheek, and then made his way to the door. I tried not to project my annoyance at him for feeding Morgan's fantasy of living out the rest of her days on the Island.

"Lilley, are you coming with me?" Thomas called. Lilley cast one long look at me, her ocean blue eyes clearly troubled by something. I stared back at her, thinking she would say something. But then she looked away and left the room, as if she thought better of it.

Dad, please take Amelia. I don't have the strength to comfort her right now, I told him wearily.

He turned slowly and extended a hand to Amelia, who was still on the floor. "Amelia, let's go up on the roof and see the view." She turned her sad, tear-soaked gaze on me, almost begging me not to make her leave. But I nodded slightly at her to go with him. With a frustrated sigh, she let Dad pull her to her feet.

As the door was shutting behind them, I heard Dad in my head. *Be merciful, Baby Doll. She needs your love and support to get through this.*

When the room had cleared, Caleb went around to the other side of Morgan's bed so that we were on either side of her. He folded his hands in front of him and in a very calm voice, he said to her, "Morgan, you have been my friend for a long time now. We know each other pretty well…Sometimes you know things about me before I even figure them out myself." He gave her a pointed look, and helpless tears escaped from her eyes and rolled down her face as she listened to him. "I know you're exhausted, but I feel like you're still running away from us because you don't want to be completely honest. I feel like you're not even being honest with yourself...Whitnee and I want to help you, but if you keep hiding your real feelings about all of this, there's nothing we can do."

The most intense sob I'd ever heard from Morgan choked out in a half-scream, and then no sound could be heard as her body rocked with silent weeping. It was as if everything about her was falling apart before our eyes. I couldn't stand it. I crawled up onto the bed beside her, pulling her pillow and her head across my lap. Caleb rested his hand on her tense back, tracing comforting circles. I held her and stroked her hair as she muffled her screams in the pillow, her white-knuckled hand fisting into the cushy material. Her whole body was rigid. Caleb and I held each other's gaze as she let it all out. I could see his eyes watering, and I blinked fast to keep myself from doing the same thing. We knew we had to be strong.

"We love you, Morgan," I reminded her, my voice wavering. "You're not alone. Ever."

Slowly, I could feel her releasing the tightness in her muscles and relaxing her grip on the pillow. Her flood of emotion seemed to drain her of all energy. She came up gasping for air, and her screams turned to soft moans.

When she finally voiced her thoughts, she was almost hard to understand through the thickness of her emotion. "I'm not afraid to die. But I am afraid that my life will have meant nothing. I'm afraid that I let what happened to Carrie change me into this person who never really lived...It's almost like I can accept dying now because I feel like I really died on the inside when I was eleven."

I opened my mouth to respond to that, but Caleb shook his head at me to wait. I deferred to his wisdom and just kept smoothing Morgan's hair silently.

She continued, her face still turned away from us, "Sometimes I think it makes sense that I would die young. Maybe God knows

I wouldn't make it through watching another loved one go before me. Maybe He's being merciful with me by taking me early...not that it makes much of a difference. I've always felt like the black sheep in my family. I don't really have a lot of goals for the future. And as you two grow closer, you won't need me as much anymore...I don't want to become a third wheel." She stopped talking and burst into tears again. Caleb and I exchanged guilty looks.

"I am so sorry if we ever made you feel like a third wheel," Caleb said.

"You haven't," she replied weakly. "But I can see it heading that direction. I'm glad to know that when I'm gone, you will at least have each other. Maybe my only job was to bring the two of you together at Camp Fusion and help grow your friendship—"

"Stop right there," I interrupted her firmly. "Not that I'm ungrateful you introduced me to Caleb that summer...but your purpose in life is much more than *that*. I feel like you are so preoccupied with dying that you've forgotten all the wonderful things about living, Morgan. You can't give up on us like this—we need you."

"Yeah...who would help me in Spanish class?" Caleb pointed out. "You know how my pronunciation is. I'd fail every exam without your help."

"Who would tutor Angel and Marci on their reading skills? Those poor first graders look forward to those afternoons just to see you!" My mind flashed across all the things Morgan did for other people. I might be the one in the spotlight, but she was always busy doing the behind-the-scenes stuff that made other people successful.

"Who would drop off movies and soup for me when I'm home sick from school?" Caleb added.

"And who would jam to loud music in the car with me? You know Caleb doesn't always like my song choices."

"*Ugh*. No kidding," Caleb agreed. "And I know it's selfish, but I always look for you and Whitnee in the stands before my games. Who would cheer for lucky number thirteen if you weren't there?"

"And who would mediate the fights between Caleb and me? We'd kill each other without you." She wasn't responding, but I felt her relax as she listened to us go back and forth. Finally, I said softly, "Morgan, if you're the third wheel, then we're a tricycle. And a tricycle doesn't work without all three wheels."

"We'll help you fight this, Morgan. Even if it's as bad as you think it is," Caleb assured her. "Staying on the Island is just running away from the problem."

Slowly she pulled herself up into a sitting position. With swollen eyes and puffy cheeks, she faced both of us and drew a deep, ragged breath.

"How do I go back home…and watch you and everyone else suffer because of me?" Her voice was hoarse. "Because the reality is…I do have cancer. There. I admitted it. And it's very aggressive. And if it doesn't ultimately kill me, the days ahead are still going to be bad. I watched my uncle go through chemo for this same kind of cancer. He didn't make it six months after he was diagnosed. And he was so sick the whole time—worse than before he started the treatments. You both have already been through so much…I just *can't* put you through this with me. I'd rather stay here and die away from everyone I love."

"What about Thomas? Are you willing to make him suffer and watch you die?"

"Thomas cares about me…but it won't hurt him the way it will hurt my family or you two. I was never meant to be a permanent part of his life anyway. Maybe I came to this Island this summer just to find a place I felt comfortable dying." She sounded as if she had actually been giving this thought. I didn't know what to say as her words sank in. I couldn't lose Morgan in my life. I just could not accept a future without her.

"Morgan," I made her look me straight in the eye. I had to ask her…because I simply did not understand. "Is there any part of you that *wants* to live?"

She tried to hold my gaze, but eventually her eyes dropped to her fidgeting hands. "I don't even know anymore. But does it matter what I want? This is what's happening, right?" Her tone was so resigned, so depressed. I guess I had just wanted to hear her admit that she *wanted* her life…that we were important enough to her to try fighting longer.

"I know death is part of life," Caleb finally said. "We're all going to die at some point—even Whitnee or I could die before you do. Nobody knows how much time they have left. But you are *still alive* right now. You might feel like you died six years ago, but you've been very much alive to *us*. There are still moments and memories to create, Morgan." He sighed. "Don't try to die before it's time."

Caleb and Morgan both had more experience dealing with actual death than I did—and had probably spent more time thinking through it. The difference was that Caleb had a healthy perception of it while Morgan had spun a web of dark thoughts in her mind for too long.

"Go home with us, Morgan," I begged her. "Whatever comes, we'll get through it. And we'll keep making memories together for as long as we have." I reached for her hand, and Caleb took the other. When I tucked my hand in his, we formed a tight circle of love and friendship. I used the opportunity to transfer to my best friends the comforting tranquility that came with Fire abilities. Warmth spread from my hands to theirs, and the soft golden glow lit up the space in our little circle.

Morgan's lips curled into a small regretful smile as she stared at our linked hands. "If I go home…I'll lose my hair." A few lagging tears trickled down her cheeks as she confessed, "I know it's ridiculous to worry about that on top of everything else. But I like my hair." As a girl, I totally understood what she meant.

Caleb smiled. "I'll shave my head…and then we can go buy matching wigs!" His voice became effeminate as he pretended to toss his hair. "It'll be so totally cute. We can braid each other's hair and act like rock stars!"

Morgan let out a therapeutic laugh, and I was able to conjure a small smile. "It does give you a chance to try out different hair colors and styles…" I tried to sound positive, but my throat felt constricted. "And think about how nice it will be to not have to blow-dry and fix your hair everyday. By the time it grows back, you'll miss being bald!"

"Maybe." She sighed. "I really don't want to go through this."

My heart felt just as heavy as I watched her become resigned to a new fate full of hospital trips and painful treatments.

"If there was anything I could do to take this away from you, Morgan, I would," I said, but my words seemed empty. Because there was *nothing* I could do. How many other people had said the same thing, wishing they could take away their loved one's pain and suffering? I knew I wasn't the only one, but it still hurt. I resented the fact that I had all these special powers here on this Island, but I could not give life to a dying person.

Morgan's voice was deflated as she said, "I know you would, Whit. But for whatever reason, it's the road I have to walk."

"I would rather walk this road with you than miss out on any part of your life, Morgan."

"Ditto," Caleb echoed.

Morgan bit her lip as she studied both of our faces thoughtfully. After a moment, she nodded resolutely and said, "Okay."

UNDERSTANDING IS ELEMENTAL

I left Morgan's room as soon as she fell asleep again. Caleb offered to stay with her until they came in with the next Water therapy treatment, a process meant to keep the pain away. I think Caleb assumed I needed time with Dad or to check on Amelia. And, initially, I was going to find them. But when I spotted the guard standing outside Gabriel's door, I made a detour.

Gabriel's room was still and quiet when I entered. He didn't stir when the door clicked shut behind me. It was intensely sad to see him all alone in a hospital room with nobody waiting patiently by his side for him to wake up. These were the moments when family members and friends should have been gathered around, praying and weeping.

Instead there was nobody but me.

I stood over the bed, my arms wrapped protectively around my stomach as if I was trying to keep the emotions from spilling out. I'd always thought it was weird to talk out loud to someone who clearly couldn't hear you. But what if he *could* hear me? What if he just needed one friendly voice to remind him why he should come back from wherever his mind was?

"Hey, it's me, Whitnee..." I started, feeling a little awkward about my lonely voice echoing in the room. "I'm really sorry...

I feel like this is my fault that you're...like this." There was no movement, no fluttering of his eyelids. Those long eyelashes just rested softly against his cheekbones. His full lips were slightly parted, and he breathed in and out steadily. Amazing how strong my desire was to be close to him. Something in me wondered if I needed Gabriel the way Morgan needed Thomas...just for moments like these.

I tried to keep talking. "I found my dad—thanks to you, actually. If you hadn't believed everything I was telling you, and if you hadn't trusted me about the ruins...well, you know. I guess I'm saying thank you and...I can't wait for you to meet him. Now would be a really good time to stop being such a brooding Pyra and just wake up." I attempted a smile even though he would never see it. "We kind of need you around here, you know. Even Eden misses you...she'd never admit it, but I know she cares about you."

I let my words trail off for a moment, pondering the relationship between Eden and Gabriel, letting my mind envision a future there. But the pang of jealousy I felt at picturing Gabriel with anyone else made me stop. I knew it was selfish, but it was how I felt.

I cleared my throat and started again. "We found out Morgan has cancer...something that you know of as Poison. I'm honestly trying not to panic about it. She wanted to stay here on the Island, but there's no chance she'd survive if she did. At least at home, they might be able to help her...I don't know. I have to get her home as soon as possible, but I don't feel right leaving until I know for sure my dad is going with me. And until I know you're okay..." My voice caught as I tried to find the right words in my heart. I swallowed down the ball in my throat and lowered myself to rest on the edge of the bed. "I mean, I keep thinking about what you said...about how you want me to consider staying here permanently. You were right about me feeling something strong for you. Honestly, I tried to ignore those feelings all summer. But it's so hard. When I'm here, it's like there they are...all in my face again. You were and still are a big reason I needed to come back."

Geez, I was putting it all out there now, but it felt good to confess these things even if he never knew about it. "Honestly, Gabriel, I feel a little lost around here without your opinions and your plans...and your horrible stubbornness." I smiled wistfully. "Being here makes no sense without you. I actually miss that look on your face when you're frustrated with me. And I love the way I can actually feel the heat from your skin when you get mad... And, okay, the whole eyes-turning-gold-thing when you're making Fire...I confess it's super sexy. Not that you deserve to know that or anything." I ran my fingers along the palm of his hand, picturing all those moments and more. But then a sobering feeling came over me as I stared down at his lifeless body. "I *really* wish that things were simple between us. I wish that staying or leaving here was an easy choice. I wish that your parents hadn't hurt you the way they did—" This time the tears pooled in my eyes. "It's so unfair the way you've been treated. I hate it. I wish that I could be the one to make you happy and love you the way you need it, but..."

BUT I have to get my friends and my dad home. BUT I still like my life on the Mainland. BUT I'm scared of settling on a future. BUT there's Caleb...

All the 'buts' that could have completed my thoughts didn't come out of my mouth.

Instead, I leaned down and rested my face on his neck. "Please don't give up," I whispered near his ear, breathing in his delicious scent. "If you promise to wake up, I promise to stay until you do. You are going to do great things, Gabriel. I believe in you. Come back to us soon, okay?" I dropped a quick kiss on his neck because I wanted him to feel my presence. But the threat of utter meltdown was approaching.

I jerked myself away quickly and wiped my eyes. I gave him one last longing look before leaving the room. I had to get out of this place. I needed fresh air. I needed time to myself. Deliberately, I went straight to my room and donned the black cloak and the festival mask that had been tossed in the corner earlier. I rushed to the back exit of the Healing Center, knowing that I was not allowed to leave the building but really not caring about safety and rules in the midst of my rampant emotions.

"Excuse me, mistress!" a Hydroguard called out behind me. I ignored him and sped faster to the door. Just as I was about to barrel outside, he placed a hand out in front of me. "I cannot let you leave. I am sorry."

"I just want some fresh air. Please step back!" I responded impatiently.

"Very well. I can escort you to the roof where the others are."

"I really just want to be alone…"

"I am sorry." He took me by the arm and started to pull me away from the door. I was so sick of being forced into action by other people that I jerked my arm away defensively.

"Don't touch me!"

He was about to argue again when someone else interrupted.

"What is the problem here?" Through my mask, I saw the man with the long white hair and white beard. His blue eyes were bright and wise as they sized me up.

"Simeon, sir, she is not supposed to leave…" the Hydroguard began, but Simeon held up a patient hand.

"You may go back to your post. I will handle this."

The guard obeyed, and when he left, I held my shaky hand out to Simeon, the Councilman for Hydrodora. He took it and gave it a comforting squeeze. "I thought that was you, Whitnee," he whispered knowingly. I hadn't seen him since the last time I'd been on the Island. And even though I should have given him a proper greeting, I was just feeling so suffocated.

"Simeon, I just need to get away for a little bit. I can't stay here with all the sickness and sadness and…" I tried to sound in control of myself, but I think he could sense my panic.

"It is troubling around here, I know. I just heard about Morgan's diagnosis." He still had my hand in his old, wrinkly one. I didn't respond because that darn ball was back in my throat. With a sigh and a glance around him, he said softly, "If you walk out that door and follow the shore, you'll soon see a huge rock with the Hydro sign carved into it. Behind that rock is a trail that will lead you to a quiet place—a place you might find safe enough to…release some energy." He smiled sympathetically. "I can only offer you a few minutes head start before I have to tell your father where you are."

I stared at him in surprise. Was he really going to let me go out there alone? When I hesitated, he explained simply, "It is a private hot spring that I own. Nobody will be there. I went there frequently when my wife was sick and I needed a break from this place."

I cast one grateful glance at him before bursting out the door and running away, my cloak trailing after me. I followed his directions and ran beside the sparkling river away from the village until I found the marked rock. Sure enough, there was a barely worn trail directly behind it that wound through the forested area bordering the Blue River. Without hesitation, I sprinted down the trail, wanting to feel the burn of my muscles and lungs, trying to expel the panic in my chest. There was nothing but forest and trail for a little bit until I came to a little clearing with a hot, bubbling spring. Thin wisps of steam released every time a bubble popped on the surface, permeating the area with a fresh, misty smell. White flowers grew along the edges of the water. The whole place was secluded by thick trees with small white blossoms dripping from their branches. It was a small piece of heaven.

I turned in a circle, ensuring that I really was alone. And then I ripped off the cloak and the mask and tried to focus on catching my breath. A dark rage welled up within me.

My best friend is going to die.

I threw a Firedart into the spring, its force landing like a cannonball that splashed angrily back at me.

Gabriel might die.

Another Firedart exploded.

Where's the justice? Firedart. *Why do bad things happen to the good people?* Firedart. *How can somebody like Eli—someone with no real love, no real humanity—have so much power over people?* Firedart.

He's the one who should be suffering! I screamed inside. The explosions were creating a mess, but I didn't care.

Seriously, I wanted to know what idiot thought up the idea that 'everything happens for a reason?' I could not imagine a good reason for me losing six years with my dad, for Morgan dying young, for Gabriel being born to such awful parents, for having unexplainable powers, for finding an Island that complicated my life forever...Was I just some cosmic accident when the Island merged with the Mainland? What was the point of *all* this?!

I held my hands out in front of me, palms down, life force rippling out of me. The spring bubbled more violently and then started churning like a whirlpool. With my thumb and middle finger, I acted as if I was pulling an invisible string. The Water reacted by stretching and gurgling upward with fluid movements. I manipulated it into different shapes, and then swished it all up into a raging river rapid in midair. Then I slowed it down until it was just crystallized water droplets floating slowly past my face.

When I released it into a cascading Waterfall back to the earth, I clapped my hands together once and launched a ball of Fire to the center point of the Waterfall. The two elements reacted to each other in a thick blast of steam. The heat rushed at me, but I immediately forced the pressure into a squall of Wind that swirled all around the small clearing. I kept the circulation going, my hair whipping around my face, droplets forming on my skin. I stepped into the center of the spring until I was just a centerpiece in the midst of the surging elements. The Water was warm like a bath, and it popped and sizzled everywhere I stepped. I released Firelights into the swirling Wind, so that their blurry movement rushed past me like headlights on the highway.

I reached both hands out to the sky and beckoned the trees to come closer, to lean down and join us. With groans, the limbs stretched toward me, creating a cocoon of nature. Though I wasn't touching the trees, I felt the tickle of the white blossoms as some floated down and danced around me.

In that magical moment, the four life forces were surrounding me, protecting me, strengthening me. I could feel each of them uniquely, like four friends with four different personalities. I needed their power around me and in me. I needed to breathe with the Wind, to see with the Fire…to hear the Earth, and feel the Water. I wasn't combining them into one power this time… just appreciating the unique sensations of all four.

Maybe everything did happen for a reason, or maybe it was up to us to find a reason for our circumstances…to make them count for something good. I didn't understand much about my life as I stood there in that spring, but I did feel an assurance that my abilities, these life forces that rippled out of my very soul, were there for a good purpose. And sometimes purpose took a while to reveal itself. I just had to wait.

And if that was true for me, then I had to believe everything Morgan was going through, everything Gabriel had been through, everything that had ultimately brought all of us together on this Island was all for a purpose too.

I don't really remember at what point my anger had melted into tears, but my lonely cries were swept up into the vortex of energy. It was like the Island was beckoning me to release my burdens right there, promising comfort if I did. I squeezed my eyes shut and felt the silkiness of a blossom caress my face with its petals…an intentional act, I knew, in the midst of such violent energy. And I swear as each teardrop fell from my eyes, light rain sprinkled down on me from the small patch of sky above. Was I doing that? I really wasn't sure…

I leaned over, bracing myself on my knees as my tears and the drizzling rain mixed in with the Water spiraling around my legs.

Whitneeeee…

I had heard that voice the first time I transported here, though I still didn't recognize it. Suddenly, the energy surrounding the spring collapsed all around me with a shattering boom, and the pressure released. I opened my eyes and looked around tearfully.

Dad was standing there, one hand held out to me. His gray eyes saw more of my vulnerability in that moment than any other moment of my life. It was like he knew exactly what I was thinking, feeling, and fearing. If his eyes were mirrors, I was seeing an exact reflection of myself in them. It both scared me and comforted me to be seen so clearly.

I reached out to him and felt the now predictable flicker of shared energy between us. He pulled me out of the water, picked up my cloak and mask, and didn't say a word as he directed me back toward the path, my hand still in his. I cried softly the whole way back.

I wrapped my arms tightly around myself as I took in the view of the Blue River from the roof of the Healing Center. There were little gondola-shaped boats arranging themselves into some kind of formation in the water. At first I didn't see anyone manning the boats, but upon closer inspection, the people in black cloaks along the river's edge were controlling them with Water life force.

My observations were interrupted when a miniature thunderfly made totally of Fire buzzed in front of my face, flapping its wings flirtatiously and dipping and diving in circles around my head. Bewildered, I stared as it paused long enough to blow me a kiss and then disappear in a vapor of smoke.

What the...?

"I call him Firefly." Amelia spoke up from behind me. "Isn't he cute? I made him last time I was here." She came up beside me, her hazel eyes glowing gold. I had never seen her use Fire before. But that had been pretty cool. And it made me smile.

"He is *so* cute, Amelia. Good name for him too."

She smiled proudly, but then with a frown, she said, "I'm sorry I thought Morgan had an eating disorder."

I closed my eyes for a moment, feeling like that conversation had been a lifetime ago. I unwrapped one arm and draped it around her shoulders. She looped her arm around my waist, and we stood there together looking out over the village. "Are you okay?" I asked quietly.

She nodded. "Everything here seems more dangerous than I remember."

"I was scared they would hurt you if you ever came back," I admitted. "I'm so sorry you were brought into all of this...I don't know anymore how to protect the people I love." I felt my eyes welling up again, but I swallowed thickly.

"It's not your fault. I shouldn't have lied to my parents and gone back to camp. Things were actually going okay with them... but I guess I thought it wasn't enough. Now I'm worried about them and Ben and..." She looked up at my puffy face. "And poor Gabriel. I haven't even gotten to hear what happened when he saw you again—"

I cut her off before she could go further. "Let's not talk about Gabriel right now." Dad and Caleb were approaching us, and I didn't want to think about Gabriel, Ben, Morgan, death...*ugh*. My mind needed to focus on things within my control. "What do you think is going on at camp?"

"Police. Search and rescue. There's no way my parents won't know I disappeared this time, unless we go back in time again when we transport." She looked worried. Last time she had wanted her parents to know that she was missing and had been disappointed when we had been gone a day in Mainland time and only Ben knew. I took it as a good sign of her growing maturity that she felt differently now. I released her and began to pace in front of Caleb and Dad who were now listening in.

"So, Amelia's been gone two days now, right? From what I can tell so far," I mused aloud, "everybody has been transporting to and from the Mainland on the same timeline."

"Because Abrianna fixed it." Dad suddenly spoke up. My head snapped back to give him a questioning look. He explained, "She figured out a way to stabilize the time problem with the portal."

"How does the portal work exactly?" Caleb sounded skeptical. Dad thought for a second, then explained carefully. "You see those boats out there?" He pointed to the river and we followed his gaze. "Each one has a little device in it that is infused with Fire life force. When the ceremony starts, the devices will light up like torches. On the Island, we have learned how to 'charge' certain objects with life force. It's just like on the Mainland when they discovered electricity and figured out how to conduct it within an object like a light bulb…It's a helpful, proper use of our resources. However, to make a portal, you have to tap into the original source of the life force…the Island itself. Abrianna figured out a way to create an object that can channel life force directly from the heart of the Island on its own—without going through a human life on the Island. Furthermore, once she combined all four life forces, she established a connection to the Mainland…through those objects."

We stared at him in fascination. "You mean the orbs? The ones that spin when the portal kicks on?" I asked.

"Yes. Those are channeling power directly from the Island's source." His eyes were troubled. "The problem is that life forces were given to the *people*. We have the responsibility of maintaining them and governing their usage. To combine the elements and infuse them into objects, like the zephyra using Wind and Fire, is ingenious. But a zephyra is still created and controlled by humans. The life force in them runs out eventually—just like when you are gifted by someone. That's the natural order of the Island. But the portal does not work like that…it is ungoverned. It's like…I don't know how to say it exactly…like an unholy connection to the Island. On top of that, when combining all four life forces at once, it creates a power that is unbound by time and space—a power that was never supposed to be unleashed…"

I stopped pacing. "Is that why you destroyed the portal before you sailed back with Will Kinder?" My question startled him briefly.

Wow, you've really done your research, I heard his voice in my head.

Aloud, he expounded, "An active portal is not good for the Island or its people. It had to be shut down." He stared off into space. "Yet Abrianna ignored my warnings and built a new one once I was gone. Then three weeks ago, she dug too far and harnessed an ungodly amount of power within that portal room. Now the portal won't turn off. It can still be open and closed for transporting—like opening or closing a door. But unlike before, the door is always there now—the connection is permanent."

"Three weeks..." I whispered. "I used life force on the Mainland...at Papi and Mimi's house three weeks ago. And then the next night at Camp Fusion."

Dad's face registered shock, and he stood to his feet to face me. "You're just now telling me this?!"

"Well...is something wrong with that?" His reaction gave me a sick feeling.

"It's not supposed to be possible!" This time he started pacing while he thought. "And the timing...that's too much of a coincidence. It's like you're connected to it somehow..."

"Mr. Terradora," Caleb interjected. "You said that combining all four life forces creates a power that is not supposed to be unleashed...What does it mean that Whitnee can do just that?"

There was silence as we watched Dad pace, his expressions changing at the rapid pace his thoughts must have been going. Finally he mumbled, "It's almost like Whitnee is a portal herself. Or an alternate source of power..."

"Oh, great. So I'm some sort of unholy connection with the Island? If you're the Pilgrim, does that make me the Anti-Pilgrim or something?" Visions of being possessed by an evil spirit bent on destroying the Island started playing with my imagination.

Dad ignored me as he continued to pace. "I need to think about this further. Until then, Whitnee, I do not want you combining all four life forces. Under any circumstances."

Amelia jumped in, "If the time thing is fixed, then I've been gone two whole days. I have to get home! And I'm worried about Ben—he was bleeding from the head when Tamir dragged me away." She turned her large hazel eyes on me expectantly. My stomach rolled at the thought of Ben's situation. But I thought of Gabriel and my promise not to leave until he woke up...and of Morgan and her struggle to even go home.

Dad, you know I can't leave yet. But my friends need to go home... how can we get them to that portal? Can you help? I asked.

Dad halted his stride and slowly turned around. "The Tetrarch Council will be here in the village tonight for the ceremony. If I'm not completely off about the direction their politics are heading, then the Council will probably confront Abrianna and Eli immediately. More than likely, a private diplomatic meeting will be held...That is when we can demand your exit through the portal as soon as possible—maybe even by morning."

I gave him a suspicious stare. "Okay. But you do mean Caleb, Amelia, and Morgan's exit, right? I'm not ready to leave yet. And I don't go unless you go with me..."

"Whoa, whoa, whoa!" Caleb waved his arms in front of my face. "I am *not* leaving here without you. No way. If we go through that portal, we all go together."

I faced him stubbornly. "We're not repeating what happened last time, Caleb."

"Exactly," he agreed. "We don't go until we're *all* ready to go. I can live with that."

"We can't afford to let more time pass on the Mainland. And with Gabriel being the way he is, I don't feel right leaving until I know what's going to happen here with the Pilgrim Protectors. I'm sorry, but I need to tie up loose ends this time so that walking away from all of this feels right."

"I don't understand why we can't just wait for you while you handle your business."

"Amelia has to get back home before her parents create too many problems. And you know we need to get Morgan out of here before she changes her mind again. Plus, she has all those doctor appointments coming up…We don't need to waste time getting her help."

"Then just send Morgan and Amelia back. I'll stay—"

"Caleb," I sighed. I knew he would be just as stubborn about this. "I need *you* to get Morgan and Amelia back. You have to make up some story for Amelia's parents. And Morgan is too sick to handle anything on her own. Not only that, but I want you to go straight to my mother and tell her everything you know."

He was vehemently shaking his head. "Whitnee, you are crazy if you think I'm leaving you here…"

"Nothing will happen to me with my dad here now," I said firmly. "I need you to be the strong one and take care of Morgan and Amelia. I will be just a few steps behind you."

His jaw was set into a hard line as he stared at the ground, fighting what I knew was his loyal instinct to protect. The fact that he was having to choose between me and the others really was unfair. That was why I made the choice for him.

He gripped my shoulders and leaned down a little so he could watch my face carefully for a reaction. "I want you to promise me that if I do this, you *are* coming home. No matter what. Promise that nothing—or *nobody*—will convince you otherwise."

I opened my mouth to respond, but Dad's voice sounded with authority behind Caleb. "*I* promise she will go home. No matter what."

If Dad was determined to get me home, that meant he would be coming with me…because there was no way I would leave here without him.

POLITICIANS ARE SUCH FAKERS

The family reunion between Dad and Poppa Zeke and Grandmother Sarah was interesting. There was genuine joy in my grandparents, knowing that Dad was alive and well after all this time. But after the initial hugs and tears in my room at the Healing Center, I felt tension settle among us—mostly on Ezekiel's end. I think he probably felt like I did...It was hard to experience complete peace with so much time lost and so many questions unanswered. What had Dad been doing on the Island for six years? Why didn't he try to contact anybody? Why did he come back in the first place?

My grandparents were honored guests at the Lost Ceremony along with the other members of government. Though Ezekiel did not get all of his answers before he was escorted away, they had plans to meet on Simeon's ship later that night. I, however, was determined that I would wait no longer for my own answers.

And that was how Dad and I ended up back on the roof to view the ceremony from afar, hidden from the rest of the village. Caleb and Amelia chose to watch the ritual from the window in Morgan's room, keeping her company and kindly giving us some time alone. Dusk was settling on the river, and Dorians had gathered on the shores and lawns, quietly awaiting the start of the cer-emony. There was a solemn, reverent mood in the air.

I studied Dad's profile, making note of the subtle changes in his appearance…a wrinkle here or there, a slight dusting of gray hair along his temples, a deeper tan on his fair skin. Overall, he still looked as I remembered him—lean, strong, and kind. But he was also very different to me now. The dad I had once known had a whole different life, and I was keenly aware of the differences in us.

"So…what exactly happened six years ago, Dad?"

"I knew you were going to ask me that," he said, leaning back on his hands and stretching his legs out in front of him. "And it's not an easy answer, Whitnee."

"I need to understand, so try to explain. Did you miss your life here? Did you come back for Abrianna?" I pressed him.

He gave me a funny look, like he was trying to read something in my thoughts. "It was because of the Pilgrim prophecy."

"Are you the Pilgrim?"

He directed his gaze straight ahead and responded thought-fully, "If I am, I never wanted to be…I spent my entire life trying to understand why I was born different. It was interesting growing up with blond hair when everybody in my world was dark. I used to feel ashamed that I didn't have a birthmark on my shoulder like all the other kids. It made swim time kind of awkward since I never wanted to remove my tunic." He flashed a smile at me. "I just wanted to fit in, but I couldn't ignore the physical differences, nor could I ignore the fact that people were looking at me to do something special, something huge…to lead them into some new era. The implications of being the Pilgrim are a lot heavier than anyone understands, Whitnee. It was a responsibility I did not necessarily want, but I was not in a position to choose my own future."

His words reminded me of Gabriel. How interesting that they would have similar misgivings about a predestined future. I tried to picture young Nathan growing up on the Island—the only pale kid they'd ever seen. "If that's true, then why didn't you stay here? I mean, I know Abrianna pushed you through the portal the first time, but when she opened it back up…when you came back for Will Kinder, why didn't you stay? Why destroy the portal before you could use it again? Was it just because of Mom?"

"Your mom made it easier to leave the Island…but, no, it wasn't just for her." He looked right at me and said, "I'll tell you something that only one other person knows, Whit. And it might sound a little crazy."

I smirked. "Trust me, Dad. 'Crazy' took on a whole new meaning after I transported here. Very few things sound crazy to me now."

He sighed, "You sound so grown up…You've got to know how hard I'm working to not treat you like a little kid. Everything in me wants to send you to your room right now and remind you to brush your teeth before bed." I just gave him a grateful smile and waited for him to continue. "The truth is that I've always had this unexplainable communication with the Island. And I don't mean that in a figurative way. I mean the Island talks to me."

"Like a voice in your head or something?"

"Not exactly…it's more like I feel and see what the Island sees and feels. I think what the Island thinks. This is not just a land mass floating about somewhere in the world. The Island has a heart. It's a living, breathing force that provides for the people who live here. The Island loves the people, and deals out both blessing and judgment according to their actions." He paused as if hearing something, but then continued, "For some reason, I've always been sensitive to the heart of the Island. I had to destroy the portal back then because…well, because I knew what it was doing to our home, to our source of life here. And then I left on the boat that day because…it was what I was *told* to do."

He glanced at me sideways, as if to gauge my reaction. I didn't think he was crazy. But I still didn't get it. "Why would the Island tell you to do that?"

"It's complicated. I don't know if I'm ready to explain that part to anyone yet. But I knew at the time that it would be temporary. I was never meant to leave forever, even though I didn't know how I would get back. However, once I arrived on the Mainland, I forgot everything, so it didn't matter anyway."

"When did you start getting your memory back?"

"My earliest memory flashes started after your mom became pregnant with you. I thought they were just weird dreams. Your mom knew about them. But it wasn't until you were about ten years old that Abrianna found my mind through the portal. She started talking to me in my dreams. Somehow she knew you were special...or she just assumed that any child of mine would be, I don't know. But she made all kinds of threats about you and Serena if I didn't meet her in Hawaii, on the island of Kauai. She told me exactly what hotel to stay in and everything. I still thought I was dreaming, but there was enough familiarity about the dreams that I went to Ben...especially since he was in so many of my flashes."

"And Ben told you everything."

"Right." He nodded. "And I probably should have told your mom everything I knew at that point. But I was confused enough about discovering an entire new past, and I decided I needed all the facts straight first. So I started to convince my research team that I needed to do some experimental work in Hawaii, and I made sure Ben knew what was going on. The day I left you and your mom...it was like deep down something told me I might not see you again." A regretful expression settled on his face. "I cried through most of the plane ride. I still remember the lady in the seat next to me who kept asking if I was okay."

I could feel my eyes sting—I was now old enough to put myself in his shoes for a moment. He had *cried?*

"Eventually Abrianna surprised me at the hotel. We took a walk on the beach...and the next thing I knew I was on the Island with my memory completely intact. Her guards were ready for me. I was imprisoned in the tank until she convinced me to help her."

"*Convinced* you?" I know my face was disgusted. "Why would you agree to help her with anything, Dad? She's the most manipulative, horrible, evil—"

"She's *not* evil, Whit," Dad corrected. I did not appreciate him defending her. At all. "She has made bad choices, yes."

"But you always taught me that your choices define you. Evil choices make a person evil."

"Yes and no. Don't forget she is still a *person*, a life with value. I believe there is still goodness in her, a chance for her to change."

I gaped at him. "Okay, *now* I think you're crazy."

"I understand why you feel that way, Whit. Trust me, I'm not defending what she's done. Not at *all*. But consequences sometimes have a way of finding people without our interference." His eyes flicked around nervously, and he started bouncing his feet in a fidgety way.

"Maybe I don't really *understand* your relationship with Abrianna. Do you love her, Dad?" My heart thudded against my chest as I awaited an answer I wasn't sure I wanted to hear. It was kind of weird discussing these things with a parent.

He definitely wouldn't meet my eyes, but he did say, "Of course I *care* about her. I feel sorry for her. I wish she would've made different choices for her life. I've spent six years trying to clean up her messes...trying to help her find who she *really* is instead of the self-obsessed, power-driven person she's become. But I can't protect her from herself. Especially now that she's brought you into it."

I really didn't know how to respond to that. So I asked another of my burning questions: "When I was here last time...did you know about it? The dream in Hydrodora...you knew I was with friends...you knew about my abilities. How?"

"Ahh, yes...Abrianna played all of that out brilliantly," he said with a sarcastic undertone. "Apparently, Abrianna had been trying to find you through the portal, a fact I was unaware of. But when you came to Camp Fusion, I could *sense* you...the same way I sense your mind when we communicate with Wind powers. Whenever she turned that portal on, I could find your 'frequency'…like a radio tuner in my head. Same way Abrianna found mine years ago."

The light bulb went off in my head. "The dreams I had the first weekend at camp…you told me not to cross the river!"

"Yes!" Dad nodded enthusiastically. "I tried to warn you about the danger! I didn't know if you could hear me or not. So it worked, really?"

"Well, yeah…At first I thought I was just dreaming. But seriously, Dad, did you really believe that telling me not to cross the river without any explanation would stop me from doing it? It only made me more curious," I confessed with a smirk.

"I should have thought that through. But I didn't even know if it was working; the connection was so fragile. And" —he gave me a stern look— "I had no idea what a stubborn, independent teenager you had become." He held his hands out like he was mock-strangling me.

"My stubbornness got me this far," I reminded him, slapping his hands away with a smile. "But in the Camp Fusion dreams, there was always nothingness from where you were communicating from…and other weird things would go on, just like in a real dream. Did you ever hear me answering you?"

"No. I didn't hear you until you were on the Island."

"That was when I was in Hydrodora…and I could see the tank in that dream. But it was like I saw it from your eyes, not my own. I was inside the prison." I thought for a second, trying to make sense of the differences in the dreams. "Wait…after that dream, I was about to blast the prison with Fire until Morgan and Caleb woke me up. My eyes had been gold, but I had also been using Wind to communicate back, right? And then this last time, Morgan said my eyes were gold and silver when I woke up…but I wasn't going to attack anything…"

Dad's eyebrows were scrunched in concentration. "Sounds like you were combining Fire and Wind the same way a zephyra might…only instead of just casting a thought into my mind, you were able to see a mental image from my mind. The Fire ability might have helped with the image…"

I made a face at the idea of seeing into someone's mind. "That's a creepy ability."

"I would try to experiment right now, but I do not want you combining any life forces. It's too dangerous if you really are connected to the portal in some strange way."

"You're no fun." I scrunched up my nose. "So where have you been every time I've been here? And if you knew I was here, why didn't you try to see me?"

"I couldn't. Abrianna asked me to do some consulting work on her expansion plans down in the tank a few days before you transported the first time. I should have known something was about to happen because she rarely lets me go down there unless she is worried I will interfere with something. Usually I live in the little cabin you found hidden in the mountainside."

"I knew it!"

"But once I got to the tank, they locked me in there. About a week later, Abrianna suddenly ordered my immediate release back to the cabin. She came and visited me that night and told me what was going on…I was so mad at her for bringing you there that I was ready to go straight to Ezekiel with the truth about everything. But she acted so innocent. She said you were traveling to the villages, very well-protected, and that you knew nothing about me being there. She told me how smart and beautiful you were… that you could not only use all four life forces, but combine them, as well."

He sighed heavily. "I was so desperate to see you that I soaked up everything she could tell me about you. Unfortunately, I knew that I had to warn you to leave because Abrianna made no secret about what she wanted from you. Apparently, she was banking on me contacting you that night…I helped launch you right into her perfect plan. She moved me back to the tank after you went through the portal, worried that Gabriel would try to find me. I've been stuck there ever since—most of the time in a normal room with a bed and bathroom. They only put me in that cage you saw whenever they were doing things they didn't want to risk me seeing. But had I not been in there that long, I would never have realized all the ways Eli was trying to manipulate the situation for his own power. And, unfortunately, I do not have quite the influence over him that I do with Abrianna."

There was an underlying anger in his tone. I gazed out at the darkening sky. "I don't get your relationships with these people, Dad...I just don't."

"You have to trust that I've done what I had to do in order to protect this Island. I love my homeland and my people. And sometimes my presence here has made the difference in matters of life and death. The experiments that she and Eli have performed on people..." His face was horrified and disgusted as he spoke. "If I hadn't been here, it would have gone too far. Think about it, Whit. If you had the power to save people from themselves, would you? If you could save Morgan's life, even if it meant sacrificing something important for yourself, would you do it?"

"Of course I would," I responded immediately.

"Then maybe you do understand my motives more than you think."

"But Morgan has never threatened me or imprisoned me or manipulated the people I love in ways that hurt me. She deserves to be saved from this mess. Abrianna does not deserve your loyalty and help."

"Who are you to decide who deserves what, Whitnee Skye?" Dad had a reproachful tone to his words. "Is one life more valuable than another? I did not make my choices for Abrianna...I did it for a whole race of people. Be careful how you deal out judgment, Baby Doll. Mercy goes a long way. And someday it might be you who needs it."

His words made me feel ashamed. I didn't mean to sound like I didn't care about people...but I suppose I didn't have the whole picture that he did. And I probably never would. My dad's inherent compassion for people was humbling.

"Wouldn't it just make things easier if I gave her the abilities she wants?" I asked, knowing already how he would feel about that.

"Abrianna's greed for your power is dangerous. She really believes you are the answer to what she has been searching for. She tried to convince me that taking your life force abilities permanently wouldn't hurt you because you were also a Mainlander, and you would just become like every other Traveler afterwards."

"But you don't believe that?"

"I don't know what it would do, and I don't want to find out. The Island gifted *you* this way, Whitnee, not *her*. Life forces are not supposed to be used for power and greed. The Island knows the heart and motivation behind such things. Gifting others, transferring life forces...every time those things take place, it comes directly from the Island, which makes the people involved accountable for their actions. What she wants to do is not okay. And I won't let her or Eli use you."

Silence grew between us after that. For the first time, I felt like I was getting a more accurate picture of my father and the burdens he bore for an Island that seemed to have a soul. It was weird, and it didn't all make sense. But I had experienced too many supernatural occurrences myself not to believe that what he was telling me was true. If Dad was the real Pilgrim—and I was pretty certain at this point that he was—then I still didn't know how I fit into the picture and what my purpose was in having these abilities.

"And there she is..." Dad muttered, nodding toward the shore. I followed his line of vision in time to see Abrianna escorted by Hydroguards to a special seat of honor—right in line with Ezekiel and Sarah, Joseph and his wife, Joanna, and a sullen Eli. Every member of the Tetrarch Council was present—except for Simeon.

"That is one awkward row of people...look how they all put on an act for the crowd," I mumbled, watching the smiles and greetings among the members of government. They acted as if they weren't just planning rebellion, murder, and deception hours ago.

"That's politics," Dad agreed sardonically. I found myself surveying the scene for the perfect figure of Jezebel somewhere in Abrianna's entourage. When I couldn't find her, I wondered again how things had ended with Gabriel and her. Were they still engaged or what?

All lights in the village were extinguished then, and a wistful tune caught on the Wind and floated over the village—the sound of a pan flute. I trained my eyes on the dark river, waiting to see what would happen next. The flute finished its lonely song, and with a breathtaking whoosh, a spike of Water shot up out of the center of the river, its glacier blue luminescence casting a glow over the people on the shore. The point of the Water rose higher and higher, licking up toward the sky. When it finally reached a towering height, a spray of droplets curved up and out from its center and cascaded back into the river, creating the tallest, most unnatural fountain I had ever seen. The instant the falling water crashed back into the river, the startling beat of multiple drums pierced the night. The powerful rhythm made my heart pump faster, and I leaned forward in curiosity.

That was when the little boats I had seen practicing earlier started floating from upriver in perfect formation—like a wooden army marching to the center of a battle. They formed themselves into a long line, which suddenly halted in sync with a final blast on the drums. The crowd on shore clapped respectfully but did not scream and cheer.

Emerging *through* the fountain—magically dry and untouched by the Water—was a single boat with Simeon aboard. He was illuminated by Firelight as the boat came to a stop in front of the fountain.

Dad leaned over and explained, "This is the part where Simeon makes a speech honoring the dead and granting comfort to those who have lost loved ones. He's very good at it."

"Is this a ceremony just for Hydrodorians?"

"No, the Lost Ceremony is a tradition respected by the whole Island. You will see members from each tribe in attendance. However, each village tends to have its own funeral customs when someone dies. In Hydrodora, they place the body in one of those ceremonial boats and send it out to sea. The number of boats you see here represents the number of people lost on the Island since the last ceremony."

I tried to count them in the dark, but I lost track at twenty-nine. There were more that stretched out along the shore farther than I could see.

"Is it just me or are two of those boats smaller than the others? Right over there..." I pointed to the center of the line.

Dad was grave as he answered, "Yes. Those are for the children who died."

A clammy sensation seeped through my body as I stared at the two delicate boats among all the others. I don't know why, but I thought of Elon and shivered.

Suddenly, Simeon's voice rang out through the night as if magnified by a magical speaker. We heard him clearly even from our vantage point on the roof.

"Generations of loved ones have passed over into the next life, each leaving behind their own unique legacy. Pieces of these legacies remain with us..." He extended one wrinkled hand out, and a white swirl began to light up the Water around his boat. He continued thoughtfully, "We still see their faces in our own reflections, hear their voices in the laughter of our children, and maybe even tell their stories of bravery...of heartache...of a simpler time. But we all know that as time passes, memories fade, stories grow old, and names are forgotten." He dropped his hand again and the light on the Water dissipated in misty wisps. "The truth is, fellow Dorians, that years from now, our own descendants shall sit upon our shores and perform the same rituals, perhaps not understanding our accomplishments, or the struggles we faced, or even remembering our names. But there is one legacy that cannot be forgotten or misunderstood...one that transcends time..." He paused and then folded his hands as if in prayer. "Love."

The fountain behind him changed to a vivid red and began rotating in a majestic circle like a huge cyclone in the center of the river. Simeon's voice grew stronger. "The love we pass on to others is what will outlive all of us. *Love* is what draws us to these shores tonight. And I believe that on the other side of the dark sea that spans life and death, we will find a place where love abounds perfectly. I look forward to the day I will be reunited with my beloved wife. But until then, I will continue to live the only legacy she left me—a genuine love for others. Join me as we choose tonight to remember all of those who have been lost to us, knowing that on the other side, they have been found."

My eyes teared up as I realized that what had been lost to me six years ago had now been found. And the proof was sitting right next to me. Without a word, I leaned over and rested my head on Dad's shoulder. I wanted to remember this moment forever. Not many girls could say they got to sit on a rooftop with their daddy one summer night and witness an ancient ritual on a magical Island. Somewhere on the far shore, a choir began to sing. There were no words, just the beautiful pattern of voices weaving rich melodies around each other.

Dad's cheek came down to rest on the top of my head, and we watched the solemn Dorians surge forward and begin dropping things into the boats that lined the shore. Dad whispered, "Family and friends place flowers in the boats to represent their lost loved ones. In a moment, Simeon will join them on the shore, and his boat will become the symbol for all those who have died throughout history. The Guardian and Council Members will each be given the opportunity to board the bigger boat and leave their own offering of remembrance."

The processional of people with flowers was sad and reverent. The choir continued to sing, even as the crowd parted to let each Council Member go through. It began with Simeon, who boarded his boat again and knelt low, his back to the people. I wished I could have seen up close the bloom he laid in the boat. It appeared to be a vivid yellow. "What happened to Simeon's wife? He said she got sick..."

Dad sighed heavily. "She had the Poison." His words hit me like a hammer to the chest. "Only the third person on the Island to ever get it. It was a shock to everyone."

"And he couldn't heal her..." I mused, watching the old man as he kept his head bowed.

"Even if he could have healed her, she wouldn't have let him." Dad sounded distant as he reminisced. "He has since been instrumental in developing the specialized Water therapy that they are giving Morgan. Obviously I didn't know that the 'poison' here and the cancer that runs so rampant on the Mainland were one and the same until I came back six years ago. I've been passing on my limited medical knowledge through Abrianna, but the disease is very rare here...not like on the Mainland where everybody you know has dealt with it on some level."

"And Simeon has no children...right?"

"Right. But the Hydrodorians would call him father. He has been the most loved Elder they've ever had...you can see why. He loves with a heart that is sometimes blind."

I remembered last time and Simeon's steadfast belief that Abrianna wouldn't hurt us. In retrospect, he had been wrong about her motives—maybe blinded by that general love for people that Dad referred to.

Joseph and Joanna were next, and they placed in the boat what looked like a breathtaking arrangement of Eden's special Pinkberry flowers. Then I watched Poppa Zeke and Sarah lay down multicolored florals, tied up with artistic flair. When Eli came forward, I couldn't help the hatred that burned through me as I watched him place blood red flowers inside the boat. It felt so hypocritical to watch him honor the dead when his own son was a floor below me fighting for his right to live.

Abrianna was the last one to stand. The crowd was respectfully curious as she strolled gracefully among them in a white dress that caught glimmers from the natural lights of the night sky. Eli assisted her onto the boat and handed her an armful of blossoms. One by one, she kissed the tops of four simple white bouquets and then nestled them carefully among the flowers already present. I pulled away from Dad and snuck a peek at his reaction. His eyes were trained on her as if nothing else around us existed at that moment.

After a breathless pause from Abrianna, she finally turned back around. Just before she placed her hand in Eli's, I could have sworn that she glanced right at us sitting up here on the roof. I jerked reflexively, worrying that she saw me. But then Eli was escorting her back to her seat, and all eyes turned back to the river.

"Before we conclude our ceremony, I have one more thing to say..." Simeon's voice sounded again, this time from the shore. The crowd seemed surprised as they directed their attention on him again.

Even Dad cocked one eyebrow and sat up a little straighter. "There's usually no speech during this part," he mumbled.

"I want to remind you of a time not too long ago when all four tribes were united for one purpose...a time when hope was not just something we talked about, but something we felt." I saw Abrianna fix her gaze squarely on Simeon. She and Eli looked like statues with their arms linked together. Simeon ignored the questioning stares of the people and continued on with boldness. "Tonight we remember the past...but tomorrow begins the future. I fear that troubled times are heading our way, and change is on the horizon. No matter what darkness surrounds us, fellow Dorians, we must find that one purpose to unite us. I believe hope will come again...through the Pilgrim."

At the mention of the Pilgrim, the crowd reacted fiercely with whispers and comments that began rippling all over the shores. There were some cheers that sounded like war cries. There were some equally angry shouts of disagreement. But, mostly, there was just a lot of confusion and surprise. Poppa Zeke and Joseph were the only ones who stood there stoically, unsurprised by Simeon's words and the ensuing crowd reaction.

"Is that okay? To talk about the Pilgrim like that?" I wondered aloud. I thought they weren't allowed to mention that name.

Dad pulled himself up to stand and crossed his arms over his chest as he stared down at the scene below. He seemed tense now. "Simeon…what did you just do?" he whispered, shaking his head as the Hydroguards tried to pacify the crowd.

"What?" I didn't understand the full dynamic of what had just happened.

"That right there…" Dad rubbed his chin thoughtfully and pointed to Simeon. "That little speech might have just started the real rebellion." His voice was filled with finality…and a slight emotional edge.

Abrianna and Eli moved to Simeon, flanking either side of him. With a gracious smile at the crowd, Abrianna looped one dainty arm around Simeon's in pity…like he was just a pathetic old geezer who needed attention. She waved her other hand as if to show that she was in agreement with his words, and all was just fine. The crowd started to quiet down again. It almost looked like she and Eli were trying to direct Simeon away from the shore, but the old man held his ground, staring boldly forward at the river.

That was when the drums started up again, and the ceremonial boats began to float away from the shore into a new formation. As the drumbeats grew in rhythm and volume, the boats paraded in a circle around the skyscraper fountain that was still cascading majestically in the middle of the vast river. Then with a synchronized bang on the drums, every boat erupted with glittering flames shooting up and out of their centers. It was breathtaking to see so many flaming boats circling the now white tower of Water. The choir joined in, raising the emotion of the ceremony to a musical climax.

And then with perfect timing all sound ceased, and the fountain collapsed with a crashing, rippling wave. As the boats slowed their rocking from the momentum, I watched in fascination as one by one they extinguished themselves and drifted away downriver and out of sight. All that could be heard were the soft cries of people on the shore as they watched the last symbols of their loved ones float away forever.

I was especially moved to sadness when the two smaller boats finally drifted away. I thought of Morgan watching these proceedings from her room and wondered what she was feeling and thinking.

"Whitnee." Dad was very solemn. He didn't take his eyes off the crowd, and he was distant and distracted when he told me, "You need to go down to your room and stay there until I come get you. Things might turn ugly, and I need to trust you to stay out of it. Can you do that for me?"

I frowned. "I guess...but what do you think is going to happen?"

"Don't ask me questions right now. Just please do as I say." He glanced once at me with that authoritative dad-look that I didn't like so much now that I was seventeen years old. "Go now, Baby Doll. Okay?"

"Okay..." I was not happy about being locked away in my room, but because Dad had been so open with me about everything, I had no real desire to argue with him. I started to back away, but had to ask just one more question. "Dad?"

"Yes?"

"What's the story behind Abrianna's white flowers?"

Dad did give me his full attention then. "She makes those bouquets every year from her own garden. She refuses to let anyone else do it for her. Two bouquets represent her birth parents, who died when we were young. The third one honors Ben because he was the man she called father."

Indignantly, I hissed, "How could she pay her respects to him when he's not really dead?! When *she's* the one who betrayed him and forced him to leave this Island—"

"I know, Whitnee," Dad cut me off when he wrapped one fatherly arm around my shoulders and drew me close to his side. With a frown, he responded, "It doesn't seem to make sense, but I've watched her do this many times. Abrianna's bouquets are not just symbolic of the people she's lost in her life, but of her own guilt and regret tied to each of them. And as long as she refuses to make things right with her past choices, she will continue to wrap up her guilt in pretty white flowers and display them in front of the entire Island. The sad thing is that she's the one who's really lost."

I tried to mask my irritation at his words, taken aback again at the clear compassion and understanding he had for her. No matter how well he explained it, I couldn't make myself okay with his relationship to Abrianna.

When I gained control over my annoyance, I finally asked, "And the fourth bouquet was for…?"

I shouldn't have been surprised when he admitted, "Me."

But I was.

And I hated her even more.

THE DAUGHTER SHE NEVER HAD

I promise, I really was going to be the good girl that Dad expected me to be and mind my own business down in the Healing Center. But that was before Morgan got sick again, and we had to leave her in agony as Priscilla treated her...Before Amelia and Caleb moved to my room, and I volunteered to go find some comfort food for us...

Before I happened to spy the mysterious cloaked person sneaking quietly out of Gabriel's room.

I froze in place down the corridor, watching the darkly-clad figure. The usual Hydroguard on duty was nowhere in sight (warning sign number one). There was also nobody else around except the mystery guest and me (warning sign number two). The intruder didn't even glance back down the hall, just quietly clicked the door closed and rushed away toward the back of the building.

I padded softly down the hall, pausing to peer into Gabriel's room. He was still in bed—completely alone—and breathing evenly. Who had come to see him? And for what purpose? He was supposed to be under careful guard around here! My gosh, somebody really needed to tighten up security on this Island.

I darted down the hall, determined to sneak up on whoever had just left that room and find out what they had been doing there. I came around the corner of the last hallway just in time to see the back exit of the Healing Center door closing. Surely the Hydroguard there would know who it was…

Except that there was no Hydroguard there, either (warning sign number three).

With my hands ready for defense, I made the choice to disobey Dad and follow the intruder. I'd probably get in trouble for it later, but sometimes you just have to make snap decisions…and my instinct to protect Gabriel and my friends was stronger than my will to obey.

In the dark of night, it was hard to follow my subject very well. I could hear the noise from the festival downriver and suddenly felt a little exposed with my blonde hair so visible. That caused me to stick to the tree line more closely, throwing glances in all directions. Thankfully, this part of the river was deserted.

I was a little disconcerted when we came to the marked rock Simeon had directed me to earlier, and the cloaked figured began to follow the trail. Combine that with the flash of white dress that I'm pretty sure I saw swishing beneath the cloak and…

I had to pause and think.

The height, the delicate shoulders, the graceful way of moving… I was ninety-nine percent sure now I was following Abrianna. But what was she doing sneaking around all alone in disguise like that? Did she know I was following her? And if so, was this a trap? That woman was super smart, and I would be a complete idiot if I allowed myself to fall into one of her perfectly laid schemes.

Dang. I leaned against a tree and weighed my options.

Be a good girl and turn around. Go back to the safety of the Healing Center. Leave the sneaking, creeping, and mosquito bites to Abrianna and her evil plots.

*Or…*spy on where's she going all by her lonesome. Follow her and find out why she's in disguise and who she's meeting…

Oh, crap. *Who she's meeting…*Why did that thought suddenly give me a sick feeling? I knew exactly who she was meeting— someone who could conveniently distract the Hydroguards with other matters…the one person with the rumored ability to make Abrianna calm down…the very same person I hadn't seen since the rooftop earlier.

With a frustrated snarl, my decision was made. I shoved away from the tree and crept down the trail, trying to see my way through the patches of moonlight and to be as inconspicuous as possible.

Not so surprisingly, she came to the hot spring with all the white flowers. And Dad was standing there, waiting for her. I ignored the vomitous feeling in my stomach and hid myself where I could still hear and see through the surrounding foliage.

"Are you alone?" Dad spoke first, looking around suspiciously. I could see him clearly in the light of the moonbeams that filtered down through the clearing. The spring bubbled softly behind him as he surveyed the woman in the cloak.

Her voice was a little harder to hear, but I believe she said, "Of course. Eli is back on our boat." She dipped her head down and added, "Thank you for letting me see Gabriel."

"Does Eli know that I contacted you?"

"I did not admit to anything…but he knows. He always knows." So Dad and Abrianna had been communicating with each other. Again, I shouldn't have been surprised, but for some reason, I felt betrayed. I didn't care that Abrianna sounded really shaken up about something. "Nathan, I…I cannot keep him under control much longer. Look at what he did to my son! I should have known Eli would take matters into his own hands. The signs were there… I just thought I had it under control."

"Your biggest mistake was trying to control people in the first place—especially with deception and force," Dad answered her, as if he had told her this before. "It's not surprising that it has come back to hurt you."

"Please do not lecture me…not tonight." Her hand fluttered up to her face, and I watched as Dad closed the space between them and carefully pulled the hood of her cloak away. Her one silver streak of hair caught the moonlight, confirming it really was her. But Dad's face was upset as he stared at her.

"He hurt you again," he breathed, his expression angry. I couldn't see her face, but there was obviously something wrong with her.

"It has been worse than this...you know how he is. The fool cannot control his rage." She turned from him and walked a few steps away, ducking her face into the shadows, so that I still couldn't see. "And he is desperate now. He knows the Council is about to act. With Simeon's little surprise speech at the ceremony, it will be impossible to contain the people's questions now. So the real question becomes, will Eli cooperate or will he keep trying to get what he wants at all costs? The last thing I want to see is *that* man with Whitnee's abilities."

Her voice was disgusted when she spoke of her husband. *Such a lovely couple.*

"He has no choice but to cooperate now and neither do you." Dad knelt at the spring and dipped his hand in the water. "You can end all of this tonight while it is still within your power. Get rid of all your spies. Shut down the portals—"

Portals? Plural?

"—Get rid of the fake rebel forces you created just to scare the people...Don't look at me like that. I am not stupid, Bri. I know that most of this mess is your own creation."

"I asked you not to lecture me, Nathan," she interrupted him, holding up a weary hand. "I had no idea Eli would use my own people against me. I just need your help."

"I *am* helping you. Come here."

He rose again to his full height and then stretched out one arm toward her. When she moved closer to him, he cupped her neck. She leaned in submissively, tilting her face up. For a moment, I had the horrifying feeling they were going to kiss. But, no, he placed the dripping wet hand from the spring on her cheek, and the blue hue of healing life force lit up their faces.

Dad could heal! *Holy crap.* Why did he keep that a secret? What else could he do? And why was Abrianna the only one who apparently knew of his secret? She did not seem surprised at all by what he was doing. Oh, I couldn't wait to confront him! My instincts told me if he could access Water, he could use all four life forces too. Suddenly, my own abilities made sense…and didn't seem like such a big deal, after all. It was just genetics!

Now I was resisting the urge to jump out from my hiding place and start another interrogation. Apparently if you didn't ask, Dad didn't tell…*ugh*.

"If you do not follow my advice tonight, this will be the last time I help you, Bri," he continued softly. "That's not a threat; it's just the truth. You have endangered Whitnee and her friends, and I cannot continue to help someone who harms the people I love. When the Council calls a meeting in the morning, they will offer you and Eli a chance to account for what you've done."

He pulled his hands away from her and crossed his arms over his chest in authority. She shook her head in denial and tried to turn away from him again. But he stepped directly into her line of vision. "Look at me. I want you to admit your responsibility and cooperate with the Council from this point forward. They know I am here, and that will soon become public knowledge too. You cannot fight this—the Elders have an extensive support system and they are prepared to remove you from your position by force, if they must. You are outnumbered. Out of respect to you and to me, though, they are going to give you one last chance to cooperate."

"No…no." She was clearly panicking. "I have worked too hard for too many years to develop the portals and to find ways to share all the life forces…I cannot relinquish control over those things, Nathan. I refuse to give up those secrets to them."

"Those secrets are destroying you. Look what it has done to your family already…look at Gabriel! He is a victim of Eli's greed—the same greed that is controlling you, Bri. It's time to let go." She didn't respond immediately. So he continued, "I know you want to be free from all of this. So please do the right thing… while you still can."

"If I do what you ask, you will just leave me again." Her voice was pathetic, and I wanted to call out, *Heck yes, he's leaving you! Say bye-bye to all her drama, Dad.*

"You know I cannot leave," he replied, and I frowned in the darkness. What did that mean?

Her responsive sigh was tired and sad. "Now that you have spent time with her, I can see it in your eyes...you want your family back. And if you wanted to leave again, I am certain you would find a way."

He shook his head adamantly. "I can't go back. But when you are in that meeting, you *will* arrange immediately for Whitnee and her friends to leave through that portal. The longer she stays, the harder it will be for all of us...promise you will do that for me. Do whatever you can to get her home and away from Eli. And then you and I will destroy the portal once and for all and be done with it."

Angry tears flooded my eyes at his words. Why was he so ready to get rid of me? I thought we had connected on a deeper level. Didn't he know that leaving him again would kill me? Why "be done with" *me* instead of with the Island?

"Even if I agreed to destroy the portals, Nathan, Whitnee should not leave...you know what the prophecy says—"

"Don't pretend like you have ever cared once about that prophecy."

"Oh, I care about the prophecy," she spat, her words heating up with emotion. "My whole life has been dictated by the bloody prophecy, Nathan! Do not pretend like it has not in some way directed every single decision you and I have ever made. Do not pretend that the prophecy is not what drove you to leave me..."

"Abrianna—"

"If you want someone to blame for all the problems on this Island, blame *yourself*, Nathan! *You* were the one everybody loved, and you disappeared. *You* left me with no choice but to marry Eli and salvage what I could of the political mess Ben left behind."

"You keep lying to yourself, Bri. Those were *your* choices. I am sorry you cannot see yourself clearly enough to know that." Dad started to pace away from her while I watched with shameless curiosity.

"Stop acting like I do not know what my choices have cost me! I made choices to *survive* and to help our people *survive* from the biggest disappointment they had ever faced—the disappearance of their Pilgrim! I live every day with the knowledge that if it were not for that prophecy, I would have been the one you chose to love...the one you chose to stay with and rule alongside! Our lives could have been so different—it could have been *I* who bore you a daughter! Whitnee could have been *ours*—"

"Stop it!" Dad commanded forcefully and a sharp breeze ripped across the little clearing at his words. I sucked in a breath. When it died down, his voice was barely audible. "You are creating a history that was never there."

Abrianna composed herself. Uncomfortable silence settled over the area, and I became aware of the fact that I had tensed up every muscle in my body as I crouched low. I certainly couldn't move now...

Finally Abrianna spoke to him in the calm and collected manner that was more characteristic of the Guardian I knew. "Despite what you might believe about me, Nathan, it has not always been about attaining power for my own use. Yes, having abilities in all four life forces would certainly grant me the power to rule the people better...to understand their needs and their instincts better. And with it, I could finally *control* Eli. But the drive to push further, to experiment in extreme circumstances, to cross lines I never would have crossed, has not always been a selfish one. There were other reasons..."

"Like what? I don't understand your point." His tone was frustrated and dismissive.

"I am not the only one who has sacrificed a lot for this Island, Nathan. I know what the cost has been for you too. I thought that if I could find a way to take on all four life forces, then you would be free to live your life as you choose—whether that is with me or not. I have done all of this for you too. I was trying to…to save you. Give you freedom."

"Bri, are you kidding me?" Dad's head snapped back as he looked at her in exasperation. "That is *not* how it works! And if that were true, then you would have found a way to take *my* abilities a long time ago."

"Never!" she cried passionately. "Releasing your abilities would kill you. But Whitnee is different—"

"Don't talk about my daughter anymore. You are saying things you know nothing about." I recognized the controlled anger brewing beneath Dad's words.

She reached out and clung to his tunic, her voice becoming desperate again. "Think about it, Nathan…what if you were meant to go to the Mainland just so you could have a daughter from both worlds? What if I was meant to find a way to channel all these life forces just so we could use her abilities to save you from these burdens?"

"Now you're just twisting the truth of your own motivations. I am done with this discussion." He pulled away from her grasp. "By this time tomorrow, I want Whitnee gone—*that* is how you can help me. Understand?"

"What are you going to tell her? She will not leave without you. The girl has a strong will."

"She has had to say goodbye to me once. She'll find the strength to do it again," he answered with heaviness, and I felt the anger surge through me again. He began to walk away from Abrianna and toward the trail. I shrank back and held my breath so as not to be discovered.

"Nathan," Abrianna called out. "You cannot fool me. I know what you really want. I once told Whitnee that if she just gave me her abilities, you could go home with her. I meant that."

Dad shook his head in disbelief. "That is not your decision to make."

And then he disappeared into the night. My muscles were crying out for some relief, but I couldn't move. My heart felt like it had been electrocuted several times over. I really needed to get control of my new eavesdropping habit...

But the guilt didn't come in light of the new knowledge I had. That distorted picture in the puzzle was starting to make sense.

Dad was right...Abrianna was so much more complicated than I first thought. I wanted to keep my cold wall of hatred up, but I knew what a girl in love looked like...even if she was decades older than me. I couldn't tear my eyes away from her as she knelt down by the spring and plucked a white blossom from its stem. She touched it to her healed cheek, and then she leaned over and cried.

My hatred crumbled just a little bit.

"Seriously, what goes through your head every time you decide to disappear without telling someone?" Caleb grumbled as he paced in front of me. I just rolled my neck in circles and stretched the muscles wearily. For now, I was letting him vent his aggravation, because it kept me from having to explain myself. "I would really like to know how you justify your ridiculous choices sometimes, Whitnee. How do you go from, 'Hey, I'm going to grab us some food' to 'Why don't I go play my own game of hide and seek just to make everybody worry I've been kidnapped?' *Again!*"

"Oh my gosh, Caleb." I pulled my knees to my chest and watched him work out his frustration in typical Caleb-fashion. "I thought I was supposed to be the dramatic one..."

"Don't act like it's not a big deal. You're lucky I couldn't find your dad or this would be worse. One of these days, you're going to actually go missing again, and I'm not gonna care. I'll refuse to go looking for you, because I'll just assume you're on another one of your sneaky little adventures!"

Amelia's voice was bored as she bit on her nails in concentration. "I think you're just jealous, Caleb, because now her sneaky little adventures don't always include you."

My eyebrows shot up at her surprising observation. Caleb's mouth opened and closed. Then he snapped, "Stay out of it, Amelia. You're just as guilty of disappearing without warning."

She paused with a thoughtful glance at the wall and then shrugged. "Fair enough." Then she went back to chewing on her fingernails.

"Amelia, that's gross," I reminded her and then turned my gaze back on Caleb. "I promise I'm not trying to turn you into a gray-haired old man before you turn eighteen."

"So where did you go this time?"

I directed my stare at the ceiling. I just really didn't want to talk about Dad and Abrianna. I was mad and confused about the whole thing, so even if I did want to talk about it, I had no idea where to start.

"What the heck, Whitnee?" Caleb was flabbergasted at my silence.

"I just got distracted, okay?" I finally told him. "There are *things* going on around this Island that directly affect me, and I'm just trying to process all of that. No, I don't want to explain further than that. And, yes, I do expect you to leave me alone about it."

At my words, he ceased his pacing and came straight to stand in front of me. Leaning on his fists against the mattress, he looked straight into my eyes. "Why do I have the sick feeling that if I leave through that portal without you, I'll never see you again?"

"What are you talking about? What does that have to do with—"

"Just tell me, Whitnee. If you're thinking about staying here permanently, I can handle it. What I can't handle is you lying to me. I need to know how you really feel."

"Caleb," I replied with tender exasperation. "That is not what this is about. As of right now, I have no intention of staying long-term on this Island—"

"As of right now? Well, that's reassuring," he remarked sarcastically and shoved away from the bed.

"That's not what I meant…I just don't want to talk right now." I tried to reassure him, but I just didn't have much patience left.

"Well, that makes two of us," he grunted and headed straight for the door. "I'm out."

I just stared as the door closed with an ominous click behind him.

"Why won't you just tell us where you went?" Amelia questioned. I had almost forgotten she was there.

"Same reason it took you so long to tell me about that one weekend at home…" I rubbed my eyes. "Sometimes you just need to accept things first."

She seemed to understand my answer, or at least she didn't respond immediately. I was about to suggest she go to her room for the night when she spoke.

"Eventually you're gonna have to choose one."

Oh, here we go. Advice from Amelia. "Choose one what?"

Her voice was matter-of-fact. "You know…the Island or the Mainland. It's not like you can keep going back and forth the rest of your life, right? Eventually you'll have to choose one or the other. And when you do, then you'll know which guy to pick."

I blinked stupidly at her. "Which *guy?*"

She made a *duh* face. "Gabriel or Caleb? Or I guess picking the guy first could help you pick the place too. Obviously, if you end up staying on the Island, you're choosing Gabriel. But if you go back to the Mainland—"

"Okay, okay, I get what you mean…And that's really not something I want to talk about, either." I held up a hand to stop her. Something about the simplicity of her thoughts was hitting home in an uncomfortable manner.

"Well, I wish you'd figure it out because we all *really* need to get back home."

She was starting to stress me out more. "Let's just call it a night, Amelia. I'm tired."

She rolled her eyes, but pulled herself lazily to her feet and started to leave. "Denial is the first stage."

"Stop with the therapy terms, please…" I called after her, but she just gave me a small wave in return.

I sat there in silence for an immeasurable amount of time before Dad's voice in my head startled me from my stupor.

Did Tamir ever give any indication that he knew he was working for Eli, not Abrianna?

I thought back for a moment before responding. *No. He thought he was kidnapping me on her orders.*

Tell me again everything he said. With a sigh I knew he couldn't hear, I reiterated the important details I could remember about Tamir's involvement. Dad interrupted with a few questions from Poppa Zeke, and then there was a lengthy pause.

Need anything else?

Not right now. Go to sleep, Baby Doll. It's late.

When will you be back? I asked.

No answer.

Of course. *I bet if my name was Abrianna, you'd answer me immediately…*I thought to myself bitterly and then panicked that he might have heard me. I hadn't tried to cast that out there to him, so hopefully not. Who knew you'd have to be so careful with your thoughts? I assumed he was with the other Tetrarch Council members (minus Eli and Abrianna), holding a secret meeting on Simeon's ship. I could only imagine the intensity of such a gathering as they carefully thought out their next political move. With Dad's presence and insight available to them now, I wouldn't be surprised if they were up debating and discussing the rest of the night.

But I did wonder if the Council knew Dad had contacted Abrianna ahead of time and advised her on what to do. Was that part of their whole plan? Or did Dad just do that as a final grasp at helping her? Oh, Abrianna…the abusive and the abused all in one. How long had Eli been physically violent with her? And had he ever done those things to Gabriel?

Not having ever lived in an environment like that, I guess it made sense that you did what you had to do to survive, like Abrianna had said. But my mind could not fathom all of the reasons a person would stay in that kind of relationship.

I also didn't understand why Dad would stay here with Abrianna so long when she had so obviously tried to control him. Nothing about it sat right with me. And I had a feeling that as long as Dad and "Bri" had this strange co-dependent relationship, there was not much chance that Mom and I could ever fit in with his life on the Island.

"*Ugh!*" Out of frustration, I launched the pillow across the room with Wind and watched it smack the door with a light thud. Yes, I had said goodbye to my dad once…but I didn't want to do it again. It was unfair that I had a father who I *knew* loved me, but who, for unexplainable reasons, couldn't stick around to raise me!

I needed Morgan.

I made my way through the darkened hallway to her room, noting that the Hydroguard was back at Gabriel's door. His eyes slid watchfully in my direction, but I just waved before I disappeared through her door.

She was asleep in the bed and there were tubes of bright blue snaking out from under the covers. In the dim lighting of the room, the tubes glowed as they filtered pure Water therapeutically from the tub in the floor to a patch that wrapped around her stomach. Those pain-reducing, life-giving coils of Water completely freaked me out. It was the first time I actually felt like Morgan was in a hospital.

I tiptoed carefully around the tubes and lowered myself into the chair beside her bed, trying not to wake her. This detached feeling came over me as I stared at my best friend in her sleep. She was so lovely and serene—just lying there with her dark hair splayed on the pillow like a halo. I pictured the little angel figurine with the one missing wing on her dresser back home…and realized I had my own broken and beautiful angel right there beside me. I never realized that Morgan's refusal to toss that entire angel figurine in the river was an obvious sign that she had never let go…that she had never healed from the experience of losing her friend.

And just like Morgan couldn't let that angel go, neither could I let Morgan go so easily. I buried my face into her blanket and allowed my tears to soak in softly and silently. I was so quiet and alone in my grief that I froze for a second when I felt a comforting hand on my head.

"Those tears better not be for me," Morgan whispered drowsily. I turned my face to rest on one cheek where I could see her. Her eyes were still closed and her breathing even. But her wrist moved lightly as she patted my head. She was so weak—even the pressure of her hand was feather light.

"I'm sorry…I didn't mean to wake you."

"Am I awake or dreaming? I don't even really know anymore…" Her eyes slowly peeled open. The Water therapy relaxed her pain, but it also seemed to make her more sleepy and drugged.

"Just go back to sleep, Morgie," I coaxed her, closing my own eyes.

She shifted slightly in her bed and then questioned, "Do you want to tell me what's wrong?"

"No, it's okay…I just wanted to be in here with you. Do you mind if I stay, or am I bugging you?"

She ignored my denial. "Is this about me or your dad?" Her knowing eyes opened and closed sluggishly.

I bit my lip, wanting to spill everything to her, but questioning if she was in the right mental state to understand me. So I just said, "If I leave the Island, I don't think Dad will come back home with me…He wants to stay here for reasons I just don't understand."

The thing was, I meant to say it casually, like it was not a big deal. But saying the words out loud like that made my heart hurt.

"Are you sure he *wants* to stay? Not that he *has* to stay?" she clarified.

It was a good question. What would be powerful enough to make him stay? His loyalty and compassion for Abrianna? I couldn't really make myself believe that—he had left her before. Of course, the Island *told* him to leave that time so he had done it…

The Island.

Was the *Island* telling him to stay?

Whoa…brain ninja.

"I don't know, Morgie," I sighed. "I just know that if he doesn't come back with me, I'll feel like a failure. I only came back here to find him."

"And you did find him. How is that a fail?" she pointed out sleepily. I didn't have a response to that. So she said, "I'm sorry, Whit. It seems like you're just going to have to trust your dad without understanding everything."

I remembered how transparent and trusting Morgan had instantly become around my dad in the tank…and how every person who met him seemed to hold an uncanny amount of respect for him. I swear, even Eli had seemed to demonstrate a healthy fear of my dad. And it's not that I didn't trust and respect my dad…but he was my *dad*. What were other people seeing in him that was so unique?

"Why do you trust him so easily, Morgie?"

She was quiet with her eyes closed for so long that I thought she had fallen back asleep. "He didn't even know me…" she suddenly whispered. "But the first time he looked at me, he *saw* me. Exactly as I am. And he accepted me without question."

I totally knew what she was talking about. Her words marinated in my mind until she started to stir uncomfortably. I raised my head to study her pinched expression.

"What's wrong? Are you in pain?"

"Yeah, it's just…" She started to squirm and pull herself into a fetal position. "Kind of takes your breath away sometimes, you know?"

"Should I go get somebody?"

"No, no…" Her face was still scrunched up with her eyes closed in concentration. I stared down at her helplessly, wondering if the pain would pass or if she really needed a Healer's attention.

"What should I do, Morgie?"

"Just distract me," she whimpered. "Sing one of your songs or something. I like when you sing." *Oh, geez.* I was not exactly in a singing mood. Plus, singing for people on command was really awkward. Papi did it to me all the time, and the older I got, the more I resisted. "Please, Whit…"

Resisting Morgan's request was much harder. So I hummed the Spanish tune that Papi had taught me so long ago, just because it was the first that came to mind. My melody echoed off the walls of the room until her face relaxed, and she fell back into a deep sleep. Then I laid my head down in my arms and dozed off too.

A REMEDY OF REBELLION

"Whitnee…" somebody whispered. The jolting of desperate hands on my shoulders brought me to the surface of sleep. "Whitnee, come with me." It was Lilley. She gestured at me to follow her. I straightened up and stretched the cramped muscles in my back from the position in which I had fallen asleep. Morgan was curled into a ball under her covers in the dark room. The blue tubes had been removed and were coiled up in the corner. In somewhat of a stupor, I followed Lilley until she came to a small office the size of a walk-in closet. Once we were both inside, she shut the door and turned around nervously to face me.

"What's going on? Why are we in a…closet?" I asked, rubbing my eyes. She was wearing a cute dress that showed off her figure, instead of the loose-fitting uniforms of the Healing Center. With touches of makeup on her face, she actually looked older. I assumed she had been out at the Festival with Thomas all evening.

"I think I know a way you can help Morgan," she blurted in a loud whisper. "But I could get in a lot of trouble for telling you."

"Why? What is it?" She had my full attention now.

"It is a forbidden practice called Transfusion."

"Like a blood transfusion? We do those on the Mainland." I was confused as to why something like that would be forbidden.

"Transfusion is an ancient healing procedure that has only ever been documented in one place—our Dorian Records." As she spoke, she maneuvered past me and opened up a silver cube on the little desk in the room. The cube was about the size of a small cardboard box and I had seen something like it before—in Poppa Zeke's Conclave. It looked like a big version of a zephyra and could produce real-life images like a 3-D movie screen.

"One of the oaths we take as Healers is to never perform or teach others how to perform Transfusion," she said, her eyes troubled. "I have not yet taken my oaths, so…" The cube lit up with a life-size image of the thick, ancient book I had seen in person back in the Conclave of Aerodora. This time, I actually saw the cover—brown and leathery, worn with age, featuring an engraving of all four tribal birthmarks in a circular pattern. She flipped the yellowed pages of the book with a button on the device, and I thought this had to be the next step in e-book development back home. Finally she came to a page and scanned with her fingers until she found what she was looking for. She read silently, her mouth forming words she didn't say aloud. Then she looked up at me doubtfully. "This is dangerous information. I could lose my future as a HydroHealer, and you could cause yourself serious trouble if you attempt it. In all honesty, this is probably a really bad idea."

"Then why are you telling me about it?"

Her blue eyes were pretty intense as she answered me. "Because the stories Thomas has told me about you…they are incredible. I believe you are special. And I know how much Morgan means to you…and to Thomas." She dropped her gaze to the floor. "If I did not give you all the information I knew, I would have to live the rest of my life wondering if something more could have been done."

I stared at her uncertainly. "There are different kinds of treatments for cancer that we have developed on the Mainland…"

"Whitnee, you should know the truth. Morgan *will* die from this soon. There has been much damage inside her body from the Poison."

"Okay..." I took a deep breath. "Then tell me what Transfusion is."

"It can only be performed between Hydrodorians because it is a transfer of the Water life force from one healthy person to a person who is incurably sick."

"Like gifting them? How is that forbidden?"

"Not quite the same. In Transfusion, the gifter is completely giving up their Water life force to the sick person—forever."

"But I thought people on the Island die if they lose their life force..."

"Correct. That is why it is a sacrifice. The gifter is, in essence, trading their life to heal another person. The gifter quite literally agrees to take on the sickness for that person—or at least that is what the book alludes to...It is not quite clear what happens to the gifter afterwards because..."

"Because they die." It was a statement, not a question.

"It is forbidden by our newer laws to ever attempt anything that would interrupt a person's connection with a life force. That is why we do not discuss Transfusion or even act as if it is a valid means of healing someone. But with your unique connection to four life forces..."

"You think it might not kill me to do it."

"Perhaps not, but of course, I do not *know* that. And even if you did not die, you could become very ill. It is a natural cause that whenever we heal someone, we experience their symptoms too."

"We do?" This was news to me.

"Well, yes...When you have healed others, did you not feel their pain or symptoms lingering in your own body for some time after?"

I thought about it for a minute. Healing Kevin, Caleb, Gabriel, Morgan...Yes, each time I had exhibited pain in different places— my head, my back, my stomach. I thought it had been the exertion of life forces leaving me sick.

"You're right. I never knew that's what was happening. Was I damaging myself every time I did that?"

"No," she explained. "We call it the Shadow Effect. You were feeling a shadow of their pain…like echoes within your own body. The pain is real for you, but the cause is not. That is why it takes years of training for Healers to be able to withstand and desensitize the Shadow Effect. I still have to take frequent breaks when assisting Priscilla, whereas she hardly notices it anymore." She sighed and leaned against the wall. "The only thing I do not know is if you would experience a Shadow Effect or the real problem."

"Wow." I rubbed my forehead thoughtfully. "Is it guaranteed to work? Would it heal Morgan completely?"

Lilley glanced again at the book. "Judging by the few cases documented here…yes." She paused and studied my expression. "Whitnee, I have known since I was very little that I wanted to be a Healer. I love the idea of bringing comfort and health to people who are suffering, and I have spent most of my life researching and preparing for the oaths I will take in a few months."

"And you could lose all of that because of me…"

"No, that is not my point." She stood up straight and pointed at the holographic book on the desk. "In all of my studying I have done in that book—about Water, about diseases, healing, Transfusion, and yes, even the Pilgrim—there is one repetitive phrase that continues to be used…the phrase 'in accordance with the Island.' I do not confess to understand that idea completely, but I do feel that every time I heal someone, it is as if the Island is agreeing with me and allowing it to happen. It feels like I am doing something that conforms to the will of the Island…And because the Island wills it, the healing works."

I started to nod slowly at what she was saying. "And you believe that the Island would 'agree with me' to heal Morgan this way?"

"I believe you have already been gifted 'in accordance with the Island.' I have a difficult time believing that was not for a reason."

Everything happens for a reason…

"If I did Transfusion, I would no longer have Water abilities, right?" I clarified.

"According to the book, that is correct. For all Dorians, that means death. For you...probably not."

"And that's it? I just give my Water life force to her, and she's healed?" It sounded so simple.

"It says there are two aspects to Transfusion. One is the offering—the part where the gifter is willing to sacrifice his or her life force." She surveyed the ancient page again. "The second part of the process comes from the other person—the acceptance."

"What do you mean?"

She shook her head in deep thought. "They have to be willing to *let* you trade your life for theirs. If you were to offer that to Morgan, she would have to accept..."

"And that must be the hard part," I finished for her. "Most dying people will not allow a healthy loved one to die in their place."

She nodded in agreement.

And then suddenly everything fit together in my mind. Everything Dad had said about the portals and the heart of the Island...everything I knew from Abrianna about "releasing" life forces...

What Abrianna was trying to accomplish with all four life forces was using the same principles as Transfusion. That was why she said Dad would die if he released his. That was why she told me—honestly so—that she could not just "take" my abilities...I had to be the gifter. But Dad could never be the gifter for her if she refused to *accept* his abilities...which she would never do, because she was in love with him and believed it would kill him.

I now knew the biggest problem with Abrianna's methods, though, was the phrase "in accordance with the Island."

That was when the solution to all these conflicts was suddenly perfectly clear. As crystal clear as pure Water, I knew with absolute certainty what I had to do to save Morgan *and* my dad.

After Lilley and I planned it out, she left the little office to prepare her part, and I snuck back to our darkened wing. We only had a few hours left before daybreak. And there was no telling when Dad and the others would return. My window of opportunity was very small.

As I came around the corner, I was surprised to see faint light spilling out from beneath Gabriel's door. And, once again, no Hydroguard was stationed there. The corridor was quiet and deserted, so I immediately burst into his room, hoping to find that he had come out of the coma.

My heart plummeted when I discovered an empty room. He was gone—even the bed was gone! I turned in circles, fear choking me. Something bad had happened or he would be here... Where had they taken him? What if he had died, and nobody could find me? The Hydroguard had probably already escorted the body away...

The thought of Gabriel dying alone in this room with nobody by his side brought on slight hysteria. My heart sped up, my eyes burned, and I felt lightheaded very quickly. Until I had that reaction standing there alone in the middle of that room, I had not realized just how much I had believed he would be okay. How much I wanted him and needed him to be okay...

"Gabriel...I'm so sorry..." I moaned helplessly and covered my face with my hands. There was no time to freak out right now. I had to find somebody...I needed to know what happened... Somebody needed to tell Dad and the others—

"What are you sorry for?" A deep voice like dark, delicious chocolate sounded from behind me, interrupting my panic attack.

I spun around in confusion only to find Gabriel leaning against the door to the bathing room, wiping his wet hair with a towel. And wearing nothing but drawstring pants tied around his muscled waist.

Oh. My. *Gosh.*

With a half-laugh, half-cry, I somehow spanned the length of the room in less than a second and threw myself at him. The impact flattened him against the wall, and he grunted sharply; I wasn't sure if it was from pain or from surprise. All I know is that just as fiercely he lifted me up into his arms and buried his face in my hair. I held onto him, noting his bare skin was all smooth and brown and back to its steamy temperature again.

"You're alive!" I cried happily. "You look so…"

There were not even words for how he looked. There probably should have been words…a whole lot more words. Because when he pulled back to say something, I didn't even let his first word out of his mouth before I was kissing those lips with a fiery passion I didn't know was in me.

There was no argument or hesitation from him whatsoever. He was awake and alive and, wow, just as passionate about kissing me back. His hands were on my back and then in my hair and…My mind was going completely blank.

I ran my fingers through his dripping hair before locking them together behind his neck, keeping his face pulled close to mine.

"*This*," he whispered between kisses, "was worth waking up to…"

"You scared me," I gasped, the amount of emotion intensifying within me. I planted little kisses along his jawline. "How do you feel?"

His eyes were warm and glassy as they met mine just a few inches away. "It would be improper to describe to you exactly how I feel right now, Little One," he answered, his voice thick.

Awww…He called me Little One. Extra points for that.

"Then let's not talk." I knew that everything about giving into these raw feelings was pushing me into the danger zone. But when his lips found mine again, I just—

WHITNEE!

I jerked away from Gabriel at his voice. Had it just been in my head or…? But poor Gabriel only looked confused by my sudden halt.

"What is it?" he asked, turning instead to brush kisses along my neck.

"Um…" I tried to clear my head. Maybe I had just imagined Dad's voice there—

If you do not leave that room RIGHT THIS SECOND, I will come in there and put that boy back into a coma! Dad threatened.

Oh, dear lord. My heart started racing for other reasons. I jerked out of Gabriel's arms and straightened my appearance. "I have to go…I mean, I think that my Dad…"

Gabriel smiled and reached for me again. "I am glad you found him. They said he was coming to get me."

"Really?!" My voice came out pinched. "Well, you could have warned me…*Geez*, Gabriel." I ran my fingers through my hair and looked about the room. Dad wasn't in there. And I didn't hear anyone nearby. "It's just that…he and I can communicate." I pointed to my head and made a "crazy" sign.

WHITNEE! came his angry voice again.

Good grief, Dad! I'm leaving! I called back in irritation.

Gabriel made a funny face. "Apparently I have missed quite a bit…I only know Michael told them I was awake, and now they want me on Simeon's ship."

"Um, okay." I fidgeted, darting glances at the door as I put more distance between him and me. "Why didn't you come tell me as soon as you woke up?"

"I am not…moving very quickly yet…" He nodded at a walking stick that I hadn't noticed propped up against the wall. My face must have registered fear because he was quick to say, "Do not worry…Michael believes I will be fully recovered soon. I was going to send the guard to find you before I left."

"Oh." I just stared at him, realizing for the first time he was still leaning on the wall for support. "Well, I'm glad it's all good news…it was terrifying—"

Tell Gabriel to meet me at the back of the Healing Center in five minutes! Dad barked.

With annoyance, I repeated obediently, "Dad says to meet him at the back of the Healing Center in five minutes."

"He said that just now?" Gabriel's thick eyebrows knitted together in confusion.

"Listen." I lowered my voice nervously. "My dad's really protective of me, so you might not want to tell him about…you know, this kind of stuff." I gestured between the two of us. "Not that it would come up or anything…but, well, you never know. I'm not telling you to lie or whatever; I'm just saying that he doesn't have to know everything…about you. And me. And the kissing…stuff."

Gabriel gave me a skeptical look. I was about to exit the room, but he just looked so dang good, and I just felt so *light* inside knowing he was okay…I ran across the room one last time and rose on my tiptoes to kiss him quickly on the lips. "For the record, I *really* missed you."

"I see that. And I look forward to exploring that topic more later." He grinned, his face practically glowing at my attention. I flashed one flustered smile at him before flying out of the room.

And running smack into Dad who was waiting for me in the hallway. Oops. I hadn't realized he was *right there.*

Not good.

He gripped me firmly by the elbow and began steering me away, his angry thought finding its way into my mind…*Too late. I already know about the kissing STUFF.*

I didn't reply, but allowed him to direct me to a private room away from all the sleeping patients on our hall. No sooner had he shut and locked the door did he spin around and explode at me.

"What are you thinking?! You are not allowed to…to *get involved* with somebody like *him!*" He pointed violently back down the hall.

I tried to remain calm…and innocent. "What are you talking about, Dad?"

"I'm talking about Gabriel! And you! I walked in and…there you were!" His face was bright red—with anger or embarrassment, I didn't know. But I could feel the same color creeping up my neck as I realized what he had seen. "I have got to get that image out of my head. I mean, good lord, Whitnee, does your mother know about…?"

"Know about what, Dad?" This was so completely awkward. I'm not sure which of us was more traumatized by the experience. "Does she know that I've kissed a guy on a magical Island that I happened to transport to this summer? What do *you* think?!"

"*I* think that there's no way I'm going to allow *that* to go on!" His eyes and gestures were wild as he sputtered, "He's Abrianna and Eli's son, and he's too old for you—"

"He's only two years older than—"

"Too old!" He snapped in a high-pitched voice. "And he's engaged—"

"Um, because of his parents' choice, not his—"

"And I don't even want to think about what he's thinking when he's…*arghh*!" Dad turned away from me and ran his hands over his head in aggravation. "Whitnee, there are things you don't understand about the way a guy's mind works—"

"Are you serious?" I cried in exasperation. "Dad, I'm seventeen years old!"

"Yeah, well, clearly there is still a lot you have to learn." I understood this was difficult for him, but *give me a break*. I was not a child! He continued with fervor, "And if I had been there, I would have had a lot more strict dating guidelines for you. I cannot even imagine your mother allowing—"

"But you *haven't* been there, Dad!" I erupted. "And there is clearly still a lot that you have to learn too! Quit assuming I'm some promiscuous girl with no standards and that Gabriel is some creeper who is only after one thing! You have *no* idea what that guy has sacrificed to help me survive on this Island. He's the one who helped me find *you*. Give him some credit!"

Dad took a deep breath and paced in front of me a few times. When he paused to speak, his intensity had lowered a notch. "Whitnee, you are a precious, beautiful, smart, amazingly gifted girl. I am sure that there are any number of boys out there you could choose." But then he threw his hands out dramatically and pointed back down the hall as he punctuated his words, "Just not *that one!*"

I glared back at him. He was being completely unfair, especially since I knew how complicated his own relationships were on the Island. Just to test his reaction, I said, "Gabriel cares about me, Dad. He wants me to stay here permanently on the Island with him."

"Of course he does!" Dad threw his hands up in the air. "Look at all the power you have!"

"Are you *implying* that he might do something like, I don't know, try to use his feelings to manipulate me into staying here and helping him govern the Island with my gifts?" I pointed out, lacing my words with double meaning. Dad paused and frowned at me. I took his silence as my cue. "Gabriel is *not* like his parents. You know that, Dad…you can see goodness in him. Just be honest about the fact that your real problem with Gabriel and me is that you don't want me to form any kind of emotional connection to this place. You want me to leave as soon as possible, don't you?"

The weight of my accusation hung heavy between us. I waited to see if he would lie or be honest with me about his intentions. Finally he spoke. "Yes and no. You-with-Gabriel is never going to be okay with me—for a *lot* of reasons. But, yes, I want you to leave. I don't want you burdened by the problems on this Island. I don't want people trying to use you and manipulate you because of your abilities. I don't want you limited, Whitnee! I want your choices to be your own."

"You say that, but you're trying to take away my choices…what if I wanted to be with Gabriel the rest of my life?" He opened his mouth in protest again, but I was quick to add, "I'm not saying I do, but what if? What if I felt just as responsible for what happens on the Island as you do? What if I wanted to be wherever you are, Dad? Would you take that choice away from me?"

"You do not know what you would be choosing," he pointed out harshly. "And as your father, there are still some choices I can make for you, Whitnee Skye."

That did it. "Listen, Dad. I mean this with respect..." I mustered up as much maturity as I could. "But I'm not the eleven-year-old girl you left behind. There are some choices you have to let me make for myself and trust that I'll do the right thing. I know that's hard for you because you haven't been around for six years. The only choice you should worry about right now is whether or not to be a part of my life again." He wouldn't meet my eyes, so I softened my voice. "Dad, I want you in my life! And if you want that, too, then I know we can figure out how to make it work...whether here or back at home. But if you let me go again, then you've lost the right to care about my choices."

His expression was absolutely torn as he looked at me. With a defeated shake of his head, he said quietly, "I have to go. But when I come back in a few hours, you and your friends should be ready to leave."

I dropped my gaze to the floor, realizing what he really meant. He came to me then and tried to hug me, but I didn't move. "I love you, Whitnee. I know you don't understand right now...and maybe you never will. But I love you too much to let you stay here." When I refused to return his hug, he pulled away and held the door open for me. "Go to your room now."

Outwardly I obeyed. But in my heart, the cry of rebellion had already begun.

"Are you certain you want to do this?" Lilley prompted me one last time. Her blue eyes were glowing across the dark room as she stirred the tub of Water in Morgan's room.

I stood over Morgan's bed and thought about Lilley's question. Was I certain I wanted to save my best friend's life? Absolutely.

Countless people had watched their friends or family members suffer from cancer, wishing they could do something about it. And here I was with a gift that could take it all away from her. It's not that I was some noble, self-sacrificing hero…I just happened to have the means to do what so many others only wished for. The only scary part was taking that leap of faith without knowing what specific fate would lie on the other side. If we did it right, Morgan would be healed. But what would happen to me? Neither Lilley nor I believed I would die…but death wasn't the only outcome to worry about. Was it wishful thinking to believe that I could accomplish something like this without side effects? It seemed to me that all difficult choices had their costs. I thought of Dad. He would never agree to this—none of the men in my life right now would—but I was doing it for him too.

"I am absolutely sure," I finally replied. I watched the Hydrodorian girl—only a couple of years younger than me—as she re-positioned the Water therapy tubes. "Are you sure about this, Lilley?" She was the one who would lose her future career over this.

"Yes," she said simply.

I had to ask. "Why are you willing to do this when it could get you in so much trouble?"

She looked up at me from her work, and her words were surprisingly thoughtful and passionate. "Because I believe that love and sacrifice are more important than following an oath that makes no sense. You can help your friend, so I am going to help you."

"And are you sacrificing your future out of love for me and Morgan—or your love for Thomas?"

Her hands froze momentarily at my insight. But instead of denying what I had figured out about her the first time we met, she said casually, "Thomas cares about Morgan."

"And you care about Thomas," I pointed out unnecessarily.

"I am not doing this just for him," she protested. "I believe in the Pilgrim and in everything this Island once held to be important. Since when did sacrificing on behalf of others become something we should not talk about or share?"

"I know, Lilley," I assured her. "You speak like a true Pilgrim Protector. And I am grateful for your help." We both took a deep breath at the same time, and I said, "Let's do this."

She nodded. "I have everything ready. Though it is not necessary for Transfusion to take place, I would prefer that both of you be in the Water. If something goes wrong, I will have better precision with the treatment."

If something goes wrong...great. Maybe I should have been concerned that I was placing my life and Morgan's into the hands of a fifteen-year-old Healer-in-training. But something about Lilley made her seem older and wiser than her age. And I really did believe the convictions she espoused about the Pilgrim. The girl's heart was pure.

"Help me with her..." I pulled the soft blankets away from Morgan who only stirred slightly. Together, Lilley and I lifted her off the mattress. It was no easy feat, even though Morgan was much lighter than I expected. How much weight had that girl lost? Trying to lower her gracefully into the Water was pretty much impossible.

This was when I really could have used Caleb's help. But after serious thought, I had opted to keep him in the dark about what I was doing. Not just because I worried he would discourage me from it—but because I wanted to keep Caleb's conscience clear of having to choose between Morgan's life and mine. I could not let him carry around any guilt if he went along with it and something bad happened. The only way to protect him was to let him sleep fitfully in his room. Lilley and I would be the only ones to blame if this went awry.

Morgan awoke from her drugged slumber when we settled her abruptly into the Water.

"Whit...? What're you doin'?" she slurred as we propped her up into a sitting position inside the little pool. We purposely kept the lights dim in the room so as not to alert anyone in the hallway. And we had locked the door so no one would be able to interrupt.

"It's okay, Morgie," I reassured her. Lilley tossed me the Water therapy patch with two tubes hanging from it.

"Place that around your stomach," she instructed and dipped one end of a tube into the pool of Water. The other she connected to a silver box. "I will be monitoring both of you the whole time. Hopefully you will only experience a Shadow Effect…But if there is any indication that a physical transfer of the Poison is taking place, I might be able to suction it out with Water before it takes root in you."

I did as she told me, asking skeptically, "You really think that would work?"

"I suppose we shall find out…" Her tone was solemn, but also alive with the kind of fascination that you only hear from doctors when they're given a new challenge or medical mystery to unravel.

"Lilley." I had a sudden thought I needed to clarify. "If you sense that the cancer—er, Poison—is transferring to me, and there's nothing you can do about it…please don't try to interrupt the Transfusion." She nodded slowly at me, accepting my will in the matter.

On that thought, I stepped inside the lukewarm pool water and lowered myself directly across from Morgan so that our legs overlapped. She gazed over at me as if trying to decide if she was dreaming.

"First, you have to offer her your gift. Then she has to accept it," Lilley narrated.

"Okay…Morgan, are you awake?" I sat up straight, the Water patch making me feel like I had high-rise pants on that were way too tight.

Morgan looked back at me in confusion. "I think so—am I? Why are we in the Water, Whitnee?" She brought her hands up out of the Water and let them drip in front of her face, staring at them in confusion.

"This is really important, so I need you to focus on me and listen, okay?" She dropped her hands back into the Water and zeroed in on my face. I wasn't quite sure if there were certain magical words to go with the offering or not. Nothing had been specified about that part in the Dorian Records. But I had a feeling that the Island didn't care for certain words—only for certain attitudes and motivations.

So I opened up my heart to her. "You are my best friend, Morgie, and I consider your life even more important than my own. In fact, I've always thought you were a better person than me. With all your peacemaking and unselfishness…I've always wanted to be more like you." Saying those words to her brought me to humble tears. I'm not sure I had ever told her that. I was more overcome with emotion about this moment than I realized, and I was not surprised to see her begin to cry with me. "I have something to give you, Morgie," I continued through my emotion. "I think that there's a way I can take away all the pain you've been in for so long…but you're going to have to trust me completely."

"Hold out your hands, Whitnee," Lilley reminded me softly, her own hands dipped readily into the pool.

I held up my hands, palms facing out at Morgan. "If you will accept my gift of healing to you, then take my hands."

Morgan sobbed as she stared back at me in exhaustion. "I thought they couldn't heal the Poison here…am I dreaming?"

"No. This is real. I can help you, but you have to let me."

"Whitnee…there's nothing you can do—"

"Morgan, please! Just let me help *you* for once. Give me your hands!" I begged.

She squeezed her eyes shut, and more tears ran down her cheeks. Then she slowly reached both hands out and pressed her palms to mine. Our fingers laced and locked together.

And Transfusion began…all on its own.

As if the Island had been waiting for this moment.

At first, it just felt like a growing pressure on my chest…but then as the Water in the pool bubbled and gurgled and flashed around us, it became more like a piece of myself was being torn away like duct tape ripped off of sensitive skin. It took my breath away—painful and terrifying all at once.

I don't remember much except that it felt like it took hours, even though I had no concept of time after thirty seconds of the experience. I think Morgan and I both were screaming at one point. And Dad was there…or at least his voice was in my head, shouting. Panicking. Questioning. He could sense exactly what was happening but could do nothing to stop my rebellion against him.

*Now I'm not a threat…*I think I tried to reassure him in the middle of the chaos. *Abrianna can't use me against you…you're free. And so is Morgan.* But I don't know if my words ever made it to his mind. I could hear Lilley, of course…and sometimes even feel her pulling on me or sending me doses of her life force. Everything became a blur of pain and energy. Eventually I lost my vision and my hearing.

I was drowning in Water and so very thirsty at the same time. I was freezing cold and yet radiating blasts of heat. My whole body was being shredded and reconstructed.

Baby Doll, what have you done…? Dad's fearful voice was there. *Just hang on. I'm coming…*

Right before I crossed over into a terrifying abyss of darkness, I cried, *Please don't send me away, Daddy.*

SECOND CHANCE

I am not eloquent like Whitnee. I don't have philosophical deep thoughts, and even when I do, I lack the best ways to express them. But there are two things in life that I now know: (A) You never know—and I mean, *never* know—what the next day will bring you, whether good or bad. And, (B) Second chances are like forgiveness, like a brand new, shiny start at making things better. If you're ever given a second chance at life, *don't waste it.*

My second chance started the moment I stood up in that pool of Water, and Whitnee didn't. I was in shock—I couldn't even speak as I took in everything happening around me. The Water rolled off of me differently—as if it were not just dripping on my skin, but inside me too. Something inside my body felt...*new.*

There was shouting and banging on the door until it finally exploded off its hinges, and all these people sloshed into the room, which had flooded in the violent wake of energy. I was still in shock, even as Nathan helped Lilley hold unconscious Whitnee's head above water. Even as Gabriel (um, Gabriel was awake?) brightened the room with light. Even as Simeon helped me out of the pool, threw a towel over me, and made me sit on the bed...

I watched with surreal detachment as Nathan and Lilley laid hands on Whitnee, trying to revive her. Everyone was moving about the room in a flutter of panic, barking questions and looking for answers. I had none...I had no idea what Whitnee had just done. Priscilla and Michael shoved their way through the crowd and blocked my view of my best friend when they knelt down. There was a lot of blue light and a lot of Water. At some point, Caleb came to my side. I think he was asking me questions, but I wasn't hearing them.

"I tried to pull it all out..." Lilley was muttering as she checked the connections on the tubes.

"I feel Poison," Priscilla declared, her hands glowing blue on Whitnee's abdomen. This startled everybody in the room. All eyes turned toward me, and I just stared back in utter astonishment.

"Morgan did not know. I take the blame for this," Lilley stated, her chin held high.

Priscilla started yelling at Lilley while Michael tried to explain to Gabriel and the others something about a "transfusion." Caleb was simultaneously listening to them and commenting to me. That was when Thomas entered and flanked my other side with arms that tried to comfort me. The noise and chaos level of the room was starting to break into my awareness. Why did I have a horrible feeling that whatever had just happened was my fault?

Suddenly, with a cry of mourning and frustration, Nathan threw his hands out, and all the Water in the pool parted dramatically away from Whitnee, like Moses parting the sea. The room grew silent at the display of Water life force skills that had come from Whitnee's dad...who we thought was just an Aerodorian all this time.

"Nathan...?" Ezekiel spoke in wonder.

Nathan ignored him and the stares of everyone in the room. He stepped down into the damp pool, picked up his unconscious daughter, and carried her out of the room.

Ezekiel and Gabriel tried to follow, but I heard him call back down the hall. "Leave me." Then the Water spilled back into the pool, splashing all of us.

That was my breaking point. The shock came crashing down as I realized there was one more thing I now knew...(C) A true best friend will love you to the end—even to the point of giving up her life for you.

"I cannot find it." Priscilla shook her head in frustration, smoothing my tunic back down over my stomach and putting her hands on her hips.

"You mean the Poison is gone?" Simeon clarified.

"It appears to be," she said as if this was the worst news ever. "Of course, it could be temporarily hidden...could return when she goes back to the Mainland...could be all kinds of explanations except really gone."

"Or she could have been totally and completely healed by Whitnee through Transfusion," Simeon responded quietly, patting my hand reassuringly.

"I would like to run more tests after I speak with Lilley," she told me and exited the room in a huff.

"Is Lilley in trouble for this?" I worried.

Simeon shrugged. "Depends on the outcome, I suppose...I will watch how Priscilla handles her apprentice before I step in. Lilley is one of the brightest Healers we have had come along—she shows great promise."

"And what has happened to Whitnee?" It was all I wanted to know from the moment Nathan carried her out of there.

"Mr. Terradora has not come out of her room and refuses to let anyone else in. So...we don't know." Caleb spoke up from where he leaned against the wall, his arms folded over his chest. His eyes met mine, and the fear passed between us with just one look.

"I promise I didn't know what she was doing...she just said she wanted to help me, and I needed to accept it. So I trusted her. Caleb, are you mad at me?" I sat up in the bed, not taking my eyes off of him.

"Of course not." He sighed.

"Whitnee will be just fine," Simeon assured us. "She could not have performed Transfusion unless the Island gave her permission. People like Whitnee and Nathan receive special revelations from the Island. It guides both of them in their choices." He struggled to his aged feet, and Caleb came around to help him up.

"What do we do now, sir?" Caleb asked.

Simeon grasped Caleb's shoulder. "I do believe you will be leaving soon. I would make sure you have all of your belongings together. Say your goodbyes." He glanced at me meaningfully. "And leave here knowing that all of your hard work the last few days has made quite an impact on our Island. I am hopeful for the future now that so much of the hidden evil has been brought into the light. You will be praised among Pilgrim Protectors for years to come." He smiled, but Caleb and I just couldn't conjure return smiles. Our hearts were hurting and overwhelmed.

Simeon gripped my shoulder gently with his other hand. "Morgan, you have been given a second chance. More than anybody else on this Island right now, you understand what true love and sacrifice mean. I suggest you hold your head high and never forget the gift that was given to you. Fear is your only enemy now."

I nodded as I stared into his piercing, clear blue eyes. "Yes, sir."

"I must meet with the others. We are set to confront Abrianna and Eli in just an hour—before the last day of the Festival kicks off. If all goes according to plan, you will be walking through that portal by mid-morning. Just be ready." And he shuffled out of the room.

I jumped from the bed to my feet, feeling an energy in my body that I hadn't felt in months...maybe even years. I walked straight into Caleb's arms and pressed my cheek to his shoulder. He hugged me back, and we just stood there for a moment in silence.

"Is your cancer really gone? Do you feel any different at all?" he finally whispered.

"Yes. I feel like a new person, Caleb," I responded timidly, worried that this would upset him...worried that he'd rather have Whitnee healthy and happy in his arms instead of me.

But he just squeezed me back and sighed, "Thank God."

A smile touched the corners of my mouth. Yes, my heart was doing a lot of thanking right then.

"I still do not understand why you have to leave so quickly," Thomas muttered as we strolled hand in hand along the river. It felt so good to be outside—especially after eating a big, yummy breakfast. I couldn't remember the last time I had eaten and not felt sick immediately afterwards.

I tried to explain my thoughts to him. "Because if I'm going back, I have to go now...before my parents find out I'm gone. I have doctors' appointments all week."

"But you are healed now."

"We *think* I'm healed...but I will feel better when the doctors confirm that for my parents." I thought of Whitnee lying sick and immobile in her room. Nathan had allowed only Caleb, Amelia, and me to see her, refusing to explain or speak to us beyond a warning that she needed quiet. He had just left for the Tetrarch Council meeting, but only after they had doubled up on Hydroguards in and around the Healing Center. Caleb was the one who had encouraged me to get some fresh air. Everybody kept assuring me I should not feel guilty about Whitnee's state.

But of course I did.

I had asked Thomas to fill me in more about his village and their Festival of Springs traditions, so we had headed north toward the Waterpark. It was risky to be out in the open like we were, but with my hair dyed dark this year and my skin glazed with a summer tan, I could easily blend in with the Dorians. Except for the occasional worker, most of the Festival action was taking place downriver where the parade would start later.

Thomas finally questioned, "Do you not wish to stay here on the Island with me?" His voice was insecure, and it caused me to look up into his boyish face. Those sparkling blue eyes of his would not meet mine, and I felt terrible about the fact that I had been willing to stay when it was only to die here.

"You know, Caleb pointed out that my wish to stay on the Island was just me being afraid and running away from my problems." I gazed back out over the lapping of the river on the shore. The grass was still glittering with morning dew as the sun stretched out a lazy good morning greeting across the water. I continued thoughtfully, "He was right. I wanted to find a place to die without having to deal with all the other aspects of it. It was actually really selfish of me... selfish to do that to my family, my friends...and to ask that of you. I just didn't realize it until my friends confronted me."

"You did not answer my question...How do you feel? About me?" Thomas pushed.

"Thomas, I feel a lot of things for you." I smiled up at him. "I'm so attracted to you, it's ridiculous. I feel gratitude to you for being there for me during one of the darkest summers of my life. You took care of me, and you didn't question my wishes. Ever. If I wanted to stay here—and I mean, if I really wanted to stay for the right reasons—I know you would have made that happen. And I know that if I want to go home for the right reasons that you'll support that too."

"I do not want you to leave," he blurted.

I tilted my head sympathetically. "Thomas, can I ask you something?"

"Yes."

"If you could go back to the Mainland with me and make a life there, would you do it?"

He glanced over at me with uncertainty. "As much as I would want to be with you, that would be difficult. I feel like I belong *here*, Morgan."

I nodded with understanding. "And I feel like I belong on the Mainland."

There was an uncomfortable silence between us as we drew closer to the Waterpark. Finally, he stopped and pulled me forward so we could face each other directly.

"So what happens when two people who care about each other belong in two different places?"

I stared at him sadly. "It sucks, doesn't it?"

Suddenly, he leaned over and kissed me. His hands were still holding onto mine at our sides, and I just allowed myself to feel the moment. I loved the way he smelled, the way he tasted, the way his kiss felt as magical as the land itself.

When he slowly pulled back, he stared into my face for a moment. I memorized his thoughtful expression and the exact shade of cerulean that his eyes had become with the river and sky in the backdrop.

"What will you do when you get back?" he asked softly.

"I've got some things I need to let go of...some things I need to change in my life," I said truthfully. I thought of Carrie, and all the fears and doubts I had carried with me for too long. It was time for change. "And if the cancer really is gone...I'm going to make my last year in high school the best one of my life. What about you? What's next for your life, Thomas?"

"I plan to stay involved with the Pilgrim Protectors...help turn things around on this Island. I enjoy Water purification and the way my job allows me to travel to the villages so frequently. But who knows? Gabriel has mentioned some ideas he has for me once he becomes the Guardian next year...I guess we shall see."

"Maybe he wants you to train the Water Beast," I teased.

He grinned. "And you thought I was just telling you an old myth."

With a laugh, I exclaimed, "Whatever! You were the one who said it wasn't real. That thing was definitely real!" I started chanting the *Jaws* theme music again, and this time he joined me. I reached out and tickled him, enjoying immensely how he jerked away with laughter. "You know, you really are too flirty for your own good," I told him.

"So are you, my blue-eyed Traveler."

"I try not to get serious in relationships."

"Me too!" He looked at me as if he had never before seen the similarities between us. But I had seen them. I had known that, while his feelings for me seemed real to him, they were also driven by the fascination of another world. "But I could have allowed myself to get serious about you, Morgan," he admitted softly.

"Me too," I agreed, with a bit of regret.

"No matter what happens," Thomas said, throwing a playful arm around my shoulders and directing me forward again into the Waterpark. "I will always remember the way you flirted with *me*. And if you ever come back, it should continue to be a tradition of ours."

"Deal. From one flirt to another." I laughed, the uncomfortable pressure of saying goodbye to him releasing somewhat. But that was before my eyes found an alarmingly familiar person lurking around the Waterpark, acting as if he was part of the crew setting up for the Festival activities there tonight. I immediately pulled Thomas in front of me to hide my face. I didn't know if the man had spotted me yet.

"What is it?" Thomas was confused.

"Just act normal," I shushed him, peeking over his shoulder as the man sauntered further away. "There's a man over there named Jude. He's one of the rebels from the tank—the one who drugged Whitnee when they kidnapped her. What do you think he's doing here?"

Thomas immediately tensed up. "I do not know, but I would not be so naïve as to believe it is innocent. Should we follow him?"

Normally, I would have said no. But my days of fearful hesitation were over. With a nod, we started to stroll casually after him. Thomas pointed out little facts about the Waterpark, all of its winding Water rides and tubes twisting in what seemed like dangerous and high-impact drop-offs and curves. I feigned extreme interest in every word, while we trained our eyes watchfully on Jude's progress further into the park. He took a deserted path that led up a hill. Thomas halted my progress.

"Maybe you should go back and get help. I will keep following him."

"What? Heck no, we're not letting him get away. If they're planning something, we need to know what it is—especially since the Tetrarch Council is meeting and making major changes *this morning*."

"Very well. But please be careful. Here." He grasped my hands as if to gift me with Water life force...but nothing happened. We stared at each other in confusion. His hand was lit up, but it was as if my body would not accept it.

"No time!" he growled. "Stay behind me."

We started up the winding hill, the sounds of rapids approaching. When we reached the top, Jude was no longer in sight. Only the entry point for what looked like an adventurous water slide stood before us.

"Do you think he went down the slide?" I mused, turning around in circles. But no sooner had the words escaped me than a Water spear shot out straight at Thomas's heart. I reacted so quickly, I almost didn't know it was me who counteracted the spear with my own defensive shot. The two forces hit with the deafening sound a wave makes just as it breaks. Thomas and I both fell backwards with the impact of the splash but quickly righted ourselves, hands outstretched in defense.

Jude stepped out from behind a tree, his own hands ready to attack. "So..." he said, sizing me up. "You made it out alive. I thought you would be dead by now, as sick as you were."

Thomas conjured another Water attack, which Jude deflected just as quickly.

"Tell your boyfriend to settle down, or we will kill both of you," Jude warned, and that was the cue for a man and a woman I did not recognize to appear from the trail behind us. They stood there like guards, blocking our way back down.

"Why are you here?" I questioned.

"Our business is not finished. Now both of you are going to come quietly with us if you want your lives spared."

I barely glanced at Thomas before he called, "Fish Out of Water!"

Fish Out of Water...a ridiculously-named attack plan we had constructed during our training. I knew exactly what to do. I thrust my arms back and then pulled forward every ounce of Water from the rapids behind me like a heavy blanket. The Water reacted violently, and pushed me straight up on its curling wave. Thomas dove with

263

a headfirst flip right into the towering wave beneath me. The Water became a shield that allowed him to shoot rapid, bullet-like Water attacks from within. Meanwhile, I aimed my Water spears perfectly from up high, and all three of our enemies were on the ground before they could even react. With an artistic little spin move I had created, I released the wave and landed steadily on my feet beside Thomas who was soaking wet and catching his breath. I held up a dripping hand for a high-five—a Mainland tradition I had taught him—and he slapped it with a sigh of relief.

"Way to go with the quick thinking," I complimented him. "Now, how do we get these guys back to our people?" I was in awe by the fact that I wasn't out of breath or energy after such exertion.

"We could send them down the ride and then use Water to project them onto the shore..." he suggested. "Speaking of Water...how were you able to do all of that? Did somebody already gift you?"

"Um..." I spoke slowly as I contemplated how different it had felt using life force this time. "I think that Whitnee permanently gifted me. I mean, I can't explain it, but I feel like a real Hydrodorian. It's not like a gas tank that needs filling anymore...It's like, fully *connected* now."

He didn't know what to say so he just smiled and shook his head. "That is quite a gift—" But his words were interrupted when a Water spear hit him in the stomach and sent him hurtling backwards—right into the rapids.

LOOSE ENDS

"Thomas!" I screamed as the Water whooshed him away too quickly. He was gasping and holding his abdomen when he disappeared from view. Jude rose to his feet and the two other people were stirring from their positions on the ground.

Time to go.

I flew through the air and launched myself into the rapids after Thomas. Jude shot another spear, but it missed me as I landed painfully on the body slide. I was tossed around a sharp turn that propelled my body high up on the walls of the slide. Water sprayed in my face, and I could feel myself picking up speed. Had I not been terrified of being under attack, I might have been thrilled by this ride.

I hollered Thomas's name again, and I thought I heard him call back to me. I would have tried to push myself faster to catch up to him, but that seemed like a dangerously stupid thing to do given the pace that I was traveling.

The ride dropped down steeply through a black tunnel with racing multi-colored lights in the ceiling, clearly designed to give the appearance that you were moving faster than you actually were. Darn those Pyras for helping the Hydros make everything in this village! I lost my stomach somewhere back at the top of the tunnel, and I couldn't help releasing a scream as I raced through the darkness.

Finally a light appeared at the end of the tunnel...and no, I don't mean that figuratively. I was relieved to know I'd at least be able to see where I was again. But unfortunately, that was the end of the ride. I shot so fast out of the tunnel that I flew through the air, my arms and legs flailing at the sudden fifty-foot drop-off into the river.

Yep. I screamed again before I hit the Water.

When I finally came up for air, Thomas was trying to stay afloat. He was in an obvious amount of pain. In fact, there was a murky, bloody cloud in the water around him. There were people shouting at us from above. Obviously, the Waterpark was not supposed to be in use. Jude came flying out of the tunnel after us, but he somehow manipulated the Water to give him a softer fall. Then he was moving abnormally fast toward me in the river. I began to swim away with the aid of Water life force.

I forced a rolling wave in Thomas's direction and propelled him carefully away from danger toward the shore, like I had with Whitnee in the ocean. It was much easier to accomplish that in the fresh water of the river. Once Thomas was safely on shore, I directed my attention to Jude who was almost on my heels.

The anger that filled me then at what he had done to both Whitnee and now to Thomas was the edge I needed. I halted unexpectedly, used the Water life force to propel myself up out of the river, and performed a mid-air back flip that positioned me directly behind him.

He had barely turned around when I yelled, "You should have gotten rid of me in the tank!" And then with both hands, I swirled the Water around him, wrapping it like tentacles around his body. His arms were caught at his sides as the tentacles twisted tightly up to his neck. He looked frightened for the first time, unable to control the Water. He fought hard against it, but for once, I was the stronger one. With great force I never could have conjured before, I blasted him right out of the river where he landed near Thomas and struck his head hard enough on the ground that it knocked him out. The cords of my Water life force remained a prison around him.

Thomas lifted his head off the ground, blood seeping out through his hand, and stared at me in awe. "Morgan, you really are a flirt.

That kind of power makes me want to kiss you again," he joked. I reached his side, kissed him roughly since he had mentioned it, and then helped heal some of his pain.

Jude was still unconscious. But I won't lie. Justice felt good.

By the time we handed Jude over to Hydroguards and explained what had happened—giving detailed descriptions of the other two rebels who were still loose—the Tetrarch Council had returned to the Healing Center equally victorious. They were accompanied by Gabriel, Eden and Levi—even Hannah came out of her room to greet everyone. Her burns had been healed, but she was scarred all along her neck and arm.

We were quickly informed that Abrianna and Eli had been cooperative and willing to shut down the rebel operation they had admitted to forming as a "puppet" terrorist group. They also agreed to release the Pilgrim Protectors who had been taken captive the other night. Unfortunately, though, three Protectors had been killed—including Jeremiah, the Pyra who had found the cabin—and Eli and Abrianna claimed to not know Tamir's whereabouts at that point.

Gabriel would be overseeing the task of locking up those rebels who were at large and considered dangerous. Abrianna had agreed to send us home immediately and had already headed back to the Palladium to prepare the portal. The Council agreed to keep quiet publicly about Abrianna and Eli's corruption as long as they continued to cooperate with them in private. They felt that it was better for the people's morale to protect the reputation of their Guardian. There were specific trusted delegates from each tribe (Pilgrim Protectors, by our label) that would be moving into the Palladium indefinitely to keep watch over affairs while the Council cleaned house of all the deception that had been going on for years.

It became clear that these changes would take a lot of time. For years, the Guardian had been given so much control that I wouldn't be surprised if it took years to clean up. It had been decided that Nathan's presence on the Island would remain secret from the people for now until they could figure out the best way to handle it—"one mess at a time" seemed to be the motto.

And speaking of messes...Despite all the good that had been accomplished, and all the successes in a relatively short time, Whitnee's situation still cast a cloud of uncertainty and fear over our group. Caleb reported that she still had not come out of it, but had been going back and forth between vomiting, fever, chills, and terrors in her sleep. He was pretty shaken up—especially when Nathan called Amelia, Caleb, Ezekiel, and me into Whitnee's room for a private gathering. I did not miss the fact that Nathan never included Gabriel.

It was also the first time I had heard Nathan speak more than a few words at a time since he had found Whitnee in the healing pool. And what he had to say did not make me feel much better.

"In just a few minutes, you will be leaving by thunderfly to go to the Palladium. Ezekiel will be going with you, along with a few of your other friends. Under no circumstances are you to try to change plans or *not* leave this Island immediately. Do you understand?" Caleb, Amelia, and I nodded at his parental tone. I glanced at Whitnee who was curled up into a sleeping ball under the covers. Every once in a while, I could see her start to shake with little tremors. I wondered how we would be transporting her and what would happen once we were back on the other side of the river at Camp Fusion.

Nathan kept one hand protectively on her head as he spoke. His voice grew soft at his next words, as if he was delivering bad news. "I am not ready to send Whitnee home with you yet. She is going to stay here—"

"But, sir—" Caleb interrupted as Amelia and I gasped. Ezekiel remained quiet at the news. But Nathan held up a patient hand.

"I know that scares you, but I am not keeping her here permanently—I *promise*." He looked Caleb right in the eyes. "She belongs at home with you and her mother. But I need a little more time with my daughter before she goes back and I never see her again."

"I guess that means you're not coming back with her." Caleb's voice was almost robotic at this realization.

"That's not fair, Mr. Terradora!" Amelia spoke up vehemently. "The whole reason we came back was to find you! Whitnee deserves a daddy at her graduation and her wedding and...Why are you doing this to her?"

The pain on Nathan's face at Amelia's words stirred my heart. "Amelia, be respectful," I warned.

"Some things just can't be explained easily, Amelia." He gave a regretful sigh and then looked into our eyes one at a time. "I will never be able to thank each of you enough for being such loyal friends to Whitnee. Even though I cannot leave the Island, you have given me something I never thought I'd have again...a chance to see my daughter." Then he smiled comfortingly at Amelia. "You might have thought you were coming here to take me back, but you really came here to bring me hope. And I will cherish each one of you in my heart for the rest of my days."

We didn't know what to say. Things just weren't playing out the way we expected. Nathan continued, "I need you to do a few more things for me. When you get home, please go straight to Whitnee's mom and tell her everything you know. If Ben is still alive and well— and let's hope and pray that's the case—then tell him and Serena that exactly three days from tonight, Whitnee will be coming back through that portal and to be ready for her."

I thought Caleb looked like the sick one then as he sat there listening to these instructions. "Caleb." Nathan addressed him carefully. "I need you to tell Serena that—" he cleared his throat, "—that Whitnee is going to need some medical attention when she gets home. Serena needs to be prepared mentally and emotionally to help Whitnee deal with some lingering cancer in her system."

"What!" I cried, my eyes welling up instantly with guilty tears. "No! No, I didn't want her to take the cancer from me...Please tell me that's not true!" I broke down into horrified sobs. How could Whitnee do that?! I would never have allowed it...never trusted her...

Nathan left Whitnee's side and came to me. I couldn't even look at him out of guilt. "Mr. Terradora," I sobbed. "I'm so sorry...I didn't know. I didn't know what was happening." He placed tender arms around me and patted my back.

"Morgan, this is not your fault—"

"Yes, it is! How can you say that?! I'm the one who had the cancer...and now I don't!"

"Morgan!" Nathan pulled back and made me look into his kind, gray eyes that were so much like Whitnee's, it hurt. There was no condemnation there, none of the blame I expected to see for giving his daughter cancer. "You need to listen to me. Whitnee does not have the advanced cancer that you had. Lilley was able to siphon most of it out of her body. What is left there seems very treatable, especially if they treat it now."

"No..." I whimpered.

"She saved your life, Morgan. And she will eventually be okay, too. If you walk around with guilt, then you're cheapening the gift that my daughter gave you. She did it because you're important to her, and she loves you. She wanted you to live a full and meaningful life, free from the burden of disease." He shook me slightly when I still refused to accept the truth. With gentleness, he said, "Sweet Morgan...guilt and fear can be a cancer too. Don't let it replace the cancer that was in your body. Promise me?"

I wasn't sure how to *not* feel guilty at this point. But I knew what he meant. I couldn't get rid of one enslaving chain in my life just to replace it with another. I had to keep my mind and emotions healthy this time.

I just nodded at him and leaned into his arms one last time. I truly trusted Whitnee's father. If he said it, I believed it. If he said her cancer was treatable, I believed him. And if he believed it was best for Whitnee to stay three days with him, then I would trust him.

After that, we were each given privacy with Whitnee to say our own goodbyes, even though she probably wouldn't hear or remember. While the others went first, I sought out a piece of paper and something to write with. I wasn't always great with words, but I needed to leave her a note—something she would have to read when she woke up...something that she would most definitely remember.

Quickly I scribbled my words down, tears blurring my vision the whole time. When I finished, I folded it up and waited my turn to say goodbye. Thomas found me in the hallway. He was looking much better now that he had changed out of his bloody, torn tunic.

"Are you going with us to the portal?" I asked.

"Of course. I want to be there this time when my blue-eyed Traveler leaves my world." He winked, but then he grew more serious. "Do you think you will ever come back, Morgan?"

I shrugged. "I certainly don't know the future." With a smile, I added, "At least I'm not planning to die anytime soon, so...you never know."

He smiled back and kissed the top of my head. And it was comfortable between the two of us. I was sad to leave him the same way I would be sad to leave any new friend who meant something to me. But my world wasn't ending.

"How is she doing?" Levi asked as he joined us in the hallway.

"Still won't wake up," I told him glumly.

"I am sorry you have to leave...especially before she wakes up," Levi said comfortingly. "But do not worry. Whitnee has already proven she is a fighter." He patted my shoulder and then started to walk away. As if he had a second thought, he turned back around and there was a smile on his face. "Morgan?"

"Hmm?"

"I like big butts, and I cannot lie."

For a second, I thought I had misunderstood him. Surely Levi did not just quote Sir Mix-A-Lot. But his smile was so mischievous that I realized he had said exactly what I thought he said. We both burst into laughter at the same time. Thomas just looked confused.

"I am going to kill Whitnee when she wakes up!" I shook my head in amusement.

"I was supposed to surprise you with it at some point...now seemed like a good time." He laughed again. "You Mainlanders listen to some strange music." And then he walked away. *Oh, Whitnee,* I thought, smiling to myself.

Thomas gave me an inquiring look. "Don't ask," I told him with a final shake of my head.

When Nathan came around the corridor as Levi disappeared, I made a spur-of-the-moment decision to offer him something. "Mr. Terradora," I called out and met him a few feet away from Thomas. He raised his eyebrows in question. I fidgeted with the note in my hands. "Um, I was wondering if there was any other message you wanted me to pass on to your wife? I mean, if there was anything you wanted Serena to know specifically from *you,* I would be happy to tell her. I know she misses you...and I just thought..." I trailed off, feeling kind of awkward now that I had brought it up.

Nathan nodded slowly at my words. Finally, he replied, "Tell her that I love her, and I'm really proud of her. And tell her..." He paused and shifted his gaze to the floor before looking back at me. "Tell her that I'll meet her on the other side someday. She'll know what that means." And then he turned away kind of quickly, as if to hide any emotion. He got halfway down the hall before he turned back around and said sincerely, "Thank you, Morgan."

I tried to smile, but then Caleb came out of Whit's room, his eyes red-rimmed. Poor Caleb was in agony over all of this. Apparently, he and Whitnee had a fight last night and his last words haunted him. I grabbed his hand and squeezed it sympathetically as he passed me without a glance.

It was a solemn affair when I entered Whitnee's room by myself. Knowing I was leaving her evoked very different feelings than leaving Thomas. I approached her bed quietly and stared down at her as she slumbered. The most disturbing thing to me was not the greenish pallor of her skin or the occasional expression of pain that crossed her face. No, it was the fact that the halo of light I had seen around her since we had been here was now gone.

I brushed the stray hair from her face and then placed the folded note by her bed with her handwritten name facing up. I had even drawn the little flower blossom around the dot of the 'i' in her name—

the way she always signed it. I decided I was not going to use this time with her to say goodbye.

Instead, I choked out, "See you in three days, okay, Whit?" And then I rushed out of there before I could sink into depressing, fearful thoughts.

I might have said more or stayed longer had I known that it would end up being a lot longer than three days before I would see my best friend again.

RESTORATION

A FISH AND A DYING WISH

Dad! Are you there?!
   Right here, Baby Doll... Can you open your eyes? Whit?

Oh my gosh, it hurts so bad! What's happening to me?!
You're sick, Baby Doll. Tell me where it hurts...
Everywhere! Am I dying? Make it stop!
Hold on, Whitnee...hold on...

Daddy, wait! Don't get on that plane! You can't go to Hawaii...
you can't leave us...
   Shhh. It's okay. You're just dreaming. I'm not leaving.

Whitnee, we're giving you another Water treatment...Can you
hear me in there?
   Is Morgan okay?
   She's perfectly healthy. You healed her, Baby Doll.
   Oh, good...Tell her how much she matters—she listens to you.
   I will.

Dad, I need something.
Anything, Baby Doll.

If you love me, please don't make me leave the Island yet. I need more time with you.

…Okay, Whitnee.

Something was weird. I felt off-balance…like the feeling you get when you spin in the same direction for too long and try to walk to your left but your body propels you instead to the right. And then you fall.

I woke up alone, stood too quickly, and then fell hard on the stone floor of my room.

I landed on my elbow, and when I instinctively grabbed it, my other hand came back slick with blood. I tilted my arm so I could see the damage and had a sudden flashback to the moment I woke up on this Island the first time. Same injured elbow, same oozing blood.

I crawled dizzily over to the pool of Pure Water in the center of my room. The effort that it cost me was almost ridiculous. By the time I lowered my arm into the Water and watched the blood spread out like vanishing smoke, I was exhausted and felt ready to pass out. Like it was second nature, I conjured the Water life force to heal my boo-boo…

But I felt nothing. There was no connection with Water—at all. And trying to feel for it just made me sicker. I snapped my fingers, and a flame burst forth and landed in the pool with sizzling steam. That confirmed it. I still had life force abilities…except for one.

That was when I vomited into the pool with no warning at all. And it was the most painful kind of heaving I'd ever experienced…like my major organs were trying to shove their way out of their happy little home inside my body.

"Oh! You're awake. It's okay…it's okay!" Dad came running in and threw himself down beside the tub where I was sprawled. He held my hair back out of my face and tried to soothe me until I was finished. Not that much actually came up—but the hurling was painful enough without it. I splashed Water on my face and in my mouth before rolling over on my back to catch my breath.

Finally, I gasped with a hoarse voice. "I don't have Water life force anymore. It's gone."

"I figured." Dad smoothed my forehead as he sat beside me. Then he carefully inspected my bleeding elbow. When his hand connected with mine, there was nothing there—no flash of power or energy between us anymore. Something about that fact gave me a dreadful feeling inside. I know he noticed it too, but instead of commenting, he simply placed a cool hand in the Water and then pressed it to my arm.

This time, he was the one who healed the gash for me.

"You can use all four life forces," I stated. "Why didn't you tell me?"

"Nobody knew."

"Except for Abrianna?"

He cocked one eyebrow and nodded. "But I can't combine them like you. I can just use them one at a time…the way you did out at the spring."

Well, that was an interesting distinction.

"Now I only have three." I sighed.

"Are you sure you still have the others? Have you tried?" he asked doubtfully.

I flicked another little flame up into the air and then used Wind to spin it in a circle above our heads. As it fell back down, I conjured a little green Earth shield for it to detonate against. The whole demonstration took me a total of thirty seconds, and when I was done, I felt sick again.

"Easy there, Show-Off," Dad remarked when he saw my face scrunch up in pain. "Let's get you back up into that bed."

"I don't want to get back in bed. Help me stand up for a bit."

Though he was skeptical, he helped me to my feet. I lost my balance again when the room tilted before my eyes.

"Ah. I see how the elbow injury happened now." Dad grinned. "Get back in bed, you stubborn thing. I bet once you eat and drink something, some of these symptoms will get better."

As he helped me back over to the bed, I mused aloud, "So, Transfusion must have worked, if I don't have Water abilities and Morgan is all better. But now I'm wondering what exactly is wrong with me." Dad's face turned grim, and I made him stop moving and look at me. The Here Comes Bad News Look was back. "Dad? Did Morgan's cancer spread to me?"

He hesitated, but must have decided that beating around the bush wouldn't help. "A little. Lilley was able to stop most of it from transferring."

I was stunned. "So...am I dying now?"

"No, Baby Doll. You'll be fine—it's a very treatable amount. If not, I would have sent you home immediately."

"Are you mad at me for what I did?"

"It's hard to be mad when your daughter shows just how loving and unselfish she can be," he answered.

"I had selfish reasons too..." I admitted. "I want my best friend around for a long time. And I want a relationship with my dad that doesn't revolve around protecting me from people who are after my abilities."

"I'm pretty sure I understand all the reasons you did it, Whitnee. That doesn't mean I like this at all." He sounded worn out. "But I do understand."

"I was prepared for the worst, just in case. But still...I can't believe I actually have cancer now," I breathed, letting him direct me back to the bed again. "I want to see Morgan. Where is she?"

"They left this morning."

I blinked at him in confusion. "Left?"

"Through the portal..."

"You mean Caleb too? And Amelia? They're all gone?"

He frowned slightly at my surprise. "I was going to send you back with them, but I just couldn't do it yet...And I didn't know when you would finally wake up...They needed to get home." He paused as he took in the expression on my face. "You did want to stay a little longer, didn't you?"

"Well, yeah…" I answered, a little disoriented. "It's just weird to know they're *gone*." I stretched back out on the bed and pulled the covers up, contemplating how far away Morgan and Caleb felt now. "You're sure they actually went through, and Abrianna's not holding them hostage somewhere, right?"

"Oh, I'm sure. Ezekiel witnessed." He watched my reaction carefully. "But you only get three days here. And then you're going back, too."

"Without you?"

He gave me a tired look and didn't answer. "If you're feeling up to it tonight, I'd like to take you to my cabin on the mountain for the next three days. Kind of like a father-daughter retreat. I thought about what you said, and you were right…we both still have a lot to learn from each other. So this is our chance. What do you think?" He seemed a little unsure of himself.

A slow smile spread across my face. "I think I would really like that, Dad."

His return smile was relieved. "Good. I'm going to find you some food. Can I trust you to just sit still for a little bit and not get in any trouble?"

"I'll try." Now that I was back in the bed, I definitely wasn't moving again until the dizzy, nauseous feeling passed.

From the doorway, he called back, "I think you have a note by your bed."

I glanced over at the little stand next to me. My name was scrawled onto a piece of blue parchment in handwriting I knew very well. With shaky hands, I unfolded the note.

Whitnee,

You asked me at one point if I even wanted to live, and I said it didn't matter. But I lied. I had no idea how much I wanted to live until it was a real possibility. Thanks to you, I have been cancer-free for five hours now. And for the first time in a long time, I'm REALLY living. (I totally beat the BEEP out of Jude this morning—sucka! Ask your dad for the story.) I know you are convinced that your dad is the real Pilgrim, but I still stand by my belief that YOU are the Pilgrim. In my life, you have been the blonde-headed, all-gifted, birthmark-free Dorian who saved ME and gave ME peace in the midst of my own dark times.

I believe in you. Come home soon.

Hugs,
Morgie

Despite my discomfort and pain, that felt good. That felt *very good.*

And I smiled with absolutely no regret in my heart.

"I mean, really, is there not any creature I can be other than the fish?! The turtle is pretty cute," I whined from underneath my horrid costume.

"The turtle has to move, which is why I am the turtle and you are not. The fish just gets to hover there under the seaweed and look pretty," Dad pointed out.

"Pretty?" I echoed in disgust. "Look at all those children out there—how we do know some of them don't have horrible sea creature phobias? Look at their parents forcing them to act happy and wave at the creepy, fake fish on the parade boat. These are the things that create psychological issues for some of us."

Gabriel smirked as he stood handsomely beside me, barely leaning on his cane. "Fish do not speak, so maybe you should just hover quietly," he quipped.

"Says the guy who gets to stand on the boat and wave to the crowd as himself," I hissed. "You try sitting here inside this ridiculously pompous costume, sweating and itching. Don't be surprised if this fish goes belly-up before we reach the Waterpark." At least the dizziness had gotten better, but I still felt so weak and so not myself.

"You sure are whiny when you do not get your way." Gabriel patted one of my stupid fins condescendingly.

"Come on, Whitnee, it's an adventure." Dad swatted me with one of his rubbery turtle legs. I would have swatted back at both of them had I been able to move. I think that was their real plan through all of this—imprison me inside a fish suit so I couldn't do anything stupid again. I really didn't mean to act so grumpy. I felt like crap, and now I was dressed like my worst enemy...but still. I was alive. I was with my dad. And he was actually being civil toward Gabriel...who looked mighty fine in his dark dressy Island clothes.

"Hope I don't throw up inside this thing..." I huffed and sat back like a good little fish among the giant-sized seaweed.

"Everybody in their places!" Simeon clapped his wrinkled hands. "The parade is beginning!" He moved to our little portion of the stage just as the boat started to pull away from its dock. "How is my special little fish feeling over here?" he asked me with a twinkle in his blue eyes.

"Aside from the costume? Better."

"I apologize that I could not visit you this afternoon," Simeon said. "But I want you to know how proud I am of you, Whitnee. I know that was a difficult decision to make. You were able to do for Morgan what my wife would not allow me to do for her. You are special, indeed."

"Oh, I don't know about that..." I started to say, glancing uncomfortably at Gabriel. Dad and I decided to keep my new cancer a secret from Gabriel and anyone else outside of the Councilmen. Gabriel had been upset enough that I had endangered my life and lost a life force. I certainly didn't want him to know that I had also acquired the incurable Poison during the process.

"You might not be able to use Water anymore, but you will always be a true Hydrodorian because of what you sacrificed." He found my hand and squeezed it through the costume.

"Thank you."

Before I could say any more, he reminded me, "I know you are uncomfortable in there, but this will not last long. Once the parade ends at the Waterpark, everybody on this boat will unload there, and the boat will take you directly upriver to Pyradora. From there, Eden will meet you with a wagon and take Gabriel to the Palladium and you two"—he pointed to the turtle and me—"to the cabin."

"Are the decoys in place?" Dad asked in a hushed voice.

"Oh, yes," Simeon nodded. "Priscilla and Lilley are the only ones who know the real plan. If any of the rebels like Jude have been in the village watching, they will still believe you are in the Healing Center. This really is the safest—and most creative—way to get you out of the village."

"Definitely creative," I mumbled. Dad had a theory that sometimes the most obvious place you could put yourself was usually the last place your enemies would look for you. I just took his word for it since he had made a career of hiding from everyone on the Island for the last six years.

"Simeon," I called before the old man could leave. "Will you please make sure Lilley does not get in trouble for what I did? She was just trying to help, and I really—"

"Yes, yes…do not worry. I have already seen to it that she will not lose her position at the Healing Center," he assured me, and I thanked him wholeheartedly. I had not seen Lilley again before I left, but I would always be grateful for her honesty and loyalty when it came to things that really mattered.

"Are there other Pilgrim Protectors on board?" I asked Gabriel, feeling a little queasy.

He nodded carefully up ahead. "The sea horse is Levi. And the back pair of legs on the eel is Thomas." I breathed a little easier knowing my Dorian friends were close by.

My gaze shifted to the front of the boat where the sea horse was dancing around animatedly while the two people acting as the eel wove theatrically around the props and other costumed people on the boat. Watching Thomas's legs skip around as he hid underneath that monstrous green eel made me wonder how things had ended between Morgan and him. I couldn't wait to get the scoop from her when I returned. Thomas had been gone most of the day, but he had returned to the Healing Center right before it was time to leave. He had been more subdued than usual…something I completely understood. Leaving somebody through a portal was a nasty, depressing business. I couldn't help imagining how Caleb felt when he walked through the portal today. Our conversation last night had never been resolved, which left me with this empty ache in my heart. A part of me really hoped he had felt it too.

Once the parade started up, the noise level intensified. It was all quite magical for the audience, especially with the "Pyratechnics"—fireworks—that were just as brilliant in the early evening sun as they probably would have been in the dark.

Simeon and Gabriel waved to the crowd and even had flowers thrown at them from far away…probably with the aid of Aeros in the audience. Once again, you could tell how Simeon was loved by all. I imagined him to be the white-haired grandfather that everyone wanted to claim. It still amazed me that he had been the one to publicly ignite the fire of rebellion regarding the Pilgrim. That was probably why he had gotten away with it—nobody expected the peaceful Hydrodorian Tribal Elder to stir up trouble for the Guardian. It was brilliant, actually, because people followed Simeon wholeheartedly. There would be no turning back once he opened up the topic of the Pilgrim.

As I watched him smile benevolently to the people, I found myself feeling queasy again and worried I really was going to have to swim my little fish self away where I could barf in privacy. But whether my reaction was purely physical or a little bit emotional, I wasn't sure.

To make the queasiness worse, it became obvious very quickly that Gabriel was something of a celebrity. I had never seen him in this context, but it was absolutely ridiculous how many girls screamed his name in that scary fangirl way.

He just flashed his white teeth and wide, gorgeous smile at all of them and played the part of an unaware little heartthrob. Since it would expose his weakened state if he moved around with his walking stick, he pretty much stayed by my side—giving me the perfect excuse to watch him obsessively. I admit to making a few catty comments in my head at certain obnoxious, adoring girls in the audience. But then I stopped just in case one of them had special Aerodorian abilities too, that would allow my thought to enter their minds.

At one point, he asked me behind smiling, gritted teeth, "Are you still awake in there?"

"Oh, you bet I am…pretty impossible to fall asleep with girls screaming 'Gabriel' as if their lives depended on it. Why didn't you tell me you had so many admirers?" I think I sounded bitter and cranky again. *Geez*…maybe it was the rotten cancer growing inside me. I was starting to understand Morgan's mood changes a lot better now.

"It is just because of my status as the next Guardian," he replied dismissively.

"Right. I'm sure it has nothing to do with your cute butt. Or your widely-accepted status as Island Hottie," I blurted before I could think about what exactly I was admitting. Gabriel's hand froze mid-wave before he laughed right out loud.

"I had no idea you thought my butt was *cute*," I heard him exclaim as if this was the funniest thing he had ever heard me say. "Maybe I should be standing more like this…" He shifted his body around so that I was forced to stare directly at the cute butt currently in question.

"I didn't say that *I* thought that…I just meant…Gabriel, stop!" I started to laugh because he had started swaying side to side in front of me. "In about ten seconds, I'm going to do something that will make you fall on that *butt* in front of all these people…and then we'll see what people are saying about you…"

"Well, I would not want to disappoint the *admirers*, so I shall behave." I narrowed my eyes at him through my mask, but I was pretty sure he was just goading me. With barely a glance my direction, he added, "Besides, there is really only one admirer I care about...and she makes quite a cute little fish. Even if she is a jealous little fish right now."

"Stop calling me a fish!" I snapped, my cheeks flushing at his words.

"Who said I was talking about you?" he teased, but his hand came out and rested casually on my fin again, a reassurance that I was the most important girl (fish) in his life.

You two are about to make me sick. Dad's voice came into my head. *Maybe you could spare me all the flirting before I regret letting you stay here longer...*

Now who's being the Grumpy Pants? If you go frolic around the ship like a happy turtle, you won't have to listen to us, I reminded him sweetly. I think I heard him groan.

The eel came dancing past us at that point, and Gabriel called out, "Brilliant effort, Thomas. You might have a future career as an entertainer." I chuckled, deciding that it was fun to be a part of the festivities, even if the reasons were kind of weird.

"Shake those hips!" I couldn't resist teasing Thomas, especially because I was sure he needed a little smile after Morgan had left. He didn't respond because he moved away again. But Dad's voice entered my head...*Be careful, Whit. We don't want other people to know you're here.*

I rolled my eyes. *Thomas knows I'm here.*

But the other person under that eel costume doesn't.

Fine, Dad...but for all they know I'm just some Island girl under here.

Our conversation stopped because it was obvious we were nearing the Waterpark. The music aboard the boat grew louder and more energetic the closer we came to the end of the parade. Simeon was at the front of the boat, waving and laughing as the eel began circling him manically, gyrating in time with the music. The cheering of the crowd climaxed in volume. Then an almost deafening pop sounded, and beautiful cascades of sparkling Firelights fell into the river all around the boat.

At first, I was too busy admiring the fireworks to realize something had just gone terribly wrong.

One minute Simeon was standing there, and the next minute he was on the floor of the ship. Gabriel had seen it the moment it happened and had leaped to the front of the boat at the same time Dad tackled me in his turtle costume.

Stay down! Dad shouted in my head. Through my costume, I barely saw Gabriel duck to miss a Firedart that came *from the back of the eel.* Just as the seaweed above us exploded, something told me that it probably hadn't been Thomas under the eel after all...

We were under attack.

The strange thing was that in the midst of all the music and the fireworks, the crowd was slow to catch on that something bad was happening.

Levi ripped off his sea horse costume and was able to tackle the eel, knocking down both people. The guy at the front of the eel appeared confused and immediately submissive. But the guy at the back shoved his way out of the costume and shot again in Gabriel and Simeon's direction. I couldn't see who he was, but he had to have been a Pyra. Gabriel launched an attack back at him. A chase broke out on the ship. Once the billows of smoke started spreading out from the seaweed, the crowd reaction changed to screams of horror. The other costumed people aboard jumped ship to escape the flames.

Don't move! Dad instructed as he pulled himself awkwardly off the ship floor. He ran to the guy who had been steering the ship. "Do not dock here! Go! Go! Head straight upriver! NOW!" he yelled. The guy looked terrified, but he obeyed Dad without question.

The whole ship sped up so quickly that almost everyone lost their footing. We left the traumatized crowd behind with a trail of smoke that was filling up the inside of my costume and suffocating me. I had no choice but to wriggle out of the costume so I could breathe.

Lying flat on my back, I ripped the mask off my head and saw Simeon sprawled unnaturally on the floor of the ship. I crawled through the crashing debris until I came to his side.

"Hold on, Simeon." His pure white beard and wrinkled neck were splattered with blood. Quickly my eyes found the injury... part of his shoulder looked as if it had been blown off. *Oh my gosh.* My stomach rolled, and I felt lightheaded. He was staring at me like he was in shock. I gripped his hand firmly and cursed the fact that I could no longer heal. Suddenly his eyes widened, and he tried to speak but only choked.

I was yanked away from him by hands that should not have been familiar. The terrifying smell of sulphur invoked a paralyzing fear in me. Saul had my arms wrapped tightly around my chest so quickly that I couldn't move or fight back. One of his palms was pressed to the bare skin along my forearm, and he was burning me...literally. I screamed in horrified pain as the white-hot sensation grew in intensity.

"I will kill her!" Saul yelled at Dad and Gabriel, who had stopped short when they realized what was happening. "If she really only has three life forces now, she is no longer necessary! If you come closer or try to stop me, she dies. I swear."

How did he know about the three life forces?! And, *oh my gosh, somebody make the burning stop!* My screams turned into moaning cries.

"What do you want, Saul?!" Gabriel yelled.

"I just came to do a job." He motioned at Simeon struggling on the ground. "A little reminder that rebellion can get you in a lot of trouble. And now you are going to let me leave, or Whitnee gets to die like Simeon. And we all know she cannot heal herself now...you will be unable to get either of them help fast enough."

Whitnee, can you use any life forces? Dad's voice was desperate, but I couldn't even answer back. It felt like Saul was burning a hole right through my flesh. I made a weak attempt at escaping, but that did exactly what I worried it would do. Saul just fed off of my fear.

"It sure would be a waste to kill you..." He sniffed at my hair, and I felt his mouth and unshaven chin brush roughly on my cheek.

Gabriel took a step forward, and his hands ignited with flames.

"Don't! You could hurt Whitnee!" Dad stopped him. "Let her go, and we'll let you go!" he commanded Saul, disgust and anger distorting his voice.

"I might be changing my mind now," Saul remarked near my ear and then without warning, he shot another attack at Dad. I yelped as Dad's Earth shield went up, deflecting the shot so that it exploded on a thick wooden pole. The top of the pole with all of its decorations came crashing down on top of Dad before he could dodge it.

DADDY! I cried inwardly as I watched him fall to the deck with the impact. The ship continued to speed forward, and Levi appeared behind Gabriel. With one sweep of the situation, Levi was poised for attack. I peered through teary eyes at Gabriel, wondering what I should do. They would not attack Saul first if they thought he was serious about killing me. And Saul was using me as a shield at the moment. Gabriel stared back at me, his eyes clearly debating what to do. At this point, I was pretty sure Saul had done permanent damage to my arm.

I thought I saw Gabriel's eyes flick over at Dad uncertainly. "Gabriel," I sobbed. "My dad..." The thought of losing Dad right before my eyes, combined with the torturous pain Saul was inflicting on me, brought me to my knees.

"Get up!" Saul dragged me further away from Gabriel and closer to the ship's side. I tried to regain my balance despite my limited vision through watering eyes and windblown hair. Gabriel stayed where he was, acting as if he were listening for something.

Whitnee, when I count to three, I want you to throw yourself to your left and shut your eyes, okay? Dad commanded suddenly. I didn't have time to question because he started counting. *One...two... THREE!*

I squeezed my eyes closed and pitched all of my waning strength to my left. Something impacted Saul violently, and I was sprayed with a sticky substance. His grip started to loosen around me, but not fast enough. He fell back against the ship's edge with me still in his arms. When I opened my eyes again, Gabriel's glowing golden irises were all I could see as he lunged forward. I was ripped out of Saul's grasp just before he took me overboard with him.

I cradled my burned arm against my chest and fell into the safety of Gabriel's arms. He held me tight and pulled me away from the side of the boat. "He can never hurt you again, Little One," he assured me, the Fire burning dangerously in his eyes.

The sticky substance...it was Saul's blood. All over me. The smell and the feel of it were like a disease. I looked up at Gabriel with frightened tears. "Did you...?" I couldn't complete my question. He just stared back at me grimly.

But I knew. Gabriel had just killed a man for the first time.

Thirty minutes later, we had docked, met Eden, and changed our course to head straight for Jezebel's house. Dad's back was in a lot of pain—but he was the only one with healing capabilities and there was no time to concentrate on helping Simeon until we got to a secure and still place. Dad kept giving him doses of Water life force to try to alleviate pain, but Simeon seemed to be rejecting it. I wouldn't even let Dad touch my arm—I did not want him wasting energy on me when Simeon was in such dire need.

The ride up the mountain felt alarmingly unsafe as we sped along the narrow, cliff-hanging roads. Dad and I stayed low with Simeon in the back of the wagon so as not to attract the attention of the few Pyras who had remained in the village instead of attending the Festival of Springs. Would I ever get a chance to visit this village and actually enjoy my time here?

Jezebel was waiting for us, clearly distraught about Simeon's condition and, at the same time, openly curious about my dad. She kept watching him as if she expected him to do something unexpected or crazy.

"So much blood…" Jezebel had wet towels and blankets ready when they carried the old man into the house and laid him down on a bed. Her eyes sized me up. "That looks like a Pyra burn."

I just nodded, thinking distantly how unfair it was that every time she saw me I looked so completely horrible. Gabriel interrupted her curious stares. "Jez, do you have any pain medicine for Whitnee? And when will a Healer be here?"

"The closest Healer I could find was Michael, who had just arrived back at the Palladium. So he cannot be here for a while. And I suppose I will have to hunt around here for the burn medicine." She seemed disgruntled about that—not by the dying man who was bleeding all over her bed, but by the fact that she would have to go look for something to help *me*. I was in too much pain to care. "Gabriel, does your mother know about this?" she questioned casually.

Before he could respond, Dad piped up. "Yes, she knows. She is coming here with Michael."

My annoyance over Dad and Abrianna's frequent communication flared up. "Then who do you think sent Saul?" I questioned.

"Same person who sent Jude and the others," Dad muttered. Clearly he didn't believe Abrianna had done it.

"Eli?" I guessed and glanced at Gabriel for his reaction.

"Eli will not admit to it," Gabriel informed us. "He claims the rebels are acting on their own now. Unfortunately, there is no way to know if he is telling the truth."

"My guess is that he is not," Eden said. Nobody disagreed.

"And where is Saul now? Please tell me somebody caught that beast of a man," Jezebel wanted to know. Clearly, she was not a fan of his either.

"He is dead," Gabriel mumbled. His eyes found mine, and I shivered again at the memory.

"You did the right thing, Gabriel. He was going to kill Whitnee…or worse." Dad's voice was surprisingly compassionate. I was wondering what Dad considered worse than my death, but just as my thoughts started going there, I stopped them with a sickening swallow of bile.

Simeon let out a cry of pain and started shaking. "We cannot wait for Michael, and Simeon cannot heal himself of such an injury," Dad realized. "I need everyone out of here right now." Sad that I could no longer help with healing, I hesitantly left the room with the others, still clutching my arm and concentrating on just placing one foot in front of the other.

Once my adrenaline started to subside, the sick feeling intensified. I had a bubbling and blistering burn along one arm. No matter how much I rubbed and wiped, I still felt and smelled Saul's blood on me. Combine that with the smell of my own burned flesh, and the nausea in my stomach had heightened to knife-like pains ripping across my abdomen. Instead of following the others to the living room, I had to rush to the bathing room and vomit violently over and over again.

The vomiting slowed, but the crying started. I was completely miserable and terrified by what had happened in twenty-four hours. I went from healthy to sick. From protected to hunted.

From invincible to damaged.

I was sitting on that floor in a completely helpless state when Eden found me. With firm, steady hands that were accustomed to work, she knelt down and started dressing my arm with some kind of smelly medicine. I tried to stop crying, but the misery was so heavy. I had to hide my face in one hand and bite my lip through the painful sting. Without a word, she wet a towel and started wiping my face and exposed skin of the remaining blood. The longer she took care of me, the more I calmed down.

Finally I spoke. "You've done so much for me, Eden. I'm sorry I let you down."

"Let me down? What are you talking about?"

"I mean, I'm not the Pilgrim…I only have three life forces now. And I'm leaving in three days. I've done the exact opposite of everything you hoped for when you formed the Pilgrim Protectors." I hated disappointing Eden. She was so strong and independent and noble.

"Whitnee…I do not profess to know what your purpose here is." The green of her eyes was vivid as she spoke. "Only you can know that. But being around you and your father has confirmed to me that the Island still sees. Still hears. And still provides. That is enough for me right now. Anything else is between you…and the Island."

The Island…They always spoke of it like it was a person.

She got up to wash her hands, and I changed the subject as I examined my charred skin. All I could feel was the low, painful throb of my distressed pulse. "Did they find Thomas?"

She didn't look at me when she responded, "No. Not yet." I wasn't sure how to take that news.

"You don't think he betrayed us, do you?" I felt so guilty asking that, but it was suspicious that Saul had been able to take Thomas's place on the boat that fast. I had to know what she thought about it.

"As soon as we find him, I suppose we will know," she answered without emotion.

"But somebody told Saul we were on the boat."

She frowned in the mirror as she dried her hands. "What makes you think that? I assumed he was there to kill Simeon and accidentally discovered you on the boat."

"Oh. Maybe." I thought about that. "Eden, did you know about the Transfusion between Morgan and me before you met us at the dock? That I only had three life forces?" I asked, a niggling sensation that something was off about Saul's presence on the boat.

"No," she answered and gave me her full attention. "They would never pass information like that through the zephyras. Only the Pilgrim Protectors with you at the Healing Center knew."

"Saul knew."

When my eyes met hers, I know we were thinking the same thing. Was there someone else we trusted working for the other side? *Please don't let it be Thomas...* I thought desperately.

Dad interrupted my thoughts. *Whitnee, Simeon wants to see you.*

I sighed and tried to pull myself up from the floor. "I think my dad wants me in there now. Thank you for taking care of me," I said sincerely. She helped me up when it was clear how much I was struggling. Slowly, I veered back to the bedroom, my eyes meeting Gabriel's ever so briefly when I passed the living room where he was pacing. He paused in his stride, his expression worried. But I continued on my way, barely catching the low tone of Eden's concerned voice as she addressed Gabriel.

Dad kissed my forehead when I entered the room. "Will you sit with Simeon for a moment? He is asking for you. I am going to get more Water." He left quickly.

I stumbled weakly over to the poor old man lying on the bed.

"Whitnee, please come here," he said hoarsely.

"I'm right here, Simeon," I responded gently, wondering why he wanted *me* there, of all people.

He tried to wet his lips as he spoke, but they were almost sticking together. "I am an old man, Whitnee. I have lived a full life, and now I am tired..." I listened to him struggle with his words, afraid to know where this conversation was heading. When he spoke again, he stared at the ceiling as if seeing a movie of his life. "My wife was a Healer...the most gifted Healer of her time. She paid attention to the details of her craft that others ignored. She loved people so much...always made allowances for their faults, claiming that everybody needed grace."

"She sounds like you, Simeon," I said softly.

"She was better than me. She loved so purely, and all she ever wanted for herself was children of her own. When it became obvious that would never happen, she refused to let it embitter her. She threw her life and love into her healing work, choosing to treat every patient as if he or she was a child of hers..." His breath caught, and he started coughing. I didn't know what to do for him—where was Dad? The coughing fit finally subsided, and he continued, "One day a patient was brought to her—a sweet little girl—whose houseboat had collapsed. She was half-drowned, and her body had been crushed beyond repair. There was no way she would live through the night. My wife was advised to just ease her pain so she could pass quickly and easily. But my wife had a stubborn side and that little girl had captured her heart the moment she laid eyes on her broken body."

Simeon was still staring at the ceiling, and I was taken in by his story, even if I wasn't sure why he wanted me to know all of this. "She set to work, believing that she could save the girl's life. By the end of the day, she had somehow stopped all of the bleeding inside and repaired enough of the major damage to buy the girl some more time. The only problem was that the girl was paralyzed from her neck down. She was alive, but her body was useless. My wife was exhausted and in a terrible amount of pain from the Shadow Effect. I begged her to come home and rest, but she refused to leave the girl's side. To this day, I still do not know what exactly happened that night the little girl should have died, but I do know that the next day, the girl got up out of her bed and walked around her room in perfect health…as if the accident had never happened."

"Wow…" I breathed. "How was your wife able to heal her like that?"

"She would never say anything except that it was a miracle from the Island. I always wondered, though, if she had made some kind of bargain with the Island for the girl's health…She often interceded on behalf of others, sometimes to the point of risking her own comfort. And if you bargain with the Island, there comes a point when you must uphold your side of the promise. It was about five years after that incident that my wife grew ill with the Poison." His voice grew thick with emotion and his eyes clouded with tears. "I could not understand why someone who had been given such a gift in healing would suffer from a disease with no possible cure. I begged her to accept Transfusion from me, which, of course, she never would. She claimed that everything happened for a reason. I just could not fathom what that reason was..." Goosebumps broke out all over my body. I could relate to this story.

"My wife was visited by so many of her former patients when she grew ill. But that girl visited every day, spending hours at a time with her, caring for her like my wife was her own mother... right until the day she finally died. Years later, the girl got married to a nice man and was able to have two perfectly healthy children. Her first was a son. But fifteen years ago, she gave birth to a daughter." Simeon paused with a hopeful smile on his face. "She named her daughter Lilley...after my wife. And that fifteen-year-old Lilley is quite a gifted Healer just like her namesake. I do not believe that is a coincidence."

His eyes finally moved to meet mine, and I realized now whom he was talking about. It was Lilley and Mark's mom who had been miraculously healed by Simeon's Lilley. "I called my wife my Water Lilley, and I believe that her legacy still lives on in the lives of her patients. Her ability to save that little girl's life so long ago made it possible for our little Lilley back at the Healing Center to help you save Morgan's life today."

I leaned back and blinked a few times at him, pondering the way our lives intersected with others at different times and for different reasons.

"And now I want to give *you* something, Whitnee," Simeon said seriously.

"Right now? What is it?"

He held up his trembling hands. "I do not have much time left before I am no longer a candidate...just please say you will accept."

I stared at him in shock as I realized what he was offering me. "Oh, no, Simeon...No way. Michael will be here soon, and he will heal you—"

"Whitnee—"

"No, I refuse that gift, Simeon! You have a tribe to lead..."

"Please," he begged with wide eyes. "Give a dying man his wish…"

"You're not dying."

"Not right now…but soon I will be. Not even Michael will be able to heal this by the time he gets here. And if we do not act soon, I will no longer be healthy enough to make the Transfusion. The gifter has to be in good health."

"But with Transfusion, you're guaranteed to die, Simeon! I just can't do that to you…I'm sorry." I stood up from the bed as if the matter were settled.

When I turned away, his voice was so broken and sad. "Why will you not let me do for you what you did for Morgan? It is the last thing I have to give. I am ready to see my wife again. I have no children…no legacy to leave behind other than the sacrifice of my own life. Please do not deny me that, Whitnee. It is my choice… and it is in accordance with the Island." I froze there in the middle of the room, my heart racing at those words. Simeon added, "You are meant to have all four life forces. I was meant to give you back the fourth. Everything in our lives has cycled in this direction for a reason. You know that in your heart."

I could feel the same incomprehensible assurance steal over me that I had felt when I had been the gifter for Morgan. But being on the accepting end was far more difficult. How could you let somebody else give their life to you like that? Even if they were old? Even if they were injured?

But I did feel the truth in my heart, just like he said. It was always meant to happen this way. We just didn't know it until we got to this point.

*It's okay, Baby Doll…*came Dad's voice in my head. *He's right.*

With unsteady feet, I joined Simeon again and stared into his compassionate eyes. "Thank you, Simeon." My voice caught as I realized what I was going to do.

He just held out his beautifully aged hands to me and replied, "Thank *you*." Right before I closed my eyes, I saw him smile the most satisfied, peaceful smile I'd ever seen cross a person's face.

The moment our hands met, the Island agreed. Unlike before, I was not the one being ripped apart this time. I was being given new life, new strength, new power. And at the same time, the diseased and broken parts of my body were washed clean by the Pure Water. It was not painful for me at all...but I could tangibly feel the cancer leave my body.

Once again, I had no concept of how long it took, but when it was over and I opened my eyes again, I knew I was just staring at the shell of Simeon's body. I remembered Caleb describing the moment his dad passed away...He said one minute he was there, and the next he wasn't. You just knew when the spirit left the body. That's how it was. Simeon was gone. Forever. And his death was so fresh that the smile was still on his face. I hoped he was already being reunited with his Water Lilley on the other side.

I just stood there as the tears collected in my eyes. I felt a responsibility now for Simeon's life and death. Even though it was in accordance with the Island—even though we knew it had been the right thing to do—the heaviness of the gift that had just been given to me anchored me to that spot. Carefully I pulled away from his lifeless grip and neatly folded his hands over his still chest...those hands that had channeled the healing and loving power of Water for so long.

After giving his hands one last squeeze, I discovered the perfectly smooth skin that now covered what had been my horribly scorched and singed arm.

His death had brought me life.

"Oh, Simeon..." I burst into mournful tears for the lost Elder.

I didn't hear Dad enter the room until he was standing behind me, his hands pressed to my shoulders. I didn't have any words. "Mourn for his life, Whitnee...not for his death," Dad advised kindly. "It was going to happen with or without Transfusion. Instead, he got to die the way he wanted."

"But the people will never know what he sacrificed for me..." I had a feeling Dad would want to keep it quiet that I now had all four life forces. Even though I *felt* like myself again, I realized that this put me back in the same sticky situation with Dad and Abrianna.

"You're right," Dad sighed and then he knelt down beside me and rested a hand on the old man's head. "Saul and Eli thought they were shutting down a rebellion by silencing Simeon. But they picked the wrong man to punish…the people will not cower in fear. They will unite over this."

"How do you know?"

Dad's voice was hard when he replied, "Because the most beloved Elder on our Island was assassinated. And Gabriel will see to it that the truth comes out."

BEACH RETREAT

Dad gave Gabriel very specific instructions about what to do next—what to tell his mother, what to say to the Pilgrim Protectors, how to protect himself...It almost felt like Gabriel was stepping into his new leadership role from that moment forward. And he took every bit of advice Dad gave him.

Goodbyes were quick, because Dad did not want me there when Abrianna and Michael arrived. He assured me somewhat reluctantly that Gabriel would be invited out to the cabin before I transported. So we left the situation with Simeon in Gabriel's capable hands (with Eden and Levi assisting him) and made our way to Dad's cabin in the middle of the night.

We found that Abrianna had made the changes Dad must have requested. The cabin was freshly cleaned and stocked with food and supplies. Even the furniture had been arranged to provide an extra bed on the opposite side of the single room. The windows had been opened to the fresh ocean air, and everything was cozy and comfortable.

After bathing and eating a light snack, we kicked off our father-daughter retreat with some serious sleep. It was honestly the most peaceful and deep sleep I'd had in a long time. I felt completely safe in my dad's cabin, and my body was at total rest after

Transfusion. I awoke the next afternoon to a growling stomach and the sound of muffled voices on the porch.

"...seventeen years old! On the Island, she is considered an adult, Nathan," a familiar grandfatherly voice was saying. "The choice to stay or go should be hers—"

Bleary-eyed, I stepped out into the afternoon sun to find Dad relaxing on the floor of the porch underneath the Aerodorian Wind chime. Poppa Zeke and Sarah rested in the chairs. Judging by the immediate break in conversation, I knew who they'd been discussing.

"Look who's alive," Dad remarked with a smile. My grandparents stood to greet me with hugs. Then I settled on the floor beside Dad and started picking through the fresh fruit displayed on the little table. The view of the ocean was beautiful and private, and the breeze was just the right intensity for four Aerodorians to feel perfectly relaxed.

"What are y'all doing here?" I asked sleepily, savoring the burst of juiciness that flowed from biting into a pineapple slice.

"Catching up on nearly thirty years..." Poppa Zeke replied with a weary smile. "And we brought our granddaughter some gifts."

I raised my eyebrows in excitement. Sarah handed me a beautifully woven bag featuring the Aero symbol on its side. The bag was made from different shades of purple weave (their word for a cotton-like crop grown in Geodora). I cooed over the design until she urged me to open it.

Inside the bag were several different Dorian outfits in the wispy fashions of the Wind tribe. Some of them I recognized from the last time I was here. I squealed with joy when I pulled out the gorgeous lavender dress I had worn the night we went to the Nightingale—the one with the long, flowing sleeves that were cut open along my shoulders. "This is my favorite dress ever!" I cried.

Sarah smiled at my obvious excitement. "I recovered it after you left—we kept everything that was yours. Keep looking inside."

In addition to the clothes, there were some bracelets, a pair of rhinestone sandals with leather straps designed to wrap around and tie above the ankle, some rhinestone hair decorations, and then my own bathing set of lavender-scented perfumes.

"I threw in some mouthwash, too...after your incident last time you were here." Sarah laughed with me as we told Dad the story of how I practically burned my tongue off the first time I used their mouthwash.

Poppa Zeke handed me a box from underneath his chair. "These are from me."

I gasped when I found the first item resting safely inside its own smaller box. "It's beautiful." I pulled out a gorgeous brown and purple Wind chime made from different-sized reeds. Thunderfly charms hung from it, and when the breeze picked up the hanging pieces, the sound was rich and comforting. Suddenly I missed the tree houses of Aerodora more than words could describe.

Poppa Zeke pointed to the two smaller boxes at the bottom. "Those are two custom-made drums from the Music Center—one each for Amelia and Kevin. I figured a small drum was a safer option than Amelia's singing voice." He laughed, but I was so moved by their thoughtfulness that I stood up and hugged them both again, saying thank you with as much gratitude as I could convey. I was blessed with such giving grandparents—on both sides of the world.

"One more thing..." Poppa Zeke said. This time he pulled out a small leather pouch with the Geo symbol sketched onto it. "Before Caleb left through the portal, he asked me to give this to you from him. He said it was a peace offering."

The mention of Caleb's name made my heart stop. With gentle hands, I took the pouch from Poppa Zeke. What in the world would Caleb leave for me?

I opened the pouch, and resting upon a cushion of leaves was a perfectly-carved flower, rounded petals and all, made from the glittering white rock of the Island mountain. It reminded me of a flower I had seen somewhere before...I stared at it for a moment before cautiously scooping it from its little earth bed. It caught the sunlight and sparkled at me.

"A petrified Saint flower..." Dad breathed. "Where did he find that, I wonder...?"

Poppa Zeke smiled. "He told me he made it for her."

"What do you mean? Like he carved it?" I asked, glancing back and forth between the two of them. I didn't know Caleb had any artistic ability.

Dad was impressed. "Not carved. That is a real flower that he turned to white stone with the Earth life force. It's an extremely difficult aging process. That is a special gift, Whitnee. Few Geodorians are able to accomplish the art of petrifying a plant. Be very careful with it so it doesn't break."

"Wow." I grazed my fingers lightly over the little flower that had last rested in Caleb's hands. As I was about to place it back in its pouch, I saw a little folded piece of paper peeking out from the leaves. I couldn't open it up fast enough. All it said was:

I didn't mean it. I'll always care, always try to find you—whether you want me to or not. Don't stay missing for long this time.

–C

P.S. About Morgan...I understand, and I would have done the same thing.

I could not control the tender smile on my face. Caleb always knew exactly what I needed to hear. Stupid butterflies started dancing a little jig in my stomach as I tucked the note and the exotic flower back into the pouch. "Where have I seen this kind of flower before?" I asked just to take my family's attention away from my reaction to Caleb's note.

Dad answered meaningfully, "Simeon grew them around his hot spring. And they are the same white flowers that Abrianna uses for the Lost Ceremony every year. They call them Saint flowers because they are the only blossoms on the Island that grow naturally white without the aid of a Geo. Pure white Saints."

There were so many things I could have thought or felt at Dad's words. Instead, I just decided to treasure the fact that Caleb had unknowingly left me such a lovely symbolic gift that could mean so many things to me. I missed him terribly after that.

"So this was your hang-out spot," I mused aloud as Dad and I walked down the beach barefoot. The tips of the ocean waves had turned orange with the fading sun off to the west, and the water itself looked pink. It was gorgeous here, with the mountain behind us and the water rolling peacefully onto the shore.

"Ben had the cabin built when I turned twelve. With three strong Aero personalities at the Palladium, it became kind of a calming retreat when one of us needed time away." Dad explained. "I used it more than Ben and Abrianna. I loved the simplicity and privacy of it. Abrianna hated to be away from the center of activity and refused to come out here without me or Ben. The location is protected by screens that make it blend in with the mountain. Look back…"

I turned around to see where the cabin should have been not too far down the beach, but it wasn't there! There was only an uninterrupted panorama of the mountainside vegetation and beach. "That's crazy!" I exclaimed.

"It's just an optical illusion. Once you get closer, it will appear— yet another reason it was suspicious that Tamir found you and Gabriel there so easily. Only Abrianna or Eli could have told him exactly how."

We picked up our pace again as we talked. "Thanks for having Poppa Zeke and Sarah over. I love them so much. Wish I could take everyone back to the Mainland with me." My grandparents had been forced to leave before dinner. There were matters to handle concerning Simeon's death. Hydrodora had closed out the Festival of Springs in mourning over their Tribal Elder's murder. The rumors had spread quickly after the burning ship in the parade had sped away. Gabriel was giving a public announcement of clarification to the whole Island via zephyras an hour from now. Poppa Zeke had to meet him in the Aerodora Communication Center to ensure that nothing went wrong with the broadcast.

Gabriel had followed Dad's advice and given his parents no choice but to let him deliver the news to the people. Fortunately, Thomas had been found in a closet near the boat docking station for the parade. He had been beaten and left for dead but was now in Lilley's healing hands. I had no doubt he would be just fine—and I was more relieved to know he had not been a part of the plans. We didn't need another heartbreaking betrayal among the Pilgrim Protectors.

Eli still would not admit to being the instigator behind the assassination. But the remaining Council members had pressured Abrianna and Eli into just biding their time as "puppet" leaders this year until Gabriel was anointed as official Guardian. All of the decision-making and power was actually in the hands of Gabriel and the Pilgrim Protectors now, with guidance from Ezekiel and Joseph. Abrianna and Eli had no choice but to play along, because the alternative was imprisonment and destroyed reputations for both of them.

I was very curious to hear Gabriel's broadcast and to see how he would handle the questions of the people. In my heart, I had no doubt that he would do a wonderful job, especially with the support he had been receiving.

Dad interrupted my thoughts with a heavy sigh. "Your grandparents want you to stay here and for me to bring Serena to the Island."

"But you disagree because it's too dangerous for us here?" I guessed.

He glanced over at me. "Yes. But is living here even something you would really want, Whitnee? It's not that problems are less complicated on the Mainland than they are here. But your responsibility over them would be more complicated here—because of who you are and the abilities that you have."

"Are you telling me I actually get to make the choice?" I clarified.

"Not necessarily, no…I guess I'm just curious how you feel about it."

"I don't know, Dad…All I want is for our family to be together again. Is there really no way you could leave the Island? What if we did a split thing? Like summers here and school years on the Mainland?"

He smiled. "Wouldn't that be nice…But, no, that's not how it works, Whit. The portals have to be shut down. And I mean forever shut down. Once that happens, the connection to the Mainland will be gone—never to be opened again."

"Be honest with me, Dad." I stopped walking and dug my toes into the wet sand, as if trying to plant myself permanently there. "Will the Island not let you leave?"

Dad paused and then faced the water as he answered, "My job right now is to keep things in balance and to help preserve the longevity of the Island and its people at whatever cost. I don't know what the future of that job looks like, of course…but I am not *permitted* to leave."

"But can't you bargain with the Island? Simeon said something about—"

"No, Whit. Bargaining is not without consequences."

I thought of Simeon's wife being only the third person on the Island to die of cancer. Had that been her consequence? That added a whole new dimension to the phrase "be careful what you ask for."

I changed the subject. "Tell me what happened when Will Kinder was here. When we met him, he had drawings of the cave near Jezebel's house and he knew about the tank and the Water Beast and…he kept talking about destroying things with Fire."

"I can't believe he remembers all of that." Dad shook his head. "When he landed on the Southern Beach, Eli found him before I got there."

"And Eli and Abrianna were not married then, right?"

"Nope." Dad looked annoyed as he remembered. "Eli always pursued Abrianna because she was beautiful and powerful. After Ben disappeared, I was the only one there to look out for her. She was always stubborn about Eli, simply because she knew I didn't like him. Eli told her everything she wanted to hear, and she used him and his loyalty whenever it suited her. At that time, he was helping her construct the tank. Will showed up, and Eli and his band of cruel friends questioned him and then gifted him with Fire to see what would happen—like he was a science experiment or something. Combine Will's mental problems with the way they were treating him, and the results were damaging. Eli moved Will to Pyradora and hid him in that cave on Jezebel's property...except that her house was not there at the time. The property belonged to the family of Jesse, Eli's best friend and trouble-causing side-kick. Jesse is also Jezebel's father—one of the wealthiest men on the Island."

"This is all starting to make sense," I muttered. "But what happened in the cave? Will said that was where y'all fought."

"When I finally found Will, I also discovered the tunnel that led to a new portal room that Abrianna had been developing in secret. I was furious with her—even though the portal wasn't working at that point. I was adamant that she should not create another one. There was a big fight between us. Eli got involved, taking her side, of course. I tried to collapse the room behind us, but Eli got violent, and I had to get Will out of there. I went straight to the Palladium before Abrianna knew what I was doing. I damaged the portal there enough that it wouldn't work. She was shocked at what I had done, and the things she said after that were a real eye-opener for me. The ideas that had been brewing in her mind for so long had been rooted in so much selfishness and greed that I knew I had to leave. The Island *wanted* me to leave, because she would try to use my abilities for evil. And my abilities were given to me for a specific purpose. So we sailed away as quickly as we could. I barely had time to say goodbye to my parents. And the rest you know."

I voiced my first thought: "We should have Abrianna and Eli assassinated."

"Whitnee!" Dad was reproachful. "I don't want to ever hear you say such a thing again."

"Dad, I was kidding...kind of." I shrugged and rolled my eyes. The sun had finally set, and I paused a moment to look up at the fresh, twinkling stars.

"Dad!" I gasped. "Is that the Big Dipper?" I tilted my head at an awkward angle to see better.

Dad's voice was sad. "It certainly looks like it, doesn't it? It's the only thing I've had to remind me of the Mainland."

"How can we see it here too? Where exactly are we in the world?"

"I don't know...but it's always in the northern sky. Keeps me company when I miss you and your mother."

Maybe Will Kinder wasn't as crazy as everyone thought. The man had noticed and remembered more details in his short time here than I had.

"So that room in the mountain is a portal, after all?"

"Yep. The portal in Hawaii."

Interesting...I must have been seeing a Hawaiian beach when I had activated it. "And the tables with the straps are for..."

Dad's face turned dark. "Horrible things that should never exist...That's where they have experimented with taking people's life forces." He visibly shivered. "Do not ask me for more details than that."

"And were you never tempted to use that portal to come back? I mean, the tunnel freaking connects to your cabin! Or did you not know?"

"Oh, I knew. But I actually can't go near either portal now. As in, I am physically unable to get within a certain distance of it. There is an invisible barrier I cannot cross in that tunnel." He looked over at me to observe my reaction.

"Seriously? Why?"

He thought for a moment and then said with a shrug, "I guess you could say it's the Island's way of ensuring no one takes my abilities. It has only been there since I returned."

I frowned at this news. If that was true, then there really was no hope of him being able to come home with me. Suddenly, the fact that I was leaving him in a couple of days became a reality.

"So...in two days I go back through that portal knowing I'll never see you again," I stated flatly.

"In two days, you go back to your mother and your friends and your life on the Mainland knowing that I am alive and that I love you. Something you weren't sure of before..." he corrected me softly.

I'm not sure which of us was sadder about that.

The next day belonged completely to Dad and me. It was by far one of the best days of my life. We spent a lot of time talking about the differences between the Island and the Mainland. We took frequent walks on the beach and even played with the life forces. He knew the secrets of each life force, things that nobody had taught me. I learned how to use Wind to change the climate of my immediate environment. If I needed a temperature change or cloud cover, I could do it—but only within a certain radius of myself. He showed me how to infuse an object with Firelight. I practiced on a mountain rock and eventually learned that I could even control the color of light inside the rock.

We were sitting on the beach when Dad called a flower to himself. (Yes, he *called* it, and the flower detached and flew through the air to his outstretched hand.) "Do you want me to show you how to petrify a flower?" Dad asked, but then glanced at me knowingly. "Or should I let Caleb explain that process another time?"

I shrugged and took the blossom from Dad's hand. "It's not like Caleb can ever come back here." Wistfully, I pictured Caleb with his eyes lit up green and the white flower turning to stone in his hands. It bothered me to know he was so far away, that if I needed to talk to him or see him, I couldn't.

The flower hovered in midair above my hand as thoughts entered my head that I had long ignored. "You like Caleb, right, Dad?" I don't know why I asked. Maybe something in me needed his approval before he was no longer in my life. I didn't look at Dad, but I could sense his furtive glances in my direction.

"Sure. Caleb seems like a good kid."

I nodded and made the flower twirl in front of us. So many things I wanted to say...*I really haven't dated much, Dad, because I want you around. I'm scared. I want to be Daddy's Little Girl and know that if a guy breaks my heart, it will be okay...because you're there to protect it.* But I didn't say it aloud. And I shielded the thoughts from transferring between our minds too. My throat felt thick with the realization of what would never be.

As if he could sense my discomfort, Dad suddenly rose and pulled me to my feet.

"I've got to teach you something you will absolutely love, Whitnee. But you're gonna have to get in the water." He gestured at the ocean.

"Yeah, right." I rolled my eyes.

"Trust me. I can teach you how to talk to *fish*."

"Pretty sure I have nothing nice to say to them, Dad."

"Even if you could command them to stay a certain distance from you...?"

When my curiosity won over my hesitance, Dad showed me how children trained their "pets" for the Water rodeo. It wasn't talking to the fish so much as using Water to communicate certain commands. By the end of the lesson, every fish in that ocean was staying at least five feet away from me as if there were an invisible force field around me. It was a dream come true! Too bad I hadn't learned that before then...

Once Dad and I had exhausted ourselves for the day with good food, good company, and good life force action, we went to sleep with the moonlight reflecting in our cabin. I should have been able to sleep perfectly that night.

But when daylight broke on the day I would leave through the portal, I was restless and pensive. I had woken up in the middle of the night with an annoying headache—only to find that it had been brought on by Abrianna. That evil woman figured out how to break into my thoughts with her poisonous words.

Whitnee, your father wants to go home with you, but he is being forced by the Island to stay, she had said. While Dad's "frequency" had felt like soft, white light, hers was guarded and cloaked in deep, dark purples within my mind.

Somewhat sarcastically, I had replied with...*Well, hello, Abrianna. I don't remember inviting your voice into my thoughts.*

There had been a pause before she spoke again. *I am trying to make things right by helping you. You do want your father to come home with you, do you not?*

Of course I do. But he made it clear that he has to stay. I trust him.

He only has to stay because he can access all four life forces. He is like a balance scale for the Island. The Island needs him here, so he cannot leave.

That had been part of what Dad had explained, but it didn't seem like his only reason. My mind was already turning, trying to figure out why she was contacting me.

Abrianna, what do you want?

I want your father to be happy, and he has been different since being reunited with you. I am afraid that losing you again will devastate him. You might not understand, but I do love your father, Whitnee.

Gross. I really didn't need to hear that.

You have a funny way of showing love to people, Abrianna. Imprisonment, abuse, lies, manipulation...Your love sounds like more of a punishment.

Her voice in my head was not amused. If anything, she came back sounding offended. *I am offering to give you and your father a way home—a way that would be in accordance with the Island's wishes.*

Humor me, I responded doubtfully.

The Island is only requiring one all-gifted person to bring balance to the life forces right now. You and Nathan are the only two people with this gift. That means even you could stay here on the Island in your father's place. But I am willing to take that role if you will just transfer your abilities to me. I do not believe you would be harmed in any way. And this would enable your father to go home with you.

I sat up in bed with fury in my heart. *You are such a liar!*

I know I have lied in the past, but my career is practically over and my secrets are no longer my own. My own son hates me, and I am sure you can tell there is no love lost between my husband and me. I have nothing left, Whitnee. The only person who matters to me in this world is your father.

With frustration, I replied, *Yeah, that would change the second you took all of my life forces. Give me a break. There is no way I would ever give you that kind of power—*

If you refuse to give them to me, what about giving them to Gabriel? Do you trust him with that kind of power? He is our leader now.

That threw me off completely. If this wasn't really about her gaining her own power, then could it be that she really cared about my dad's happiness? I didn't respond immediately.

Just think about it, Whitnee. Today is your last day, the drakons have been removed, and the guards will be dispatched tomorrow to destroy that portal. We could make the transfer this afternoon in time for your father to go with you tonight.

There was a pause as if she expected me to say something back, but I remained silent. She continued, *Nathan has done more for me than I could ever repay him for... The only thing I know he wants for himself is to be with you and your mother. And you have the power to make that happen. If I could give that to him, I would be willing— whatever the cost. Even if it means losing him to another family.*

I had to say something to that. *Yeah, well, of course he wants to be with his real family! He disappeared on us six years ago—because of you!*

I understand how you feel... Do not forget that he disappeared from my life long before he disappeared from yours.

I was too upset to continue the conversation after that. Because, ultimately, she was right. She was his original family and part of his original home. I hated that.

The last thing she said before her presence drifted away was...
If you change your mind, I believe you know how to contact me.
There was no way I was contacting her. If she and I never spoke again, I was okay with that. But what she said stuck to me like bubble gum on the bottom of my shoe. Every step I took, there it was sticking to the ground and driving me nuts.

Dad had graciously invited Gabriel out to the cabin for the afternoon before my evening departure from the Palladium portal. Hopefully, Ben and my friends would be waiting for me on the other side. I had way too many mixed emotions about leaving this time. And the thoughts brewing in my head certainly complicated things.

I decided after all the unattractive ways I had looked during this particular trip, I wanted to dress up—not just for Gabriel's last memory of me, but because it was my last day on the Island. So I spent extra time making my hair smooth and straight. I finally pulled out the pink extensions and used one of the silver hairpins Sarah had given me to fasten one side. The Aerodorian dress still fit perfectly, and I enjoyed how it swished around my legs and accentuated my figure. I dabbed on some Island makeup and donned a silver bracelet.

When I came out of the bathing room, Dad's face lit up. "My little girl is so grown up," he mumbled. "I have something for you...something that might go perfectly with that dress."

He went to his armoire and pulled out something small and delicate. "I had Ezekiel bring it when he came this morning, but I made a minor adjustment." He held out his hand, and a glittering necklace swung there. I took it from him and noted the intricate silver beading and white stones. The charm that hung in the center was a clear glass thunderfly. When I touched the thunderfly with my fingertips, it came to life with a gorgeous shade of violet light.

"You infused it with Firelight, didn't you?" I smiled at the exquisite nature of such a gift.

"Yes. It will only light up when you touch it. And I placed a special material on the back so it would not burn your skin...Do you like it?"

"Daddy, I love it," I breathed. "Help me put it on." When he had finished, the mirror confirmed that, yes, it was the final touch to completing my outfit.

He stared at me through the mirror. "I figured it's tradition to give you a necklace from every place I go, you know...Hopefully this one will be associated with better memories."

I spun around and threw my arms around him. "I don't want to leave you!" I cried, fighting the urge to sob and ruin my makeup.

"I love you, Whit." He hugged me back and then pulled away with a tender expression. "You have turned into such a lovely young lady...I see so much of your mother in you. Strong, beautiful, smart." His voice suddenly broke and I could see the regret in his eyes. As if he needed to focus on something more within his control, he changed his tone completely. "Gabriel better behave himself today, or I will make you change into sackcloth. None of the kissing stuff, Whitnee, I'm serious."

"Oh my gosh, we are not talking about that again..." I sighed and moved across the room to give my luggage some attention. I double-checked to make sure I had packed everything, even reaching into my Island survival bag that Morgan had brought with her. I had forgotten my cell phone was in there. Just for kicks, I tried to turn it on to see if it miraculously received a signal. But, no. Nothing. In fact, the screen was like static. Nothing about the phone wanted to work. So I shut it off again, thinking I might need what was left of the battery later...assuming it worked again on the other side.

Then I found Dad's old jeans and U2 t-shirt that I had taken from the cabin. With a pleading look, I turned back around and tossed the clothes to him. "Wear these today."

He gazed sadly at the clothes. "I don't even know if they still fit."

"Come on...it's my last day! I could use the magic of your lucky shirt."

He kind of laughed but then gave me a what-the-heck shrug and moved to the bathing room.

While he was changing, Gabriel arrived at the door—with his *mother*.

"Uh…" I couldn't control my startled expression. Not only did Gabriel look wonderfully handsome—and without a walking stick—but Abrianna was all perfectly put together as usual in a red formal dress. "I didn't know *she* was coming," I said with confusion, forgetting how rude that sounded.

Gabriel did not appear too happy about it either. "Nor did I."

"I did not, either." Dad spoke up from behind me. His Mainland clothes still fit, and I was struck by how suddenly he had just become the dad of my childhood. Not a powerful hero born on an Island. Just my normal, concert-going, t-shirt-wearing dad with ripped jeans. "Hello, Bri," he greeted her cautiously.

"I am not trying to impose on the three of you…I just thought since it was Whitnee's last day, I would like to come and spend time with her too. Under no false pretenses." She smiled humbly before resting her cool, gray eyes on Dad. "And I thought I could keep you company when Gabriel and Whitnee want some time alone together."

"There will be no alone time for Gabriel and Whitnee," Dad stated sternly, and I just shot him a warning look.

Seventeen years old…I reminded him.

Still my daughter…he flung back.

Then we simultaneously turned cordial smiles on our guests. "Come on in." I held the door open, and Gabriel and I exchanged a skeptical, this-will-be-interesting look. *Under no false pretenses… ha!* I had no doubt that Abrianna was there in case I changed my mind about the transfer of life forces. But she was ridiculous for hoping—I would never give them to her.

WHEN THE CRAZY THING IS
THE RIGHT THING

"Do you see that? The way the water reacts to him?" Gabriel nodded in awe at Dad and Abrianna, who were walking along the beach at a comfortable distance ahead of us.

I squinted through the late sunlight to see what he was talking about. "What?"

"Look at the tide…it follows him. I have never seen anything like that."

Sure enough, it was obvious from this vantage point that all the waves rolled in *toward* Dad. The water lapped up the shore in his direction every time, even as he moved further down the beach. Gabriel was right. It was like nature itself followed my dad.

"That's weird," I agreed, befuddled by the phenomenon. Every once in a while, Dad would turn around and check on Gabriel and me—probably just to make sure we weren't making out in the sand. *Geez.*

But now that we were somewhat alone, Gabriel and I were able to talk more openly about things.

"Are you certain you cannot wait one more day for Simeon's funeral? I will be speaking at the ceremony…I would rather have you there with me," Gabriel said.

"I wish I could, but my mom and friends are expecting me home tonight," I replied with a sigh. I couldn't believe it was time to leave. "I was really impressed with how you broke the news about Simeon," I complimented him. "Even if you had to just blame it on the 'rebels,' I still felt like you gave the people hope and comfort while ensuring their security. And I loved the part when you told them about Saul and how you would 'personally see to it that every person associated with his cause is hunted down.' I love it when you talk *justice*...it's hot," I teased, elbowing him in the ribs.

He took the opportunity to grab my hand and tuck it into the crook of his arm. We continued to stroll beside the water. "They were not just words. I am intent on ridding this Island of violence and chaos."

"I know you are. You are going to be an amazing Guardian, one that will be praised in history books someday...I really believe that," I admitted sincerely, resting my head against his shoulder and watching the way our bare feet left behind our contrasting footprints in the sand.

"I would be a better leader if you stayed...You could be my personal advisor." His voice was casual, like he was testing out the idea with me.

"You and I both know that Eden is the girl for that job," I responded, and then hated the pang of jealousy I felt. That was the moment that I think I recognized how well-suited Eden and Gabriel were for each other...And it hurt to think that once I was gone, he would start to notice that too.

"Very well. Do not stay to be my advisor. Stay to be *with me*... as more than my friend."

Oh, good lord, he had just come right out and said it!

I avoided answering him directly. "I don't think my dad is giving me much choice to stay at this point." My heart pounded as I thought of what Amelia had said...that ultimately wherever I chose to live would probably indicate which guy I would choose. And choosing the guy, choosing the place, was all tied in with choosing the life I wanted. But at this point, it didn't seem like my choice. And even if it was, who said a girl had to settle down at my age?

"I absolutely respect your father and his wishes, but I believe that if you really wanted to stay, you could find a way to convince him," Gabriel insisted. "I think your problem is that you do not know what you want."

I cast my gaze up at him, admiring the cut of his jaw and the way the muscle there tensed when he was thinking about something serious. I felt like it was time to just be honest and open about this. "You're right. I don't know what I want. I don't know if I want to be on the Island for the rest of my life. I also don't know how to say goodbye to this place, knowing I can never come back. It feels like an impossible choice. So, yeah, part of me is glad the choice is being made for me."

"And if there was no Caleb in your life, would the choice be easier?"

He had to go there.

Again, I just decided on honesty. "In some ways, yes. Caleb means a lot to me, Gabriel. I'm not willing to lose him."

"I know. I have always known that. And I am the fool who placed you right back into his arms," Gabriel replied calmly. "Yet I am the one who receives your kisses and affections, not Caleb. Could it be that you are just mistaking your friendship with him for more than it actually is?"

"Gabriel," I sputtered. "It is not your place to question my relationship with Caleb. That's between him and me." I was taken aback, but mostly because his words were making me confused. On the Island, Gabriel was so obviously my match. But in every other part of the world, Caleb was my soulmate.

"I do not apologize for it," Gabriel replied stubbornly. "I feel like you and I are supposed to be together, Whitnee. I need you here with me. I need your laughter in my life to keep me from losing my sanity. I need your wisdom and perspective to help me govern these people." He stopped walking and gathered me unapologetically close. "I need to be close to you...to know there is someone—just one person—I trust wholeheartedly. I need the distraction of your kisses, so I do not make my entire life about duty and responsibility. You make me feel alive and able to conquer any conflict that arises. Whitnee Skye Terradora, I just need *you*. Please stay."

I stared at him wide-eyed, stunned to hear him put it all out there like that. I genuinely believed that he cared about me in a very real way...just like I knew my feelings for him were real too. But something about it didn't feel *right*. With careful thought, I replied, "There is just one problem with everything you said..." I turned my head and nodded in Dad and Abrianna's direction as they continued to walk slowly down the beach, deep in conversation. "Them."

"What do you mean?"

"I don't want to end up like *them*, Gabriel."

"We are not like them—" he growled.

"But we are in some ways, and that scares me. You just gave me a long list of reasons why you *need* me...not why you *want* me. I already told you—you don't need me here to do the right thing, to be successful as the Guardian. And I cannot stay here out of a sense of duty that I just do not feel."

"Then stay because you love me!" he cried, jolting me with intensity. Instead of responding with empty words, I just leaned into his chest and wrapped comforting arms around him. I could sense just how desperately he wanted love in his life. It broke my heart to know I just couldn't give it to him. Not right now. Maybe if I could have stayed—or if there had been a way to converge my two worlds—maybe then I could figure out if I could love Gabriel the way he wanted. But I couldn't force a commitment that wasn't ready.

"I do care about you..." I whispered. He pulled away and stared longingly into my eyes. I figured I had about five seconds before he tried to kiss me, and then, God help us, I would not be able to walk through that portal again. With a sudden impulse, I said, "I want to give you something before I leave. Come on." I took him by the hand and started leading him back down the beach, throwing watchful glances back at Dad and Abrianna.

When we entered the cabin, I moved immediately to my bed and started removing my jewelry. I didn't want anything to get damaged, and we had to do this before Dad and Abrianna figured out we had left. Gabriel halted and gave me a funny look. "Whitnee, I know relationships are different on the Mainland… but here on the Island we have traditions about this kind of thing."

I stopped in the middle of the room. "Huh? What are you talking about?"

"I am just saying that you do not need to prove your feelings. *That*" —and he pointed at the bed with an awkward expression— "is something we save for after the marriage festivities. Besides, your father…my mother…they are just outside…"

I stared at him in confusion. "I don't underst—" But then my mouth dropped open as I realized what he thought I was doing. "Gabriel!" I hid my face in my hands and felt it burn red hot.

"Not that I do not want to…do *that* with you," he was quick to assure me. "I just prefer that it be under the right circumstances, like if you agreed to become my w—"

"*Don't* finish that sentence!" I held up a hand before this could turn into a marriage proposal on top of everything else. "Are you thinking what I think you're thinking?" I almost couldn't look at him from my embarrassment.

"Well, you started undressing—"

"I wasn't *undressing*! I was taking off my jewelry!" I exclaimed in exasperation, awkward laughter threatening to bubble up out of me.

"Oh." It was the first time Gabriel appeared embarrassed too.

I knelt down on the floor and ripped the rug away, revealing the hidden trap door. I felt around for the tricky lever that would spring the door open, muttering in amusement, "I can't believe you thought I was bringing you here to…I mean, not that I'm not physically attracted to you and all…but, really!"

The door slid open, and I peered down into the darkened tunnel below, trying to ignore how right Dad had been about where a guy's mind went...

"What are you doing?" Gabriel frowned at me.

"You mean, besides seducing you?" I looked up at him, flustered. "You know, for the record...I'm saving myself for marriage too!"

He squatted across from me with a serious expression. "I am glad we clarified that...I would hate to think of you doing *that* with anybody but the man who won your complete heart and commitment."

My stomach jolted involuntarily. Why did he have to say things like that? And wasn't it slightly ironic that a guy saving himself until marriage was such a turn-on? Wow...

Gabriel leaned over and brushed a quick kiss on my lips. "I want to always remember this look on your face."

"You mean the one of complete embarrassment?"

"No. The one of complete innocence," he said and then directed his attention down the tunnel. "Now, tell me what you are doing and what exactly you want to give me if it was not...well, you know."

I took a deep breath, willing my blushing face to cool off. "Just follow me and trust me, okay?"

"Follow you blindly, yes. Trust you without knowing what you are doing...no."

"I'll explain in a sec." I didn't wait for his agreement before I jumped down into the tunnel and climbed down the grooved wall to the floor. He was quick to follow. As soon as I started out at a brisk pace through the tunnel, Dad's voice came into my head.

Where did you two go? I thought I made it clear...no alone time.

I stepped on a rock and scratched my foot...Gabriel took me back to the cabin. Oh, man, I had totally just lied to my dad.

You totally just lied to me, Dad replied with irritation.

Give me a break. We're not making out in here or anything, okay? We just decided to come back. Take your time with "Bri"–Ugh, I hated how he called her that— *and we'll see you in a little bit.*

Um, no. We're coming back to the cabin then too.

I panicked. I didn't want Dad or Abrianna interrupting what we were about to do. So I did the very thing I swore I wouldn't. I found Abrianna's frequency.

I need you to distract my dad. Gabriel and I want to be alone. Will you do that for me?

A few seconds later, she said. *Of course…I hope you are behaving yourselves.*

I made no promises.

Gabriel's voice sounded behind me. "Whitnee, why are we going to the portal?"

I didn't answer him until we got closer to the place where the tunnel spilled out into the huge circular cavern with its four pillars. Sure enough, the cavern was completely deserted and quiet. No drakons this time. I walked around and stared down the stairs into the center of the four pillars. The two tables were still there. I wasn't sure exactly how this would work without accidentally triggering the portal…hmm.

I started slowly down the steps. "Whitnee. Stop. Explain yourself," Gabriel demanded. I turned around halfway down the steps and looked back at him. His face was angry, and his arms were folded authoritatively over his chest.

"I want to give you all four of my life forces, and this is where we can do that."

"Under no circumstances will you be giving me any of your life forces. It could kill you—"

"Transfusion proved that it won't. But you are the only person on this Island who I trust with this kind of power…You could use them for so much good as the Guardian."

"I do not want that kind of power!" he growled at me like I was crazy. "Come away from there, and we will go back to the cabin. You are not thinking clearly."

That's when I blurted, "If I give them to you, my dad can come home with me tonight."

Gabriel was skeptical. "Did he tell you that?"

"Well, no. But it makes sense. Your mother said that if—"

"My mother put this idea into your head?" he gasped. "You cannot trust anything she says, Whitnee! I thought you were smarter than that!"

Ouch. That hurt.

"Time to go," he commanded and motioned for me to join him.

"No, Gabriel!" I yelled. "I don't want these abilities anymore. They've only caused me problems. And you need them—you could definitely control them better than me! Please, I want my dad to come home with me! If you do this for me, you'd be giving me my family back." Tears had sprung to my eyes. Gabriel softened. He descended the steps to meet me, but instead of continuing down to the platform with me, he made me stop and look him in the eyes.

"If I could help you find a way to be with your father forever, I would. But this is not right," he said gently and wiped an escaped tear from my cheek.

"Please..." I begged him. "Don't you even want to know what it's like to use all four life forces? Wouldn't that help—"

"Enough!" His tone was firm. "It is just like you said. I do not want to become like *them*...like my parents. Please do not ever tempt me like that again, Whitnee. This gift was given to you, not me. I refuse to accept it for myself."

And again...that was why Gabriel was the best leader for this Island.

I let him take me by the hand and lead me away from the portal. But as soon as he arrived at the top, he was seized by masked people. Before either of us could react, they had knocked him out with a swift blow to the head and thrown armbands on him. I started launching Wind attacks but was overwhelmed when I looked around the cavern and found masked rebels flanking the entire circumference, hands blazing with violent life forces ready to explode. I spun around in shock.

A tall, bald man with dark eyes pushed through the wall of people on the other side.

"Eli!" I screamed in anger and let loose about three lightning arrows aimed at his face. He deflected each of them, causing rock to explode where they landed.

"Lower your hands, Whitnee! Gabriel dies if you do one more thing without my permission!" As if to make his point clear, he nodded permissively at the guy holding the unconscious Gabriel. The guy shot Gabriel in the leg at point blank range. The shock and pain brought Gabriel out of his unconscious state, and he yelled in pain.

"Gabriel!" I cried out in fear. Eli would kill him. I had no doubt now.

"I think you know what I want," Eli called as more people spilled out of the tunnel that led to Jezebel's house. So that was how they had gotten in there..."Now, get down there on that platform!" With slow, uncertain movements, I started back down the steps.

Dad! We need your help in the cavern! Eli is going to kill Gabriel. He wants my life forces...I'm trapped! I called out. When I didn't receive an immediate answer, I panicked. *Abrianna, come help us! Eli has us in the cavern—*

"Yes, I am aware." Abrianna's voice sounded from the tunnel entrance leading to Dad's cabin. Relief flooded me. For about three seconds. Dad was not with her, and she appeared way too calm, given the situation. "Now, Eli, you were not going to try to do this without me, were you?" she called out coolly.

"Where's Dad?" I kept trying to reach him in our minds, and he wasn't responding.

"Make the transfer, then you and Nathan can go home," she told me simply.

"No! It is a lie!" Gabriel roared.

"Shut your mouth, Gabriel," Abrianna warned him, her eyes still focused coldly on Eli. "You know how your father can be. We want him to play nice today."

"I only play nice when I get what I want. Seize her!" Eli commanded. The guards lunged for Abrianna, but she was actually pretty quick. With a flash of Wind, she picked several men up off their feet and slammed them against the walls. Then she threw a lightning arrow at Eli. He counteracted it with a Firedart, and the two exploded loudly in the center of the cave. I took that distraction as an opportunity to help Gabriel. It was easy to hit the guy holding him captive, but much harder to get Gabriel to his feet with one useless leg. Man, we sure had bad luck every time we came to this cavern.

I was doing pretty well until I felt a force hit me square on the back and knock the breath out of me. Gabriel and I collapsed onto the floor. He was ripped away from me again when Eli himself picked me up with rough hands and threw me over his shoulder. I could hear Gabriel shouting and trying to fight back.

Forget life forces. I started beating the crap out of Eli with my fists. I stopped only when I saw both Gabriel and Abrianna pinned against the wall with four people prepared to strike them down.

"Your cooperation is not that essential, Whitnee," Eli replied with a disgusting lack of concern for his family. "I need an excuse to get rid of them anyway. Go ahead and give me one."

If he was trying to employ reverse psychology, it worked. Or maybe he was that demented. Either way, I gave up and let him carry me down the stairs. I braced myself for the moment the portal would click on automatically but was surprised when nothing happened, perhaps since I was not touching the platform... Eli threw me harshly on the table, and a woman started forcing me down on my stomach and tying me up with straps. Eli took the same position on the other table, and they strapped him down too. I watched with a sick feeling when he fit his hands to the handprints already in the table.

"Time for you to gift me with your life forces, Whitnee." Eli was speaking very matter-of-factly. "Or my wife, your boyfriend, and your father will all die in the next two minutes. There is no time to waste trying to make up your mind."

I thought I heard Gabriel shouting his protests at me, but I wasn't sure. I was in an impossible situation. The only fact that gave me comfort was even if Eli did take all of my life forces, it didn't mean he couldn't die. He would become powerful but not invincible. And I would make sure somebody murdered that man before I left this Island.

"Time to decide, Whitnee!" Eli shouted, but his voice was drowned out by a sudden rapid firing of life forces above our heads. The cavern broke out into chaos, and Eli's eyes widened with confusion. "Make her do it now!" he commanded the woman who was holding me down. She pressed my hands down. But something was going on up above...something unexpected.

Instead of gifting Eli, I called on all four life forces at the same time. Several things happened the moment they started surging through me. First, I started glowing all over again, and that strange sixth sense came over me just like before—where I felt like I could see through time and space in the room. Second, the pillars started vibrating, and a great Wind picked up in the cavern. The portal had activated.

With unnatural strength, I broke out of the straps and knocked the woman several feet away from me with one sweep of my arm. I had become the freaking Hulk. When I turned on Eli, he was watching me in fearful fascination. A shot of white hot energy blazed out of my hands and exploded the stone table beneath him. He flew through the air. But instead of letting him crash to the floor, I zapped him with some kind of electric force, levitating him from a distance. He acted as if he couldn't breathe right, like he was completely frozen there in midair.

My voice was distorted with rage. "You've been responsible for so many deaths, so many problems on this Island! I hope you're ready to face whatever is waiting on the other side for you, Eli."

"You are not a killer," he choked out, even though he looked terrified.

"You wanted these powers, and now you're about to find out just how dangerous they can be." I didn't even really know what I could or would do, but the amount of power in me was inhuman.

I started squeezing Eli with the electric binding, and he gasped for air.

"Whitnee, no!" Eden shouted at me. "Let go of the life forces before you accidentally transport! Everything is under control now."

I whipped my head around to find her running toward me, her hair flying around her face. I kept my hands poised. "He deserves to die for all he's done!" I cried, thinking of Will Kinder and my dad and Abrianna and Gabriel and...

"Whitnee," Eden pleaded one last time, and then she held up armbands. "Just let go. You do not want his blood on your hands."

Something about her words broke through my haze of revenge. I did want Eli to suffer, to die, to face consequences. But Eden was right...Ultimately, I didn't want to be the one who decided that fate for him. I glanced up to see the activated portal coming to life. With a sharp drop of my hands, I let him fall hard on the ground. Under my threatening stare, Eden and Levi slapped armbands on Eli and dragged him away. I followed them up the stairs just as the curtain of the portal filtered down to the cave floor. There it was: a beautiful snapshot of a Hawaiian beach, glimmering in the center of the room like a mirage. I gave it one curious glance before noticing the Pilgrim Protectors who had overtaken the entire cavern, subduing the rebels with armbands and threats.

"How did y'all know...?" I asked, the white glow of the life forces still lingering on my skin.

"Jezebel," Eden answered with a nod at the girl who was now attending to Gabriel across the room. "She contacted me when the rebels stormed through her property earlier. I tried to warn you, but none of you answered your zephyra. I suppose she really is one of us..." Eden and I exchanged looks with a raise of our eyebrows.

"Eden, my dad. I don't know where he is..." I told her and started moving in Abrianna's direction.

Eden nodded. "We already sent Protectors up to the cabin. We will find him." And she hopped into action, shouting orders at different people.

As soon as I approached Abrianna, who was standing there guarded by a Pilgrim Protector, I had to contain my anger again. "Where is my dad?"

"In the cabin. Slightly drugged. He would not have been able to come down here anyway. I just saved him the trouble of worrying about you."

I gaped at her. "You *drugged* him?"

"You *asked* me to distract him. You were the one who lied and manipulated the situation. You are more like me than you care to admit."

A tiny flicker of guilt ran through me. I did lie to Dad…but with good intentions. Right?

"How could you do this? You planted the idea in my head to give my abilities to Gabriel just so you could get me down here! You never quit, do you!"

She was unmoved by my emotion. "If you make your weaknesses known, people can use them to defeat you. I know you better than you think, Whitnee."

"You don't know anything about me."

"I know how much you love your father and how much you love Gabriel. I knew you would bring him here and try to sacrifice your abilities on behalf of both of them." She gave me a pitying look. "I used to be like you. I used to love others freely too. But just like you, I had to learn the hard way that love is just a weakness to be used against you."

"That is the saddest thing I've ever heard," I replied with pity of my own. "Does any part of you care that Gabriel could have just been killed?"

She matched my gaze with cool collectedness. "He is still alive. And so are you."

"And so are you—because of the Pilgrim Protectors." My heart was filled with contempt as I added with a shake of my head, "And my dad actually believes there's good in you…" Her eyes flickered with something at my words. Regret? Shame? I hoped so. I popped my hand up like I was going to slap her, but instead, one quick burst of white, hot energy snapped out like a whip. She cringed and then gasped from the little shock I'm sure it delivered, the passiveness gone from her face. "*That* was for Amelia," I announced and gave her one scathing look before marching away. When I was out of her sight, I paused to lean against the wall. I felt shaky all over as I came off the adrenaline high. Or maybe it was the fact that all the life forces had drained out of me by then. Either way, I stood there in a daze, staring at the open portal below. When I started to feel suffocated, I tried to conjure a breeze aimed at my face.

But it didn't work. I couldn't access the life forces again because the portal had messed up my connection. So weird. Gabriel looked past Jezebel and Michael, who was now trying to fix his leg, and caught my gaze from across the room. I just shook my head at him and then looked back at the portal. That had been too close.

Poppa Zeke arrived pretty quickly after that. He found me first and made sure I was okay. When I told him I was just resting, he moved to question Abrianna. I stood there by myself long enough to see Eli and most of the rebels escorted out of the cavern. I watched Michael completely heal Gabriel and make him test his leg out. I got to observe the way Jezebel attached herself to Gabriel and the way he tried to be patient with her attention. I gazed in annoyance as Abrianna answered questions and acted as if she had been a victim through the whole thing. I observed how well Eden handled every situation and the way she went to Gabriel with questions or to update him with new information. They did seem to have everything under control.

Just as I felt that I had enough stamina to head back to the cabin, Dad came barreling out of the tunnel with all of my bags and boxes in hand. He was still in his ripped jeans and U2 shirt, and his bloodshot eyes darted nervously around the cavern, searching.

"Daddy!" I cried and ran around the circular chamber. He grew relieved when he spotted me.

Dropping everything to give me a hug, he cried, "I've been trying to contact you! Why are you ignoring me?"

"Sorry, I accidentally activated the portal and don't have my life forces back yet," I explained. "Why do you have all my stuff? And I thought you couldn't get this close to a portal—"

He cut me off breathlessly. "Say your goodbyes. We're leaving."

"For the Palladium?"

"No...through that portal right there." He pointed at the rolling ocean waves of Hawaii.

I looked at him like he was crazy. "I can't go to Hawaii!"

"I'm going too. Home."

I just stared at him in shock. Was this a joke? "I don't understand..."

"Don't ask me questions, Whitnee. We have to leave in the next few minutes if I'm going with you." He searched around the cavern until he found Abrianna. I watched his expression harden, and I think they started talking in their minds. I saw her face change dramatically too. "Give me a second, Whitnee." And Dad and Abrianna started walking toward each other. Poppa Zeke followed her, and there was an intense conversation between the three of them. I was so busy watching them that I jumped when Gabriel touched me at the small of my back.

"What is happening?"

I was still somewhat disbelieving. "Dad and I are leaving... through that portal."

"He is going with you? Right now? How?"

"I don't know. But I'm not questioning it." I hugged my arms to myself and turned to face Gabriel with finality. "I think it's time to say goodbye."

"No..."

So many things to tell him and not enough time...how was I supposed to say goodbye for what was probably forever? As my eyes wandered, I found Jezebel watching us from a distance. "You're still engaged to her, aren't you, Gabriel?"

He looked unsurprised as he followed my line of vision. Then he answered solemnly, "Maintaining the engagement was the only way to guarantee her trust."

I just nodded like I understood. I wanted to tell him to break it off immediately—that it wasn't right. That *she* was all wrong for him. But I couldn't. I was leaving and it was his life. Instead I said, "When we leave here, you'll need to shut down the portals behind us. My dad says they're damaging the Island. If you keep them open, it will only cause more problems."

He looked at me like my suggestion was ludicrous. "If I shut them down, you can never come back."

I just let my eyes convey the clear message that not coming back was the point. "One more thing…You need to listen to Eden," I gulped, swallowing down my selfishness. "She is the one person on this Island I know you can trust—*wholeheartedly.*" I knew he got the reference I made to his own words earlier. He gave me a funny look, but I continued, "And promise me that you'll move on with your life and you'll always do the right thing no matter how crazy or difficult it might seem. Promise me that you'll—"

"Do not do this," he interrupted, his eyes becoming emotional. He drew me close and cradled my head against his chest where I could feel his heart beat. The heat of his body encompassed me in warmth—a sensation I would never get to experience again. "Do not say goodbye," he pleaded.

Time to go, Baby Doll, Dad whispered. *Once that portal closes, I've lost my chance.*

I pulled away from Gabriel and turned to see Dad moving back my direction. He picked up my boxes and his own small satchel. Then he held out my bag to me. With reluctance, I slung it across one shoulder, still processing the permanence of leaving. I hugged Poppa Zeke for the last time and watched as tears clouded his old eyes.

"I'll give Ben your message," I promised him, hoping Ben was still well enough to receive it. He smiled through his tears. Then I said goodbye to Eden. When she hugged me, I whispered in her ear, "Take care of Gabriel." She nodded resolutely. I thanked Jezebel formally for her hospitality and for saving our lives with her quick thinking. She just gave me a flippant wave, managing to conjure a fake smile. The last person standing there was Abrianna. Her face was completely expressionless, but her eyes…oh, her eyes were such a different story…like dark wells of sad memories and thoughts. I had nothing more to say to her, so our eyes just met without a word exchanged.

"We gotta go, Whit," Dad urged me and started down the stairs.

I glanced again at Gabriel. His face was a mask of pain, his hazel eyes tortured. I turned away and followed Dad down the stairs. If we didn't go through that portal in the next few seconds, I was going to lose all control over my emotions.

I almost made it to the platform when Gabriel called my name. I froze and turned around to find him sprinting down the steps. "Wait!" Even Dad stopped to see what he wanted.

"It is my turn!" Gabriel's face was intensely trained on mine as he came to a stop on the step above me. I gazed up at him expectantly. "Whitnee, truth or dare?"

I felt like I had been kicked in the stomach. Why was he doing this to me? We were supposed to just leave and be okay. I had my dad. He had his Guardianship. Everything had worked out for the best, right?

"Truth or dare!" he repeated adamantly.

Afraid to speak the truth about how I was really feeling, I blurted, "Dare."

He paused, understanding intuitively why I hadn't gone with truth. Then he said fervently, "I *dare* you to come back…someday."

I glanced at Dad who was listening in with a pensive look on his face. Then I looked Gabriel straight in the eye and choked, "I guess this means you win the game."

His face fell at my words. "Then why do I feel like I just lost?"

I reached up and pressed my palm to his cheek, brushing my thumb lightly across his lips. "When I'm gone, I think you'll realize just how much you've gained. So proud of you, Gabriel."

I watched his face harden into a cold wall of indifference, and once again, I was jealous at how easily he could just turn off those emotions. It wasn't fair.

He took a step back and his tone was dark when he said, "You should know that I will not come looking for you again. Ever."

I nodded slowly. As long as I lived, I would never forget that look on his face and those last words. I understood why he was trying to hurt me…because, unfortunately, that was the only way he knew how to deal with his own disappointment.

I mouthed the word "goodbye" because saying it would have taken me over the edge. I charged down the stairs past my dad, swallowing back the huge ball in my throat and trying to hide my tears. I know Abrianna said something to Dad in his mind, because he paused, too, and looked back at her. She trained her glittering eyes on him as if nobody else in the room mattered. Then he grabbed my hand, and the flash of power between us was there.

Without a glance back, we stepped into the wispy postcard before us.

Transporting with Dad was totally different. I did not lose consciousness but instead experienced every trippy moment of jumping into another time and place. The colors of the rainbow flashed before my eyes, and I felt like I was being squeezed uncomfortably and thrown into empty space all at the same time.

But when the weird, unexplainable stuff was over, we just *materialized.* There was no crashing into the sand. Instead, my hand was still tightly gripping Dad's when the ocean appeared before us.

"Did we make it? Are we in Hawaii or still on the Island?" The two beaches looked rather similar to me.

With a big sigh, Dad let go of me and started trudging to the left. "We're on the island of Kauai, the last I saw of this part of the world."

I followed behind him in silence as I took in my surroundings. Then I couldn't help asking, "We did the right thing, didn't we? Leaving the Island so quickly like that? That felt kind of crazy."

He kept moving forward. "Sometimes the crazy thing is the right thing."

"Dad, stop." He turned around slowly and looked at me. "Why'd you leave? Did you make a deal with the Island? What did it cost you?"

Dad looked completely exhausted and overwhelmed, but his eyes burned with intensity when he said, "You need a father more than the Island needs a Pilgrim right now. That's all you need to know. Now we need to get to that hotel and call your mother."

He started walking again, and I watched his retreating back, wondering at what point his consequences would catch up to him. "Oh, wait! I have my cell phone!" I called out. I dropped to the sand and dug around in my bag. With excitement, I pulled out my phone and waited while it found service. Oh my gosh, my mom was going to die when she heard his voice! I was dialing her number when I caught the expression on Dad's face.

"What's wrong?"

"Nothing…I just haven't talked to her in so long. What if she doesn't want me back in her life after all this time? I just assumed…"

I shook my head. "Just wait, Dad." It was the first time I had seen him somewhat unsure of himself. The phone rang once before Mom's voice was there.

"WHITNEE!"

"Hi, Mom—" But she cut me off with a slew of half-English, half-Spanish words and phrases that ran together. She was crying.

"Whoa, it's okay. I'm totally okay," I tried to reassure her, not really understanding everything she was saying.

"Oh, *mija*! You were supposed to come back two weeks ago! What happened?! Where are you?!" she shrieked.

I was shocked. "Two weeks? I've been gone that long?"

Dad mumbled, "This portal has not been stabilized. We must've jumped ahead."

"Wait, Mom, did Caleb and Morgan tell you about—"

"Yes, yes…they told me everything! And Ben gave me your dad's ring and we waited by the portal for you that night but you never showed up!! I have just been sick with worry—you better have a good explanation for this, Whitnee. Your poor friends…I swear, they've been over here every day hoping you'd call! With school starting next week, I didn't know what to do!"

"Mom. Just stop for a second!" I interrupted her. "I have somebody who wants to talk to you…"

With a giddy smile, I held the phone out to Dad. He stared at it like it might bite him. But then slowly, he stepped forward and took it from my hands. When he pressed it to his ear, his voice was shaking. "Serena?"

That was all it took. I could hear Mom screaming into the phone even from where I was sitting in the sand. "Serena, sweetheart, I missed you…" And then Dad's knees buckled underneath him, and he sank to the ground and cried like a baby.

I crawled to his side, listening as best as I could while my parents cried and assured each other over and over again of their love and commitment.

Dad flung an arm around me and pulled me in close. "I love my girls…" he sobbed into the phone, gripping me tightly at the same time. Mom was talking rapidly into the receiver. "Well," he sniffled. "We're actually in Hawaii—of all places!" And then he just started laughing, which caused me to laugh. I'm pretty sure Mom was doing the half-laugh, half-sob thing too.

And that was when I finally let myself cry. This moment made *everything* worth it.

"We close our program today with breaking news about Texas native Nathan Terradora, whose strange disappearance captured America's attention six years ago. After a baffling case of amnesia, Terradora was actually found by his wife and seventeen-year-old daughter on the coast of Kauai—the same Hawaiian island where he had been conducting geological research when authorities reported him missing. Though the man claims to not remember the accident that sparked his amnesia and resulted in a nationwide search for him, he expressed his clear gratitude over being reunited with his family and regaining his memory. The family has remained private about the mysterious details surrounding Terradora's reappearance. Hawaiian authorities commented jokingly that time-travel more easily explained his six-year vacation from reality, after he was coincidentally found wearing the exact same clothing he was last seen in. Despite the unanswered questions, the family of three claims they are looking forward to catching up on lost time. Regardless of what did or didn't happen, it is nice to know this is just one more missing persons case that can now be closed with a happy ending."

THREE MONTHS LATER

I gave my hair one last spritz with finishing shine spray and decided my blonde locks were as straight as they were going to get on this Saturday night. With a light coat of lip gloss and a few dabs of my favorite perfume, I was just about ready to go.

Then Morgan's text message came in. *Can't go tonight. Sick to my stomach. Mom is freaking out.*

I frowned as I texted back. *Should I be worried?*

I straightened up my bathroom while I waited for a response. Morgan and I both had been completely cleared of any type of cancer after we left the Island. Morgan's parents and doctors called her their miracle. All they knew was that one week she had stage four cancer, and the next week she was a perfectly healthy teenage girl. Not one trace of the disease was in her system no matter how many times they repeated tests. Of course, we couldn't tell them the truth, so it had been kind of fun to see the brilliant minds of modern medicine scratch their heads in total bafflement.

The only evidence that Morgan and I had of our cancerous moments was the lingering irritable stomach problems. I had never had those problems before, but now they acted up frequently—particularly when something stressed me out. I had a feeling that my new chronic symptoms were just part of those "consequences" that came with Transfusion. But it was worth it to get to spend my senior year with a happy, healthy best friend.

Morgan's next text made me smile. *Truthfully? I totally binged on chocolate chip cookies that Mags and I made…can't tell Mom.* There was a smiley face at the end.

Morgan had done well putting some healthy weight back on her body. And she often amused Caleb and me with the dramatic ways she enjoyed her meals. It was like she was rediscovering the pleasure of food. So, yeah, bingeing on cookies until it made her sick was not surprising.

Feel better! We'll miss you, I responded.

I'm sure Caleb won't mind having you all to himself for a night, she replied. *You kids be good!*

I just rolled my eyes and threw my phone and makeup bag into my purse. I swished one last time with the Island mouthwash; it was almost all gone. It had not worked as strongly on the Mainland as it did on the Island. But I still loved using it—the taste brought back powerful memories every time. My thunderfly necklace hung loosely around my neck, and I touched it with my right hand as I had every day since the summer…just to see if it would light up with Firelight. It never did—just another reminder that the portals were no longer active. With every passing day, the Island felt farther away.

With a sigh, I gave Caleb's petrified Saint flower one longing look. I had preserved it in a shadow box frame to display in my room. Its crystallized petals glittered next to my lava lamp as a beautiful reminder of the Island and of Saint Simeon whose ultimate sacrifice had brought me healing. I swore I would never forget.

I shut the lights off and closed my door before smiling at the sounds of fierce competition coming from the living room.

"Oh, that was a low blow!" Caleb scolded my dad.

"Some day you'll beat me, little boy. Keep practicing!" Dad teased.

"Yeah, I could win if I cheated like you, old man!" Caleb quipped.

"Are we fencing or boxing tonight?" I asked as I walked right in front of the TV where they were playing video games. One look told me it was a fencing night. Boys and their swords…Once Dad had discovered the new gaming systems could be controlled with bodily actions, he and Caleb had made up as many excuses as they could to battle each other regularly. I think the movement and control of the game made Dad feel in some weird way like he was still controlling life forces. And Caleb's company was good for Dad—he was like the son Dad never had. And I guess Dad was like the father Caleb had lost.

"One more game!" Dad decided.

"I'm not going easy on you this time." They assumed their battling positions.

"Caleb, we don't want to be late," I warned as I continued on toward the kitchen where the tantalizing smells of Mom's cooking were wafting.

"I had to wait for you to get ready; you can wait long enough to witness the spanking I'm about to give your dad," Caleb retorted. "You smell nice, by the way," he added as my perfume finally drifted his way.

Mom and I exchanged amused glances. "I love how he pretends that he doesn't purposely come over here early just so he can play with Dad," I told her. "Sometimes I think he'd rather hang out with him than me."

"It's a guy thing," Mom agreed. "So where are y'all heading tonight?"

"Dinner and a movie…maybe Starbucks afterwards."

"As long as you get up for church tomorrow," Mom reminded me as she opened the oven and pulled out her casserole. "Don't forget Uncle Ben is driving out here for the afternoon. And I want those scholarship applications finished by Monday."

"Yes, ma'am." I saluted her. Thank God Ben had been just fine by the time I returned. For an almost eighty-year-old Aerodorian, he was quite a survivor—and now a permanent part of our family. I will never forget the silent way he accepted the message of forgiveness from his brother, Poppa Zeke. His eyes changed, and I knew it had affected him in ways he would never show me. Something felt really good about setting people free from a burden.

I watched my mom put the finishing touches on her work. She made me help her set the food out on the table where she and Dad were apparently having dinner by candlelight after we left.

Mom had been amazing about everything. Honestly, I'm not sure I would have handled things as well as she had. After she flew out to Hawaii to get us, we spent a few days there together as a family in order to fill Mom in on *everything*. While she had asked plenty of questions, she had never once doubted the Island's existence.

Our time in Hawaii saw some rough moments. Mom was not a fan of Abrianna—for a *lot* of reasons—and I know Abrianna was the subject of several private conversations between my parents. Dad had trouble sleeping in Hawaii. Sometimes it was insomnia, sometimes nightmares. I think he had a lot of fears about waking up to find us gone. Then, right before we boarded the plane back to Texas, I had my first post-Island meltdown in the airport. It was the first time it really hit me that I would never go back to the Island. I made myself sleep most of the plane ride just to forget the ache inside.

By the time we made it back to Texas, school was starting. I had to scramble to get myself ready. My summer projects were not complete, but Mom was able to get me a week-long extension with all of my teachers. It certainly helped that our family had been all over the national news once again. Yep, that's what happened when a missing person was found. Case finally closed...but only after a lot of media and police drama.

But we had survived it. Mom had given Robert a polite rejection and never thought about him again. (Ha! I knew it.) Dad's former geological research foundation called him up after all the news coverage and offered him a job again. Dad took it, but only because it was somewhat of a desk job. None of us were really ready for him to start traveling again. Jaxson and our camp friends had kept in touch at first—especially when they saw the news. But we didn't hear from them as frequently once school started.

And then there was school…senior year…and all the firsts and lasts that came with it. Honestly, after everything my friends and I had been through on that Island—matters of life and death— the drama of typical high school life oftentimes seemed petty and irritating. It took Morgan, Caleb, and me some time to readjust to the social scene. Good thing we had each other. I couldn't imagine dealing with so many changes in my life if my best friends hadn't been such a key part of it all.

Things finally settled into normalcy. Mom and Dad went on a second honeymoon down to their favorite spot in Mexico. That had become the weird part about our family being together again. Well, weird for *me*. I tried not to think about it, but I knew my parents were all in love and wanted alone time. Fortunately, I was a senior with a very busy schedule, which conveniently excused me from the house enough for them to have their privacy. I just decided to remain ignorant of the fact that my parents acted more like newlyweds than a couple nearing their fifties. Morgan and Caleb thought it was cute. It made me want to barf.

The last three months had been really great…most of the time. I won't lie and say that it was perfect. Learning to live as a family of three again was an adjustment. I didn't realize how much Mom and I had established our own comfortable routines over the years. Not only that, but sometimes Dad still treated me like I was eleven years old. I didn't blame him for that—I knew he tried really hard to give me my space. But he was still adjusting to having a teenage daughter with opinions and responsibilities of her own. I loved him for trying, but there were definitely moments when our strong-willed Aero personalities clashed.

Speaking of Aero…I went to the closet and pulled out the Aeropostale jacket that Dad had purchased for me. The first time he discovered the store, he had freaked out, insisting we both needed clothes with "AERO" on them. He got a real kick out of the double meaning. And, hey, if he was going to buy me more clothes, I was not going to argue.

"Caleb, we need to go!" I called again. I was drowned out by the shouts and smack-talking between him and Dad. Donning my jacket and purse, I planted myself by the front door, bouncing on my heels impatiently. Finally, they finished. Caleb won. He did a victory lap around the house and held up his hands for Mom and me to slap. I did, but then didn't let go and jerked him back.

At a raise of my eyebrows, he concluded the celebration. "Sorry, I'm coming." He grabbed his own jacket and opened the door for me. Mom and Dad followed us out.

"Morgan can't come...she's sick," I informed him. "Cookie binge," I had to explain when everyone looked concerned.

"So, it's just you two?" Dad clarified meaningfully. I turned wide eyes on him, wishing we could still communicate between our minds. I would remind him not to embarrass me. "That sounds like a date," he added. And there was the embarrassment. *Thank you, Dad.*

"Nathan," Mom chastised.

"Two friends going out for some fun does *not* make it a date, Dad! See you later." I rushed away and stood impatiently by the passenger side of Caleb's car.

Caleb waved at my parents. "I'll have her home by midnight," he shouted back before opening the car door for me and helping me inside.

It was actually a little chilly out. Fall weather always excited me, though. It meant Friday night football games, tailgate parties, and hoodies with jeans. And this season of football had already been extremely promising. Our team had won last night, which had maintained our undefeated status all season. Caleb himself had even scored two of the touchdowns. Laura in her flirty cheer-leading uniform had been all over that victory after the game, but Caleb had seemed oblivious. Not that I cared or anything...

Once we were inside the car, Caleb grumbled, "You know you don't have to act like going on a date with me would be the most horrible thing ever."

"I didn't act like that!" I said defensively. "It's just my dad, you know. I don't want him to get all crazy and protective."

"Your dad likes me. I don't think he would have a problem if we dated."

I just remained quiet and started messing with the radio in his car, looking for a good song. Caleb didn't know about all the ways Dad had freaked out over Gabriel and me on the Island. And I would never tell him, either, because then I'd have to admit to all the feelings I had for Gabriel.

Leaving Gabriel bothered me sometimes, but it still *felt* right. And even though Amelia had said that choosing the place meant choosing the guy, I had pretty much decided that I wouldn't let that be the case. Just because I was going to live on the Mainland didn't mean that I had to launch into a relationship with Caleb. That needed time. I needed to make sure that what I felt for Caleb was real too…and not just based on the fact that he felt so strongly for me.

I kept thinking about what Mom had said—about how Caleb deserved all of my emotions when the time was right. And I agreed. Part of me still belonged on that Island with Gabriel. Until that part of me was no longer there, I could not in good conscience enter into a real dating relationship with Caleb. It just wasn't fair to him or to me. But I'll be honest…keeping things completely platonic between us wasn't always easy. Caleb made no secret of his feelings for me, and it wasn't like I didn't have my own feelings for him.

When I had finally discussed the Caleb/Gabriel situation in its entirety with Mom, she had been good about listening and withholding any opinions that might sway me in one direction (unlike Dad). After hearing me describe Gabriel in detail the first time, she gushed with me and admitted that she wished she could meet him. In her words, "He sounds so dreamy, *mija*!"

But she had been more than supportive of my decision to not get involved romantically with Caleb yet, insisting that I would know when (or if) the time was right. And until it was, then I was fortunate to have him as a friend and should work at maintaining that.

However, when I shifted my eyes over to Caleb as he drove, I still felt the little twinge of butterflies in my stomach. He was so cute. "I like that jacket," I complimented him. *Especially the way you look in it...* I added inwardly.

"Thanks." He glanced down at which one he was wearing. "I talked to Kevin today. He still brings up how mad he was that he didn't get to go back with us...blames it on the fact that he is not as much of a rule-breaker as Amelia." Caleb chuckled. "I think finally meeting your dad and getting that drum from Ezekiel was like a peace offering for him, though."

"Poor Kevin," I grinned. "Amelia's birthday is next week—we'll have to call her." I thought of my soon-to-be thirteen-year-old camper. Amelia had finally gotten to see how her parents reacted to her disappearance. By the time she returned to camp, there had been a massive search going on for her. When Ben had been found unconscious, they assumed the worst about Amelia's fate. She played up her kidnapping story, claiming not to remember much that happened to her. Morgan told me later that Amelia was a fabulous liar, but Amelia insisted she was just a good *actress*. On a positive note, her kidnapping forced her parents to reassess their priorities, and things had been much better among the three of them. They never found Amelia's kidnapper (duh), but their search efforts did help discover a serial rapist hiding out in a nearby county. We thought about that whenever we felt bad about all the lying.

"I can't imagine what my life would be like now if we hadn't taken the jobs at Camp Fusion," I mused. Suddenly, I felt my phone vibrate in my purse. I pulled it out and read the text. "Dad says, 'Tell Caleb I will never let him win again if he doesn't behave on your date!' Oh my gosh, he is so obnoxious." Caleb grinned as I texted back, *It's NOT a DATE.*

"You know," he began with a mischievous tone to his voice. "We could pretend it's a date…"

I played along. "Okay. What exactly would a date look like to you, Mr. Austin?"

"Oh, I don't know. I'd probably buy your dinner and your movie."

"Sounds good to me!" I agreed readily. "Would that be all?"

"No, of course not. I'd open doors for you—"

"You do that anyway."

"Yeah, well, I'm just a nice guy. I'd probably hold your hand too."

"I already let you hold my hand sometimes," I pointed out.

"I hold your hand like friends hold hands." And he grabbed my hand to demonstrate. "But if we were on a real date, I'd hold it like this…" He took his fingers and intertwined them with mine intimately.

I gasped with mock surprise. "That's 'indigitating'…Only *real* couples do *that*."

He brought the car to a stop at a red light. "I would find ways to be close to you in the movie…kind of like this…" And he leaned over to where his face was in my hair and his lips were a mere inch away from my ear. I was overcome again by the yum vortex and the sensation of his breath on my neck. "I would most definitely want to kiss you, but I would wait until you were the one practically begging for it." His thumb began tracing a slow pattern on my wrist.

Oh my gosh, he was evil. Those darn butterflies were doing a tango inside my stomach. I just sat there frozen in place, not breathing. His mouth moved closer to my lips until I was sure he was going to do it. Caleb was going to kiss me! His lips were close enough to mine that I could smell the spearmint gum in his mouth.

But then he pulled away suddenly and gunned the engine, leaving me stunned in the front seat. The light had turned. With a wicked grin, he said, "Good thing we're not really on a date."

I glared at him and tried to slow my heart rate. "You are the devil."

"And you like it."

"That stuff doesn't work on me," I assured him and gazed out my window, focusing all my energy on keeping my expression composed.

He snickered. "Oh, Whit…it's just too *easy* with you!"

"What does that mean?"

"Meaning I can read you like a book…you *wanted* me to kiss you."

"And you wanted to kiss me!" I shot back. "Don't act like you were just trying to seduce me for my own benefit. Believe it or not, I can read you pretty well too. And you're completely naughty, Caleb Austin!"

He just kept laughing. I noticed our hands were conveniently still indigitating. But I pretended it was no big deal because, truthfully, I liked it. My fingers snuggled very comfortably with his.

"So," I began, a coy tone in my voice. "Would it be a pretend date or a real date if I went to prom with you?"

His eyebrows shot up. He hadn't seen that one coming. He glanced over at me with a sly grin. "Whitnee Terradora, are *you* asking *me* to prom?"

I responded coolly. "Well, we just technically 'indigitated' for the first time." I squeezed his hand. "Prom seemed like a good next step in our relationship."

"Fine then…but only if it's a real date." He winked at me.

Prom was still months away. Maybe by then I would be ready to date him for real. But just to get back at him, I leaned over casually and whispered near his ear, "I'll think about it." With no warning, I brushed a feather of a kiss on his cheek, allowing my face to linger there for just a moment.

He shivered. Caleb Austin actually *visibly* shivered! I pulled back with a satisfied smirk. "That's right. Two can play at your little game."

"Whitnee." He shook his head. "One of these days I'm just gonna do it, you know. I'm just gonna kiss you, and then you'll be forced to admit that you want to be with me."

"No, you wouldn't. You respect me too much to do that," I said.

He shrugged with a smile. "Maybe you're right…maybe you're not. Guess you'll find out." But I knew I was right—because I knew the qualities that made Caleb so special to me.

I narrowed my eyes at him as if calling his bluff, and turned up the music, because my current favorite song was on. When I started to sing along and direct my attention back out the window, I realized the smile on my face wouldn't go away. I had a feeling senior year was going to be full of surprises. After all, everything in life was an adventure…

Even pretend dates with my best guy friend.

Absentmindedly, I touched my free hand to my necklace again. When it flashed purple in the reflection of the window, I looked down in surprise. It must have been a trick of the eye…or a street lamp or headlight outside. I tapped it again…

Instead of Firelight glowing from within, it was still just a simple glass thunderfly.

Discover more about the world of Phantom Island!
www.KrissiDallas.com

ACKNOWLEDGMENTS

In the strange way that art can mirror real life, I was sick through most of the year that I was writing *Watermark*. Not only that, but cancer and disease struck loved ones of mine during that time, and I was forced to take a deep glimpse into the despair that comes with terminal illness. *Watermark* comes from a deep well in my soul that needed to seep through the pages of a story, to weep with characters in need of healing, and to somehow capture the hope and restoration that we all want in this life and the next.

Special thanks to Tyler Matjeka for challenging my prayer life and reminding us all that each day we have here is a precious gift from the Lord. You truly embody Proverbs 3:5-8. May God grant "healing for your body and strengthening for your bones."

There are hardly enough words in the world to thank Katrina Elsea for all she has done to strengthen this series. (And if I could write enough words, she'd find a way to chop them down and make them more concise.) Pretty sure there is nobody else—next to me—who knows and loves these characters like you do, Kat. Thank you.

Thank you to my best friend, Melody, for allowing me to plunge into her darkest fears…and write about them. You are such an inspiration.

Thank you to my mom, Bonnie Inman, and my husband, Sam Dallas…you endured with me through many restless nights, emotional upheavals over fictional characters, and a lot of self-doubt. Thanks for keeping me off the ledge.

To my Phantom Island Team…Renea McKenzie, Loni Fancher, Ali Moore, Allison Duke, Courtney Ussery (Fuzzy Coffee Books), and Amber Stokes (Seasons of Humility)…Thank you for reading and believing.

Kristen Verser, you are not just my cover artist, graphic and website designer, and a creative soul who totally gets my vision… you have become my friend. Thank you for all the extra time and love you put into the world of Phantom Island!

Heartfelt thanks to Springtown Middle School and U.M.E. Preparatory Academy—two educational communities who not only allowed me to teach their middle schoolers, but unselfishly supported every endeavor and risk I knew I needed to take. I'm so thankful for the love and encouragement from my students and their families that continue to follow me on this journey.

And to you—yes, *you*, my reader—thank you for keeping the magic alive in this series. You are in my heart and prayers with every piece of this story.